AUTHOR	CLASS
22. PHILLIPS, S.	F

TITLE Blonde ambition

Blonde Ambition

BLONDE AMBITION

Samantha Phillips

Century · London

First published by Century in 1996

1 3 5 7 9 10 8 6 4 2

Copyright © Samantha Phillips 1996

Samantha Phillips has asserted her right under the Copyright,
Designs and Patents Act, 1988 to be identified as the author of this work

First published in the United Kingdom in 1996 by Century Ltd
Random House, 20 Vauxhall Bridge Road, London SW1V 2SA

Random House Australia (Pty) Limited
16 Dalmore Drive, Scoresby, Victoria 3179, Australia

Random House New Zealand Limited
18 Poland Road, Glenfield
Auckland 10, New Zealand

Random House South Africa (Pty) Limited
PO Box 2263, Rosebank 2121, South Africa

Random House UK Limited Reg. No. 954009

A CIP catalogue record for this book is available from the
British Library

ISBN 0 7126 7614 7

Papers used by Random House UK are natural, recyclable
products made from wood grown in sustainable forests. The
manufacturing processes conform to the environmental
regulations of the country of origin.

Typeset by SX Composing DTP, Rayleigh, Essex
Printed and bound by Mackays of Chatham plc, Chatham, Kent

Biographical note

Samantha Phillips was born in Derbyshire, is a graduate of the University of London and has a Masters from the Sorbonne in Paris. Following a background in ship broking and advertising in Paris she joined Lloyd's in 1989, employed by Willis Faber & Dumas as a broker in their aviation division.

In November 1992 she left Willis Faber and began legal action against the company. Two weeks later she published the first edition of *Inside Eye*, a magazine that revealed what went on behind the scenes at Lloyd's. After a two year struggle she won a highly publicised court case against her former employers. Samantha Phillips lives in London and now writes full time.

Acknowledgements

It all started at a cocktail party when Richard Charkin suggested I wrote a book about Lloyd's. So I ought to begin by thanking him. I must also thank my dearest friend Vanessa Corringham without whose help and support I would never have got through the ordeal of the court case which coincided with my father's death in Cairo. Thank you also to Patrick Walsh my agent whose unwaning enthusiasm and bonhomie kept me on track. To Jessie Carr-Martindale for his wisdom, and script for the BBC, to Amanda Hemingway for all she has done, to Kate Parkin and Louise Hartley-Davies at Random House for their sheer brilliance and support in the final stages of the text, to Nicky Eaton for her skilful guidance, to all my friends at Lloyd's and to Peter Middleton to whom I am eternally grateful. Finally to my wonderful family – my mother, Paul and Peter – and all my friends and in particular to Carolyn Jordan for her undying support whilst working into the small hours. I love them very much and they have been my anchor over these past two years.

To Daddy

PROLOGUE

It was an empty building in a street full of other empty buildings. Hardly a car drifted down the road; the well-lit night, a night of street-lamps and neon, of arc-lights, spotlights, standard illumination on every façade, showed unoccupied rooms behind uncurtained windows, multi-locked doors on to echoing vestibules, an occasional glimpse of silent corridors, untrodden stairs. By day the buildings hummed with computers, trilled with telephones, bawled, shouted, mumbled with the many notes of the human voice; by night they were as quiet as a sepulchre, a vault full of sleeping technology, where corpse or coffin would have been out of place. The light slanted in from outside and lay in pale bands across desk and floor. Beyond its reach the gloom was untouched. The girl and the man were the only people in the building apart from an unseen security guard on ground level; they might have been the only people in the whole City. It was 1a.m. and the hush of their surroundings made their encounter seem not merely clandestine but desperate, even sinister. The girl was seated at a desk on the fourteenth floor, out of range of the street glimmer, a single lamp shining down on the old-fashioned typewriter which clicked and zoomed under her dancing fingers. The girl, accustomed to the speed and correction facility of a computer keyboard, made several mistakes, swearing frequently under her breath. The de la Tour lighting contoured her profile, caught a red lustre in her hair, a silver lustre on her long nails. She was young: the curve of her cheek was perfect, the furrow between her brows still fresh. The lamplight made an irregular circle around her, cut with shadows. Beyond, a long thin ray reached out from a half-open door to a separate office at the back of the room. The man emerged from the office, his shoulders wide against the light, his face in darkness. The beam broadened and narrowed with the swing of the door, then vanished as the man's body intervened. It was only when he was very close that she could see familiar features.

'Is it done?'

She shook her head, a quick jerking movement which was all she could spare: the machine absorbed her whole attention. He stood over her while she worked, behind the lamp, a looming, ominous figure. When she had finished he took the sheet of paper from her, tilted the desk lamp so he could read it *in situ*. 'Fine,' he said at last, 'You've done a good job. You're the only person I trust with this.'

She did not respond but some quality in her expression made her upturned face look suddenly older, its spotless youth shaded with cunning, almost shrewish. He put down the document, snapped the light round, the yellow glow pooling vacant desk and silent computer. Man and girl were left in semi-darkness. Her head was on level with his waist, her lifted eyes enormous from that angle, the whites faintly sheened, her mouth dark as a bruise against the triangular pallor of her visage. He knew her lips were parted because he could see the furtive glitter of teeth. He imagined a vampire snarl adorning avid innocence, an appetite beyond satiation corrupting features normally pretty, spoiled only by too much makeup. His hand cupped her skull, closed on the nape of her neck; then he thrust her face hard against his crotch. The woollen trousers rasped at her cheek, took the red from her lips. He pulled her head back for a moment, his grip tight in her hair; the other hand fumbled with fly-button and zip. Then he had tugged down his pants and his penis lifted of its own accord: a living, growing hardness: it kissed her lips, pressed between them, feeling resistance, hesitation, the tentative probing of an uncertain tongue. Then the lingual exploration became more persistent, doubt turned to desire, hunger became famine; he looked down and saw her eyes half closed in ecstasy. He seized her by the temples and rammed her head against his abdomen, choking her, filling her. When his climax had subsided a shiver of afterlust ran through him. Pleasure mingled with a sweet irresistible fear that one day she would eat him to the core, and there would be nothing left.

She got to her feet, reaching in her bag for a tissue to wipe her face.

'I'll call you a taxi,' he said, picking up the nearest phone.

She waited patiently while he made the call, accepted a dismissive kiss. She did not attempt to reapply her makeup or tidy her hair. On her way out, she did not greet the security guard. She stood on the pavement beside the taxi and spat.

In the Gents on the fourteenth floor, the man was scrubbing and scrubbing at his trousers with a damped cloth, trying to remove the last trace of lipstick.

CHAPTER ONE

The girl emerged from the Underground into a grey London morning. Grey streets teeming with grey suits and the pallid light of a grey summer over all. Grey building soared above her, their windows reflecting hurrying bands of cloud; the wind flapped at her unfastened jacket, tugged her bag; a fleeting bar of clear sky passed overhead, sending a few rays of sunshine chasing one another across a pavement gleaming with recent rain.

But despite her sombre surroundings and the temperamental weather the girl felt her heart lift. This was where it all happened – the wheeling and dealing, the high-tech, high-flying international transactions, the shrilling of telephones, the flicker of computer screens switching millions from continent to continent at the touch of a button. Just to be there was to taste power, under the grey suits, behind cloud-mirror windows, the heady excitement of juggling with zeros that launched fleets, built dams, overthrew governments. She ached to be part of it.

The crowd divided around her, heading for the tube, hailing taxis, fragments of split conversation receding behind her. The bond market – the FT index – that dreadful *boeuf en croute* at Lucilla's dinner party – George's gold – Hubert's polo – the imminent collapse of marriages, share issues, British industry.

Several of the men glanced round, watching the slim legs balanced on slimmer heels, picking their way among puddles and people like a gazelle in a vegetable patch. She was a legs girl, only of medium height but most of it below the waist, long elegant limbs emerging from short elegant skirt, shapely with slender muscles, sheer with Dior tights.

The girl did not notice their stares. She was rushing to her appointment, afraid of unpunctuality – she was chronically unpunctual – desperate not to miss it, terrified to arrive. Above the legs she was a honey-coloured girl, golden tones of skin and hair set off by an outfit of severe and professional black. The secretaries who passed her were many-hued, gaudy and chattering

1

like parakeets: the austerity of her costume singled her out. Her face was misleadingly youthful, its infantile curves belied by the squareness of her small chin and the determined, potentially stubborn, set of her mouth. She paused to check a street name on the wall above, breasted the crowd again, clutching briefcase and bag.

As is always the way when you are in a hurry, everyone else seemed to be going in the opposite direction. Her goal was across the street, the Fitzgerald Denton building, an Edwardian edifice of daunting proportions bearing all the hallmarks of imperial architecture. Massive columns, laborious carving, an entrance that would not have disgraced the Roman Senate approached by a grandiose flight of unnecessarily broad steps and flanked by two bronze sphinxes. This was a monument to historic power, created for the masters of empire, its vast portals now masking power of another kind, rulers using not military but financial muscle, whizz-kid descendants of Cecil Rhodes and Clive of India. Mounted high above the entrance were two flagpoles: on the left a Union Jack, on the right what she assumed to be the corporate flag of Fitzgerald Denton. They flapped and shrank in the freakish wind, recalling brave pennants on many-masted ships, trading for Britain in every port of the world. She was heading for the Marine Division which insured the ships of today, metal monsters engined, funnelled, fuelled, free of the weather's whim, but the images those flags awoke in her mind were older, of beating sails and dipping bows, pirates and parrots, and for a minute she fantasised that past and present were joined here, part of the continuing romance of commerce and the sea.

She crossed the road, dodging traffic, and ran up the wide steps. She felt very small as she entered the shadow of those looming columns, an impertinent urchin daring to invade this ancient and majestic milieu. But she thrust self-doubt aside and walked smartly through the open doors into reception.

A security guard in naval uniform addressed her, his friendly cockney voice presenting a marked contrast to the marble magnificence of the vestibule. 'Can I help you, miss?'

'The Marine Division?'

'Fourteenth floor on the new quad.' Behind the automatic

2

response he was wondering what her chances were in that particular den of hyenas. 'Do you have an appointment?'

'Nine-thirty.' She glanced apprehensively at her watch as he opened the door for her. 'Is there a Ladies around here?'

'On the right as you come out of the lift. Don't worry: you've got time. That lot don't often get the chance to wait for a lady.'

He gave her a grin and a wink and she found herself responding, obscurely reassured. Perhaps it had something to do with the uniform, recalling an image of her father a few years ago, just before he retired from the Marines. White peaked cap, medal ribbons, dark blue serge tunic. Her apprehension receded.

He checked her name off on a list, admitted her to the lift and proffered another grin by way of encouragement before she disappeared from view. She pressed the button for the fourteenth floor, noting that triskaidekaphobia had crept in: there was no thirteenth. It was strange to register the existence of an old and meaningless superstition in an environment ruled by facts and figures, rationality and technology. Superstition even here, sneaked in by the back door.

The lift stopped on the third, breaking her train of thought, and a man entered. Mid forties, tall, angular body; what little spare flesh he possessed seemed to have sagged from his hunched shoulders and accumulated around his belly, causing his shirt, elsewhere inadequately filled, to bulge slightly above his waistband. His jacket was unbuttoned, perhaps due to carelessness, haste, hangover, a too-late night followed by a too-early morning. His face had also sagged, the cheeks dropping below the ridge of his jaw, dissipated lines dragging at his eyes and the corners of his mouth, his lips bloodless, set hard as if clenched against the collapse of the rest of his physiognomy. His coat was cashmere and his suit Savile Row but he still looked ineradicably seedy, an internal more than an external seediness, a seediness of the mind that was betrayed by the sideways flicker of his gaze, the way he appeared to be summing her up, mentally undressing her, not with a leer but with a curiously clinical precision. She avoided eye contact, feeling suddenly claustrophobic, trapped in the confines of this aluminium box.

He pressed the button already lit for fourteen and she inadvertently held her breath for a couple of floors, possibly because of the faint odour he exuded, stale cigarette smoke, stale beer, stale rooms. His presence damped down some of her anticipatory nerves, quelling excitement with an unexpected distaste. On the whole, she would have preferred to take her excitement unadulterated. At fourteen the doors reopened. She hung back, knowing she was already late, doubtful of the unknown territory ahead. But when he had gone her native resolution and sense of commitment returned. She walked out of the lift, turned right, and went into the Ladies. Her watch showed her it was just on 9.30.

Hugo Wingate, Managing Director of Fitzgerald Denton's Marine Department, combed his hair briskly off his forehead. The hair in question was thick and fair, there was plenty of it, hair ran in his family: his grandfather had died with a full white mane. It was a strictly private cause for gratification, particularly when he saw the creeping baldness that afflicted so many of his colleagues. That morning, his locks were still slightly damp, not from the flurry of rain that had pattered briefly at the windows of his taxi but from a post-workout shower at the Broadgate Health Club near Liverpool Street. He was just under six feet tall, solidly built with a firm, athletic brand of solidity, any excess flab massaged and exercised out of existence. Most women would have described him as good-looking, if rather oppressively masculine, his features a little too heavy, his chin cleft, his naturally ruddy complexion deepened to a careful bronze from skiing and occasional sunbed. The upper-class background, which was the one thing he lacked, mattered only to him. Even while he faked it with all the right labels he both envied and despised those among his compeers whose blood was a few shades bluer than his. 'Now and then,' someone had once remarked to him, 'you can catch a glimpse of the chipboard beneath the walnut.' A dismissive aside, now almost apocryphal, repeated frequently on the floor of Lloyd's; but never within Hugo's hearing.

The interview panel's search for a trainee broker was in its last day. They had started a couple of months earlier with over two hundred applicants, most of whom had come via headhunters. These had been pruned to a shortlist of twelve, the final

4

five of whom were being seen that morning. The panel consisted of three brokers: Hugo presiding, at the head of the boardroom table, Colin Sewell, a senior broker who had been with the firm most of his working life, and a man with hooked shoulders and pouched belly recently ejected from the lift, whose name was Bill Spooner. In attendance was a youth whose principal function was to operate the video camera mounted on a tripod and positioned to the left of the table, its blank eye fixed with sinister purpose on an empty, solitary, straight-backed chair.

The girl came out of the Ladies with her nose repowdered, her lips reglossed, her windswept hair brushed into place. She had tried scraping it back into a ponytail, hoping it would make her look more professional, but it merely served to remind her of her schooldays – 'Hair below the collar *must* be tied back' – with exposed ears and a general air of disastrous youth. That would never do: she wanted to appear young and ambitious, elegant and in control, but not adolescent. She had loosened her hair again in haste, studied her mirrored face under the stark, uncomplimentary lighting favoured by male designers of ladies' loos, bitten her lips, glanced at her watch. Time for the deep breathe and the plunge. The door swung to behind her.

Spooner glanced over the morning's list of candidates with little interest. Five of them before lunch – five pink-faced, snub-nosed eager wannabees before his first vodka tonic. He was going to need that drink very badly by then. Anticipation might well increase pleasure, but you could have too much of a good thing. He had found some time ago the best way of dealing with the pressures of his position, but it was too early in the day for him to have given his system its accustomed boost and he viewed his surroundings with an unreasonably aggressive gaze. In due course he would retire to the Partners' loo, or powder room as it had been christened by the office staff, and revive himself, returning to survey the world with a brighter and beadier eye. Until then he shifted restlessly in his seat, humped one shoulder higher than the other. Hugo was tapping irritably on his blotter with a biro. Sewell checked the time: 9.37.

'The first one's late,' he said.

5

'Mm.' Hugo was skimming the relevant application form. 'Charlie Christie. Well qualified, but obviously a lousy time-keeper. We don't need that.'

'Where'd he go to school?' Spooner queried automatically, his tight mouth splitting into a provocative yawn. Interviewing bored him: unfledged young men with clean collars and shining aspirations were not his choice of company. He was a veteran with a nicotine-stained finger on the pulse of business, getting higher on the daily challenge of his job than on the wonderdust which kept him going. Sitting on this panel he felt like an examiner at a viva voce. It was not a role which appealed to him.

Hugo was checking the CV.

'Millfield.'

'That any good?' Spooner had been educated outside the public school system and did not care who knew it. He was Hugo's contemporary, but belonged to a newer breed, shorn of pretension, foreigners admitted to an exclusive club, there to do their worst or their best. He laid no claim to class or culture, wielding only a Masonic handshake and an air of being in on a secret that no one else knew, a secret he might be persuaded to impart to a privileged ear if the time was right, if the deal was worth it, if the ear was sufficiently attentive. It was this air of being in the know which made him invaluable. Nobody liked him, nobody trusted him, but everyone was sure he was one move ahead of the game.

'It's in the top ten,' Hugo was saying.

'High fees?'

'Very.'

'I can't understand it,' Spooner said. 'Paying the earth to have your son locked away from all women but Matron, and turned into a raving poof who's no good at anything but cricket.'

'A pouffe,' said Sewell tersely, 'is an article of furniture.' Office rumour suggested he was that way inclined himself.

'Millfield's co-ed,' said Hugo, oiling troubled waters.

The intrusion of his secretary offered a welcome diversion.

'The 9.30's here now,' she said.

'Show him in.'

For no reason that Hugo could analyse, she bit back a smile. Their relationship was not entirely professional but she usually

6

affected a demureness in front of senior colleagues which pre-cluded her smiling out of turn. She went out, reappearing a moment later to announce: 'Charlie Christie.'

It was the girl from the lift.

The secretary retreated, and Charlie was left confronting three pairs of eyes, startled, antagonistic, reluctantly appreciative. For several seconds there was complete silence, edged rather than broken by the almost inaudible murmur of the video camera. She registered Spooner with a sinking of the heart: his probing gaze, once the initial shock had passed, explored her so closely, with such chilly intimacy, it felt like a touch. She felt suddenly that her skirt was too short, her restrained black suit innately vulgar; but she pulled herself together and lifted her chin with a hint of defiance.

'Charlie . . .' Hugo's eyes dipped pointlessly to the deceptive CV. 'I take it that must be short for Charlotte?'

'Yes.'

'I beg your pardon, but . . . I'm afraid we expected a man.'

'Did you?' She really mustn't be impertinent. She made herself relax into a smile. 'Well, if it's a problem . . .'

'No. No, of course not. But –' He glanced at the other two for support and received none. Sewell was still clearly unnerved and Spooner continued to study the candidate as if he were a farmer contemplating a prize heifer. 'It's the CV,' Hugo explained. 'Those idiots in personnel have ticked "M" on the covering sheet. That's what threw us. I'm sorry if we appeared rather disconcerted.' By implication, he at least had adjusted his outlook, even if his colleagues had been left behind.

She responded quickly, her confidence reviving. 'Look, if this is too tricky then perhaps I should leave. However, I was hoping –' now was her chance to seize the initiative, now while two-thirds of her interrogators were still too stunned to inter-rupt – 'I was hoping you would give me a few minutes to tell you why I might be suitable for the post you want to fill. May I take a seat?'

She sat without waiting for permission, under the baleful stare of the camera. In front of her the panel collectively straightened in their chairs; Hugo leaned forward, signifying courteous attention, potential interest. She concentrated principally on him, instinctively aware that he was the most influential person present, targeting his blue eyes with her own direct regard. 'First, in case personnel have ticked any more of the wrong boxes, I've brought my academic certificates.' She produced them from a folder in her briefcase: nine Os, four As, and degrees from Oxford and Insead. As she refastened the case on her knee it rucked up her skirt a little: the prying camera dipped slightly to focus on a partially exposed thigh. But Charlie was oblivious to the mechanical watcher, launching into her pitch with growing assurance, talking frankly and fluently about her hopes, her ambitions, her ideas concerning the job. As she was speaking a slow inward smile lightened Hugo's expression: this, he was thinking, could be their secret weapon against rival brokers, feminine charm and an intelligence more than equal to most of the men. She might be exactly what they needed. He could just imagine the reaction in the Room as he sprang her on Lloyd's for the first time, Abanazar rubbing the lamp to conjure an unexpected genie. It would be something of a shock to a world that had been male-dominated since Edward Lloyd's early coffee-shop days of the early eighteenth century.

Charlie had a sound knowledge of the insurance business and had obviously done her homework on both the operation of Lloyd's and Fitzgerald Denton's international structure and market status. It was an efficient performance to which they accorded their uninterrupted attention. Finally, she asked them if they had any doubts or questions. Hugo came up with a couple of routine queries; Sewell added his mite for the sake of participation; Spooner emitted a noncommittal grunt when she supplied answers. The starting salary was elicited: it was small in comparison to other City jobs of the same calibre but Charlie believed it was worth going short for a while in order to snatch a career opportunity that meant so much to her. She told them she was available to begin immediately, and she would look forward to being contacted *prontissimo*. Thank you for your time, gentlemen; she trusted they would meet again soon. She concluded with a smile that conveyed a relaxed certainty which she did not feel, nodded to the camera as an afterthought, and made her exit.

Hugo watched her legs depart.

'Well, well,' he said. He glanced at his colleagues and went on, carefully dispassionate: 'What do you think?'

'She's good.' This was Sewell. 'She's very good. If it were my decision alone, I wouldn't have let her out of the room, just in case she was on her way to another interview. If we don't snap her up quickly someone else will. She's head and shoulders above the other applicants. That's the upside. The downside is how long she'll stay. She's highly ambitious and we don't want to waste time training her if she's going to move on more or less immediately.'

Hugo shrugged. 'That's a risk you take with any bright employee. A plodder will stay put – but we don't need any more of those. Bill? What about you? You haven't said much.'

'I couldn't get a word in edgeways,' Spooner retorted. 'Never met a bird who knew when to shut up. Let her loose on the floor and she'll talk them all into a cardiac arrest. That'll be good for business.'

'We were interviewing her,' Hugo said testily. 'She was supposed to talk. What've you got against her? Her sex?'

'No,' said Spooner, 'and yes. The packaging is fine: I'd fuck her any day of the week. But I wouldn't employ her for anything else. There's more to this job than fancy packaging.'

'Her academic qualifications are excellent,' Sewell pointed out prosaically, endeavouring to raise the tone of the discussion.

'There's more to the job than passing exams, too,' Spooner snapped. 'So she was a clever little schoolgirl. So what? She'd be playing out of her league here.'

'I don't agree.' Hugo interceded in a decisive manner. 'I thought she was pretty impressive. I don't advocate tokenism, but maybe it's time we had a woman aboard. The City's changing. We don't want to be left behind.'

'Precisely,' Sewell assented.

Spooner gave way grudgingly. 'We've got four more to see,' he reminded them. 'One of them might be of interest. Assuming Simon Canning is not a Simone, Andy Leeson isn't short for Andrea, and –'

'Yes, all right, point taken. We won't make our minds up till we've seen what else is on offer.' Hugo consulted the list of remaining interviewees, cast a cursory eye over the next CV.

9

Privately, he had all but decided in Charlie's favour. She was the prime contender: he wanted to give her a chance to prove herself and anticipated with some pleasure her impact both on Fitzgerald Denton and on Lloyd's. But now was not the moment for further argument. After all, he had the casting vote.

Spooner glanced aimlessly at his watch, excused himself, and left the room. 'Nature calls.' The other two were not deceived. When he returned they knew he would be indefinably more relaxed, more tolerant, approachable yet alert, subjecting the leftover applicants to a less jaundiced scrutiny, dismissing them with less scorn. By the end of the morning he might even be accessible to the dangerous notion of a female trainee broker.

When Charlie came out of the lift the friendly naval uniform greeted her with a grin and held the door open for her benefit. She thanked him, smiled back.

'Go off all right, did it?' he asked her. 'I bet you knocked 'em dead.'

'Well,' she said, a little taken aback, 'it was interesting.'

Outside, one of the cloud-gaps had opened up into a wide avenue of blue, shedding sunshine on to the wet pavements, the fragments of pool and puddle, the glossy bonnets of available cabs. The City gleamed, its grey shades turned to silver. Tired of public transport, she hailed one of the taxis and threw herself luxuriously into the back seat, an irrepressible smile, originating she knew not where, illuminating her features.

'Where to, miss?'

'Lime Street, please.'

She scrambled out of the cab and for several minutes just stood, staring. The building rose up in front of her like a gigantic food processor – a money processor, a people processor – a vessel of steel and glass festooned with service pipes, air-conditioning tubes, external elevators, as if it had been ruthlessly disembowelled and garlanded with its own intestines. She remembered reading an art critic, somewhere quite recently, who had described it as 'a metaphor for a society consumed with endemic bulimia, routinely spilling its guts, ripping out its own organs, exposing in its self-destructive passion all that was once coyly

10

private or safely taboo'. She couldn't remember where she had seen the piece – possibly in the *Guardian* at the house of an acquaintance, or in Pseud's Corner in *Private Eye* – but although she had dismissed it as nonsense, now, despite the pretentious phraseology, it seemed to her to mean something. The Lloyd's building was indeed architecture as art, a functional structure turned inside out, an eyesore or a symbol, she didn't know which.

This was where she would work, should her job application succeed; here were the secrets into which she would be initiated, the strings she would learn to manipulate, the game of Chinese Whispers she would have to play. She imagined herself making her daily pilgrimage up the main flight of steps, under the glass canopy, nodding to the scarlet-coated individual who stood on guard, with gold-braided top hat and immaculate white gloves. There was a mounted policeman nearby, and a pair of blue-blazered custodians, like low-profile bouncers outside a recherché nightclub, studied the comings and goings of the crowd. A constant stream of suits hurried to and fro, clasping folders thick with vital documentation, like worker ants commuting to the nest with a precious cargo of leaf-shreds and morsels of food. Passing tourists stopped to photograph the scene.

'Men,' thought Charlie, on a sudden bubble of inward laughter. 'That's what this is all about. A secret society for schoolboys with all the trappings that they love: fancy dress, tribal exclusivity, probably codewords and rituals. It's nothing but an elaborate charade – but what goes on underneath? That's the question. If I want to find out, I'll have to learn how to play their game, by their rules. If I get the chance.'

A bus pulled up from Gibbs Hartley Cooper, disgorging a posse of brokers, pin-striped and laden with the inevitable folders, out-of-towners unable or unwilling to pay the premium for office space within walking distance of Mecca. There was a girl with them, good-looking in a carefully groomed, businesslike style, with Spanish black hair cut into a geometric bob and a designer jacket whose apricot hue flamed against the surrounding plumage of monochrome grey. She was struggling with a teetering stack of papers many of which seemed to be escaping from their covers, almost eluding her grasp. Some of the men

11

were empty-handed. Her bundle was plainly not just awkward but cumbersome; as they crossed the road she could barely see over it. No one helped her. She tottered up the steps and into the building, watched in her precarious progress by assorted suits, the mounted policemen, the blue-blazered bouncers, the scarlet-coated sentinel. Their collective expression showed appraisal and even admiration, the bouncers swapped a comment that was clearly aimed below the belt, but no assistance was offered, there was no trace of old-fashioned chivalry or sexist *politesse*.

Charlie found the incident curiously significant. The double standard obviously operated in this male-dominated environment, but only the negatives, the customary ogling and lavatory jokes, the schoolboy mentality again. The positive aspects – the holding of doors, the carrying of burdens – had been dumped as antiquated gestures. Charlie could imagine the remarks: 'This is a man's world. She chose to break in. Let her sink or swim on her own.' For the first time she experienced a qualm that was more than nerves, the shadow of a premonition.

'Hell of a building, ain't it?' An American voice intruded on her thoughts, a tourist with a camcorder who had apparently been shooting Richard Rogers's artwork, the advent of the bus and the overburdened girl. He must have been standing beside Charlie for some time, but she had been too absorbed to notice. 'You on vacation?'

'No.'

'Looks like a modern edition of the Tower of Babel if you ask me. Hell in a glass case, all tied up with metal tubes. You going to work there?'

He must have correctly interpreted the look on her face, whatever that might be. Doubt, expectancy, eagerness or longing.

She said: 'I hope so.'

'I wish you luck, honey. You're going to need it.'

12

CHAPTER TWO

The sunlight panned between the girders of Tower Bridge as the taxi made its way over the Thames. It came to a halt inside the Blue Circle, a grandiose warehouse conversion that formed the centrepiece of Butler's Wharf. Charlie paid the driver, tipped lavishly in accordance with her mood, and went into reception. Unlike the traditional splendour of the example at Fitzgerald Denton, the security man here sported grey worsted and lank, overlong hair, and lounged in a swivel chair flipping through a tabloid newspaper. He, too, did not favour vintage courtesy. He recognised Charlie from previous visits and wondered, not for the first time, who she was. The object of her calls, David Chater, was one of the original residents from 1975, a lawyer living in a single-bedroom apartment on the second floor. On the wrong side of fifty and clearly comfortable with his bachelor status, he had the reputation of being something of a ladies' man. He was visibly well off, rather *soigné*, despite a retreating hairline and an incipient embonpoint. The women in his life were predominantly around his own age, executive types looking for a part-time companion rather than romance; the security man could not place Charlie among their ranks. He even speculated – since he had that kind of mind – if she were a high-class hooker. He had heard that nowadays superior tarts were all ex-public school.

Unaware of occasioning such improbable fantasies, Charlie entered the lift, her thoughts still preoccupied with the events of the morning. Even if she didn't get the job – and she felt she had to touch wood with every seductive stirring of confidence – she had had an intriguing meeting and a glimpse into the world to which she yearned to belong. What she had seen had been no Elysium, a world of hazards and pitfalls, unequal opportunities, infinite possibilities, treacherous hopes; but it had been nothing if not stimulating. She checked her reflection in the mirror-surround and saw a flush of excitement in her cheeks that outdid her blusher. When the lift stopped on the second floor a man was waiting outside; she was assailed by the ghost of Spooner, a shadow crossing her sunlight, but it was nobody, nobody special, and her momentary twinge of fear vanished as she stepped past him into the empty corridor. The walls were solid, the carpet thick, deadening her footfalls, shutting off the rumour of the metropolis outside. For a few seconds she stood still, listening to the quiet, conscious of feeling inexplicably reassured – inexplicably because, surely, there was no need for reassurance, nothing to trouble her but the lingering memory of a man she had not liked. She walked down the corridor and turned the corner to David Chater's apartment.

The security man had rung to announce her arrival: the door was ajar in readiness for her. Chater, hearing her come in, added a small measure of tonic to a large one of gin and called out: 'Hello, darling. In here –' and welcomed her with a triple kiss, a fashion borrowed from his Parisian mother, long since dead. She felt his carefully razed cheek cling to hers and smelt the aftershave she had given him at Christmas – and then, over his shoulder, she saw the stranger. He was standing at the arched picture window that overlooked the yacht haven, the incoming light casting his profile in sharp relief. A profile like a medieval woodcut, hawk-nosed, thin-lipped, austere, the jaw a clean line that disdained the blurring of age.

She drew back from Chater, awaiting an introduction, but he was more concerned with questions.

'How did it go? Did you knock 'em dead?' The same phrase the old sailor at Fitzgerald Denton had used. Why did it feel unlucky?

'I don't know. They say they'll be in touch: the usual line. I thought it went really well, but . . . I suppose I'm afraid to be too sure.' She took a mouthful of her drink and the flush in her cheeks deepened still further. 'Ouch. Can't you squeeze in a little more tonic? That doesn't just pack a punch: it's instant concussion.'

David took back her glass. 'I'm just getting you into practice. If you're going to work at Lloyd's you'll need a head like a rock. Oh, I'm sorry,' he turned to the man at the window, 'Charlie, I'd like you to meet a very old friend of mine, Henry Marriott.

Henry, this is Charlotte Christie. I've known her since they dropped her in the font and fancied her since she first put on lipstick – she was nine at the time, the lipstick was her mother's – but due to the fact that I'm her godparent I'm afraid she's out of bounds.'

Charlie, accustomed to his flirtatious attitude, wrinkled her nose as if to say 'Don't be silly', and turned her attention to Henry.

'Hello,' he said, extending a hand. His grip was light and strong, his voice low down the scale, a soft voice with a hard edge, iron under velvet. She judged he must be a contemporary of Chater's but here there was no creeping paunch, no loosening beneath the chin; the years had merely tempered him, honing flesh against the bone, emphasising the fine-drawn features, refining and not deteriorating. He had the rarefied air of a hermit or an ascetic, a man habituated to solitude, preferring his own company, yet capable of sympathy and sensitivity. A knight of the crusading kind, who might prefer outwitting dragons to the crude brutality of slaying them, one who would never take advantage of a damsel in distress but would restore her to her weeping family without laying a finger on her. This was a man, Charlie felt, who would always put a cause before a woman, embracing the concept of self-sacrifice. A man it would be easy to respect, difficult to approach, dangerous to love. His eyes were light in colour, grey as the clouds which had marred the early morning, river-clear. Something in his gaze seemed to pierce right into her mind.

Fantasy, all fantasy. He was a stranger; she knew nothing about him. The map of a man's face tells you only how well he has learned to deceive.

'Henry is an underwriter at Lloyd's,' Chater continued. 'They say he's the biggest brigand in the ship. All right, I know: more tonic. Coming up.'

He left the room to replenish her glass and Charlie summoned a suitable response. 'That's quite a reputation to live down to.'

'David's a lawyer,' Henry reminded her. 'Entertaining untruths are part of his stock-in-trade. No one wants a solicitor who's unswervingly honest: it's a contradiction in terms.

15

Besides, the truth is so often dull – or worse, disappointing. My real biographical details wouldn't arouse your interest at all.'

Charlie was about to contradict him but he did not give her the chance, moving on smoothly to her own affairs. 'So you're having a shot at joining Lloyd's?'

'That's the idea.'

'Fitzgerald Denton is certainly a good place to start. With their name behind you I doubt if you'll have too many problems.'

'I don't know if I've got the job yet,' Charlie demurred. 'The interview went OK but I'm sure I was one of a crowd.'

'You would always stand out in a crowd,' he said lightly, and for an instant, looking into those cloud-silver eyes, she lost her grip on the subject under discussion. Possibly he detected her confusion; whatever the reason, he added without waiting for her reply: 'I'm certain you'll become a major asset to Fitzgerald Denton in no time.'

David came back into the room bearing rather more dilute gin and the conversation lost its intimate flavour. They moved on to a small balcony with a view of the dock and a miscellany of yachts, motor launches and old sailing barges, moored to a chain of pontoons. All of them were dipping and bumping in the wind-ruffled water as if impatient to break loose and speed with the river current towards the distant sea. Charlie was distracted by signs of activity aboard one of the barges: cases of liquor, supported by clutching arms and staggering legs in nautical trousers, tottered up the gangplank, followed by more boxes, presumably of glassware, and trays wrapped in clingfilm borne on different legs, bare and shapely and rather more sure-footed. 'Looks like the makings of a good party,' Chater remarked. 'Might gangway-crash later. More drinks?'

He disappeared in search of refills and Henry said: 'Your godfather seems to be addicted to single bliss.'

'Oh yes,' Charlie smiled. 'We keep waiting to hear wedding bells but all we ever get is the occasional fire alarm. Whenever an affair looks as if it might get serious he takes flight. He values his freedom too much; I think he'd find marriage rather flat. Or at any rate, rather flattening.'

'Marriage is not necessarily a flattening experience,' Henry

16

said with curious detachment, answering the question she had not asked.

Charlie, embarrassed, found herself faltering an apology. 'I'm sorry, I didn't mean . . . I didn't know you were married.'

'Only when the wind is nor'nor'easterly. My wife has been very ill for some time.' Charlie, tumbling still deeper into embarrassment, groped in vain for a change of subject. Her companion went on as though determined to finish his explanation, to have done with it, his gaze fixed not on Charlie but somewhere between the river and the sky. 'My son was killed in a motorbike accident and she never really came to terms with it. She now lives in a protected environment. They look after her very well.'

'How dreadful,' Charlie gasped, racked with guilt for letting the conversation slip into such painful sidelines. 'I really am sorry . . .'

'Don't be.' He was almost curt. 'It happened nearly ten years ago. It's history now. We all have to learn to live with our history.' He smiled suddenly, a smile of regulation politeness, setting tragedy aside, resuming what must be his customary social veneer. 'Forgive me for having the bad taste to burden you with it. We've only just met: I had no right.'

'Please – *please* – don't call it bad taste,' Charlie stammered. 'It's always an honour if – if people choose to confide in you.'

'He'd have been about your age now,' Henry said slowly, his smile easing, responding to her evident sincerity. 'I suppose that's one reason why I was thinking of him. He was only seventeen when he died.'

'Please tell me about it,' she said, hoping she didn't sound presumptuous, adding, anxiously: 'If you wish.'

'Not much to tell.' His expression was wry, hurtful to watch. 'I bought him the bike. As far as my wife was concerned, that made it my fault. He was hell-bent on a bike – you know what teenage boys are like. He wanted a metal steed on which to vaunt his prowess. Natural enough. I understood; his mother didn't. I wish I hadn't been so bloody understanding. We had a row but I overruled her, made James promise to be careful, take proper lessons, that sort of thing.' His face changed, pent-up breath escaped in a gentle sigh. 'Stupid. Adolescents don't care; it's

17

against their creed. They all think they're going to live forever. As it is, all it took was a wet road and a lorry. The lorry must have been going too fast, but they couldn't prove it. And so . . . farewell, James.'

Charlie couldn't speak. She ached to touch his hand but was afraid it might appear forward. He lit a cigarette with peculiar deliberation, inhaled deeply. At last she said, to break the silence: 'Can I have one too?'

'I beg your pardon. I should have offered . . .'

'Not at all.'

They smoked together in unexpected companionship, giving the ghosts time to fade. Charlie wondered what was keeping David, and whether he was being deliberately tactful. Why exactly had he invited her to meet this man? Was it only because Henry was an underwriter at Lloyd's?

'These are David's,' Henry remarked, flicking the cigarette box with one finger. 'I must buy him some next time I'm in the duty-free. He always complains I never smoke my own. He says I'm too mean.'

'I thought you were frightfully rich?' Charlie said involuntarily.

'Of course. You need to be mean to get rich. Conversely, you need to be rich in order to have something to be mean about.' A trace of real humour quirked his mouth, and she hoped the phantom of his son had receded, at least for the moment.

David Chater returned on cue.

'How about lunch?' he suggested, with an enforced heartiness which implied he might have overheard, or guessed at, part of the preceding discussion. 'I thought maybe the Dickens Inn, or the Yacht Club.'

'Charlie should be celebrating in style,' Henry interceded, though celebration, she felt, was a little premature. 'She'd like the Pont de la Tour. My treat.'

They entered the restaurant through huge glass doors; to their left, assorted crustaceans goggled at them from a bed of crushed ice adorned with black seaweed; to their right, an attentive waiter materialised to greet a favoured regular. They negotiated bar and brasserie and penetrated the inner sanctum of the main restaurant where, in an atmosphere of sybaritic dedication, gourmets and gourmands, foodies and faddists, sat poring over their menus and debating the finer points of sauces and side dishes with helpful acolytes. The waiter escorted Henry's party to what was clearly his usual table and Charlie found herself manoeuvred into a chair and confronted with a catalogue of unpriced dishes. She wondered if there was anything cheap – when in doubt, her grandmother had once told her, a true lady will always order an omelette – but omelettes were not in evidence and the only eggs that featured belonged to the sturgeon. Henry watched in faint amusement as she hesitated, plainly confused by his impromptu extravagance. 'I think . . . I think I'll have the smoke salmon,' she faltered eventually. 'And – pressed duck . . .'

He shook his head. 'Leave it to me. We'll both have the Caspian beluga, followed by the *filet*, very rare. David?'

Charlie opened her mouth and then shut it again. She really would have preferred the duck but Henry was paying and that left her little choice. He might not be as mean as he had claimed, but his generosity was obviously conditional, a calculated gesture designed to put him in control. As the recipient of both the generosity and the control she experienced a mixed reaction, part indignation, part an elusive excitement, an arousal that was almost sexual. She was not certain that it pleased her. David's presence, as umpire or chaperon, added a restraining element that in some perverted way increased the stimulus.

Henry left him to dally with the menu and returned to the subject of Charlie's prospective employment.

'So tell me,' he said, '*à propos* of today's interview, do you really think we have reason to celebrate?'

'Touch wood.' She suited the action to the words. 'I told you, I hope so, *but* . . .'

'Of course, you're attractive and intelligent. That might be a problem.'

'Thanks for the compliment.' She lapsed into self-mockery. 'It *is* rather difficult, but I bear up. Seriously, why *should* that be a problem – supposing it's true?'

His smile flickered into life at her response. 'It might be for them.'

'Why?'

'You're too bright, too quick, potentially too successful. You might get out of hand: a firecracker in their midst – a live grenade with the pin out – a blonde bombshell ticking its way to explosion. Very risky. Also – I may be mistaken, but I believe you show indications of conscience. That could be inconvenient. A broker needs a conscience like an athlete needs a wooden leg. It drags him down, slows his progress: other people stare at it and then look away hastily in pity and repulsion. All he requires is the semblance of honesty and a scruple or two for special occasions. A conscience is an unprofessional handicap.' His sarcasm was too savage for jest and Charlie felt uncomfortable: if this was irony she could have done without it.

David, in confabulation with the waiter, had missed most of their exchange for more important matters. The calves' liver, or the sole *bonne femme*. These decisions were so difficult.

Charlie studied her host uncertainly, troubled eyes reflecting her doubt. Seeing it, he changed key, murmuring 'Forget it', and 'Compromise is a fact of life. We all have to do it', which was not quite what she wanted to hear. 'Do you still want the job?'

'*Want* it? Of course I – It's a challenge, anyway. I like challenges.'

'Then I'm sure you'll get it.' He finished the lingering smile, creasing his thin cheek into laughter lines too faint to be commonplace. That total smile, she thought, must be a rarity, his laugh probably an endangered species. Perhaps because of his personal tragedy, perhaps something in his nature.

'Liver,' David announced, the incongruous word invading a short pause. 'I'll go with the liver.'

The waiter retreated and for a while conversation became general.

The caviar arrived presently, a lavish mound of it heaped on a silver platter and sustained by the inevitable crushed ice. Hitherto Charlie had only seen it served with nervous delicacy in crystal thimbles. It was accompanied by an unopened bottle of traditional Russian vodka, unsealed by the waiter with due reverence, a crucial part of the pre-prandial ritual. Henry poured the clear liquor and served the beluga himself, not entrusting such an essential task to a mere menial. They ate in

20

hushed appreciation. 'Men,' Charlie thought for the second time that day. Girls would have laughed at the price, gloated at the savour, munched, gossiped, launched into a parody of orgasmic satisfaction. Men took it all so seriously: the food, the flavour, the rites of consumption. As if the extortionate cost in itself merited a unique brand of respect.

'Is this something else I'll have to get used to if I'm working at Lloyd's?' she enquired of her companions. 'Not just intensive drinking but expensive eating.'

'Naturally.' Henry reached out and removed a stray black globule which had evaded her tongue and attached itself to her cheek. Rather to her surprise, he sucked it from his fingertip with unexpected sensuality. 'Waste not, want not.' The platitude covered a flicker of intimacy. 'Anyway, there's nothing like a diet of caviar to erode the conscience.'

'Do you have one?'

'A conscience? Maybe. But I never take it out to lunch.'

'You really are mean, aren't you?' The vodka was following the gin into her bloodstream and she was growing reckless. 'I'll bet you never give without expecting something in return.'

'Probably.'

'So why all this? What do you want from me?'

He hesitated, not in doubt but because he wished to arrange his answer. 'Call it in the nature of an investment.'

'And if there are no dividends?' she persisted. 'What then? Are you insured against all risks?'

'Everything,' he said, 'except an Act of God.' His gaze met hers and held it, eyeball to eyeball, interlocked.

'Delicious,' said David, presumably referring to the comestibles. 'Are you two flirting, talking business, or both?'

'Neither,' said Henry. 'This is far too serious for flirtation. Or, for that matter, for business.'

The waiter removed the debris of their starter; the vodka bottle, disastrously depleted, was replaced by a '67 Richebourg. A further ceremony ensued as it was uncorked and allowed to breathe before the advent of the main course. Henry, having signified his approval, excused himself and left the room.

'You've made a hit,' David said when he was out of earshot. 'Marriott's not a man who's easily impressed.'

Charlie said nothing. She was intoxicated with alcohol, seduced with food, unwilling to give herself away.

On the tenth floor, Cynthia Greenslade was in charge of the switchboard of Fitzgerald Denton. She'd been there for nearly seven years, and had her finger on the wire, if not the pulse, of the whole company. It was said that whatever was going on, Cynthia was always the first to know and often the first to tell. When the light on the incoming board flashed she discarded the matinée coat she was knitting for a prospective niece, flipped the switch, and responded automatically: 'Good afternoon. Fitzgerald Denton. How can I help you?' It was her mantra: she'd once calculated that in an eight-hour day she would repeat it, with slight variations (*Hello*, *Good morning*) 1,440 times, assuming an average of three calls per minute. There were occasions when she felt like a mechanical device.

'Who shall I say is calling? Thank you. Just one moment, sir. It's ringing for you.' She held the call until it was answered and duly recorded in the telephone log that at 13.42 Hugo Wingate had received a call from Mr Marriott. It was a slack day, no doubt because of Wimbledon, and she had time to resume her knitting before the light started its insistent summons again.

The Richebourg went the way of the vodka while Charlie toyed with her *filet*. Her appetite had vanished with the caviar and she was mesmerised by Henry's eyes, surveying her from beyond the barrier of the table, searching her mind, baring her soul, eyes palely burning as if lit by some secretive inner fire. She no longer cared how drunk she was, though she knew such a lethal mix of grain and grape would assuredly catch up with her later. She was aware she was ignoring David, not because she was being rude but because she kept forgetting he was there. Henry's dominating presence focused all her attention. There was some quality about him which troubled her, a factor behind his understated arrogance, his effortless mastery of the situation, which she was struggling to isolate, sensing that whatever it was, it constituted a vital element in his personality. This was a puzzle which she must solve if she was ever to understand him. She needed to comprehend, to compete, to meet him on an equal footing. The glamour of advanced intoxication haloed him in an aura of elusive power: she saw him suddenly as a medieval saint, etched in suffering by the brush of a Mantegna, his high ideals and intrinsic rectitude hardened in the face of pain. Neither temptation nor failure could sway him: he knew that he was right. That was his mystery, the key to his strength. *He knew he was right.* In doubt and disaster, personal loss or public disgrace, he would choose his course and adhere to it, discounting qualms. This was no bigot or fanatic but a reasonable man profoundly convinced of his own superior judgement, his ability to seize any dilemma by both horns. In that instant of revelation Charlie found herself afraid of him, fascinated and afraid, realising it was this core of certainty which made him, more than the job she dreamed of or the world she dared to enter, a dangerous challenge. In a flash of deceptive clarity of the kind that only occurs well down the bottle she saw all three in an irresistible conjunction; Henry Marriott came with the package. If Lloyd's was her future, so was he.

Wine succeeded wine, in this case a Barsac-Sauternes from 1969, heavy as syrup, golden as a summer in the Midi. The *crème brûlée* which it was intended to complement tasted unnecessary, a flavour too far; Charlie pushed it aside.

'It's not the best year,' she said haughtily, airing her knowledge. 'Didn't they have a '67?'

Henry laughed outright.

When the meal was over and Henry was settling the bill *en route* to the Gents Charlie concluded with something of an effort that it was time she went back to her flat. Ladbroke Gardens represented a haven where she could collapse into a horizontal position and succumb to an agreeable unconsciousness. 'David,' she turned to her godfather, 'would you – would you both think me terribly rude if I just went home now? Otherwise I'm afraid I may keel over or something. It's been quite a day.'

David blinked at her, bewilderment edged with concern. 'Are you all right? Is it your – you know –' his voice sank to a whisper '– your Woman's Time?'

Bachelordom, Charlie reflected with a glimmering of lucidity, shows itself in curious ways. 'No, darling,' she said. 'I'm just pissed.'

'Pissed?' David appeared even more baffled.

'Gin and tonic, vodka, Richebourg, Barsac: it's quite a list. Quite a Brahms and Liszt.' She caught herself short on a giggle which she knew to be inane. 'Sorry. Lousy pun. I think it was the Barsac that finished me off. It was a heavenly way to go, but . . .'

'You didn't eat enough,' David said instantly. 'You hardly touched the *filet*, and left the dessert.'

'I didn't feel hungry,' Charlie murmured.

'We'll get you a taxi,' David said. 'You're a bit hyper after the interview: that always lowers your stamina. Don't worry, darling: Henry will understand. I'll make sure of it.'

On his return to their table she made her apologies; he seemed undisturbed. 'I hope you've enjoyed yourself, even if you have overdone it a little.'

'It's been marvellous,' she replied. 'It only seems a pity we had nothing definite to celebrate.'

'Ah, but we had.' He reseated himself just as the waiter arrived with three glasses of pink champagne on a silver tray.

'What's this?' Charlie blenched.

'This is just for a quick toast.' He handed one of them to her. 'Dom Perignon: it's quite harmless, I promise you. Fizz with flavour.' He raised his glass. 'Welcome to the City. I trust the career you've chosen is the right one and I know you'll be a big success. Cheers.'

'But,' Charlie stammered, confused, 'but – well, I've only had an interview. I mean – this is very sweet of you, Henry, but I won't hear till the end of the week.'

'You're hearing it now. I called Fitzgerald Denton earlier. You've got the job.'

'*What?*'

'There'll be a letter of appointment in the post this evening.' His smile was still slightly crooked, misleading in its gentleness; he clinked his goblet against hers. Her head cleared alarmingly: the restaurant came abruptly into focus. 'I couldn't resist breaking the news to you. Well done.'

'Thank you,' said Charlie. 'I – good God.'

'Yes,' said Henry with peculiar gravity. 'He can be. Sometimes.' He swallowed a mouthful of champagne, replaced his glass on the table. 'And now I'm afraid I must go. I have an important meeting at 4.30, so if you'll excuse me . . . Incidentally, I took the liberty of ordering a cab for you both. It should be here soon, but do stay on if you like. You must finish the bottle. David, I'll give you a call next week. Charlie, it's been a pleasure. Perhaps when you've got your feet under the table at Fitzgerald Denton I could give you a ring.'

'I'd like that.'

He passed her his card, took her hand for the second time. Out of mere courtesy she tried to stand up, supporting herself against the rim of the table. The room was not quite steady around her and this outward instability seemed to parallel her inner confusion. His departure was too abrupt, the news of her achievement too startling. She suspected him of using his influence in her cause, and resented it even while it gratified her. She wanted to be convinced she had succeeded entirely on her own merits.

When he had gone she sat down again, much too quickly.

'Congratulations,' said her godfather. 'Not simply on the new job. That is a man whose friendship cannot be bought.'

'Really?' She was responding mechanically, her thoughts in a spiral.

'That's pretty unusual, believe me.'

'I suppose most people have their price.' The trite observation escaped her on a reflex. She was still thinking of Henry Marriott, a man whose integrity was apparently priceless.

'Of course they do,' David said happily. 'We're all donkeys in pursuit of a nice fat carrot. Me too. And you, darling. Today has just whetted your appetite. You've got the taste for it: I can tell.' He looked round for the waiter. 'Now, how about polishing off the rest of that champagne?'

Charlie leaned back in her chair, resigning herself to an alcoholic fate, and reviewed the events of the day. She assumed, with what little pragmatism she had left, that it was unlikely to be typical of the City broker's regular diary.

She was wrong.

CHAPTER THREE

Charlie had lived in Notting Hill for a year. Before that she had rented a flat in Barons Court, but the apartment in Ladbroke Gardens had been acquired on a mortgage, her first serious financial commitment, the bottom rung in the ladder to an executive lifestyle. The area had once been the location of the king's race course; now, it was ageing gracefully, slightly faded but not yet gone to seed. Portobello Road was nearby, an alfresco Aladdin's cave with antiques both genuine and fake, junk and jumble, gew-gaws and kickshaws, knick-knacks and bric-à-brac. Charlie had bought a Wedgwood coffee service there, a Victorian cheval glass with candle-brackets on either side, a slipware bird too chipped to be valuable. When burglars broke in they had taken all her Japanese technology but left the china. She had been surprised at the depth of her relief: these were things she had chosen herself, treasures unearthed from the Portobello hoard, part of her intimate environment. It was impossible to feel an emotional attachment to a television set. After the burglary, she had called a security firm, installed the necessary accoutrements of urban life: mortice, Chubb, entry-phone and alarm. The alarm was particularly irritating, shrilling into action at the slightest provocation.

That afternoon, she stumbled up the steps to the front door, thrust the wrong key in the right lock (or vice versa), and spent several minutes trying to sort out which was which before the various locks yielded reluctantly and the door swung open. Junk mail scrunched underfoot. She tried to bend down to rifle through it but decided she might be unable to straighten up again afterwards, kicked the envelopes aside with a wayward foot, and headed for her own apartment, fortunately situated on the ground floor. More keys, more locks. The new Chubb was stiff, grudging admittance. When the door finally opened the alarm, galvanised into action by what was clearly a forced entry, beeped a rapid admonition before beginning its raucous ululation, reverberating hideously through her skull. She groped her way to the control in her coat cupboard, colliding with a table in transit, and fumbled with the switch. The merciless bell was silenced. Peace. Home. She crumpled thankfully on to the sofa.

The flat was the largest in the house, with a double aspect drawing room commanding a wide view across the private gardens to the rear. There were few flowers but the shaven lawn was fringed with plane trees whose broad leaves snared the summer breeze, shifting and rustling in the restless air. She loved the trees, the thick trunks marked as if painted in sprawling brushstrokes, the palmate leaves, each big as a dinner plate, the deep green shadow beneath the boughs. It was really why she had bought the flat, that little sanctuary of countryside remembered. The trees and the brindled bark and the sun and the whispering. They were like old friends, steadfast and reliable, who would always be there for her. There were communal gardens nearby, well laid out and superficially serene, but under the bushes by the railing she had seen dirty syringes, used condoms, the ugly jetsam from the underside of life. Beneath the plane trees there was tranquillity, secluded and free from slatternly detritus. But that day the sun was undependable; passing showers had left the foliage dripping and shining with a veneer of moisture. The vista of transient cloud and moving sky seemed suddenly depressing. Of course, it was Wimbledon fortnight; no wonder there was so much rain. She checked her answer machine, ignored the messages, damned all intrusive technology. Then she switched on the television set – her brand new, ultra-protected television set – and watched the sickening arc of the tennis ball as it spun from one side of the court to the other.

When she could stand, she made for the bathroom, stepping out of her shoes, shedding clothes in her wake. Jacket, blouse, skirt, bra, discarded in a wilting trail across the carpet. She leaned against the tiled wall to wriggle out of tights and briefs, tottered under the shower, reeling when the water hit her. The temperature fluctuated wildly as she jiggled the taps; warm, scalding, cold. When the heat steadied she turned her face up to the jet, felt her hair flattened against her forehead, runnels of water coursing down her neck, dividing on her shoulders, veining her arms, glittering arteries streaming over belly and thighs. Her foundation was washed away, her mascara liquified and ran. A wave of nausea rushed over her, doubling her up. It had all been too much, the drink, the caviar, the overdose of sybaritica: her body could not keep it down. She threw up till she was empty, rinsed her mouth out, swathed her shaking limbs in a towel. She did not have the strength for vigorous rubbing and she threw herself under her duvet still damp, towel-wrapped, while the distant drone of the tennis commentary lulled her to sleep.

Several hours must have passed when the ringing of the telephone dragged her back into consciousness. It was dark beyond the open curtains and the voice of the television had changed. At first she imagined it was the alarm again, and she cursed as oblivion receded; then the machine cut in and reality dawned. She heard her own voice, nearer and louder than the ramblings of the BBC, sounding different as voices always do on a tape. 'Hello; this is Charlie. I expect I'm in the bath. Leave a message' – and then the insistent bleep. Modern life seemed to be punctuated with bleeps and bells, tapes and transmissions, an endless chorus of twittering automata drowning out the birdsong of an idyllic past. She strained her ears to identify the caller, trying to isolate the words from background interference. It was her father, but she could not make out what he was saying. Sorry, Daddy. Can't get up yet. I'll call back. Afterwards, very gingerly, she pushed back the duvet, swung her legs over the edge of the bed. This would never do. She was supposed to be a tough twentieth-century woman who could wine-and-dine her way through a long evening and wake up the next day with stars in her eyes. Her body simply wasn't used to a midday session. Unaccustomed as I am to lunchtime drinking . . .

She got to her feet, leaving the rumpled towel in the bed, pulled on a sumptuous dressing gown, formerly the property of her ex-fiancé, and went into the drawing room. Tripping over the remote control for the TV she switched it off and then on again, with the sound down, so she could catch the ten o'clock news. She drew the curtains across the main windows, shutting out the night under the plane trees. Then she played back her father's message. 'Hello darling. It's only me. David told me about the job. Bloody good show. When you've got a mo give your mother a ring. If you could make it this weekend we'd love to see you. She's says it's been nearly five weeks and we're beginning to forget what you look like. Anyway, lots of love. Roger and out.' Charlie pressed the appropriate button and the tape rewound. She was desperately thirsty and still felt too feeble for verbal communication. She explored the fridge, found Evian, orange juice, ice. The combination tasted like an oasis in a desert. Back on the sofa, face to face with Trevor McDonald, she decided she might be able to survive the stresses of City life after all.

By 8.30 the next morning she felt partially restored, though her stomach still felt slightly queasy. She had forgotten to close her bedroom curtains and she blinked in the onslaught of remorseless sunlight. In the kitchen she assembled the ingredients of her father's cure-all for alcoholic after-effects: two raw eggs, a splash of Worcester sauce, and a screw of ground black pepper. She whisked the obnoxious mixture into a froth and braced herself to swallow it in one go. 'I learned two things in the forces,' her father used to say. 'An infallible hangover remedy and how to talk bullshit. Both have proved essential in civilian life, too.' Charlie, with an inherited flair, had learned from him. She warmed the glass to prevent the mixture sticking, stiffened her sinews, and tossed it valiantly down her throat. Once it had eluded her taste-buds she began to feel revived. She set coffee in motion and went to check the post and the phone.

There was no letter of appointment. Marriott would surely not have lied but he might have been mistaken. 'We're considering her,' Fitzgerald Denton might have said. 'She's well to the top of the list' – something like that. Too easy to misinterpret. But no: Henry Marriott was not the kind of person given to misinterpretation. Over coffee, she did her best to banish speculation, returning phone calls and arranging to meet one of her friends, Caroline Elliott-Browne, at her health club in the Fulham Road. She dressed carefully, anxious not to disturb her stomach, in swimsuit, tracksuit, pumps. On the street she hailed a cab to Holmes Place.

By the time she got there her insides felt quasi-normal – the

29

miracle cure working again – but she had no intention of offering her system unnecessary provocation in the form of exercise. She avoided the gym and entered the sauna. To her relief it was empty; she did not feel inclined for the customary keep-fit smalltalk about mileage achieved on the treadmill, litreage heaved on the bench-press, the number of lengths completed in the pool. She sat down in the muffled quiet of the tiny log cabin, hoping she could sweat in private for a while. The image of Henry Marriott kept intruding on her thoughts: she wondered if she would ever see him again, and how soon, and whether, once she was part of the City scene, he would behave any differently towards her.

Ten minutes later she was glossy with perspiration and the intense heat was becoming claustrophobic. Had Henry in some way secured her the job at Fitzgerald Denton? Would she have got it if he had not made that phone call? *Had* she really got the job at all? She left the wooden shed, steeled herself, and jumped into the ice-cold plunge pool. The contrast snatched her breath; she gasped silently like a fish at the impact of the freezing water. Scrambling out again, shuddering, she could not believe this bizarre regime of torture was doing her any good, except for the fact that the physical shock had cleared the doubts from her mind, leaving it temporarily as numb as the rest of her. She returned to the sauna and towelled herself furiously, pouring a ladleful of green, pine-scented water over the smouldering coals of the fire. They hissed, belching steam; the humidity soared. Dizziness surged over her: she sank down on to the lowest plank-bench and ducked her head between her knees. To her dismay, she heard the door opening. A waft of cooler air dispelled her vertigo, succeeded by the unmistakable reek of Chanel 19. It was Caroline Elliott-Browne.

'Darling! What splendid news!' She plucked Charlie from her semi-prone position and kissed her relentlessly on both cheeks, almost occasioning a relapse. 'You look splendid too. God, I must catch up. I've got the most horrendous hangover. What did you say?'

'Splendid,' Charlie echoed hollowly.

'Darling, don't be a dog in the manger. Just because you're

into sobriety and early rising – why *were* you up so early? You rang me before nine.'

'I went to bed early,' Charlie said palely. 'To be precise, after lunch.'

'My God,' Caroline exclaimed. 'What sort of a lunch was that?'

Charlie told her. Caroline declined the doubtful pleasure of the plunge pool – 'When I cultivate masochism it'll be whips and chains, not icy water' – and while they showered and dressed she cross-examined her friend on the subject of Henry Marriott.

'I'll swear I've heard the name. Something to do with a merger, or a takeover. Anyway, I'll sound out the grapevine. How old is he?'

'Not sure. Fifty-odd. I haven't got close enough to count the rings.'

'Yet,' supplied Caroline. 'Married? Must be. They always are.'

'Separated.'

'How separated?' Caroline persisted. 'Be more specific. By a wall, a chastity belt, a thin layer of Janet Reger? There are so many degrees of separation.'

'She's in some sort of asylum,' Charlie said, unwilling to explain further.

'Dear me. Sounds like Mr Rochester. Are you sure he doesn't have a Gothic mansion in the heart of the countryside, and keep her locked away in the attics in the care of a sinister nurse?'

'Of course not,' Charlie snapped. 'He's frightfully civilised. He minds terribly: I could feel it. There's all this pent-up suffering inside him –'

'Oh *shit*!' Caroline swore, sighed, pulled on the top half of a tracksuit that had never seen a track. 'All right, I get the picture. Hard outside, soft centre, with a dash of bitter in the sweet. Just like my favourite liqueur chocolates. Let's hope the bitter isn't essence of cyanide. That kind are always irresistible – like the chocs. Now, how about a celebration? There's a bottle of champers in the fridge at home. I feel far too healthy after that shower. I need to wake up my liver.'

'*Healthy?*' Charlie was indignant. 'You didn't even get in the pool.'

31

'This is a health club,' Caroline pointed out. 'I feel healthy. Come on, my car's outside. Did you bring yours?'

'No: I took a cab. Why on earth did you come by car? You only live round the corner.'

'I wasn't going to *walk* here: it's bad for you. All those exhaust fumes: pure carbon mon. Have you got your bag? Good. I'll drive us back.'

Inevitably, Caroline worked in PR. Her business hours were filled with corporate functions, product launches, press parties; her social life with launch parties, press functions, corporate dinners. She finished every evening with a nightclub and started every morning with strong black coffee. Friends had been hospitalised trying to keep up. She had, they said, not so much an appetite for life as an addiction; an evening in was a famine to her. Her looks flourished on the momentum: at five foot ten, she had a figure tending to opulence, narrow waist counterbalanced with well-arranged padding, making the most conservative clothes appear flamboyant and sexy. A vast alcoholic intake gave her complexion a peach-bloom lustre, her hair a mahogany sheen. Charlie, one of the few people who could survive long periods in her company, felt unusually fragile beside her, sometimes even subdued.

Caroline owned a house in Hollywood Road bought by a wealthy and fortunately naive first husband who dropped out of her life, probably suffering from exhaustion, after about six months. She filed for divorce and kept the house. Husband number two brought in an army of interior designers who converted, redecorated and refurnished at breathtaking expense, vastly exceeding their allotted budget. Caroline threw the husband out with the designers after finding him *in flagrante delicto* in the spare bedroom with the charming young man responsible for soft furnishings. She was left with the spoils of matrimony, free to concentrate on a life and a career in the fast lane.

They cracked the Bollinger, toasted Charlie's future success. 'We might as well finish it,' Caroline said some time later. 'After all, it doesn't keep.' She invited Charlie to a country-house junket the following weekend, offering as a dubious incentive the

32

prediction that it was bound to be too, too ghastly. 'I need some moral support, darling: you can't let me down. Imagine it, a whole weekend with a load of guests who are into rusticity and real ale. It's a recipe for tedium.'

'Do you *know* that's what they're into?' Charlie said, blanching.

'Not exactly,' Caroline admitted. 'I can just feel it – *here*.' She pressed her superb bosom. 'Anyway, you're on a roll at the moment. You can take this one in your stride. We're friends, aren't we?'

'I refuse to commit myself,' said Charlie, 'on the grounds that it may incriminate me.'

'*Please*, darling,' Caroline wailed.

By the bottom of the bottle, Charlie had succumbed. She excused herself from a prolonged session on the plea that she had to see her parents, but agreed to go to the party on Saturday and drive to the ancestral home for Sunday lunch.

The letter of appointment was on the mat when she opened the front door. She knew at once what it must be. She picked it up and went out into the garden, opening it only when she was seated on the grass under the plane trees. Fitzgerald Denton were pleased to inform her that she would be joining their team, starting, if possible, at the beginning of September. The initial salary was not large, though sufficient to cover her mortgage, but the prospects unfolding before her seemed suddenly unlimited. She would be a denizen of that enchanted kingdom of money and power, an executive-class traveller to the great cities of the world, a gambler for whom every hand was full of aces. 'A top broker can make well over 100 K,' Henry Marriott had said at one point, somewhere between the *filet* and the *crème brûlée*. Seductive words, a siren song to open ears with no one to lash her to the mast and speed her ship safely by. 'Bloody man,' she thought, and read the letter again. And again. She remained in the garden until the light began to fail and the whispering of the trees grew imperceptibly louder. The evening breeze had sprung from nowhere, and suddenly all the warmth of the day disappeared. Clouds smothered the dying sun. It was like the day before, outside the tube station, grey changeful weather, wind and sky hurrying, hurrying, tugging her, pulling her, on to a perilous future. A shiver ran through her; she heard the first drops of rain pattering on to the leaves above her. She should have gone in ten minutes ago. She ran into the flat, to the sort of quiet night Caroline would never contemplate, promising herself to phone her mother.

The party on Saturday was tolerable – Caroline's predictions of social disaster rarely materialised – and the next day Charlie drove down to her parents' house in Chichester. Once there, she was glad she had come: her grandmother, whom she had not seen for nearly a year, was there too, and Charlie sat down on the sofa beside her, holding her hand, trying to say she was sorry for an unintended neglect. Granny looked rather frail, she thought, her small face shrunken from a resolute nose, the lines of a lifetime's worry and laughter flickering and multiplying in her cheeks. The hand in Charlie's clasp felt insubstantial, a fairy claw thinly mantled in skin.

'It must be ten months since I was last at Ballards,' Charlie calculated. 'That's awful. I don't know where the time's gone.'

'Youth.' Her grandmother smiled a faint, sweet smile, as if her sense of humour had been laid up in lavender. 'You're so busy rushing headlong at life you don't stop to count the days. It's worse when you're older, you'll find, when you're counting the months and years, trying to hold on to the time that keeps slipping through your fingers. When you're young, you think you have for ever. It's a curious contradiction: you're racing forward to get to a place you believe you'll never reach, middle age, old age, death. By the time you get there, it's too late to slow down. You're in the spring flood of life: enjoy it. I did. I would never tell you to go gently, be careful, look both ways, anything like that. Advice from the old is so dreary. I don't want you to think of me as a dull old woman who moralises at you; besides, that sort of thing never does any good.'

'You're never dull, Granny,' Charlie said remorsefully, tightening the clasp on her hand very cautiously. 'I'd welcome any advice you wanted to give: you know that. I think of you often. I suppose the problem with family is that they've always been there and you tend to assume that they always will be, sort of steady and permanent, like trees, only . . .'

'Only I won't always be here,' her grandmother said gently. 'None of us will. Heigh-ho, what it is to be young.' And suddenly her blue eyes sparkled with remembered mischief. 'You're all bright and shiny with hopefulness. I like that. When you're near, some of the shine rubs off on me.'

Charlie laughed massaging her thin fingers. 'Have some shine,' she said. 'If this new job proves lucrative, I should have lots to spare. When I've got my routine sorted out I'll come down for the weekend: we'll go to that little café where you used to take me for tea at half-term. The one where the waitresses all wore white aprons and starched caps, like French maids in the theatre. I bet it's all different now. They probably have pink hair and chewing gum and jeans.'

'It's gone,' the old lady said, and Charlie almost thought she shivered. 'I used to go there every Friday with your grandpa when he was alive. He liked it such a lot; I wasn't sure why. It wasn't really his kind of place at all.'

'No, it wasn't,' Charlie agreed. 'Tea at the Ritz would have been more his style: Royal Doulton and extravagant cakes. Or champagne and anchovy sandwiches. He must have found a country café a little underwhelming.'

'Not entirely.' The vague smile returned, suddenly ghostly. 'He was having an affair with one of the waitresses. The French maid in his life – of course. That must have been how he saw her. How clever of you, dear. I never understood before.'

Charlie was staring at her, appalled. 'But – how did you know?'

'I didn't, really. Then she came to his funeral, all in black, very ostentatious. Vulgar. Grey would have been discreet and in much better taste. Anyway, when I saw her there, I knew. Naturally, I'd suspected for a long time, but . . .'

'Woman's intuition?' Charlie suggested.

'Oh no. It was much simpler than that. Your grandfather loved me a great deal, but when he – well, lost interest in certain things, I knew there could only be two reasons. Either he'd genuinely – lost interest, or he had an interest elsewhere. A French maid, you see. A naughty secret. Your grandfather liked naughty secrets. It kept him young; I didn't grudge him that. I tried very hard not to mind.' The glimmer of a tear eclipsed the sparkle; she fumbled for a handkerchief, let Charlie take it from her and daub away the offending droplet. It was a beautiful handkerchief if rather worn, the antique lace fraying, cream dimmed to yellow. Old and exquisite, like its owner. Charlie tried to think of an appropriate response and couldn't. The silence stretched out into something companionable, easy.

At length Granny retrieved the handkerchief and tucked it back into her sleeve. 'I don't know if your father mentioned it,' she said, 'but I'm putting Ballards on the market. If you want to see me there, you'd better come soon. We've discussed it a lot, your parents and I, and we're agreed: it's too big and too inconvenient, I might be taken ill there and unable to call for help, you hear such dreadful stories. It's much better to sell up and invest the proceeds in case I should ever need to go into a Home.' She gave the word a distinct capital letter. 'Actually, I hope it won't happen. I'd much rather pop off quickly and have something extra to leave to all of you.'

'Don't!' Charlie said distressfully. 'Please don't talk like that. Granny, you've always loved Ballards. Do you *have* to sell?'

'It's the best thing.' Her grandmother sounded tired rather than convinced. 'I'm going to move in here. That old box room on the half-landing can be converted into a little kitchen so I'll be able to do my own cooking and have visitors up for tea without disturbing anyone. I wouldn't want to be a bother to you all.'

'You couldn't be,' Charlie insisted. 'It's not a *bother* to look after someone you love.' There was a pause while she assimilated the forthcoming change. 'Granny, how much do you think you'll get for Ballards?'

'The agent valued it at about £280,000, but apparently the market's still very sluggish – that was his word, sluggish, like a slug I suppose – and I might have to settle for less. I don't mind. Your grandfather bought the house after the war. You'll never believe what he paid. Seven thousand pounds! Mind you, it was a lot in those days. You could buy a perfectly good place for a few hundred then, so Ballards was rather grand by any standards. Of course, it hasn't changed really, it isn't worth any more, it's only that the money is worth less. I find that a little frightening somehow. You all work so hard nowadays to put money in the bank, and once it's there it seems to shrink until a sum that used to buy a three-course dinner won't get you a cup of tea. Does that worry you?'

'Not really,' said Charlie. 'It's just economics. You have to make the money work and grow. You have to invest it.'

'I know,' said her grandmother. 'I have a charming financial adviser who's always telling me so. But it's very confusing.'

The four of them sat down to dinner. Eating at the Christies' was always a formal affair; that was how her father liked it. Napkins and side-plates and a silver cruet. He expected the family to change, not necessarily into evening clothes but at least into something different, it was part of a ritual which was important to him. Another masculine ritual, Charlie thought. Drinks in the drawing room, dinner in the dining room, the appropriate knives and forks queuing up for each course, glassware in waiting for the wine. Conversation revolved around Granny's move, the box room conversion, Charlie's new job. By ten o'clock her grandmother was growing tired, and Susan Christie took her up to bed.

Charlie's father watched them leave, his expression betraying a hovering anxiety tinged with habitual impatience. Charlie realised for the first time that the impatience was with himself, his own feelings, his private doubt or distress. His upbringing had taught him that manhood entailed absolute self-control, emotional restraint, above all the unquestioning assurance essential for the dominant male. It was a persona in which qualms of any kind had no place. But he was human, he saw his mother fading, and it both troubled and frightened him, reactions which he did not want, could not handle. Then he became brisk, practical, dismissive.

'I don't think Granny's got long left,' he said abruptly.

'She's all right,' Charlie maintained stoutly, not wishing to contemplate losing her. It had taken her months to come to terms with the loss of her grandfather. 'She looks sort of ethereal these days, but that's natural, isn't it? Old people very often do. She's pretty on the ball; she always was.'

'Her ticker's a bit dodgy.' George Christie addressed his daughter without looking at her, his gaze on his empty glass.

'She's had a couple of bad goes lately; angina, apparently. Needs care. That's why I thought it best we have her here. Your mother will keep an eye on her.' He shrugged off the disagreeable subject, glanced up again. 'How about a small port? I got a bottle of tawny from Warre's the other day; took me twenty minutes to decant. Lovely stuff.' He went to the sideboard where his favourites were kept and produced a cut glass decanter.

Charlie thought of pursuing the issue of why her mother should be exclusively responsible for Granny's welfare, but abandoned the idea. Her father was too set in his ways to accept earth-shaking changes of attitude. She sipped the port, then said hesitantly: 'Did you ever know about Grandpa and the waitress in that café near Ballards?'

'Who told you about that?'

'Granny did. Before supper.'

'Good Lord. Oh well, I suppose she feels you're old enough now to discuss things woman to woman, so to speak. Still . . .'

'You did know?' Charlie said.

'Yes, of course. It was one of those things that everyone knew but nobody mentioned, if you see what I mean. Good thing, too. There are too many things talked about nowadays that might be better kept quiet, if you ask me. Openness is all very well, but a certain degree of reticence can be a damn sight more comfortable. Take your grandma: she must have guessed what was going on but at least she never had to suffer the embarrassment of being told. No nasty scenes, no messy divorce. Thank God. Anyway, I don't think there was much in it, really. Not so much an affair, more a flirtation.'

'That isn't what Granny thinks,' Charlie said.

There was a brief, slightly awkward silence; then she changed the subject.

'What'll be done with the money from the sale of Ballards?'

'It'll go into some sort of deposit account, I suppose. High interest and all that. I don't know much about that kind of thing. I'm not some pettifogging accountant.'

'This financial adviser of Granny's,' Charlie queried, 'do we know if he's any good?'

'Should be. Recommended by a chum of your grandfather's

from the regiment, so I understand. You could try talking to her if you're bothered. But you know, people of her generation don't like to put their financial affairs on public parade. She might think you were prying. Anyhow, she may not welcome advice from a chit of a girl.' He gave her a broad grin, half teasing, half affectionate.

'How about some more port?'

CHAPTER FOUR

The rest of the summer was hectic: Charlie's diary was a clutter of scribbled engagements, lunches running into cocktail parties, early evening drinks overspilling into dinner. She attended Ascot with Caroline Elliott-Browne, the two of them sashaying around the Royal Enclosure in gigantic hats designed by a mutual friend. Charlie was hidden under a vast dark blue brim with a band of ruched organza and a real orchid; Caroline had salmon-pink chiffon atop black straw rounded off with an impossible orange concoction resembling an exploding chrysanthemum. The sun shone, the champagne flowed, the orchid wilted. Once in a while they cast a careless glance at the racetrack. Charlie backed the Queen's horse Aureole in the Hardwick Stakes because she thought it looked so handsome – a judgement Caroline dismissed as frivolous – and was gratified when it scraped home in a photofinish, winning her sixty pounds. She returned to Holland Park exhausted, only to find herself confronted by another party, another dinner, another step on the road to alcoholism.

Meanwhile, the agents found a buyer for Ballards, dropped the price a few thousand, and contracts were exchanged before the end of the month. The box room conversion was under way, and Granny began the laborious business of sorting through the accumulated possessions of a lifetime, packing essentials, deciding what to sell, what to keep, what to throw away. Most of the furniture was to be auctioned, but she said that if there was anything the family wanted they should help themselves. Charlie got a favourite chair, a small marquetry table, and an oil painting of wild horses galloping through a storm which had always captured her imagination as a child. Her grandfather used to tell one of his best stories about the table, how he had bought it from a fakir when he was serving with the Tenth Balouch Rifles on the North-West Frontier, how his batman had carried it on his back for over a hundred miles, and how it had saved both their lives when they were attacked by a rebel tribe. Then he'd turn the table upside-down and point out the mark on the underside where the bullet had impacted. 'That bullet had my name on it,' he would say, 'or Ranjit's,' and Charlie would feel the dent in the wood and savour the fantasy of adventure and danger. Granny never told her that he had bought the table for seven-and-six from a junk shop in north Finchley while on sick leave. She would see the rapt look on Charlie's face, and smile to herself. She was not the kind of person to spoil a good story.

Grandpa had been a great one for stories. He had read Charlie all the classics: *The Swiss Family Robinson*, *Treasure Island*, *Jim Davis*, and most of the tales of Edgar Rice Burroughs and John Buchan. Boys' stories in the main, ripping yarns of pirates and explorers, smugglers and swashbucklers. Charlie, bored by Enid Blyton and the pony books of her contemporaries, loved them all. Sometimes, she would sit with her grandfather in the fading daylight listening to sagas of romance and derring-do, knightly quests and desperate deeds, carried away on the wings of fancy to strange places with exotic names, Timbuktu and Katmandu, Samarkand and Trebizond, Chimborazo, Cotopaxi, Coromandel. He would embellish and exaggerate his own experiences, breathe atmosphere into the slowest narrative, alter his voice and accent for different characters. He and Charlie would play a special game where he would quote a line or two with a particular intonation and she would have to guess from which book it originated, the character depicted, and the author. It was a game as private to them as a personal code; they used to play it even when Charlie was grown up.

He died in his sleep, quite suddenly and without warning. She learned later that he and Granny had gone up to bed that night, he'd given her his customary peck on the cheek and at about three in the morning she woke abruptly to feel a great shudder going through him. She switched on the light, thinking to reassure him after a nightmare, but he was already dead. She got up, put on her dressing gown, and sat with him a while. Then she went downstairs and made herself a pot of tea. She carried it up to the bedroom on a tray and sat waiting for it to draw, and it wasn't until she came to pour that she noticed she'd brought two cups and two saucers. She stayed with Grandpa, holding his hand until it grew cold. When the dawn crept in between the curtains she telephoned Charlie's father.

'George, it's Mummy,' she had said, and he'd often recall that her voice was perfectly clear and controlled. 'Sorry to wake you so early, dear, but I'm afraid I have bad news. Your father died in the night. Could you come over now?'

Charlie had loved her grandfather very much. Having the table was like holding on to a piece of him, a wishstone with which she could conjure up all his stories. These days, it was kept in her flat and she trusted to the alarm and the Chubb and the mortice to keep it safe. People, she reflected, were not so easy to treasure.

Towards the end of July Charlie visited Chantilly on the outskirts of Paris for the Coupe de Diane. She was invited by her ex-fiancé, Michel de Boismenu, who was trying to reanimate their affair, or at least to lay it to rest in a bedroom rather than a graveyard. Race days in France were invariably designer occasions, the men in Armani, the women in Claud Montana, but for all the glamour Charlie did not enjoy herself. Unspecified worries niggled at the back of her mind, she lost 300 francs on the favourite, and Michel took advantage of a sudden rainstorm to force her into a clinch in a doorway. She extricated herself with a combination of muscle and tact, concluding that the aftertaste of love may linger but when lust is gone it's gone for good.

Michel came from an old and extremely wealthy family owning major vineyards in the Loire. He, however, had a soul above viticulture and preferred a spurious struggle with imagined penury on the Left Bank, leading what he fondly believed to be a Bohemian existence as a misunderstood artist. Since he had an extravagant nature, expensive tastes, and little interest in the mundane business of earning money, parental funds sustained his lifestyle and shrewd *galleriens* occasionally exhibited his work. Much of this consisted of nude studies of Charlie, fortunately rendered unrecognisable by artistic mannerisms and questionable draughtmanship. She was never sure what her mother and father would have made of them although, paradoxically, she thought Granny might have enjoyed a quiet giggle. Posing had, of course, been merely the preliminary to sex, plenty of sex, pushing back the parameters of eroticism into what was, for Charlie, unexplored territory, employing esoteric sexual aids, watching pornographic videos, acting out grotesque charades with Charlie as Madame de Montespan on a black velvet altar and Michel in the dual role of Sun King and satanic Nemesis. The whole process felt potentially dangerous, probably harmless, wicked enough for a thrill, wanton enough for decadence, a vital part of the legend that was Paris.

For a while, finding herself involved in a Warholistic scenario where flesh ruled, on canvas or off it, Charlie had felt she was seeing life, tasting passion, recreating the glory of Simonetta Vespucci and a hundred others, models whose bodies were immortalised in eternal talent and unpeeling paint. But gradually the games began to pall, infatuation waned, and she saw both passion and painting in a more realistic light. Now, on the late flight out of Charles de Gaulle, she knew their engagement had been simply another excuse to party, their projected marriage no more real than an opium dream. She hoped she would always care about Michel – it was alarming to think that an ardour so violent and all-consuming could vanish without trace – but she understood now that they could never be 'just good friends', never socialise together on companionable terms; leftover tenderness and regret were too near and too painful to be easily eluded. It was a mistake to cling to the past, or – as in Michel's case – to let the past cling to you. As Paris reeled away beneath her, obliterated by a drift of cloud, disappearing in a puff of smoke as if the whole city were no more substantial than a mirage, she turned her thoughts to the future. A new job, a new world.

Another dream to chase.

CHAPTER FIVE

On the first Monday of September Charlie awoke half an hour before her alarm went off. She felt absurdly nervous, as if it were the start of term at a new school and she was the outsider, wearing the right uniform but knowing none of the other pupils and understanding none of the jokes. She had taken some pains with her choice of clothes, trying on a range of possibles the previous night and eventually settling for a white silk shirt and tailor-made suit, her own version of standard City garb. She got up quickly, immediately alert, dived into the shower, dripped into the kitchen. There was no milk for her coffee and she felt too hyper to drink it black. She tried to use up some adrenalin scrubbing the enamel off her teeth, moisturised her skin, glossed her lips, patted her blusher into place. When she was dressed she had to resist a frantic impulse to take everything off and start again, convinced she had got it wrong. No time. No point. She blasted Chanel on to a couple of pulse-spots, glanced in the mirror, and walked out of the door.

She took the tube to Bank, emerged on to the platform, and was swept along like flotsam in a tide of suits. Spilling out into the daylight the stream divided and subdivided, into threes and twos and individuals, and Charlie found herself separated from the crowd, making her own way to the offices of Fitzgerald Denton. It was a mild day and the buildings were sun-mellowed, façades of buff and beige taking warm tones from the light, windows filled with the sheen of late summer. The cough and purr of traffic, the scurrying of passers-by, the preoccupied faces and pattering feet all contributed to the atmosphere of a vast, complex hive where a huge swarm of pin-striped bees came and went about their endless affairs. Charlie found the hustle stimulating and the brisk walk steadied her nerves. At the entrance to Fitzgerald Denton she smiled at the doorman; he responded in kind but for a minute his expression was blank; clearly he was taking a few moments to place her in the catalogue of his recollections. So many morning faces passed his way, though they were rarely decorated with such a genuine smile.

The lift was crowded and slow, stopping at every floor. Charlie got out on the fourteenth in a gaggle of secretaries and headed for the Ladies for a final check. The mirror told her she looked efficient; she did not bother with a retouch. The face beside her, she noticed with a covert glance, was applying an extra thickness of lipstick, blinking through its mascara. A faintly familiar face. Charlie looked again, this time more openly. The girl forked a cigarette from a packet of Marlboro', applied a match, and inhaled deeply. Her gaze met Charlie's; she said carelessly: 'Hi. I forgot you were starting today. Welcome to the club.'

She didn't sound particularly welcoming. She hadn't sounded welcoming at the interview, Charlie remembered. This was the secretary who had conducted her to the interrogation chamber. Young, glossily packaged, with a spectacular mane of hair rather redder than nature had intended and an obtrusive bosom straining at a skimpy top. There was an undercurrent to her accent that was probably Romford, something that would not have mattered had she made less effort to conceal it.

'Hello,' Charlie said, determined to be friendly. 'I met you at the interview, didn't I?'

'Uh-huh. They thought you were a man: that was funny. I nearly laughed out loud. Hugo's face – ! I'm his secretary, by the way. Well, his personal assistant.'

'Hugo?' Charlie had yet to fit names to her prospective colleagues.

'*Mister* Wingate. The managing director.' She doled out information with studied indifference, as if determined not to show that she was trying to impress. The cigarette shrank visibly with every indrawn breath. 'I'm Bianca Leach. I can't remember your name.'

'Charlie Christie.' Bianca after Bianca Jagger? she speculated.

'Oh yeah. Charlie. No wonder they got confused. You're one of their glamorous graduates, right?'

'Trainee broker,' Charlie supplied.

'Like hell. The only thing they'll let you break is the

photocopier: you'll see. Three months of it at least. Your baptism of ink.'

'I don't think so,' Charlie said. 'It's hardly part of the job description.'

'There's a lot goes on here,' said Bianca with significance, 'that isn't in the job description. Believe me.' She tossed the end of her cigarette into a loo, did not bother to flush it, and turned back to the mirror for a final preen. 'Come on then,' she said with a flicker of comradeship. 'Into the jungle.'

Charlie followed her lead.

They passed rows of desks, banks of computers, clicking keyboards, winking screens. At the sight of Charlie the tapping fingers slowed, inquisitive eyes swivelled in her direction. Charlie, affecting detachment, received unexpected encouragement from Bianca, who tossed a smile over her shoulder and remarked: 'This is the kiddies' enclosure. Hamsters and bunnies. Pay no attention.'

She entered Hugo Wingate's office without knocking, catching him on the telephone, his voice slightly raised in the unmistakable tones of domestic dispute. He swung his chair away from them and dropped an octave to say: 'Emily, I've already explained to you, I just can't make it. I've got a business dinner. Tell the Simpsons I'm sorry. No: I have to go now. I'll call you later.' He hung up without waiting for an answer and spun the chair round again, rising to his feet to offer Charlie a handshake and a greeting. Charm purred in his voice and etched his smile.

'Grab a seat. Bianca will get us some coffee.'

When Bianca was dispatched and the door closed he launched into what was clearly a routine spiel, welcoming her to the company and outlining in general terms the programme for her future training. 'You won't be reporting directly to me, you understand. I've allocated you to a line manager who'll show you the ropes. But if you have any problems, anything at all, don't hesitate to come and see me.' His manner was relaxed and competent, his charm unobtrusive enough to be effective. The coffee arrived in a cafetière with cream in a jug and bone china cups. Bianca dispensed it and Hugo thanked her automatically, adding: 'I need those documents by 10 a.m. so you'd better get down and do some real work for a change.' There was an element of banter in his voice; his smile was redirected towards her.

'If I'm allowed the time,' Bianca retorted. 'Should you require any more waitressing –'

'I'll interrupt you,' Hugo grinned.

'Service,' Bianca said impudently, 'is not included.'

She left the room with a wiggle of her hips and a snapping of the door. Charlie, seeing the expression that was swiftly banished from Hugo's face, knew they were sleeping together, or had slept together, and thought she guessed what Bianca had meant about duties beyond the range of the job description.

After coffee, Hugo said he would escort her to the office manager who would be responsible for giving her a basic grounding in what he called the operational systems at Fitzgerald Denton. 'Administration may not be very exciting but it's vital to the efficient running of any company. Everyone has to do their stint.'

Charlie was duly introduced to the photocopier.

During the course of the day, however, she met several of the brokers. The Rt. Hon. Rupert Lambeth was to be her guide around the market and would show her the Lloyd's side of the business. He was a tall, skinny young man with a leisurely attitude to life and a countenance so ingenuous as to border on the naive; a permanent hangover was the only cloud on his brow. He had an air of cultivated disarray: his hair resembled a hayfield after a hurricane, his cuffs were frayed, his jacket, though expensive and gaudily lined, sat awry on his shoulders, tugged on in a hurry and never adjusted to sartorial correctness. His shoes alone showed signs of care, polished to an impressive shine, a trait left over from his time in the Royal Horse Guards. He promptly invited Charlie to lunch but she begged a raincheck, needing some spare time to digest the ramifications of the copier, a machine rather more complex than a mainframe computer. After Rupert, she was taken to her new line manager, the senior broker on the team she was to join. At the sight of him, she felt an involuntary recoil. It was the third of her tribune of interviewers, the man she had first encountered alone in the lift. Bill Spooner.

His handclasp was strong yet clammy, an uncomfortable

combination. She wondered in passing if the greeting had been invented, not as a gesture of peace that entailed potential combatants releasing their grip on their sword-hilts, but as a preliminary test of character. Every handshake was a revelation. At the touch of Spooner's fingers, Charlie's very flesh seemed to shrink. From the beginning, she had felt for him not so much dislike as distaste, as if she sensed intuitively a rottenness at the core of his spirit.

She told herself she was being fanciful, and turned thankfully from his perfunctory welcome and hooded gaze to his subordinate, Andrew Kendall, a far more attractive proposition. He was another young broker, with the muscles of a rugger blue and the sort of clean-cut features that would have made him a Forties film star. A shy smile qualified the firmness of his mouth; his eyes were intelligent without active dynamism; his suit, unlike Rupert's, was immaculately pressed and fitted precisely across his broad shoulders. Charlie thought he looked trustworthy – if such a concept was not too alien for a broker – but unexciting. Possibly the problem was that the two qualities were too often unable to exist side by side.

Between bouts of photocopying she met most of her other colleagues, but with so many new faces and names she found it difficult to keep track of them all. They remembered her more easily: one woman in a line-up which had been exclusively male. They appraised her with avid eyes, admiring her physical assets yet suspicious of the very femininity which allured them. The cook had come out of the kitchen, the courtesan had left her boudoir, the typist had abandoned her typewriter. The enemy was in their ranks. It was challenging, chancy, an inevitable step into the future, the thin end of the wedge. Charlie, aware of uneasy vibes, noted with irritation the photo of Princess Di above the copier, on which some artistic talent had drawn, at lip level, an oversized representation of the male genitalia. But she decided it was diplomatic to ignore it.

Hugo Wingate watched reactions with amused gratification. Among the optimists, bets were being placed as to who would be first to get Charlie into bed, but he declined to join in, adopting a lofty detachment which fooled no one. On Tuesday night he would take Bianca to the mews house which was his town residence, dress her in one of his old rugger shirts, and make love to her in the spotless bed with a towel spread over the sheet in case of leakage. The towel usually became rather rucked up, but it was an extra large one, bath size from Harrods, and thick enough to absorb any stray evidence of misbehaviour. The towel, like the sheets, was regularly laundered, but he didn't believe in taking risks. His father-in-law, recently deceased, had been the latest in a long line of Dentons, bequeathing the bulk of his shares to his daughter; Hugo was very happy in his marriage, it had fulfilled all his professional needs. His sexual requirements were regularly satisfied in the cul-de-sac house, by Bianca and her predecessors. His wife used the place rarely, staying over once in a while after a Friday night at the theatre, but in case of an impromptu visit he was always scrupulously careful to leave no clues, rummaging with meticulous paranoia through the rubbish bin in case there was an eggshell too many or a second yoghurt carton among the litter. Genius, he had read, is an infinite capacity for taking pains, and behind his superficial sophistication Hugo believed, with some justification, that he had a genius for opportunism, for seizing the moment, the flood-tide that leads on to fortune. He had come a long way from his grammar school education and an upbringing in undistinguished suburbia. At times, he could almost imagine he had bridged the terrible chasm between lower and upper middle class.

He and Bianca Leach had much in common. She too was on the make, though starting further down the ladder and aiming less high, concentrating on picking up slipshod aitches, ironing out vowels, packaging her sex appeal with sufficient style to pull a broker rather than a clerk. She dreamed of the good life in Hugo's six-bedroomed Godstone home, ousting his wife from bed and board, stepmothering his children, patting his dogs. She knew it was unlikely but she clung to the hope that in the end his heart, or at least his loins, would rule his head. She was especially good at fellatio, and when she took his member in her mouth, when she tongued his scrotum and slid his penis halfway down her throat, she knew he would promise her almost anything. In cooler moments he might think the liaison too

49

dangerous to pursue, he might calculate that he could replace her secretarial skills and fill her space on the towel, but there are some talents which cannot be taught, and Bianca made the most of hers. Her tongue would take her far. Like her lover she also had a capacity for taking pains. Whether she would be happy living in rural bliss, surrounded by stepchildren and dogs, was a question that never occurred to her. She was too busy concentrating on the means to do more than idealise the end.

She didn't usually pester him to leave his wife, she merely made herself essential, trying to feel that in the mews house at least she was on her own territory, even if she couldn't leave so much as a fingerprint on the bathroom mirror. But the advent of Charlie gave her an occasional qualm. The office was her kingdom, where she and Hugo had an official relationship, privately sanctioned, publicly understood. She did not want competition on her own patch. On the day of Charlie's arrival she went home in a state of distraction, telling herself there was no need to worry.

Hugo dined at the Ivy with a friend, determined to avoid the Simpsons.

By early evening the City was as empty as a ghost town. The frenetic industry of the daytime had fizzled away, the myriad workers being filtered through a mesh of oyster bars, brasseries and wine cellars until they could be absorbed into the commuter system, whence they would disappear from view. The lees remained, sitting in corners drinking and swapping scandal till they, too, trickled westward in search of the wilder shores of clubland. The streets were silent, exhaling the day's intake of heat in a nightlong sigh; isolated footfalls echoed hollowly on pavement and tarmac. The Lloyd's building brooded over all like a monstrous factory, lit from below with a spectral iridescence, its topmost tower taking fire in the sunset, its gleaming windowscape betraying sinister inactivity. Even in repose it seemed like an ominous machine, glittering with earthly temptations, waiting for its daily intake of victims who could be ground up in its belly, reconstituted as its own creatures, and spewed out again to take over the world. In the morning its lifts would rise and fall like pistons, its air conditioning would pulse into action, its minions would stream up the open-tread steps through portals of glass into the hidden matrix. They gambled millions on the spin of a microchip, the fall of a sparrow, refracted morality through an enchanted prism. It was a new twist to an old tale, an ancient game with broken rules, played out in a tower of steel and sorcery where the knights were foresworn and the dragons wore suits. By night, the slumber of the City was pregnant, and the streets dreamed.

Formerly, Lloyd's had been the domain of the privileged, where Names merited their capital N, signifying a long inheritance of wealth, position, reputation. Deals were guaranteed with a pledged word and sealed over a copita of Amontillado. A conspiracy of the rich covered any default, concerned to preserve their image of rectitude and responsibility. The reach of the press was short; the proletariat lived on another planet. But the Thatcherite ethos had taught that greed was not the exclusive prerogative of the upper classes. Technology arrived to invade, control, betray; barriers which had survived two world wars crumbled at the touch of a button. The accents that came to market were from far down the social stratum, their suits made in Milan not Savile Row, their heritage not the burden of prestige but a race-memory of deprivation, a class-memory of rage. They dismissed honour as hypocrisy and took what they wanted, coming tardily to the feast, determined to make up for centuries of lost time.

Spooner was of their breed, a particularly unattractive specimen; his hunger was of his kind, his corruption was his own, a corrosion of the soul nourished on envy, cynicism, the necessary compromises of ambition. His self-loathing, regularly aggravated by the women who turned him down, the goals he would never achieve, the principles he had thrown away, was inevitably redirected against those irritants: morality, status, women. Cunning beyond calculation in his own field, he had few resources outside it, taking sex wherever it was for sale and patronising the arts only in the name of corporate entertainment. He would drink Carlsberg as easily as Corton, eat a beefburger with the same relish as a steak Diane. He liked expensive restaurants only because they were expensive, spending lavishly in the cause of business, using any lie to market the risk, all for

51

a quick fix, a fast deal, a high commission, the temporary cathar-
sis of making money. Robbing the rich to feed his insatiable
appetite, the famine that was nurtured through generations of
poverty. He had no traditional sense of responsibility, no
respect for the past, no thought for the future. Fitzgerald
Denton had promoted him because he increased their bank balance; colleagues despised him, admired him, tolerated him,
detested him, but whatever their dominant reaction, all of them
were slightly wary of him, distrusting a mind sharpened by
avarice and a sensibility blunted on cocaine. This was the period
of the 'soft' market: too many underwriters were chasing too
little business, no one could afford to alienate such a successful
player. His worse enemies bided their time, waiting for the
ambience to change.

But change was coming, a change no one had foreseen, a catastrophe beyond the range of standard cover. In a world of elaborate economics nobody had done any simple arithmetic for a
long, long while, and now they were learning over-late that the
sums would not add up. Too many ships had sunk, too many
typhoons had raged, too many birds of ill-omen had come home
to roost. Men had died when asbestos furred their lungs, chem-
ical plants had leaked poison, drug companies had overdosed.
The planet was falling apart and Lloyd's had promised to foot
the bill. For decades they had thrived on the fear of unlimited
risk, making enormous profits on routine survival, occasional
losses on intermittent disaster. But now God had tipped the
glass and the sands were running out. The meteoric rise of the
insurance *arrivistes* was about to encounter a serious glitch.
Spooner, a listener whose ears were always open, had already
caught an intimation of something desperately wrong.

About six months earlier he had stood in for Hugo at a Mansion
House dinner given by the Lord Mayor. One of the Wingate
children had been rushed to hospital with a high temperature,
meningitis had been briefly suspected, and Hugo had passed his
invitation to Spooner principally because he was the only man
left in the office. The meal was over and the port was on the
move when Spooner's sensitised faculties filtered out a single
conversation among many, big talk among small, alcoholic

52

lubrication loosening tongues that should have remained still. It was a name that first caught his attention, not merely a name but a Name, a high-profile MP apparently involved in a particular syndicate, snared in the net of unlimited liability and facing possible bankruptcy and parliamentary ruin. Other Names followed, from backbench and cabinet, courtroom and boardroom, most of them known to the eavesdropper. Spooner identified the speakers as a senior civil servant from the Treasury and the Chief Whip. Then he let his eyes close as if vision might impinge on hearing, tuning out extraneous noise, concentrating his whole being on the task of listening. His face presented an aspect of sleepy intoxication but his grip was tight on the stem of his glass and tension clamped his sagging jaw. He was a ferret by nature, a scrabbler in dark holes, a predator of anything into which he could hook his teeth. Now, all his rodent instincts were on the alert: his nose twitched at the whiff of corruption. Something taut in the hunching of his shoulders may have betrayed him: the progress of the port decanter caused a turning of heads and the man from the Treasury was watching Spooner's profile, wondering at the diner apparently too inebriated for tabletalk. Spooner sipped his liquor, picked up a conversational fag-end nearby. The conspirators, if such they were, had suddenly become more prudent: there was nothing else to overhear. When dinner was over the Chief Whip slipped unobtrusively away and made a telephone call.

Spooner left the Mansion House, paid a routine visit to a couple of clubs, and went back to his flat in Docklands in the company of a Chinese prostitute called Soo Chang. That, too, was a matter of routine. He liked the Oriental face for its differentness, its doll-like immobility, the black eyes which appeared to be without expression against the unlined skin, the flattened cheekbones and the ivory curve of the nostrils below the low-bridged nose. Soo Chang was a near-perfect example of this type, her eyebrows thin or plucked, her painted lips full and red as a peony: to Spooner, she might have been a dummy in a shop window, a mask with little or nothing behind it. Her features did not alter as he lifted her skirt, pulled down her briefs, turned her on to her belly. The crease between her buttocks was like the cleft in a peach, the junction of two half-moons of golden flesh.

He explored her diligently, opening the crease, probing her anus. There was a belt coiled on the bedside table and he picked it up, his mouth stretching into a rictus of arousal, lashing her without warning, leaving a red welt on her skin which faded only slowly. At that, her face changed; she said over her shoulder: 'You're hurting me. Is extra.' Her voice was clear and childlike and hard as ice, giving nothing away.

'I'll pay extra. Greedy bitch.'

'You pay now. Bad names are extra too.'

Bitch. Whore. Fuck me. He thought but did not speak, fumbling for his wallet with shaking hands, spilling notes on to the bed. She amassed and began to count them even as he returned to his exertions, wielding the belt with bitter restraint, wanting to inflict real pain, passionate pain, an orgasm of agony, knowing, with regret, that opportunities for total abandon were rare. He knew her pimp and, more to the point, the pimp knew him. When his penis was threatening to burst his fly he unzipped, preparing for rear entry.

'Condom,' she said by way of a reminder, tucking the wad of notes into her bra. Had she been less tactful, she might have been reading a magazine.

He had just put one on when they broke the front door down.

They were professionals; they wasted no time. The drill crunched wood into sawdust and the lock was being dismantled even as Spooner groped for his trousers. They had reached the bedroom before he was ready, catching him bent double as he tried to stuff his cocaine case under the mattress. Soo Chang, still lying on her stomach, displayed neither confusion nor interest. 'If you want to watch,' she said, 'is extra.' The intruders, perhaps, were of a similar breed. They ignored her exquisite bottom, dispatching Spooner with a couple of swift, scientific punches. 'Dress,' they told her. She dressed. They asked her name, her address, the name of her pimp, brusque questions to which she supplied succinct answers. The impassivity Spooner so much admired was unaffected even when he began to regain consciousness, groaning automatically, blood leaking from his torn mouth. It was none of her business. 'Very sensible,' they said. 'Keep it that way.' They gave her an extra hundred, sent her outside to a waiting cab. In the back, she sat on her sore bottom, re-counted her money. For Soo Chang, it had been a profitable night.

In the bedroom, the visitors completed their work on Spooner. They offered no explanation, nor did he ask for one. They were quiet, unremarkable men of nondescript age and face, wearing jeans, bomber jackets, trainers. One had thinning hair, the other a moustache. Spooner recognised immediately the assurance that goes with official backing if not formal status. Much later, recapitulating events through a mist of unexciting pain, he was able to pinpoint why. They had not worn gloves. In the unlikely circumstance of a complaint, no one in authority was going to identify their fingerprints. They did not need to be careful. 'Your ears are too sharp,' they told him, smashing each orifice against the wall. 'Take care how you listen. Your mouth is too slack –' and they rectified the problem – 'Take care how you talk. A quick ear and a loose tongue can be a fatal combination.' Spooner tried to say that they need not labour the point, but communication was beyond him. They left him on the floor, his blood soaking into the carpet. When he was able, he crawled into the bathroom and retched into the lavatory pan, jerking at fractured ribs. The resulting sensation brought him near to fainting. Back in bed, anaesthetised with alcohol and painkillers, he tried to sleep. But despite his fear – and intelligent fear is an essential concomitant of survival – despite the rhythmic anguish that no amount of paracetamol could dull, his brain was still ticking over, analysing, speculating. The profit motive was as intrinsic to him as breath, and for all his injuries, Spooner was still breathing.

In the morning, a carpenter arrived around seven and fitted a new door to the flat without troubling its occupant; the locksmith came shortly after. Spooner took a fortnight off work and two months off sex. But while his ribs mended his warped mind was burrowing and burrowing into the fruitful dirt.

CHAPTER SIX

In the Sixties when swinging London was at the centre of the brave new world, art and music ruled, hand in hand with peace and love, and the West End was the place to be. The sleaze of Soho, the style of Carnaby Street, the rooftops where pop stars would play for the hell of it, the cellars where flower children watched visible dreams unfold: this was the London that foreigners read about and natives talked about, the pivot of an era, the capital of a mood. Thirty years later the dreams had evaporated, the flower children were middle-aged, the pop stars – if they showed any discrimination – had died young. Recycled flares walked the streets, reminding a generation of the bad taste that was fashion. Rioting students had become professors, politicians, executives; the issues of the day were no longer a matter for Grosvenor Square demonstration but merely dinner table dispute. Crime figures reflected the change: the statistics for post-prandial assault sky-rocketed. The pendulum had swung: the focus of attention veered from high ideals to high aspirations, from prophecy to profit. The orgies had given way to safe sex, the West End took second place to the City. The Happening was over, the office party had begun.

To the hippie culture, money was a by-product of the music revolution; protest songs and the poetry of principle brought it rolling in, and those who eulogised free love found themselves swamped in costly rewards. Some spent lavishly, on a switch-back from wealth to bankruptcy; others handed the control of such vulgar matters to unobtrusive suits, who could translate the language of finance into elementary rock-and-roll. But in the Eighties the suits became the stars: the artistic snobbery that looked down on filthy lucre was dismissed as hypocritical, impractical, sanctimonious, pseud. In offices antique and modern, merchant banks and brokerage houses, a new wave of bright young men arrived like prospectors in a gold rush, infiltrating the ancient heart of moneydom, taking over. Tradition lost out to competition, the old school tie was replaced by a casual knot of Dior silk. Boys who ten years earlier would have hung a guitar on their crotch and tried to be Mick Jagger tapped a quick tune on a computer and watched the zeros multiply. There was no need for talent or creativity, nothing to make or market: the noughts popped up like lemons on a fruit machine and dealers spinning the maelstrom of unrestricted finance started earning in telephone numbers. Gold fever spread like a plague, bringing its attendant madness: no one estimated the consequences or looked to the future. The lesson of the past is that fire follows plague, a lethal necessity, the holocaust which destroys and cleanses; but the new breed of entrepreneurs had never studied history.

Bust succeeded boom, interest rates went through the ceiling, growth factors sank through the floor. As the *commedia* unwound Lloyd's stood alone, a steel bastion, shining and impregnable, while all around it the Stock Exchange crashed, the banks wrote off millions, property values plummeted, black columns turned red, Porsches went for a song. But Lloyd's was a byword for solidity; the business of insuring Now against Tomorrow could never fail. No questions were asked, no suspicions voiced. There was not a sage in the Square Mile who had read the words of Henry Ward Beecher, or, if he had, thought to consider them: *We steal if we touch tomorrow. It is God's.* The line should have been spattered in scarlet paint on the pristine façade, it should have dripped down the windows like blood. The writing on the wall. But no street-spawned graffiti were allowed to smirch the polished frontage, no blemish could disfigure its glittering reputation. Disaster was piling on disaster, the asbestosis fiasco would turn solid ground into quicksand; Names attracted by enormous profits had signed up for unlimited liability, and now they were about to learn what it meant. An original stake of £100,000 could turn into a loss of over a million; a gamble on your savings could cost you your home, your ancestral acres, your life's work. Those at the top of the heap who saw trouble from far off did what they could to salvage the livelihood of a select few. As the City had opened its gates to the *arrivistes*, the profiteers, the carpetbaggers, so Lloyd's admitted newcomers to the club still sporting its exclusive label, dentists, lawyers, publicists, pensioners. 'Will you come into my parlour?' said the spider to the fly. Within the glass and steel processing machine the risks were layered from syndicate to syndicate, losses were passed on, the position of the inner circle would be secured by dispersing financial responsibility among the less influential. If the arithmetic would work out, if the juggler did not drop the plates – if the omens had been read aright.

Meanwhile, the game went on. But even those who bet on the gyrations of the wheel did not understand the power that made it spin. A banknote on its own is only a piece of paper: it is supply and demand, toil and trade which give it a value. Without mines, factories, farms and fields somewhere in the background a row of noughts on a screen will add up to precisely nothing. The City is a matrix of power, but a matrix must have resources on which to draw: power does not exist in a vacuum. But the whiz-kids with stars in their eyes and microchips in their brain were only beginning to find out, and the fledgeling Names let in as a favour would have to learn the hard way.

The game went on.

At the offices of Fitzgerald Denton, Charlie had mastered the photocopier and graduated on to the shredder. It did not enhance her knowledge of insurance broking. 'I told you so,' said Bianca Leach in the Ladies one lunchtime. Not, Charlie thought, in a gloating spirit, more with the gloomy satisfaction of a habitual Cassandra whose predictions of gloom are never believed until too late.

'The work I do,' Charlie fumed, 'could easily be done by a well-trained chimpanzee.'

'Most of the work in this place already is,' said Bianca. 'Hadn't you noticed?'

Charlie abandoned the exchange and went in quest of lunch, entering the lift at the same time as Andrew Kendall. As he turned to greet her she suppressed a gasp of surprise. His suit was as immaculate as ever but his clean-cut features were embellished by the most spectacular black eye she had ever seen.

'My God!' she said. 'You poor thing! You look as if you've been playing that barbaric game of yours with a herd of rhinos.'

Andrew produced a twisted grin. 'The rugger season is in

winter,' he said. 'This was squash. My opponent gave me a whack with his racquet. Complete accident. Not looking what we were doing.' She guessed he used these brief, unfinished phrases out of nervousness or native inarticulacy, to evade the potential tangle of more complex sentences. He was clearly unable to express himself well outside his own field. Or in this case, outside his own squash court. 'Wasn't his fault,' Andrew concluded. 'More likely mine. Mind you, I *was* winning.'

'I should imagine you usually do,' Charlie said thoughtfully, eyeing the breadth of the shoulders which loomed over her, making the lift seem suddenly crowded.

'Depends on the game,' Andrew said, unexpectedly serious. He shifted his weight from foot to foot, fixed his gaze on the floor-level indicator. Charlie tried very hard not stare at his eye. 'Going to lunch?'

'Sorry?' The question was so abrupt Charlie was momentarily unnerved. 'Oh. Oh, yes. Are you?'

'Sandwich.' Andrew's shorthand was getting shorter. Soon, Charlie feared, actual words might disappear altogether. That would never do.

'Sandwich?' she echoed. 'Surely not? I thought brokers had to lunch in style at the best restaurants: Wheeler's, Pont de la Tour!' For the first time in a short while, she thought about Henry Marriott. 'I was given to understand it went with the job.'

'Not always.' This time, Andrew's grin twisted in the other direction. 'Not me, anyway. Doesn't seem right running up the old expense account when I'm not entertaining.' His conscientious attitude made a pleasant change from the pocket-lining and perk-snatching Charlie normally encountered.

There was a pause before he resorted to another of his abrupt questions. 'How's it going?'

Charlie shrugged. 'Admin,' she explained. 'The copier, the shredder, et al. I don't exactly feel like a trainee broker.'

'You don't exactly look like one,' Andrew said, so seriously she could not be sure if a compliment was intended. 'Don't let it get to you. We all started there. It's a kind of custom. Like fagging at school.'

'We didn't *have* fagging at my school,' Charlie said.

'Which – ?'

'Millfield.'

The lift stopped at the ground floor and they made their way together past the security man, who called a greeting – 'Miss Christie – Mr Kendall' – and returned to the *Evening Standard*. Outside, they stood on the pavement, glancing in opposite directions in search of a cab.

'Where do you go,' Charlie asked, 'for this sandwich of yours?'

'Pub.' Andrew was more cryptic than ever. 'Or a cheap restaurant. There's a place off Bow Lane I like. Italian. My mother used to go there just after the war. Same people running it now.' He added: 'The owner had a fancy for Mum, if you ask me. Always talks about her. Chubby sort of fella, going bald, but she says he wasn't then. Suppose he must have been quite handsome when he was young. Gigolo type.'

'I've never met an ageing gigolo.' Charlie gave him a pert grin. 'Broaden my experience. Take me there.'

'It's a bit of a hike.' Andrew looked slightly nonplussed.

'Not in a taxi.' Unusually, she spotted a FOR HIRE sign cruising towards them virtually on cue. She thrust two fingers in her mouth and emitted an earsplitting whistle, which brought the vehicle swerving into the kerb.

'Christ.' Andrew blinked. 'Who taught you to do that?'

'My grandpa. He said he once brought down a whole band of charging Pathans by whistling like that. The horses reared and threw their riders. It was up near Kabul.' She climbed into the cab and Andrew followed, giving the driver their destination.

'Sounds an adventurous sort of chap,' he said.

'Yes,' Charlie concurred with pride, 'he was.' After a moment's thought, she threw in: 'He did a nice line in bullshit, too.'

'D'you take after him?' Andrew enquired.

'All round.'

At the restaurant, they sat opposite one another, with a chequered oilskin tablecloth, a huddle of sauce bottles and a single carnation in between. Charlie touched the petals and found to her surprise they were real. 'Mario's very keen on his flowers,'

Andrew said. 'Always produces a red rose from somewhere when I come in with Mum.'

'How lovely,' Charlie said.

Mario himself materialised minutes later, a rotund figure who, despite expansive belly and hairless pate, had a spark in his velvet eyes and a dimple in his olive cheek which still held the charm of his youth. His graphic gestures and high-speed delivery were typically Italian. '*Stronzo!* What have we here? The eye – it is like a squashed plum on a plate! Perhaps it is this lady's husband, yes? He come home too early; you leave too late. Or the father? So beautiful a woman, so black an eye – there must be a connection. Tell Mario the truth –'

Andrew blushed and denied everything, producing the actual explanation so falteringly that Mario clearly remained unconvinced. 'Never mind,' he said, patting Andrew's shoulder. 'No one will find you here. Our discretion, it is absolute.' His manner gave their impromptu lunch the atmosphere of an elopement. Charlie stifled a giggle. 'How is your mother? You must bring her more often. Tell her to come with you – to come alone – it is no matter. I take care of her. She is very special lady. Now –' he leaned forward, becoming more conspiratorial – 'what will you have?'

'Well . . .' Charlie began, scanning the menu card.

'The tortellini is no good. It is too rich, too heavy, not a dish for a lady. You must have something delicate, subtle, aromatic but not overwhelming. The polenta is peasant food. In Scotland, they eat porridge; in Lombardy, polenta. It is the same thing. Pizza – bah! Any street stall will give you pizza. Forget the menu. Today, for my favourite customers, I have a wonderful *agnello con olive nere*. Very tender lamb, with garlic, rosemary, tomatoes, fat black olives. It is a Tuscan recipe: I learn it from my mother. Only a few portions left. You like that?' Andrew and Charlie nodded meekly; how could they refuse? '*Bene.*' Mario whipped out a small pad and scribbled furiously. Then he bent forward again, lowering his voice still further, a rococo cherub whispering mischievous secrets into Venus's ear. 'First, I bring you some Chianti,' he confided. 'It come from the estate of an old friend of mine. His family are vintners since the days of Imperial Rome. His ancestors made wine for Emperor Augustus himself.'

61

'He was poisoned, wasn't he?' Charlie murmured innocently.

'Is a lie!' Mario declared, switching to maximum volume and drawing himself up to his full height of five foot two. 'A rumour put about by enemies of Rome.' He might have been referring to a tabloid allegation published the previous week. 'Piero Prinetti, he is a man of honour. His forefathers were men of honour. Never do they poison anyone, not even in the days of the Borgias. I bring you the Chianti; you drink his health. It is the best Chianti in Italy.'

'Brutus,' Charlie remarked as he departed, 'was an honourable man.'

But Andrew had studied rugger at Oxford, not literature. 'I'm afraid Mario's a bit bonkers,' he apologised.

'I think he's wonderful,' Charlie said.

The Chianti came in a plain glass jug: it had the woody taste of grape-pips, the bitterness of ruby vinegar, the afterglow of a blistering southern summer. The lamb was done to the consistency of butter. Mellow with alcohol, warm with food, the two of them traded life stories, ambitions, frustrations. Andrew's sentences lengthened; Charlie's office-bred irritation subsided. 'If I were you,' Andrew said, after much discussion, 'I'd beard Hugo in his den. Tell him how pissed off you are with being a sort of Girl Friday. That wasn't what you joined Fitzgerald Denton for, after all. Say you want to get on the floor, even if it's only as a spectator. At least that way you'll start learning your job.'

'The direct approach.' Charlie was pensive. 'Do you think it'll work?'

'Should do. Hugo was the one who picked you: the word is he thought you were pretty smart. It doesn't make sense for him to waste you on office chores. He'll give you a chance to prove yourself, if only to vindicate his own judgement.'

'I hope you're right.'

'Look, there were people who thought it was a mistake to take on a woman –'

'Spooner?' Charlie queried.

'And others. Hugo has to give you an opportunity to show them they're wrong.'

'And he's right,' Charlie concluded.

'Exactly.'

'I'll quote you,' she teased.

Mario arrived with the bill, apologising profusely for such a breach of good manners. 'I would like everyone to eat free; but what can you do? I must buy food, pay rent, pay many, many taxes. The bill, it is small; the pleasure, it is large.' A flamboyant gesture emphasised the largeness of the pleasure; the bill was indeed very small. He also brought a red rose from his secret store and presented it to Charlie with a bow and a kiss on her hand. Afterwards, as she and Andrew walked back to Lime Street, she found herself comparing this lunch to the one she'd had at the Pont de la Tour with David Chater and Henry Marriott. Rather to her surprise she discovered she preferred the Tuscan lamb and the chequered tablecloths.

The door of Hugo's office was open. Buoyed up by the Chianti, Charlie walked straight in. Hugo looked up from a blue file thick with documents, closing it quickly. Charlie wondered what could be so very confidential, and, in her present state of light-headedness, whether he had really been concealing a porno-graphic magazine between respectable Fitzgerald Denton covers. But if he felt any embarrassment, it didn't show in his face. He extended a hand, accompanied by an effortless smile. The usual charm offensive, Charlie thought. Two can play that game.

'Charlie, how's it going? Sorry I haven't seen much of you in the last month, but this is the busy season. Lots of policy renewals to sort out.' He motioned her to a chair; she sat down, hooking one leg over the other. Hugo's gaze wandered.

'You haven't seen anything of me,' Charlie said pointedly. 'I've been hidden behind a pile of junk for duplication or disin-tegration. I'm fast becoming an extension to your office machin-ery. You've heard of the Spinning Jenny? I'm the Copying Charlie. A right Charlie, in this case. Mr Wingate –'

'Hugo.'

'Hugo – I hope you won't think me too impertinent but I didn't join your company to train as a general dogsbody. I'm supposed to be a broker. I want to stop wasting time and start using it – on the floor. The longer I spend on things that could be equally well done by an intelligent chimpanzee, the longer it will be before I start earning my keep.' She liked that final phrase: it went straight for the businessman's soft underbelly. Money. Her wages were low for a fledgeling broker but much too high for a chimpanzee. In the wrong job, she was an expensive luxury.

Hugo took the point. 'You really should have spoken up before,' he said, avoiding apology, shifting the onus of responsibility on to her. 'You're right, of course. Leave it with me. No, better still, see if Rupert's back from lunch. If he is, send him in.' He read hesitation in her face – she knew now who had added the artwork to Princess Di's photograph – and went on: 'Don't dismiss him just because he suffers from aristocratic inbreeding. He's no chinless wonder, our Rupert. For one thing, he knows just about every underwriter who's worth knowing. He's a good, reliable performer. You can learn a lot from him.'

'I'm sure you're right, but . . .'

'But?'

'This is silly,' Charlie admitted. 'I think he's a bit keen on me. It doesn't matter. I can handle it.'

'You have to.' The charm was in abeyance: Hugo at his most forceful cut an impressive, almost brutal figure. 'I took a big gamble when I employed you. You're not the first woman on the floor but you're the first in this division: I knew there would be a few teething problems. I thought you were tough enough to cope with them. Men who think women should just be tarts and typists are going to try it on with you all the time. That's human nature: it's as rampant in the City as anywhere else, probably more so. It puts you under a lot of pressure: I know that. You can't afford to get riled, I don't expect you to be discouraged, and – if you'll excuse my frankness – you'd be a damn fool to drop your knickers. That sort of thing gets about.'

'I'm human too,' Charlie murmured coolly. 'Not that it's any of your business.'

Unexpectedly, the smile came back into play. 'Well said. Look Charlie, I want you to succeed. I'll back you any way I can. But you have to learn to take the flak. There's no room for a shrinking violet in this set-up.'

'I'm not a *shrinking violet!*' Charlie exploded, leaping to her feet. 'Just because I have a few reservations –'

'Dump them.' Hugo's good humour increased. He was enjoying her anger, the flush in her cheeks, the glitter in her eyes. 'Sit down; relax. I shouldn't have baited you – and you shouldn't respond. Your first reaction was much better. Keep your emotions at the same temperature as your gin and tonic. Maidenly indignation is an indulgence you just can't allow yourself.' She resumed her seat, shut her mouth on a further outburst. 'Good girl.' Hugo was patronising, but at least he was on her side. 'As it happens, I've been wanting to have a chat with you. You will undoubtedly be asked out to lunch by various brokers and underwriters. I don't think you should accept any invitations just yet, not until you know who's who and what they're up to. Check them out with me, anyway.' Charlie nodded, conveying polite resignation. 'I'll get you a corporate Amex for these occasions; I want your lunch dates to be strictly business. You pay; you call the shots. It puts you in the power position.'

It occurred to Charlie that Hugo was deliberately constituting himself her mentor, even her protector. She would control others; he would control her. That seemed to be the game plan. Behind her sweetest smile she turned the idea over in her mind, considering it warily.

'Now, you make a start with Rupes, and if he gets too heavy just let me know and I'll sort him out. All right?'

'Fine,' Charlie assented blandly.

She accompanied Rupert for the whole of that week, watching, listening and absorbing. The work was stimulating, his knowledge was extensive, and Charlie persistently heard only one side of his regular *double entendres*. The day began with a 9.30 meeting of the entire broking team to discuss forthcoming business, then individual brokers would brief their backroom staff and arrange appointments before setting off for the market, usually via the Croissant Express in Leadenhall. Each broker had his list of underwriters whom he was expected to cozen with frequent lunching and lavish use of his credit card. Rupert took Charlie in tow on his rounds, showed her off in restaurants, flaunted her round Lloyd's. Entry to its sacred precincts was procured by a pass: hers was silver, his gold, since he and his parents were all Names.

'For today's lesson,' he would say, 'we have an order for a TLO. Do I see a hand up at the back of the class? Yes, Christie Minor, that's a Total Loss Only insurance. In other words, the underwriter will only have to pay out if the vessel is totally destroyed; if it's just got a couple of punctures he's in the clear. This is one for the gamblers, a catastrophe risk, all or nothing. Our client is a Greek shipping owner with a fleet in excellent condition, reputable sort of chap, new to the Lloyd's market. We need TLO cover on each of ten vessels for one million pounds sterling. Now, there are several ships in good condition and the risk is low, so we should get a correspondingly low price. Say, between 0.5 and 1 per cent. Theory understood? Good. Let's try a little practical application.'

He would case the room, pushing his untidy hair into a crest and raising his eyebrows as if trying to increase his height. Then he would home in on an underwriter whose box looked free and thaw him out with smalltalk about the weather and the cricket results, until his target was sufficiently mellowed to be receptive to business. The Greek shipping owner caused the odd *frisson* of doubt when it was pointed out that seven of the vessels listed were marked tba, to be agreed, indicating they had not yet been purchased, but Rupert asserted confidently that the matter was in hand. Phrases like 'as far as I am aware' or 'to the best of my knowledge' routinely accompanied such assertions, an essential part of the broker's jargon, putting him in the clear if the client had lied. The entire deal, Charlie realised, was based purely on trust: between broker and underwriter, between broker and client. For the unscrupulous, there was plenty of room to manoeuvre. But Rupert's honesty was transparent: a poker player would have read his cards in his face. It struck Charlie that if you were going to tell a lie, it might be much more effective to dupe someone like Rupert into doing it for you.

Responsibility for the hypothetical Greek fleet was distributed among five underwriters in the space of a day, earning Rupert some £17,000-odd commission. Charlie's eyes widened at the mathematics. In between, they managed a pre-lunch glass of champagne at Corney and Barrow's, located underneath the

Lloyd's building, so Rupert could watch the rugby final on a barrage of TV screens. Laurent Perrier blended into lunch and after a short break for work they returned for coffee. At the end of the day they sent a fax confirming the deal and their task was completed.

Charlie never knew what happened a year later when the policy came up for renewal. The ghost ships had never been attached and the Greek owner had, it transpired, played the market before, changing the name of his operation to confuse the underwriters. Overstating the case was a standard dodge to get a cheaper insurance rate: the larger the fleet, the lower the premium. So much for trust.

It was one of Spooner's clients.

The architecture of the Lloyd's building might belong to the realm of futuristic fantasy but the daily ceremony of doing business was so steeped in tradition it reminded Charlie of an ancient dance of courtship. The brokers stalked their underwriters with light step and airy gesture; the underwriters, based in their boxes, hesitated and tantalised, until they were charmed, lured, flattered into scrawling the conclusive signature. Four dealing floors overlooked the chasm of the central atrium and here the dancers came and went, stumbling or swift, slow or sure-footed, but never out of step. As a woman, Charlie realised very quickly that her femininity isolated her, in some indefinable way, and always would. Superficially accepted, she knew that jokes were made behind her back which she would never be asked to share, whispers that did not reach her ears. Gradually it dawned on her that for all its coy manoeuvres the dance was not a courtship ritual after all; it was a re-enactment of the hunt, an elaborate pavane of pursuer and pursued, performed by the men and for the men in a tribe where women had little status. Machismo is the creed of the hunter: he has more time for his prey than his bedmate. In Lloyd's, women were treated as guests rather than members, allowed in on sufferance, a necessary concession to a changing society, greeted with aloof courtesy, tolerated or ignored. As if they brought with them some mysterious disease of the outside world which they might communicate to their fellows. But, although Charlie did not know it, the canker was already there.

There were underwriters who still used a quill pen in preference to a Mont Blanc; there were brokers who still abided by the motto *Uberrimae Fides*, 'In utmost good faith', on which the institution had been founded; but both were going out of fashion. Charlie soon discovered the exhilaration of making a deal, totting up the noughts on the firm's commissions: it was an emotional high, a fix, a winning gamble that set her heart racing and her eyes alight. The more she experienced that hit, the more she needed it. A successful broker sleeps on average four hours a night, and Charlie was determined to be successful. She started early and finished late, drawn into the merry-go-round of corporate entertaining, lucky to escape by midnight with both shoes on. She was particularly in demand with the male clientele and Hugo saw to it that she made herself available, doing the rounds of theatres, restaurants, discos, clubs until her brain reeled and she thought she would not survive another evening of Andrew Lloyd Webber or *Les Misérables*, escalopes and escargots, Tramp, Annabel's, Stock's. Musicals were especially good for amusing foreigners since it didn't matter if their English was less than fluent: banal lyrics and plagiarised tunes could be followed by anyone. Watching both her figure and her alcohol intake Charlie would eat light and drink slow, while all around her champagne glittered, faces reddened, sweat dripped. When she was unable to leave early she would stop drinking altogether and a surreal state of sobriety would ensue, when the latest dance beat would pound in her head and her companions, client and colleague, would take on the aspect of grotesque animals, swinish or vulpine caricatures blotched with lurid colour in the disco lighting. She would have to play grope-and-shove on the dance floor, tactfully restraining wandering hands and distancing herself from nudging crotch and heaving chest so gracefully that her partner was unable to take offence. As long as the business came rolling in, her object was attained.

Charlie's package did not yet include personal commission but she was beginning to establish a reputation and gain the respect of her compeers at Fitzgerald Denton. Hugo kept a supervisory eye on her, assuming his position gave him the authority both to criticise and protect. On those late-night sessions Charlie often felt reassured if Hugo was there. She knew herself to be his particular protégé, in some sort his responsibility; he was sufficiently her senior in age and experience for their relationship to evolve on student–professor lines, with inevitable undercurrents which, for the moment, they both affected to ignore. Charlie found him attractive at times, his powerhouse physique displaying rather than concealing the driving force within, the charm he switched on so easily – a charm which she knew to be cultivated, even calculated – catching her frequently off guard. But she was also wary of him, of the control he seemed determined to exercise over her, of a certain crudeness she sensed beneath the sophisticated veneer. He was a married man sleeping with his secretary, a hungry opportunist in an unscrupulous world. She was glad their meetings were generally in company and their association was still irregular enough to preclude the situation evolving further and complicating her life and her career.

Hugo knew what he wanted, on the rare occasions when he allowed himself to give the matter any thought, and unconsciously assumed that under the right conditions he would get it. But circumstances seemed unlikely to oblige. His marriage was essential, his mistress growing tiresome, too integral to his business to be casually fired, deep in his confidence in more ways than one. He knew he should get rid of her, boot her out, pay her off: 'Leach by name, leech by nature,' Spooner had quipped in warning, long before. Hugo refrained from telling his associate that Bianca did not cling, she sucked, and when she sucked it was all too easy for him to loose his hold on common sense, and forget everything but the passing pleasure. Bianca might not be so quick in repartee as Charlie, but nonetheless, her tongue was her fortune, and aside from their business entanglement, Hugo hesitated to throw a fortune away.

Charlie's first unofficial invitation from Hugo came unexpectedly, late in November.

It was Friday, and for Hugo that Friday feeling meant the sinking of the heart occasioned by the prospect of going home. He was late getting away – he invariably was, at weekends – and the rush hour had tailed off; Victoria Station no longer resembled a giant rugger scrum and the first-class carriage on the train to Godstone held only one other occupant. Both travellers concealed themselves, British fashion, behind copies of the *Standard*, avoiding eye contact or the exchange of comments, usually on the weather, necessitated by politeness. Hugo skimmed the headlines, giving serious attention only to the blush-pink central leaves, imitation *Financial Times*, checking Fitzgerald Denton's share price, coasting through columns of journalistic comment without registering their content.

Beyond the windows the crowded lights of suburbia gave way to a countryside wrapped in darkness. He did not really like the country: it was full of woods and nettles and shadows, cows and cowpats, slow tractors on narrow roads, people who talked about rose-growing and were involved in the community. His wife Emily was one of them. For many years now their conversations had consisted of Emily pursuing one subject while Hugo pursued another, both talking, neither listening, with no mutual interests, no communication, little argument. But a country house and a country wife were both part of the lifestyle Hugo had targeted long ago, necessary adjuncts to a well-oiled, well-heeled upper-middle-class existence. Emily had been to Cheltenham Ladies' College and finishing school, her accent was the one she had been born with, her mother was a peer's daughter and her father could trace his family fortune back to the Victorians. She cooked well, dressed badly, and was impervious to climate, which meant their centrally heated house was normally much too cold. Windows were left open to admit fresh air, radiators were turned down from an inherited passion for austerity. Hugo preferred air conditioning and his radiators on high; his wife felt that his desire for comfort betrayed his status as a member of the *nouveau riche*, but she said nothing. Saying nothing was intrinsic to their relationship, on both sides. It was only on evenings like this, faced with another country dinner party the next day, more chatter of children and nannies, roses and horses, that Hugo confronted the truth. It was the means, not the end, which excited him, filling his life, making it worth living. The scramble up the social ladder, the faces trodden underfoot, the cut-throat poker-play of wheeling and dealing: these were the things that motivated him. The conflict, not the peace to follow; the art of winning, not the prize. Bianca knew too well how to please him sexually but Charlie was the kind of woman he would have wanted if he had been free to choose, a career girl with brains beneath the glamour, hidden depths at whose possibilities he could only guess. Yet he had married Emily and, even on Fridays, he wished to stay married. Emily represented an achievement.

At the station, he got into his carefully parked Aston and drove home. It was an Aston Martin Zagalo Volante 1989. As scarlet as Margaret Mitchell's heroine, gleamingly luxurious. Another symbol of success. It had cost him almost as much as his house. Perhaps that was why, even on a Friday, he could not sit behind the wheel without a secret glow of pleasure. In the driveway he pulled up but did not hurry to get out, savouring the last few seconds of his car, his territory. In the house, he would be in Emily's kingdom, in practice if not on paper. Welcoming lights spilled from ground-floor windows. Welcoming dogs bounded from the front door. Two labradors and a retriever, all in different shades of gold, with soulful brown eyes, cold inquisitive noses, rough pink tongues. Hugo did not really like dogs but they were part of the package and he treated them accordingly, patting them in a routine sort of way and calling them by name, even though he could never recall which name went with which dog. Because of their colour they had been christened Ginger, Cinnamon and Nutmeg, otherwise Ginge, Cinders and Nutters. Hugo would give them orders which they rarely obeyed, although they came to heel at a word from his wife; he could no more understand someone talking to a dog or a cat than he could their trying to converse with a table, or discuss politics with a set of chairs. When he went inside they followed him, tails wagging as he poured himself a whisky without water, abandoning his company only when he committed the supreme offence of collapsing on to a sofa. A children's toy – a plastic horse with cavalry officer aboard – half buried behind the cushions, embedded itself in his back. He swore, and tossed it on to the floor.

'I thought Birgit was supposed to clear up after the kids,' he said as Emily came in. Birgit was the latest au pair. Happily for Hugo's peace of mind, she was very plain.

Emily, as usual, did not seem to hear. 'Christina has cried off,' she said, preoccupied with social problems. 'We're going to be one woman short tomorrow night. I know people say it doesn't matter but it ruins my seating plan. I hate it when the table's uneven.'

'What's wrong with Christina?' Hugo asked automatically, pressing the control for the television. Canned laughter, raucous yet faint, intruded in the background.

'She's in bed,' Emily said, as if this were a disease in itself. 'Something to do with her waterworks. Hugo, can you think of anybody we could invite at short notice? The trouble is, it always looks so desperate, asking people the day before. They're bound to guess they're only a stopgap. Can't you think of someone who wouldn't be offended? Someone who's – well – socially available?'

'A wallflower,' Hugo supplied, 'as desperate for an invitation as we are to invite her. Is that the idea?'

Sarcasm wafted over Emily, leaving her unaffected. 'Don't be silly,' she murmured absently. 'I was thinking of that new girl at your office. The trainee. She must be pretty anxious to please. And she might like to get out of London at the weekend. Everyone does. Would she *do*?'

'I expect she's busy,' Hugo said.

'Is she presentable?'

'Yes. Yes, of course. But –'

'If you have her number,' Emily said, 'I could call her in the morning.'

Charlie *was* busy, she had a date with a bottle of claret and Caroline Elliott-Browne; but she cancelled it. 'It's the boss,' she told Caroline. 'I really ought to go. Besides, I'm curious.' Caroline, who had a string of other invitations to draw on, was understanding.

'Tell me about it afterwards,' was her final injunction. 'All the gory details.'

'I hope,' said Charlie, 'there won't be any.'

The house was situated in six acres of ground just south of Godstone. Following Hugo's instructions, Charlie checked off the usual landmarks – pub, farm buildings, bus stop – driving slowly, looking for the name plaque. A hundred yards on the left, Hugo had told her, after the old red pillarbox. As she passed the open gateway she saw the name, Fitzdenton Place. Charlie was smiling to herself as she reversed and swung into the driveway. The house was large and unexpectedly attractive, its architectural shortcomings covered with ivy and the netted twigs of Virginia creeper, now barren of leaves. A lacework of tree branches in the background trapped a fragmented mosaic of sky. There were already three cars parked in front of the house, Hugo's Aston, a new Jaguar, and an old and very battered Land Rover. Charlie pulled over beside it and, as she opened her door, the dogs bounded to meet her, followed by Hugo. She had had a dogless childhood and was a little unsure about her welcome, worried that enthusiastic paws would ladder her tights, but the paws remained on the ground and the melting eyes and waving tails won her over. Hugo tried to call them off, apologising for their advances, but they did not respond.

'It's all right,' Charlie said. 'I'm used to unauthorised advances.'

The appearance of Emily prevented Hugo from commenting on this remark. She called off the dogs in a commanding manner which sat oddly with her air of general vagueness, using names – if they *were* names – which made Charlie feel she was on another planet. 'Here, Nutters! Cinders! Ginge!' Evidently this bizarre nomenclature went down well in dogspeak: the tails continued to wag but the pack retreated. Emily offered a gripless handshake and informed Charlie that as promised she had made up a spare bed. She could have been any age between thirty and fifty; her thin, slightly horsy face was the sort which did not alter with time, and her hairstyle had probably remained unchanged since her teens. A few daubs of makeup adhered carelessly to her features and she appeared to have dressed by accident, short drooping top, long drooping skirt, faded puce against lettuce green, with a silk scarf thrown in that bore no relation to either. Her arms were bare to the elbow but she seemed impervious to the chilly wind. She pleaded the call of the kitchen and retired, leaving Charlie to be escorted inside by Hugo.

'Nice of you to come,' he said. 'Sorry it's such short notice.'

'Someone dropped out?'

Hugo grinned at her, unfazed. 'I knew I could rely on you.'

Just like a night out with the clients, Charlie thought a little wryly.

'I'm afraid it's a very dull party. There's a couple just back from Hong Kong, a banker and his wife, she's a friend of Emily's mother, and the new local vet who treated one of the dogs during a recent health crisis. From the way Emily regards him, he probably gave it mouth-to-mouth resuscitation. Anyway, it's all pretty uninspiring. Still, I'm trusting you'll spice things up a bit.'

'A vet,' Charlie said, unenthused. 'That explains the Land Rover. I suppose he's my allocation for the evening?'

'Unfortunately,' Hugo said, taking her arm, 'that's right.'

In the drawing room they found the banker, from the Hong Kong Shanghai Bank with a portly waistline and the yellowish residue of an Oriental tan, his wife, overdressed for the occasion and sporting a very ugly necklace of what had to be family diamonds, and the vet, Charlie's allocation, half their age and on a tenth their income, in desiccated jeans and a jacket of Donegal tweed which matched his origins. His name was Reggie McAvee, and since he qualified he had worked mainly with the Irish Bloodstock Agency, physicking and nurturing the horses that he loved. But these were difficult days, even the Sport of Kings was feeling the pinch, and he had come to England to seek pastures new and potentially greener than those on the fabled Emerald Isle. Like many voluntary immigrants he relished regretting his homeland, idealising it from a safe distance, despising the English with their closed-in faces and their flattened accents, feeling fancy-free, carefree, and infinitely superior in his shabby clothing and rattletrap vehicle. Bouncing his way over perfectly smooth roads through the cosy Surrey landscape, drinking English beer in English pubs, he would wax lyrical on the rocky coast of Inishowen, and the sunset from Malin Head lacing the sea with a glittering path which seemed to lead straight to Tir na nOg. Nobody minded. It is part of the ambivalent English attitude to their western neighbours that despite decades of terrorist bombing and contemptuous jokes they still

74

expect Irish ex-pats to be poets at heart, romantic exiles remembering Erin in yearning songs and outpourings of blarney. Reggie McAvee did not disappoint. In addition to the lyric nostalgia and blithe arrogance he had the rough-hewn beauty of his people, coarse black curls framing the face of Cuchulain, quick temper and quicker laughter flickering in his sea-grey eyes. From the lofty status of his Irishness he regarded the inhabitants of Surrey with easy condescension: he liked Emily, disliked Hugo, and had come to the dinner party prepared to be cheerfully bored.

Until Charlie came in.

She was not his type, of course: he told himself that at once. A City girl in glamorous wrappings showing too much leg for the country. Very good legs, too, and she probably knew it, long and elegant, reminding him of a young filly he had treated for an ulcer a couple of years ago. If it had been summer he would have liked to take her on a hike across impossible terrain, ripping her stockings – he fondly imagined they were stockings – on passing briars, until she stopped at last, kicking off her shoes and complaining of blisters, rolling down the shredded wisps of nylon, exposing her bare limbs and citified skin to the sun. It was an agreeable fantasy instantly banished by the aloof nod with which she acknowledged Hugo's introduction. Reggie decided she was probably his host's mistress, or putative mistress, an extramarital accessory for working dinners and foreign trips. It was typical of the bastard that he could invite her to dine with his wife, as if Emily's feelings, her hurt pride and public humiliation, were unimportant. Noting Hugo's proprietary attitude, Reggie all but ground his teeth. As for Charlie, she would go for a man like that, a man who exercised only in a gym and used his credit card by way of foreplay. She wasn't Reggie's style at all.

Emerging from the kitchen, Emily, too, was wondering about Charlie. Not yet, she decided, with the unerring flair that only a wife possesses. It was possible, it might be soon, but not yet. She did not really mind – she had stopped minding long ago, thankful that an office stand-in was giving her a break. Emily tried her best but sex had always disappointed her, never living up to the bliss she had dreamed of as a teenager, when the high point of her life had been to kiss the hockey captain behind the sports pavilion. She had been within three months of marrying her first boyfriend, an eligible young man with chinless profile and plenty of blue in his blood, when Hugo had come along and, almost literally, swept her off her feet. But in the bedroom with the lights turned down the lustre of romance was dimmed, and the knowledge that he had pursued her for her connections, her position – her father – grew in the dark, working its way imperceptibly up from her subconscious, until it became a thing known and accepted, a fading ache that no longer troubled her. She was aware of the role Bianca Leach filled well before she learned her name, but realised that pretence was essential to the survival of her marriage. A secret affair, her mother told her, is a pillar of support, a tradition dating back generations; the mistress who demands public recognition, honesty, divorce is a late twentieth-century threat. Close your eyes and you are safe. And so Emily had closed her eyes, never asking herself if she would be happier if that hidden pillar were knocked away, her empty marriage crumbled, and she were left to get on with her life alone.

She felt no jealousy for Charlie, no real fear, only a vague sense of intrigue – the curiosity which had led her to press for Charlie's invitation in the first place – and a certain doubt. Charlie, she concluded, might cause problems: she appeared comfortable in the position of Hugo's protégé but Emily guessed she was not compliant by nature, too valiant for discretion, too generous for deceit. It would perhaps be a good idea if Hugo was discouraged from this particular quarry.

The meal was exquisitely cooked and impeccably served, the wine flowed, the conversation stumbled. The banker talked about the Chinese – 'Bloody good businessmen. Slitty-eyed little devils, of course' – and his wife talked about the difficulties of moving house across half the globe. Emily appeared abstracted, roused to animation only by the accidental incursion of the dogs, who flocked around Reggie making whiffling doggish noises of gratification. Hugo said: 'Get those animals out of here, dear', while Charlie stroked a golden head rather uncertainly.

'Don't you like dogs?' Reggie asked her, looking, she thought, decidedly scornful.

'I'm not sure,' she said frankly. 'I'm not very used to them. They are beautiful, but . . . you never know what they'll *do*.'

'Nonsense,' said Reggie. 'Animal behaviour is almost totally predictable. So is human behaviour, I'm afraid.'

'I love dogs,' gushed the banker's wife.

'Of course you do,' said Reggie. 'In Hong Kong, you probably ate them.'

The resultant silence was cut short by Emily's clarion call – 'Cinders! Nutters! Ginge!' – and the dogs trooped from the room to confinement in some other apartment.

'Sorry about that,' Hugo said. 'They do get out of hand.'

'They look fairly well trained to me,' Reggie countered, a pugnacious glint in his eye. 'Your wife seems to have natural authority with dumb animals.'

Quite why this remark sounded so offensive was something no one cared to work out, and Charlie, stunned to see her masterful MD caught off guard by an upstart with no tie and a single-figure income, rushed stammering into the breach. She was not even sure whom she wished to protect, or what she aimed to prevent; she only knew the situation was edging out of control. 'Emily is a great cook, isn't she?' she gasped. 'That was such a lovely dinner.' And, as Emily herself came back: 'I've just been saying what a wonderful cook you are. I'm absolutely useless in the kitchen. I never seem to have either the patience or the time.'

'Of course not,' Emily said. 'You're a career girl. Hugo's told me how dynamic you are. I'm afraid I'm not at all dynamic.' Her voice was deadpan, the note of self-deprecation so subtle even Hugo was not sure it was there. Charlie flushed with embarrassment as her compliment was turned into an insult.

Reggie McAvee sat back, folded his arms, and prepared to enjoy himself.

After coffee Charlie made her excuses, determined not to stay, whatever Hugo might say to persuade her. To her surprise, Reggie left with her. 'You can drive me home,' he said. 'I'm too pissed. I'll pick up the Land Rover tomorrow.'

'Where do you live?'

'In a village about three miles south of here. I'll direct you: the road signs are confusing.'

'Thanks,' said Charlie. 'Actually, I'm going north. To London.'

'You can go north from three miles further south,' Reggie said. 'It can't make any odds to you. Unless, of course, you're a naturally disobliging type.'

'You're very fond of that word,' Charlie remarked, getting into her car.

'What word?' He sat down beside her, clipped on the safety-belt.

'Natural. Emily has natural authority with animals, I'm naturally disobliging. If you ask me, you're naturally prejudiced and unnaturally rude.'

'I didn't ask you. I only want a lift. Left back there, not right. You'll have to turn round. Watch out: there's another car.'

'I thought you said you were going to give me directions!'

Fifteen minutes later, after Charlie had performed an awkward seven-point turn in a narrow lane, scratching her coachwork on the twiglet undergrowth beside the verge, she was driving along what appeared to be a dirt-track with a scattering of lights in the distance. 'That's where I live,' said Reggie. 'That row of cottages up ahead.' Even in the dark the cottages looked more tumbledown than picturesque. Charlie pulled over and felt the car lurch into a rut. 'Be careful,' Reggie admonished. 'There's a dip here. I should have warned you.'

'It doesn't matter,' Charlie muttered.

'I shan't ask you in,' he went on. 'You don't like me, and that way, you won't have the satisfaction of saying no. Besides, you look too tight-arsed to be a really good fuck. Or doesn't Hugo think so?'

'Hugo,' Charlie fumed, 'knows bugger all about it! Now, get the hell out of my car or –'

'Good,' said Reggie. 'That was what I hoped.' And he kissed her.

She tried to retreat but the car was too small, she was imprisoned between the man and the seat, pinioned by his mouth, penetrated by his tongue. It was the nicest thing that had happened to her in a long time and she was furious. 'Get out!' she hissed when he let her speak. 'Get out *immediately*! Just for the record, I don't go for the caveman approach.'

'There isn't any other,' said Reggie. 'Don't worry: I'm going. You know, what you need is a guard dog to protect you.'

'Not funny,' Charlie snapped. He slammed the passenger door and she did a U-turn, scooping up a portion of hedge as she went, and drove off in dudgeon towards what she hoped was the London road.

CHAPTER SEVEN

After the sale of Ballards Charlie's grandmother had felt a weight lifted from her shoulders and deposited in her bank account, where it was far more comfortable. There had been few hitches over the transaction. The surveyor, bewildered by the innocence of Granny's smile and the sweetness of her tea, missed the dry rot in the loft; contracts were exchanged; and once the trauma of leaving her long-standing home was set aside she found she was actually happier in her son's household. 'Home,' she told Charlie grandly on one of her flying visits, 'is wherever I hang my hat. By the way, dear, where *is* my hat? You know: the blue one with the veil and the little bow. I need it for London. I really can't go to London without a hat.'

'Why are you going to London?' Charlie had asked.

'Business,' said Granny with a sigh. 'Too much money can be very tedious at times. You can't just tuck it away cosily somewhere; you have to exercise it, make it work, and then, if you're not careful, it can slip its leash and get away from you and that's that. Of course, I've always tried to be careful . . .'

Charlie wanted to enquire further but she was distracted and the subject slipped her mind.

After Mr Christie's death four years earlier, a friend from his army days had taken Mrs Christie to one side and suggested that since her savings were so large she might consider becoming a member of Lloyd's. At first she shrank from the idea, never having had any financial dealings of her own, but as she turned it over in her mind its attraction grew and her reservations diminished. She was now, late in life, a woman of independent means, a phrase which, whenever she tried it out, buoyed her confidence and filled her with a novel sensation of excitement. She decided to take her future into her own hands, making preliminary enquiries, tentative telephone calls which elicited enthusiastic responses. She had always known the right people but this was the only time she had ever tried to make use of her acquaintances; networking was the modern term, she had heard it somewhere, probably on television. She said nothing to her son and daughter-in-law, perhaps hoping for the moment when she would surprise them with her ingenuity, perhaps merely secretive, after the manner of a generation which did not vaunt its financial affairs. She sailed through the vetting procedure and a rather perfunctory interview with ease, and qualified as a new Name just before the annual cut-off period in August, within months of her husband's death.

She had attended the Rota Committee meeting alone, hatted and veiled, looking like an Edwardian lady on a furtive visit to the usurer's to borrow money for her card debts. The building daunted her for a few minutes, it seemed so unlike her mental image of the grandeur that was Lloyd's. To augment her confusion she was escorted to the eighteenth-century committee room designed by Robert Adams for a house in Wiltshire and subsequently transplanted, first into the old Lloyd's, then the new. An anachronism presumably intended to reassure the old-fashioned, it was high-ceilinged and hung with chandeliers, its panels painted a tranquillising blue, its chenille carpet soft underfoot. Pictures crowded the walls, oil on canvas, generally with a maritime theme: *A Frigate off Portsmouth*, or *Harman's Action with the Shakerloo, February 1664*, or *The Royal Yacht in a light air* by Willem van de Velde the Younger. In the centre of the room was a highly polished banqueting table surrounded by an unnecessary number of chairs and a sole occupant. He rose to greet her, apologising for the absence of his colleagues. Mrs Christie felt like a time traveller, plunged from the future into the past with no pause for a stopover in the present, enclosed in a single antique shell in a giant honeycomb of metal and glass, a miniature environment which, though genuine, felt artificial, affected, contrived. The committee representative, however, was reassuring, explaining very conscientiously the issue of liability in the unlikely event of universal holocaust, then running through the catalogue of her assets. His manner was almost excessively polite, implying a gentlemanly distaste for making such personal, if pertinent, enquiries. 'You see, Mrs Christie, I have to make certain that you fulfil our requirements, just as I hope that we fulfil yours. Now, the rules of membership state that at least 60 per cent of your wealth has to be in the form of all or any of the following,' and he launched into a long list that included shares and securities, foreign currencies, bank accounts, building society accounts, insurance policies, trust funds, National Savings Certificates, and even premium bonds. Mrs Christie blinked in bewilderment at what was to her a meaningless liturgy, roused to animation only by the last item. 'No premium bonds,' she said decisively. 'I don't hold with gambling.'

'Of course not,' said the committee man, temporarily disconcerted but making a rapid recovery. 'How sensible of you.' She obviously had not understood the risk factor in her investment and he felt a fleeting qualm at the realisation that he felt unable to clarify it any further.

He moved on, mentioning letters of credit, gold bullion, gold coins: 'Gold must add up to no more than 30 per cent of your means, and it has to be estimated at 70 per cent of the current market value to allow for price fluctuations. Do you have anything like that, Mrs Christie? Some of our members have really impressive coin collections.'

'I do have a rather splendid medallion which was presented to my late husband when he retired from the Tenth Balouch Rifles,' she murmured reminiscently. 'It was when they were disbanding the rest of the Indian Army. I always thought that was a terrible mistake. Even the soldiers said as much, the poor dears. There was such a lot of resentment about keeping the Gurkhas on, you know. No end of bad feeling. It seemed such a shame.' Precisely what aspect of the situation had seemed a shame was not quite clear. 'There they are still,' Mrs Christie continued with a sigh, 'marching up and down outside Buckingham Palace. They look wonderful, of course, but awfully short. I can't believe they'd be very good at protecting the Queen, when they're so small.'

The representative arranged his features in a suitably attentive expression, accorded a respectful pause to her memories, and then resumed: 'What price would you set on the medallion, Mrs Christie.'

'Oh, I couldn't do that. It's much too special to sell.'

'Of course, of course. To you it has a sentimental value which cannot be measured. That goes without saying. But – for example – if it *were* to be sold at auction, how much do you think it might fetch? An approximate figure?'

Mrs Christie looked slightly amazed at a question she evidently considered impertinent. 'Well . . . it's difficult to say. Perhaps a hundred and fifty pounds? To a collector, that is.'

'Yes, I see. Most interesting.' He retreated into politeness again, making a cryptic scribble on the sheet of foolscap in front of him. 'Anyway, Mrs Christie, as far as your estate is concerned, I think we can safely say that the notional value of any small – er – heirlooms is irrelevant. We can exclude them from our calculations; do you agree?'

She nodded. She was beginning to find his elaborate tact irritating, and she decided it would be simpler to cut the session short. She felt his attitude matched his setting, an antique courtesy that might once have been genuine, taken out of context, distorted by the multiple pressures of a ruthless modern environment until it had all the artificial polish of a veneer. She felt a sweet pang of satisfaction watching his face when she placed her bank statement on the desk. It showed she was in credit to the tune of just over a quarter of a million pounds.

There was an agreeable silence before he spoke.

'Mrs Christie, I – er – I see this money of yours is in a current account?'

'Naturally,' she answered, reverting to her expression of mild surprise. Where else should it be? her tone implied.

'How long have you – how long has it been there?'

'Oh, a month or so. Why?'

The representative turned pale with shock. 'Because, Mrs Christie, it's earning absolutely no interest. It's just – sitting there. Useless. It should at least be placed on deposit. Otherwise its value will decrease. You have to take account of inflation.'

'I'm afraid I've never really understood all that,' she said firmly, as if inflation were a somewhat vulgar subject for general discussion. 'I don't spend any of that money, you see. I use my pension from the Post Office and that way what's in the bank can remain untouched. I do want my family to benefit from it one day.'

'Exactly,' he said eagerly, forgetting his earlier sensitivity. 'That's why it's so important to have a good investment portfolio. When you've signed the acceptance I'll take you to someone who'll be able to advise you. I do strongly recommend you listen to him, Mrs Christie. Money shouldn't be left lying about in a current account –' he spoke as if she were keeping it in a teapot – 'it must be encouraged to grow and reproduce.'

Like a vegetable garden, Mrs Christie thought, with sudden enlightenment. 'Very well,' she said. After all, she was a woman of independent means. She could afford to take advice.

She had been sponsored by two syndicate members, one to vouch for her integrity, the other as the managing agent for the syndicate she was to join. The committee representative explained to her that a period of three years had to elapse before she would receive any income; her selection of syndicates was apparently the epitome of caution and, although profits were modest compared to some of the bullish enterprises, her money was very safe and she could expect to receive a far higher return than if it had been placed in a deposit account or a building society. Then he led her from the Adam room back into the modern world, introducing her to a colleague of his who would guide her through the tangled maze of investments to a secure financial haven beyond. Despite his apparent knowledgeability he seemed very young, but then, she admitted to herself, so many people did nowadays.

For all the futuristic glamour of her surroundings, she left the premises carrying with her a curious sense of anticlimax: she had expected becoming a member of Lloyd's to involve a little more ceremony than a quiet interview with a polite older man and an earnest confabulation with an equally polite younger one. In the old days it had been a case of fanfare and ceremony, now Names were joining by the thousand. At the bottom of the steps she turned, feeling, for no particular reason, like Lot's wife, a fugitive who would be transformed into a pillar of salt for the sin of looking back. Her gaze was led irresistibly upwards, past windowless glass and mortarless wall, higher and higher to where cylindrical steel pinnacles, gleaming like missile casings, nudged at the sky.

A sudden shiver ran through her: she almost quailed at this alien structure, the cold brilliance disseminated through its transparent sides. She dropped her gaze in haste and scurried away, a compact figure, diminutive but determined, the hat she would always consider suitable for London ventures shading a face that betrayed both doubt and obstinacy. It was the obstinacy which Charlie had inherited, an older, gentler vintage, but the same essential characteristic, both a quality and a fault, depending on its application. She had done the right thing, she was sure of it, or almost sure; but she pushed away the 'almost' in a gesture of mental rejection. When the profits began to materialise she would have a major legacy to leave her family, *her* money, not that of her late husband, earned by her own ingenuity and resolution. George, Susan and Charlie would be amazed, admiring, grateful: she enjoyed imagining their reactions. Yes, she had done the right thing: the gleaming sinister building was merely the symbol of change and modernisation, not so much a threat as unfamiliar territory. Her architectural taste was behind the times, she knew that. And with that thought she turned right and found herself, with one of those strange time switches in which the City seemed to specialise, back in the past again, an artificial past as stylised as a stage set, the arcade of Leadenhall Street market. There were old-fashioned shopfronts painted in Christmas-card colours, straw-hatted butchers, their white aprons unmarked with blood, selling pristine carcasses of poultry and game, grocers displaying exotic fruits, whole cheeses, dishes of pâté.

The aroma of freshly ground coffee drew her to a corner café. She stepped inside and ordered a cappuccino. This was her first foray into a brave new world: it seemed appropriate to sample the brave new menu now she had arrived. She spooned up the froth, relishing the sweetness of the chocolate powder; but the coffee underneath tasted like any other coffee, for all its fancy dress. There was a moral there if she could only work it out. Beyond the café windows the denizens of the Lloyd's bailiwick went by, bustling about their business. Mrs Christie forgot to look for moral conclusions, telling herself that she was a part of it now – she had status, membership of the exclusive club; she belonged. She would mention her new pension arrangements to

her family but keep the rest a secret until she was ready to aston-
ish them with her gargantuan wealth. But for all her optimism
she did not feel imminently wealthy, or any sense of belonging.
She left the dregs of her coffee, took a taxi to Victoria, and got
on the train home, distancing herself from the unreal City, concentrating on her dreams of success.

CHAPTER EIGHT

During those first few months at Fitzgerald Denton much of Charlie's energy had been concentrated on learning the language, the jargon of insurance broking. The moves in the game were reduced to cryptic word-compounds or strings of initials: RITC (reinsurance to close), roll-overs, stop-loss insurance (reinsurance for a Name to protect him from serious loss), ROL (rate on line), TLO, IBNR, LMX, E&O. Sometimes, Charlie felt she was looking at a particularly useless hand in Scrabble, the kind with few vowels and a succession of hopeless consonants, making no words, no sense, only gibberish. But she realised very quickly that the jargon was simply a code, a smoke-screen of jumbled letters, concealing what was basically an elementary business practice. Take a fleet of ships, an oil rig, a power station, Marlene Dietrich's legs, obtain the lowest possible premium, spread the risk from underwriter to underwriter, syndicate to syndicate, Name to Name, pocket the commission, smile, start again. Occasionally Charlie speculated that perhaps the use of code was a deliberate attempt to add mystery and mystique, distancing the ritual from both client and investor, elevating brokers and underwriters to the level of initiates and high priests communicating in their own secret tongues. Long ago, church services were held in Latin so the peasants would not understand what was going on. Here, Charlie thought, not merely the vulgar herd but the more gullible nobility were similarly excluded. She had no idea that her grandmother had been incorporated in their number.

Christmas drew nearer, heralded in Lloyd's by a mounting wave of end-of-year renewals, hectic parties, redoubled drinks consumption, a seasonal blizzard of City snow, principally in the Members' loo. The work overload produced a species of feeding frenzy on the floor, with participants coaxing, cajoling, coercing, dangling the bait, spinning a line, scooping the pool or watching some big fish wriggle off the hook, all at impossible speed, as if

87

the citadel of insurance existed in another dimension, its inmates functioning at a different acceleration from normal human beings, fitting a year of seething activity into a standard hour – like the mayfly who lives out its life in a day yet the count of whose heartbeats is no less than that of a man at threescore and ten. Mayflies are flimsy, manic creatures; the dealers at Lloyd's believed themselves tough, thought themselves strong. Yet many of them were burnt out before they reached forty, boosting vitality and velocity with alcohol and drugs which further eroded their systems. The XL brokers, specialising in reinsurance for underwriters either in the home market or overseas, were among the most hyperactive and hyperaddicted, doing the cream of the business and creaming off the most lucrative commissions, layering the risk even as money launderers layer their illegal gains. Some underwriters had also begun to specialise in taking XL business, lured by lavish corporate entertainment and the comfortable belief that flood, fire and fever would surely never coincide outside the Book of Revelations. If they did – if Judgment Day rolled round at last – some syndicates might find themselves wiped out for good.

But in the pre-Christmas rush nobody was thinking further ahead than the festive season and the prospect of spending some of their easy-won money. Charlie was still working with Rupert, and for all her burgeoning daily know-how still felt very much the new girl. She had accepted several party invitations, declined several more, and was anticipating with some eagerness the Fitzgerald Denton bash after close of business on the Thursday before the holiday. For once, she thought, it would be interesting to see the whole team relaxing with no clients to distract them.

Spooner had spent a long time pondering the conversation he had overheard at the Mansion House dinner. He told no one about his injuries, although while his ribs mended his colleagues had found him unusually quiet, hiding suppressed pain and repressed thoughts. Wincing lines flickered round his mouth and a frown of inner tension pinched his forehead. 'You're not well,' Hugo had suggested, but Spooner denied any sickness, his normally sallow complexion bleaching at the imputation, the boot-button gleam in his depthless eyes sharpening at something more than the twinge of healing fractures.

'There's something wrong,' Andrew Kendall had opined. 'Perhaps it's his heart.'

'Impossible,' said Rupert. 'He hasn't got one.'

'Lung cancer, then,' Andrew offered hopefully.

'He'll smoke it out.'

'Aids?'

'He'll fuck it out.'

'The invincible Spooner,' Andrew grimaced. 'You could be right. In some ways he just isn't human.'

'Find me a way in which he *is* human,' Rupert retorted.

Under their reptilian lids Spooner's eyes had a peculiar quality of superficial intensity: his gaze bored into its object, as if he could see through walls and into minds, but Charlie noticed that when she returned that gaze there seemed to be little behind it. The normal glimpse of the soul was missing, there was only a wily yet shallow intelligence, a narrow, obsessive imagination. It was as though, despite his acute brain and forceful if unappealing personality, he was not quite a person; whatever spirit malingered in his body was as vestigial as his appendix. Charlie would feel his stare drilling into her even when her back was turned, like a finger probing her body. Of all the sexual attentions she received in the office, she found Spooner's eyes the most offensive, and the most disquieting.

In fact Spooner, after his initial disapproval, accepted Charlie as Hugo's latest whim, according her the same lascivious contempt, underlying loathing and sneaking fear with which he regarded all women. The opportunity offered by his dangerous eavesdropping preoccupied all his spare thoughts. His bruises had long faded and he had avoided any further meetings with the inscrutable Soo Chang, but his front door opened a little more smoothly now, providing a daily reminder, subtle as a whispered threat, of that brief, vicious warning. No other reminders ensued. He checked his answering machine regularly for unspoken messages, listened for following footsteps in the street, but there was only silence. The silence of omniscient officialdom, patient and portentous, or the silence of a locked cabinet, a closed file, a loose end swiftly tied, soon forgotten. There was only one way to find out, and as the memory of pain receded he contemplated various courses of action.

One particular fragment of the overheard conversation remained with him, offered by the Chief Whip to the Treasury representative just before they realised they had an unwanted auditor. 'Marriott assures me he has the situation well under control. With the assistance of his friends it should, I gather, be feasible to *transfer* the problem. Don't worry: he's the traditional Lloyd's vintage, an officer and a gentleman. Old-fashioned words, I know, but that's what we need right now. He understands how important it is to safeguard the ship of state above all other ships and through all kinds of weather. The Canute operation will save our bacon.'

Marriott, thought Spooner, savouring the name with all its implications. Marriott the high-minded, the White Knight of Lloyd's. Involved, clearly, in some sort of government skulduggery, even fraud, trading his integrity to salvage the futures and reputations of others. Spooner sneered automatically whenever he considered it. He could guess the aims and the *modus operandi*: the motives that might drive a man of principle down such a road did not interest him. He was self-made: he had discarded the lower-middle-class values of his background and had not sought to replace them with any other creed save that of Darwin. This is the jungle: eat to survive, steal to thrive. Terms like *officer and gentleman* he dismissed with facile scorn; Marriott had always daunted him because of his power and position, not his ethos. Maybe the time had come to prod the idol in his feet of clay.

It was the week before Christmas. Restaurants were overbooked, wine bars crowded with last-minute business and premature revelry. Spooner had reserved a table for two at Beachie's, a fish restaurant in Leadenhall market. He arrived before his guest, propping up the bar and confronting a grim reflection in the facing mirror. Seasonal celebration always took its toll. He ordered a Bloody Mary with extra haemoglobin from a barman who did not venture on either banter or smalltalk. Beachie, otherwise Beauchamp Blackett, was presiding, sporting the inevitable straw boater and pheasant plume: he prided himself on knowing all his clientele personally but although he recognised Spooner he gave him no more than a casual greeting. Spooner spent lavishly in the name of corporate entertainment but he had the insecure snobbery of the newly wealthy and he was never friendly to those he considered his social inferiors. A snapped finger summoned a long-suffering waitress and he was shown to a table by the window.

Spooner sat sipping his drink, relishing the sting of the vodka under the furry texture of the tomato juice, watching the shoppers in the arcade below. A poulterer was unhooking a turkey from a rail where a queue of similar birds waited, pimpled from recent plucking, their heads still attached with feathered ruffs and limp scarlet combs. The poulterer guillotined the bird with routine deftness and bagged up the carcass, chatting to his customer all the while. Amicable smiles were in evidence, festive camaraderie, the bustle of eleventh-hour shopping, the regulation plaint about the weather. It was too cold for snow, it was not cold enough, maybe this year, try a prayer, and what about global warming? Spooner smiled too, but his smile was bitter. Bloody Christmas. Home to his parents in Ongar, his sister and brother-in-law and their two-point-four children. Clotted gravy on overdone meat, burnt roast potatoes, soggy sprouts. He was always determined to find fault and he knew it, and knowing it did not help; he could not change. Somewhere in the fag-end of his spirit he remembered that Christmas was supposed to be a time for setting aside differences, for rediscovering love and family affection, but he could not rediscover something he had never felt, and alienation had been with him since childhood. His earliest seasonal recollection was of his vexation at receiving presents he did not want. Now, he went home on automatic pilot, and distributed extravagant gifts that no one else desired, because spending money was easy, and he had nothing else to give. And deep inside him the latent resentment grew, because he sensed he was missing a vital ingredient of life and he would never know what it was.

He spotted his guest weaving his way through the crowd below as he was ordering his second drink. Hugo disappeared into the entrance and reappeared moments later, escorted by the long-suffering waitress and equipped with a prudent gin and tonic, at

91

Spooner's table. 'Sorry I'm late, Bill; I got tied up on that deal Rupert and Charlie are putting through.'

'Fucked up, has she?' Spooner affected boredom.

'No.' Hugo sat down, turned a smile on the waitress, and requested the menu in a brisk manner that indicated he had no inclination for a long session. It was the Fitzgerald Denton party later on and he intended to save both his energies and his liver for that. 'I know you think I took a gamble with that girl but the fact is it's paying off. Decoratively speaking, she's an asset – a little decoration always goes down well with the clients – and apart from that, she's got the makings of a good broker. You're going to have to admit you were wrong, Bill.' His grin took the barb out of the comment. 'Our foray into sexual equality is going to work out fine.'

'So she's an asset,' Spooner echoed, 'with the makings of a good broker. If you want my opinion, she should leave broking to those of us who know the game. She's got the assets of a good make, that's all that matters. Or haven't you checked her out yet?'

Hugo refused to be drawn. 'I'm trying to give up mixing business with pleasure,' he said. 'My New Year's resolution.'

'Fuck me,' said Spooner. 'So you're going to dump the lovely Bianca. Never mind: there's two weeks to New Year.'

Hugo laughed obligingly, reflecting that the jibe was not so far out. After the party at Sticky Fingers, Bill Wyman's place in Kensington, he would almost certainly wind up at Tramp, wrapped around Bianca on the dance floor in the cause of Christmas conviviality. That could have only one possible consequence. His body anticipated it with pleasure but his mind was increasingly reluctant. Jesting apart, something would have to be done about Bianca. Some day.

They chose the wine, ordered lunch. Spooner kept the conversation desultory until a suitable pause arrived between the oysters and the main course. He hesitated, not in doubt but deliberation, finishing his drink and lighting a cigarette. Hugo, sensing the change of tempo, braced himself for whatever was coming, expecting a sales pitch of some kind, an attempt to enlist his support for a dubious prospect, a request for backup over past trouble. Nothing had prepared him for Spooner's opening remark. The delivery was casual, almost chatty; the aim directly below the belt.

'Hugo . . . do you know anything about a project called – what was it? –Canute? Yes, that was it: *Canute*.' His voice carried in one of those hushes that fall, every so often, even in the most crowded bar or restaurant. Hugo's expression froze, so that for an instant Spooner, not a fanciful man, had the illusion he was confronted by a mask with nobody behind it. He knew then that he had struck gold.

'Sorry?' Hugo produced the word on a reflex, after a pause too long for normal hesitation.

'Canute.' This time, though he spoke in a softer tone, there was no feigned carelessness in Spooner's manner; he was coldly precise.

'A king in the Middle Ages,' Hugo said with an effort. 'He got his feet wet demonstrating to his courtiers his inability to stop the tide coming in.'

'Bugger that for a laugh.' Spooner had little interest in irrelevant historical details. 'This version is sitting on the floor at Lloyd's, and I infer that his object *is* to stem the tide. A neap tide of unlimited liability, which might just drown some extremely important Names.'

'I don't suppose,' Hugo murmured tonelessly, 'you would care to be more specific.'

'If you insist.' Spooner's willingness was that of a man anxious to please. 'There are certain Names who have recently incurred heavy losses, losses which would probably ruin them. Many of them just happen to be MPs of the governmental persuasion. Which constitutes a problem serious enough to call for some particularly devious tide-turning. Hence – or so I gather – Canute. Exactly how it's going to be done I don't know, though I could probably take a guess. But I thought you might have more information on that point.'

'Did you?' Hugo forced himself to sound relaxed. 'Why?'

'Because I heard a mention – just a mention – of Marriott. Henry Marriott. Isn't he a chum of yours?'

The waitress, passing the table, caught Hugo's normally friendly eye and found it unseeing, his usual charm no longer apparent.

'You know he is,' he was saying tautly. Out of the window he saw the queue of turkeys, the bustle of shoppers, the happy chaos of the pre-Christmas rush, yet it all seemed suddenly remote, unreal, a film unwinding on a distant screen, while he was isolated in a separate dimension, chilly and detached. 'Let's stop fencing with each other,' he heard himself saying. 'You'd better tell me exactly what you've learned. And where you learned it.'

Rather reluctantly, Spooner divulged the story of his inadvertent eavesdropping at the Mansion House dinner. He would have preferred to remain mysterious and omniscient, but he knew he needed to reveal the extent of his knowledge if he was to profit from it. He did not refer to the unpleasant sequel. 'One of them was Henderson, the Chief Whip,' he concluded. 'The other was a heavyweight from the Treasury; I didn't catch his name. Henderson was going through his list of big losers, most of them in Marriott's syndicate. I memorised them.' Hugo did not comment. Spooner's computerised memory for useful facts was unequalled in the City. 'Just out of curiosity I checked them out later. Here –' He produced a typed list from an inside pocket. Hugo glanced at it, knowing it would be substantially correct, his thoughts occupied with desperate speculation. Should he deny or confirm, hedge or concede? And was Spooner angling for trouble, or merely a pay-off? Knowing Spooner, it would be a pay-off, probably a sizeable one. The reflection steadied him. Bribery he could deal with, provided it was discreet.

To gain time, he said: 'I can't believe Marriott would be embroiled in anything quite as clandestine as you seem to envisage. You know quite well his reputation in the City is second to none. Underhand deals – possible fraud – that isn't his style. He's whiter than white.'

'Bullshit,' Spooner retorted. 'Nobody is that pure – nobody. Anyway, he was a serving officer in the 22 SAS when I was a sergeant in 3 Para. He was a nutter: Queen and country, death or glory, he really went for that garbage. A psychopath with ideals. He'd have walked into a minefield if he thought it was worth it. Common sense just wasn't in the picture. That type never becomes a civilian: he just swaps his badge and charges off on another crazy mission. He'd call it a mission, anyway, whatever he was up to. They say his wife's in a loony bin. If you ask me, they locked up the wrong one.'

'I didn't ask you,' Hugo said. 'Sometimes, Bill, you talk too much. You know damn all about a man like Henry. Shooting your mouth off could bring you a lot of trouble.'

'So far,' Spooner was acerbic, 'I've talked to you. Only to you. So far.'

'Who else were you planning to talk to?'

'That depends.'

'On what?' Now we are getting down to basics, Hugo thought.

'The rewards of silence. This Canute business clearly depends on absolute confidentiality. A word to the press, for instance –'

'There's no need to be clumsy.' Hugo's voice sharpened. 'Only an imbecile would meddle with the press over something like this. That one really could backfire on you. If you *are* right about this masterplan – and I emphasise the word "if" – then I suppose silence might well prove golden. But it would be a mistake to overplay our hand. This sort of deal requires finesse.'

'*Our* hand?' Spooner lit another cigarette, exhaled smoke without troubling to direct it away from his companion.

Hugo chose to ignore the studied insult. 'You've confided in me,' he pointed out. 'That makes it *our* secret, not just yours. You've dealt me in on the game.'

'Don't fake it,' Spooner snapped. 'I didn't ask you here to whisper confidences. You knew it already – you know a lot more than I do – but I'm catching up. It's easy to follow a trail of shit: you just go with the smell. Wherever the dirt is hidden I'll find it. And you can tell your mates – Marriott & Co. – that my price is high and not negotiable. Do you understand me?'

'Better than you think,' said Hugo, but for all the curtness of his phraseology, his nerve quailed.

Spooner smiled his hangman's smile and drew deeply on his cigarette.

CHAPTER NINE

Charlie left the Fitzgerald Denton building that evening a little earlier than usual, planning to shower and change at home before going to the party. Her flat was near the restaurant; others at the office were not so fortunate and the ladies' loo was swamped in a fug of hairspray and perfume, with makeup kits cluttering every surface and secretaries fighting for mirror space, a scenario reminiscent of backstage at a fashion show. Speculation was rife as to who had managed to perch a full-size inflatable doll, kitted only in a Santa Claus hat and a string of tinsel, on top of the Lutine Bell. Charlie suspected Rupert as a matter of routine. She had lunched in the Leadenhall Champagne Bar, being diverted by members of the Lloyd's magic society who were finding novel ways of opening various bottles of Dom Pérignon. On her way back to what passed for work that afternoon she had caught sight of Hugo, also returning from lunch though she did not see with whom, looking, she thought, rather less than convivial, his sunbed tan untouched with Christmas pink, his expression fixed and curiously bleak. When he saw her he managed a smile, but the change was slow in coming and his greeting was abstracted. On her way home, Charlie wondered idly what on earth could be serious enough to take the gloss off his charm in the midst of the party season.

It was dark outside and a fine, soft rain was sifting through the air, noiseless and all-pervasive. Mostly it was invisible but here and there a shaft of light from street-lamp or shopfront would show a glimmering curtain, faint as mist, the tinsel-gleam on wet pavements, the dimpling of a shallow puddle. The dazzle of London kept the night sky at a distance; between looming rooftops flaking cloud revealed a fragment of redundant moon, rain-blurred and trailing a silver vapour. 'Merry Christmas!' Charlie had called to the security man on her way out, wishing the merriment was not so obligatory, feeling a sudden pang of longing for Santa Claus and stockings, the fairy-tale snow that fell to order, carol-singing children, lost innocence, lost faith. Instead, she would have a bevy of drunken brokers, an onslaught of Christmas kisses, an overdose of seasonal spirit. She gave herself a mental shake, quickening her step as she headed for the station. Come on, Charlie: this is supposed to be fun.

'Charlie!' The voice, from somewhere behind her, stopped her in her tracks. She glanced round, seeing only hurrying unfamiliar figures. 'Charlie Christie!'

A slinky dark car slid alongside her; the driver leaned across the passenger seat towards a receding window. 'Can I give you a lift anywhere?'

It was Henry Marriott.

She should have known, of course; she had glimpsed the registration, HRM 904 – 904 being the number of his syndicate. She scrambled into the car and her vague yearnings sped, shutting out the damp evening. Despite the passing traffic it was very quiet inside, as if they were now hermetically sealed in a warm private cell. The flicker of a remembered smile rucked his thin cheek; the indeterminate light glittered in his eyes. Eyes unimaginably different from Spooner's flat orbs, with depth behind depth, secret reserves of the spirit, unlit fires of the mind. Charlie fancied briefly that she saw within him, not too little soul but too much, a force that burned him from within. In the closed car which glided so smoothly through night and traffic she felt suddenly claustrophobic, shut in with a saint or a demon, she did not know which. But with Henry Marriott, even claustrophobia was exciting. She would not have traded her unease for comfort with anyone else.

'I'm going as far as Knightsbridge. Any use?'

'Terrific. I can get the tube to Holland Park.' She would have to change, but he wouldn't know that. Henry Marriott had surely never travelled by tube in his life. She could picture him in a vintage Rolls, a hansom cab, even a tank, but not on the Underground. As they headed out of the City she speculated about his timely appearance, whether it was chance, or fate, or whether perhaps there was an element of design, and he had been there, waiting in his long car like a pike in the shadows, until she had emerged from the building and he had glided forward to ambush her.

She would never know. Even if they became intimate, if they were lovers for a week or a month or for ever, she could not ask. It would be impossible. With Henry, the depths must always remain unplumbed.

He negotiated the teeming streets with an almost supernatural skill, routes opening magically ahead of him, apparently immovable logjams separating to let him through.

'Do people always get out of your way this easily?' Charlie enquired, allowing a note of teasing to colour her tone.

'Sorry?' He wasn't sure what she meant.

'The traffic seems to divide in front of you like the waves retreating from the feet of that medieval king – what was his name? – Canute.' She felt his start of surprise as an almost imperceptible vibration through the interior of the car. Charlie bit her lip at her stupidity. 'No, that's wrong – I don't mean Canute. The tide didn't turn for him, did it? I'm thinking of Moses and the parting of the Red Sea. I always get those two mixed up.'

Marriott did not respond – perhaps driving demanded his complete attention for a few minutes – and presently Charlie produced the standard question. 'What are you doing for Christmas?' When no answer was forthcoming she realised he hadn't heard her. 'Henry?'

'Did you say something?'

'I was asking what you were doing for Christmas. It's the expected enquiry at this time of year.'

'So it is.' Although the light had shifted away from his face she sensed the softening of his features, the burgeoning smile that was not for the small talk, but only for her. 'Well . . . on Christmas Eve I usually lunch with my wife at the home. They're very kind there. You remember I told you –'

'I remember.'

'After that I'll drive to Yorkshire to stay with my sister and her family, then on to Scotland for the New Year. An old chum of mine has a shooting lodge on the west coast, just over the border south of Dumfries. A few of us should be there. It's become an annual fixture.'

'An outing with the lads,' Charlie murmured.

'Precisely.' He darted a quizzical glance in her direction. 'And you? What will you be doing?'

98

'Oh, I'll be with my parents and my grandmother. She lives with them now. It'll be the usual sort of thing: too much food, too much drink, let's pretend it means something. It's worth it for Granny, but I don't think Christmas is the same when you grow up. The magic has gone. To tell you the truth, I wish I still believed in Santa Claus.'

'Don't you?' It was Henry's turn to tease. 'You should. It's a prerequisite of working at Lloyd's.'

Charlie laughed.

'Incidentally, how's the job going? I hear you're making quite an impression.'

'Really?' Charlie reverted to professional wariness. 'From whom?'

'I saw Hugo the other day. He seems to have great hopes for you.' Marriott's eyes were on the road; his attitude was reassuringly noncommittal. She didn't think he was improvising. 'I've seen you on the floor once or twice, too. With that Lambeth character.'

'Rupert.'

Marriott was uninterested in Rupert. 'The – er – general reaction is mixed. The old guard are still in shock. You are among the first of the few. It can't be easy for a woman in that kind of working environment.'

'I can cope.' Charlie lifted her chin. 'Emily Davison threw herself on a racetrack under a load of galloping horses. I only have to throw myself on the floor at Lloyd's. It's all in a good cause.'

'Emily Davison didn't survive the experience,' Henry remarked. 'I hope you will.'

'Oh, I will,' Charlie responded confidently.

They reached Knightsbridge in silence, lost in their separate thoughts.

'I was wondering,' Henry said at length, 'if you could do me a favour.'

'Try me.'

'I haven't bought my wife's Christmas present yet. I don't normally leave things till the last minute, but this year my workload has been rather excessive, and . . . well, I was going to pop into Harrods now, but I could do with some advice. If you have time, of course. I know it's the Fitzgerald Denton party later –'

'I've got plenty of time,' Charlie interjected, glancing meaninglessly at her watch, not caring how much time was at her disposal. 'I'd love to help you. Do you have any idea what sort of thing she'd like?'

'Anything that feels soft, or sparkles attractively. Mink, nylon, diamonds, paste. She doesn't notice the difference any more.'

In Harrods, they fought their way through a scrummage of desperate shoppers to the jewellery department. At Charlie's instigation, they settled on a bracelet, a gold chain starred here and there with tiny flowerets of topaz and citrine. Henry did not know his wife's ring size and admitted, upon enquiry, that he did not think she enjoyed admiring herself in the mirror. 'That cuts out a necklace or earrings,' Charlie said.

'How very astute you are. I would never even have considered that.' His appreciation warmed her. When she chose the more delicate if less expensive bracelet, in preference to a larger and clumsier affair studded with diamond chips, he expressed approval of her taste, but appeared reluctant to take the cheaper option.

'Why pay more for something you don't want?' Charlie demanded. Guilt money, she thought; but she didn't say so. 'Anyway, I thought you were supposed to be mean. You mustn't damage your reputation.'

Henry laughed, conceded, and went with Charlie's choice of ornament. When the purchase was made, wrapped and beribboned by Harrods to save the customer any further exertion, he suggested a quick drink. She declined with reluctance, this time paying real attention to the advanced hour. 'I'm still in my day clothes. I can't go to my first company function without dressing up a little. I wish –'

'That's all right,' Henry said dismissively. 'We'll get you an outfit here. Then we can have a drink at leisure, and you can go straight on to your party. A simple solution to a minor problem.'

'I can't afford –'

'I can,' Henry said.

'Your reputation,' Charlie murmured. 'Your famous parsimony . . .'

'Don't be tiresome,' Henry retorted. 'It's Christmas. I'm going to prove to you that Santa Claus is real after all.'

Forty minutes later, Charlie left the fitting rooms for the last time repackaged from the skin outwards at a total cost of a little under £2,000. La Perla briefs, Dior tights, a little black dress by Donna Karan, Italian shoes whose sculpted wedges would not have looked out of place on a podium in the Tate. Velvet scarf, handbag, gloves, even her Le Must de Cartier perfume was new. (Wear it for me, Henry had said, it's a favourite of mine.) The makeup department had retouched her blusher; lipstick and mascara she carried with her. The clothes she discarded were bundled into the store's regulation carrier bag and deposited in Henry's car on the way to the bar he had designated for their shared drink. Charlie felt both guilty and gleeful, high on excess: no one had ever spent so much money on her before and she was too human not to revel in it. She imagined herself foiled in gold leaf, tasselled in designer labels, a long-legged fairy ready to bestride a whole row of glittering Christmas trees. 'For a Scrooge,' she told Henry, 'you're wildly extravagant. I don't know how to thank you.'

'There are moments,' he replied, with one of his unexpected flashes of gravity, 'when it is fatal to hold back.' And, in a lighter vein: '*Now* do you believe in Santa Claus?'

'I believe!' she cried. 'I believe!'

Passers-by turned to stare at her as she stood with her head thrown back, the coat slipping from her bare shoulders and her honey-yellow hair sprawling in irregular skeins over her collar. The rain had stopped and all the light and laughter of Christmas was unified in her happiness. Henry secured his car and tucked her arm through his, caught unawares by the intensity of his own gratification. 'I'll keep your day clothes,' he said, 'in earnest of other things I intend to possess. At least until New Year. You look wonderful: I wish I could come with you tonight. However, I have no desire to fight the whole of Fitzgerald Denton for your attention.'

'There would be no contest,' Charlie said. You have my attention. Always. But that was something she kept to herself.

101

She was intrigued, fascinated, halfway to surrender under the barrage of his seduction technique, if such it was, his quiet certitude, his arrogant generosity. The difference in age only increased both his attraction and her respect: he seemed infinitely wiser, stronger, dominating but never domineering, armed with old-fashioned courtesy, antique chivalry, refreshing qualities after the crude innuendoes of Rupert and his ilk. He would protect her, care for her, cherish her – confine her, control her, diminish her. She would be a princess in a one-way boudoir, a saluki chained to a golden kennel. He might fall in love with her, she could fall in love with him, but there was a danger that he would overwhelm her by sheer force of personality, protect her out of all independence, submerge her doubts, her challenges, her identity in the power of his convictions. Danger is always stimulating but she feared the loss of selfhood, the deadly allure of being both mastered and belittled by this man. And the germ of guilt remained, at the core of her emotions; she had helped him choose a present for his wife while she dreamed of being his mistress, and the woman she might replace, locked in her shadow world, would accept, all unknowing, the gift of her rival's choice.

But it was Christmas, her temper was naturally ebullient, and Bollinger in the quietest corner of a quiet bar did much to dispel latent reservations.

'How do you get on with them all?' Henry enquired, reverting to the subject of work.

'Fine,' she insisted. 'Well . . . mostly fine. There's one man, Bill Spooner . . . I know it's ridiculous but there's something about him, something almost sinister. I could believe him capable of anything. He's rumoured to be a brilliant broker but I can't imagine he has any proper business principles.'

'I should very much doubt it.' Henry smiled faintly.

'Not all brokers are liars,' Charlie said. 'Some of them are just miserly with the truth. Do you know him, then?'

'I know everyone.' He sipped his drink, offering no further comment on the enigma of Spooner. 'Are you on commission yet?'

'No, but I hope I soon will be. I've been working on a big job with Rupert for a few weeks now, and Hugo seems to think this is my test case. If it comes off, maybe I'll get a share.'

'Never trust in *maybe*. You should have a fifty/fifty split: agree it with both Lambeth and Hugo straight after Christmas, and get it in writing if you have any doubts.'

'Rupert may be upset,' Charlie said hesitantly.

'Probably. He's hoping to profit from your efforts. So upset him.'

The talk shifted from work to play, from colleagues to friends. He mentioned his sister and brother-in-law, whom he obviously loved, and his host at the forthcoming shooting party in Scotland. 'I'll call you when I get back,' he promised. Charlie achieved an assumption of indifference. Her arrival at the restaurant was long overdue by the time he put her in a prepaid cab and watched her driven away. He had not kissed her and she was unsure whether or not to be disappointed.

In the back room at Sticky Fingers, Hugo and about thirty staff who worked directly under him were already sitting down to the first course. Charlie's advent was greeted with cheers and cat-calls, rather as if she had walked past a building site in a transparent bikini. She bore it with tolerance, her mind still largely preoccupied with the quiet hour she had spent in Henry's company, and the kiss he had not given her. Hugo was beckoning, and she went over obediently and sat down between him and Rupert. The latter welcomed her with an enthusiastic hug and a rather moist salutation on her cheek and proceeded to tell her, several times over and with an air of untiring originality, how stunning she looked. Charlie thanked him for the first compliment and ignored him thereafter, picking up a glass of wine to share a toast with Hugo. His earlier tension seemed to have evaporated; he smiled into her eyes and said: 'Here's looking at you, kid,' in his usual half-mocking, half-appreciative manner. It was an attitude she found more alluring and more comfortable than the wolf-whistles and taunts which had hailed her arrival.

She found herself studying Bianca, seated opposite, under-standing why she was so much attracted to her boss, less able to understand why that attraction was reciprocated. Unless Bianca's somewhat obvious good looks – full lips, smudged eyes, Coppertone hair – provided an essential contrast to Emily's immaculate breeding and deficient sexuality. She guessed Hugo had married for position and professional advancement and he needed Bianca by way of extramural indulgence, but for all her spurious sophistication it was a scenario which secretly shocked Charlie. She was a romantic at heart and she knew she herself could never marry without love. She did not want to think of Hugo, whom she had come to like, entering so cold-bloodedly into matrimony. But possibly Emily had once possessed a certain rarefied appeal, enough to seduce him into the illusion of an attachment. Charlie caught herself wondering if, ten years from now, should she somehow marry Henry, people would assume she had wedded an old man for his wealth and social status, seeing no reason for love in their union. Tonight, every question turned back on her and Henry.

Bianca was lighting a cigarillo, staring at Hugo from under drooping eyelids, mouth pursed in a kiss as she inhaled. For no cause that Charlie could perceive, the colour warmed in his cheeks and his attention, formerly fixed on her, wavered momentarily. Maybe they're serious about each other after all, Charlie thought, her imagination mellowed by alcohol and wafting her into the realms of fairyland. Maybe Hugo stays with his wife for the sake of the children – they invariably claim they do – or even the dogs. She remembered that uncomfortable dinner party, and, by a natural progression, the conceited vet who had inveigled her into giving him a lift and then mauled her so oafishly afterwards. It was a recollection she did not wish to conjure up; in some way that she could not define it smeared her image of Henry and whatever might evolve between them. Abruptly she emptied her glass and waited while Hugo, diverted from Bianca's mesmeric gaze, turned to refill it.

The wine continued to flow and Mexican-style food worked inadequately to soak it up. Tequila slammers succeeded the wine, cigarette ends accumulated in the dregs of house red, chewed lemons, uneaten lettuce, the flabby remnants of tacos littered the plates. A general atmosphere of tawdriness dominated the tables. Flamboyant gestures of inebriation sent glasses flying; Rupert wantonly smashed several pieces of crockery before someone informed him that he was not in a taverna in Kassiopi. Spooner, fortunately some distance from Charlie,

104

appeared in an especially jubilant mood, alternating fits of pensive satisfaction with rollicking outbursts of crude eloquence and lecherous repartee with the waitresses. The snapped finger was accompanied by a quip and a grin that lacked its usual bitter twist. At one point, he actually raised his glass to Charlie across the room, his basilisk eye drawing her polite acknowledgement. 'To hell with this,' she said to herself, in need of a breather, pushing back her chair. Opposite, Bianca was looking slightly green, possibly from the cigarillos which were an affectation she had only just begun to cultivate. Charlie touched her hand a little shyly, jerking her head in the direction of the loo.

They went out together.

In the Ladies, Bianca clutched at the nearest sink and retched. She had eaten very little, Charlie had noticed. She put her arm around the other girl and pulled her long hair out of the way, feeling both helpless and concerned.

'Are you all right?' she found herself saying. Stupid question. Bianca clearly wasn't.

'Not great,' Bianca gasped, between paroxysms.

When it was over she straightened up, perspiration glinting on her forehead, the smeared mascara under her eyes resembling a bruise. 'Thanks,' she said shortly. They exchanged a long look, two women who endured but did not like each other, potential rivals, with different status, different backgrounds, different goals. Normally, the pressures of their environment kept them apart, but here any divergence ceased to matter. Bianca said suddenly: 'God, everything's awful. Merry fucking Christmas,' and looked as if she were about to cry. Charlie extracted a couple of cigarettes from the pack in her bag, handing one to her companion.

'Here.'

'Ta. I don't know why I've been smoking those other things. I thought it would make a change, but they taste like shit.' And, as Charlie flicked her lighter: 'Sorry about my language. I spend too much time with the opposite sex.'

'It goes with the job,' Charlie said. 'In fact, I expect it goes with most jobs. Unless you're a nun.'

Bianca's mouth warped into what might have been meant for a smile, her lips pressed together as if she were trying to keep them from trembling. An involuntary tear spilled over her lashes and snaked its way down her cheek. Charlie was appalled. Bianca had always seemed tough, cynical, reserved, with her glossy exterior, her slightly brazen poise, a range of attitudes from the brash to the demure; it had been impossible to picture her imbued with any softer emotion, or succumbing to the weakness of tears. For the first time Charlie knew she was the stronger of the two. It did not make her feel good.

'Look, can I help in some way?' she said. 'I don't want to be nosy – you don't have to tell me anything – but there's obviously something really wrong. If I could just –'

'I'm pregnant.'

'*What*?'

'Pregnant. Bun in the oven. Up the spout. In the club.' Bianca pinched her cigarette between unsteady fingers.

Charlie said: 'I see' mainly for something to say. She didn't want to ask the identity of the father, even if she could guess.

Bianca responded to the unspoken question in shorthand. 'Hugo.'

'Yes, of course,' Charlie said before she could stop herself. 'How long – ?'

'Not sure. Couple of months, maybe. I lost some discharge last week that looked bloody but they say that can happen. I hoped I was going to have a miscarriage . . .'

'Can't you abort?'

'Yes, but . . . my best friend did it when she was sixteen. When the baby would have been due she took an overdose. They pumped her out but she still feels guilty, years later. She says you never get over it. A miscarriage, that's nature; an abortion . . . Anyway, I know it's stupid but I'd kind of like a baby. I really would. They suck it out with a thing like a vacuum cleaner, you know. That's what Raquel said. Squelch, and it's gone.' She turned back to the sink, dropping her cigarette, and retched again.

When she had recovered a little Charlie commented: 'It doesn't show. Your stomach's practically flat. Are you – are you *absolutely* sure about this?'

'Course. I went to a clinic, didn't I? Private and confidential. I don't trust those do-it-yourself tests. Anyhow, you can't always see it, specially if it's number one. My sister was five months gone before she had much of a bulge. She's got a little boy now. Cries all night, shits all day. Or vice versa. I'm so jealous I could kill her.' A rueful smile tugged at her mouth; the sparkle under her eyelashes warned of further tears.

'Have you,' Charlie broached the subject with caution, 'have you told Hugo yet?' Maybe that was why he had been looking so grey at lunchtime.

'Nope.'

'Well, shouldn't you?'

'Get real, will you? He'd give me a nice fat cheque for the vacuum job, ease me out of the office and out of his life, and I'd never be allowed back. The longer I wait, the more I can embarrass him.'

'Is that what you want?'

The only answer was a moue of dissatisfaction. 'At any rate,' Bianca said, 'he won't get rid of me easily. As they say in the movies, I know too much.'

'You mean,' Charlie was puzzled, 'you'd go and tell Emily?'

'I'd tell the press,' said Bianca. 'Or the SFO.'

Bianca returned to the restaurant first; Charlie followed a few minutes later, after a pause for rapid reflection. SFO? Serious Fraud Office? Surely not. Bianca must have misunderstood something, blown it up out of all proportion, or perhaps she was simply feeding her resentment on fantasy, making wild accusations to stir up trouble. Charlie resumed her place at the table in a state of abstraction, answering Hugo at random, oblivious to the altered tempo of the party. The lights were dimmed, the volume of conversation turned down. There was an air of expectancy in the room. A young broker three table-lengths from Charlie stood up and tapped his glass with his spoon. The last of the smalltalk faded out; heads turned.

'Charlie Christie,' the man began, and she almost jumped, startled out of her thoughts by the impromptu address. 'On behalf of all the brokers at Fitzgerald Denton, I would like to welcome you on to the team. We hope to see you in action on the floor in the coming year.' (Schoolboy titters.) 'Above all, never forget the motto of the City. *Si possis recte, si non, quocumque*

107

modo rem. If you can't screw 'em in the normal way, there's always the rectum.' (Desultory laughter. Most of the audience had not enjoyed the advantages of a classical education; those who had, could not remember it.) Charlie hesitated, unsure if she was supposed to respond, and found that Rupert was nudging her to her feet. Out of the corner of her eye she saw an evil grin spread over Spooner's face; Hugo appeared unenthused. She started to thank them but the words were cut short. A jet of aerosol foam caught her in the mouth; more foam followed, clogging her hair, spattering her new dress, trickling down her cleavage. She tried to shield her face but it was useless. Mingled with the froth were squirts of pink sauce, writhing caterpillars of chocolate, a confetti of almond flakes, a sprinkling of salt or sugar. Her eyes were tight shut but she could hear her fellow diners shrieking with mirth, cackling hyenas, screeching owls, howling demons, and she knew that this was meant to be a joke, she was supposed to laugh with the others, 'take it in the spirit in which it's meant', show herself a sport, one of the boys. The clothes Henry had bought her were not simply ruined but defiled; she felt violated as if by a rape.

A fury rose in her that was stronger than ambition, overriding her native self-restraint. As the inundation ceased she was shaking with rage and shock, her dress glued to her body, a viscid ooze creeping down her thighs. She wanted to sob, to scream, to rend their bloated smirking faces with nails grown to claws. How could they have let this happen – Hugo who was her sponsor, Andrew her friend? The hysteria subsided; there was a moment of silence in which she heard her own breathing. She could not speak. And then a lone voice began singing 'For she's a jolly good fellow', and the whole party joined in, and everyone was applauding, and she knew this was the ultimate test, her initiation ceremony, another bloody macho ritual, and all she had to do was smile in order to make the grade. But the smile stuck in her throat. 'For she's a jolly good fellow, for she's a jolly good fellow, and so say all of us.' The song ended. Charlie was panting like a runner after a long race. She tried to brush the scum from her arms, stretched her lips in the travesty of a grin. 'Thanks,' she said at last. 'Thank you all. Merry Christmas.' They let her go on a cheer as she reeled away from the table, retreated yet again to the safety of the loo.

In the mirror, she was unrecognisable, a clown after a slap-stick scene, a walking cream sundae in an advanced state of meltdown. She did not cry: there was no point. She had made her choice when she said her thanks, choking back rage and distress, grinning like a gargoyle though she ached for a Kalashnikov. Optimistically, she tried to mop up the foam with loo paper, leaving stains like weals on her beautiful dress. For her hair, she ducked her head under the tap. She could not blow-dry; the assembly would have to make do with rats' tails. When her face was clean she reapplied lipstick and powdered her nose to bolster her flayed ego before re-entering the restaurant. Her return was greeted with a burst of clapping and a glass of champagne. Hugo said: 'Well done,' and she felt suddenly that he understood her reactions and must have acquiesced only reluctantly in the evening's bloodsport. She looked for Andrew and saw him across the room, flushed with drink and evidently beyond the reach of reason. So much for friendship. And on the thought her gaze veered to Bianca who was not her friend, slouching on the other side of the table. She smiled wryly at Charlie and her lips moved on a single, inaudible, unmistakable word. *Men.*

Charlie polished off her champagne without tasting it and pushed back her chair. 'Time to go home,' she said. 'Midnight strikes. I think I just turned into a pumpkin.'

Nothing they could say would change her mind. Outside, the rain had returned in force and there were no taxis. An umbrella seemed superfluous. She walked back to Ladbroke Gardens feeling the cold drops cleansing face and hair, damping her coat. When she got home she was shivering from the chill, the wet, the aftershock of the whole hideous experience. She threw off everything, wrapped herself in pyjamas, and with a hot-water bottle tumbled thankfully into bed. Exhaustion took over and she slept without dreaming, even of Henry Marriott.

CHAPTER TEN

St Matilda's Nursing Home was the fourth establishment to whose care Henry Marriott had entrusted his wife. The first place had had Bauhaus architecture and staff to match; he had moved her after three months. Then there had been a tranquil country manor in Wiltshire which was subsequently compulsorily purchased to make way for a bypass, followed by a high-tech set-up where the chief psychiatrist had attempted to analyse Mrs Marriott into her right mind and Henry out of his. St Matilda's was a Victorian pile renovated in the Eighties with a rambling garden and a small ornamental lake populated by an assortment of waterfowl. Nature, the principal was prone to observe, had a soothing effect on the human spirit, calming to a disordered brain. Particularly when nature was well ordered, well cared for, green and peaceful. *Mens sana in campo sano*, as he was fond of paraphrasing.

Whatever its effect on the inmates, visitors like Henry were certainly reassured by the congenial surroundings and the rose-grown façade of the house. On a winter's day the low-ranging sun seemed to be permanently tangled in the topmost boughs of the trees, liquid light spilling through a crocheting of leafless twigs. Above, the sky was eggshell blue. Henry parked the car on the gravel sweep in front of the house and got out, inhaling the clean country air as if in the forlorn hope that it would do him good. For all the beauty of the afternoon his heart quailed as it always did, fearing the proximity of derangement, the fleeting view into an alternative world all too near his own, the spectre of guilt reflected in his wife's unmeaning expression. And there would be other, deeper, feelings, stirred if not woken: the memory of Helen long ago, bright-eyed and laughing, isolated cameos of happiness, youth and love lost to the ingrowing rot of bitterness and emotional decay. Once, Helen had looked like Charlie, yellow-haired and sun-gilded, vital as spring, tender as the night; now, she was a pale phantom, features blurred with

110

middle age, hair tidied but no longer styled, its original blonde faded into grey. She might not recognise him and he did not want to see her, yet more than duty drew him. He was compelled by his own repugnance, drawn to exact a penance for a fault never acknowledged, impossible to forgive. Indeed, over the years his regular visits had become a form of atonement for the failures and shortcomings of a lifetime, a gesture of self-flagellation, a desperate attempt to balance the books. Wasted effort, useless pain, but he could not continue without it; it had become necessary to his conscience, if not his heart.

He was admitted by Sister Bavistock, a briskly friendly young woman with the figure of a cottage loaf and a down-to-earth Yorkshire accent. She wished him a merry Christmas and he responded in kind, following the duck-like wagging of her behind as she led him through the house to a dining room at the back with french windows and a view of terrace and lawn, evergreen shrubs, more bare trees cobwebbing the sky. Helen was sitting at one end of a large walnut table where two places had been laid at right angles on the corner. She looked up as he came in but did not smile. He kissed her cheek, not so much an automatic salute as a gesture of commitment, a preliminary Hail Mary. 'Hello, my dear,' he said gently. 'Happy Christmas.'

There was a lingering pause; then she said: 'Henry,' as though identifying with difficulty someone she had not seen in a long while, dredging up a half-forgotten name from the mists of ancient recollection.

He sat down beside her, aware of the door closing behind Sister Bavistock, wishing she would remain, despising himself for his own cowardice. 'How are you?' Inane question.

'I am quite well.' She produced the response like a child repeating a lesson; perhaps she had tapped into a memory from the nursery. 'We are both quite well.'

'Both?'

'I told you. Why do you keep asking? We are *both* quite well. You are always asking me things. Too many questions. I don't have enough answers for so many questions. I only have a few answers, and they don't always fit. The answer must fit the question.'

Occasionally, he noticed, she would utter curious truths,

111

stray fragments of thought which in a sane person might have been termed philosophical. Yet she had never uttered such remarks in her right mind. He said: 'Yes, it must,' and 'I am glad you are well.' Further banalities. Strange that he, who was supposedly normal, could produce only mechanical phrases, while she, who was mad, achieved a grotesque originality.

'We are both well,' she reiterated quite sharply. 'Why do you keep repeating yourself? It makes conversation very tedious. I think it would be best if you went away now. We'd like to be left alone.'

Her condition must have worsened since his last visit: this 'we' was a new factor. 'Who is the other one?' he enquired, knowing it would be wiser not to ask and to himself, who is the third who walks always beside you?

'Jamie,' she said matter-of-factly. For a minute, Henry felt his very heartbeat stilled, as if her delusion had turned him to stone. 'My son, you know. He'll be in the garden now. He rides a motorbike; I can hear it in the mornings. I wish he wouldn't. He was killed on a motorbike.'

'It can't be James,' Henry said sharply. Folly – the ultimate folly – talking reason to those who have none. 'James is ten years dead. Helen –' he hardly ever used her name '- you must accept it. Death is the end.'

'Oh no,' she said, and a rare illumination sweetened her face, a flickering ghost of loveliness and youth. 'There are no endings, no beginnings. I found out. We wither like leaves, and like leaves we reopen. Autumn and spring, spring and autumn. It all comes round again.'

'It's winter,' Henry said. The season of cold and barrenness, hibernation and death.

'Don't!' For the first time in years there was pain in her voice, not real pain but an echo, pain remembered. 'It's spring: it must be spring. Jamie is back. I only wish you would warn him about the bike. He doesn't listen to me. I'm afraid it will happen again.'

'It can't happen again,' Henry said wearily, wretchedly. 'It's over.'

She did not seem to hear.

'Did *you* give him the bike? Are you encouraging him this

time, too? How could you? *How could you?*' In her face, it was as if the weather changed: a brief storm ruffled its pallor, screwing up her features, wringing tears from her eyes. The return of Sister Bavistock with appropriate tablets eventually quietened her. Henry got up and walked to the window, staring emptily outside, filled with a vague self-loathing, a meaningless remorse. Afterwards, he took the sister on one side. 'This business about James,' he said, 'this is a new development, isn't it?'

'I should have warned you,' Sister Bavistock said. 'I'm so sorry. I had hoped she'd be all right today – he's off for Christmas, you see – she's usually quite all right when he isn't there.'

'*He?*'

'Our new handyman. Such a nice boy – so sweet and under-standing, when he told me about her behaviour. A little older than your James, I should think, and probably not much like but of course there's the motorbike. I expect that's what sparked her off. Anyway, we decided – since Mike didn't mind – not to attempt any readjustment. After all, it can't do any harm if it makes her happy, the poor lass. The patients here, they go into their own worlds to escape this one, and who are we to hurt them by bursting the bubble? It doesn't bring them back, you know: it only makes them suffer.' She sighed – a sigh that had been used many times before, and grown the wearier for it. 'She's usually quite content, thinking our Mike is her Jamie. This is the only time –'

'It's my fault,' Henry said. 'I upset her. I know I said the wrong things.'

'You do your best.' Sister Bavistock took his arm, smiling her plump, cosy smile, as comforting as chocolate to a crying child. She was almost as accustomed to nursing the next-of-kin as the mentally sick. 'Helen's the only one who knows what's right and wrong in her private universe. With the rest of us, it's hit or miss. You sit down, Mr Marriott, and I'll see about lunch. She'll be quite calm now.'

He sat down obediently and his wife was, if not calm, at least quiet, a blank-faced creature who stared at nothing and barely spoke. When lunch came, she nibbled at her food; he could not eat at all. The cooking was very good – it was one of the reasons

113

he had chosen St Matilda's – but his stomach winced at the sight of it, and he pushed the sliced turkey and roast potatoes around his plate in a semblance of eating, convincing no one (whom did he need to convince?), laying knife and fork side by side as soon as he dared, relieved that the charade was over. After pudding had gone the same way he gave Helen her present, briefly warmed by the phantom of Charlie – she seemed very distant now – her head bent over the jewellery counter in Harrods, concentrating on the subtleties of selection. Sister Bavistock, misinterpreting his expression, thought: 'He still loves her, the poor man.' Everyone was *poor* in her vocabulary, her universal compassion lavished on an undeserving populace. Helen Marriott played with the bracelet for a while, a few motes of light, reflected from the yellow stones, gleaming across the blankness of her face. 'I'll show Jamie,' she said at last. 'He'll know.'

'Know what, my dear?' Henry said.

'Whom it belongs to.'

'It belongs to you,' Henry insisted, and for no cause that he could define, he felt defiled, as if he had told a lie.

It was dark by the time he reached his sister's house, just north of York, and the scattered stars sparkled like tinsel on a black paper sky. Elizabeth was waiting at the door as the car pulled up; she hugged him without reserve and scarcely allowed him time to retrieve his luggage before pushing him inside. In the drawing room there was a real open fire with crackling wood and leaping flame, holly above the mantel and mistletoe over the door (Elizabeth kissed him again beneath it), a huge tree shedding needles, beaded with fairy lights, netted with streamers, hung with a hundred baubles. Elizabeth's husband Peter, a university lecturer, offered alcoholic refreshment; a light supper of soup, bread and cheese arrived shortly after. As always, Henry felt he had come home.

In fact, this was near enough to the truth; the Dower House, on the outskirts of the village of Kirkby Pelham, had been owned by Henry's father, he and his sister had grown up there, and after their parents' death it had become their joint inheritance. In those early, blissful days with Helen he had been making a fortune in the City and at the time of Elizabeth's impending marriage he had made over his half of the property to her, on condition that if she and Peter ever wished to sell up and move she would give him first refusal. After the death of his son and Helen's subsequent illness his London house had become unbearably empty, a hollow shell which had once been a home, vacant as the *Marie Celeste*. He had moved into a succession of apartments, luxurious and impersonal as hotel rooms. The Dower House, with its family atmosphere and his sister's ready welcome, had become once more the only home he knew, his bolthole when the pressures of work grew too intense, his regular retreat. As a child, he had hunted dragons in the nearby woods, fallen in the river Aire, flown his kite from the hilltops. Nowadays, he climbed the hill to watch the dawn, strolled in what was left of the woods, fished in the river. He had his own room there; his country clothes hung permanently in the wardrobe. He had come a long way from the carefree boy who understood nothing of madness or tragedy, self-sacrifice or moral dilemma – maybe too far – but here at least was a place where he belonged, where he could retrace at leisure the footsteps of his childhood.

He was always at ease in Kirkby Pelham.

'Did you see Helen?' Elizabeth asked, reading the answer in the flinching of his regard. 'Is there any change?'

'Maybe.' His mouth thinned. 'For the worse.'

'Oh no.'

'She thinks their new handyman is – is James. He has a motorbike; apparently that's the source of the delusion. She believes I gave it to him. We reran some old dialogue. You know the sort of thing.'

'Darling, I'm so sorry.' She gave him another squeeze, her eyes filled with a sympathy that was close to tears. 'Come into the kitchen: we'll help Peter with the washing-up and open another bottle. I know alcohol can't change the world but it *can* change the way you look at it.'

Henry laughed. 'You're a dear,' he said. 'My one and only dear.'

'Pity about that,' said Elizabeth.

In the kitchen, they propped up the Aga, drank well-warmed red wine, polished a plate or two. Elizabeth put the finishing touches to the goose for tomorrow while recounting the misdeeds of her grown-up children, her newly married son, off on a skiing trip, and her daughter, doing VSO somewhere in Africa. 'I love them very much,' she said, 'but it's rather nice to have Christmas with just us oldies. Peaceful. Don't you think so?'

Henry suppressed the thought of Charlie, several counties and a whole generation away. Out of reach. 'Yes,' he said. 'Yes, of course.'

'Liar,' Elizabeth said without heat. 'Who is she?'

'I beg your pardon?'

'The woman in your life. Don't look so stunned, darling. I've been your younger sister for nearly forty-seven years; did you really think I couldn't read your mind? I don't even need woman's intuition, if it exists. Your inmost thoughts are written in large print on the flipside of your face. You're abstracted, you lapse into pensive silences in the middle of supper, you praise my carrot soup when it's pumpkin, and there's nuance in the way you talk about Helen – an extra shade of resignation – which has nothing to do with any decline in her condition. Besides, I know you too well. Who is she?'

'Thank God you don't work on the floor at Lloyd's,' Henry remarked. 'You'd steal the market.'

Peter laughed. 'Mystic Meg,' he said. 'That's my girl. Cross her palm with silver and she'll tell your fate. Leave him alone, Lizzy. It's none of our business. Henry must have had dozens of girlfriends over the past decade; a new one won't make any difference.'

'Of course he's had *affairs*,' Elizabeth conceded. 'That's not the same thing. He could always tell a pumpkin from a carrot in the past. This one is obviously more serious.'

'Not yet,' Henry said. 'All right, I admit there's someone. Someone I like; it isn't anything more than that. We aren't even having an affair. When there's anything to tell, you'll be the first to hear. Will that do?'

Elizabeth ignored discouragement. 'What's she like?'

'Lizzy –' Half-laughing disapproval from her husband.

Henry smiled faintly. 'I thought today – she's a little like Helen, the way she used to be. A long time ago.'

Like a pouncing mongoose, Elizabeth leaped on to the rele-

116

vant detail. '*How* long ago?'

'I don't know what you mean,' Henry said, knowing quite well what she meant, suddenly sensitive about the weakness of his position.

Elizabeth gave him a glance of amused scorn. 'Yes, you do. How old is she?'

Henry shrugged. 'Young, I don't know exactly.'

'Take a guess.'

He met her gaze with one of wry surrender. 'Twenty-five, maybe. Could be more.'

'Lucky devil!' Peter exclaimed.

'My daughter is nearly twenty-five,' Elizabeth said austerely.

'So he's got himself a bimbo,' said Peter. 'Good for you, Henry. I fantasise regularly about my students but I fear they don't fantasise back. Is she blonde, bosomy and beautiful?'

'More or less,' Henry admitted. 'Not excessively bosomy. Compact. And she's not a bimbo.'

'What does she do?' Elizabeth persisted.

'She's training as a broker at Lloyd's.'

'Sounds very high-powered,' Elizabeth said, reserving judgement. 'What about her family?'

'For heaven's sake!' Peter expostulated. 'You're acting like the Spanish Inquisition. Don't be so bloody nosy.'

'I believe her father was in the Marines,' Henry replied. 'No further information to date.'

'Name?'

'His or hers?'

'Don't be frivolous,' Elizabeth said.

'Charlotte.' The concession came slowly, unwillingly, as though in naming her he had voiced a conjuration, summoning their ephemeral Christmas romance into the realm of reality. 'They call her Charlie. She's David Chater's god-daughter; you remember him?'

Elizabeth nodded. 'Charlie,' she repeated. 'That's nice. These masculine diminutives are very fashionable among the girls nowadays; have you noticed? Joanna's always been Jo, of course –' Joanna was her daughter – 'and she's got a friend Harriet who's usually called Harry, not Hattie as it would have been twenty years ago. Charlotte used to be Lottie, didn't it?

117

Charlie's much nicer.'

'We approve her name, then,' Peter murmured.

'Have you slept with her?'

'*Lizzy!*'

'It's a perfectly legitimate question,' she insisted. 'This is the late twentieth century, darling: stop pretending to be so Victorian. Anyway, it's a ridiculous attitude for a university lecturer: all your students are probably at it like rabbits, that's what college has always been about. Getting a degree is incidental.'

'I'm *not being Victorian*,' Peter said emphatically. 'I'm *minding my own business*. Try it.'

'That's idiotic. Well, Henry, *have* you?'

'I told you,' he said, 'this isn't an affair. This is a hope – a fancy – maybe only a dream. I like her; I think she likes me. That's all we have for now.'

'You're a great catch,' Elizabeth said dispassionately.

'Now,' said her brother, 'you're being vulgar.'

Peter went up to bed, leaving the two of them together to share the last of the wine and an hour or so of sibling intimacy. Elizabeth produced the Ovaltine mugs they had used as children, only slightly chipped – such mementoes of the past were very precious to her – and filled them with coffee, heavily laced with cognac. '"Twas the night before Christmas,"' she quoted. 'Do you remember that? I always thought if I could only stay awake long enough I might just see Santa Claus. I never did, but I didn't stop hoping. Let's try it now. Let's put out an extra mug and see if he comes.'

'Charlie didn't believe in Santa Claus,' Henry remarked. 'I did my best to re-educate her.'

'You dressed up in a false beard and a scarlet coat trimmed with polar bear fur?'

'Not exactly.' He took a mouthful of coffee, thankful for the spirit that warmed it. 'Lizzy . . . I'm not sure what I believe in any more.'

'Are we talking elves or ethics?'

'Ethics, I'm afraid. Lloyd's is full of elves, light-fingered little creatures, all as amoral as Puck, playing their impish games with vast sums of money and other men's lives. Who was that chap who spun straw into gold?'

'Rumpelstiltskin,' Elizabeth obliged. 'He was more of a goblin than an elf.'

'That's the one. Disastrous for the economy, that sort of thing. The value of money depends on what it represents. Too much made out of nothing – Monopoly money – spun straw – knocks the entire set-up off balance. The fairytale never gives you the whole story. One day the gold will turn back into straw and then we're all for it.'

Elizabeth frowned. 'You too?'

'Me? I'm too clever. My bank account will survive but I don't know about my integrity. I'm fighting a rearguard action in the cause of national stability and the honour of Britain. Honour, in this case, being a label and stability a high-wire act. It's a disillusioning process. I'm doing something that has to be done at the behest of people I used to respect, and by the time it's over I don't suppose I'll have much respect left for anything. Including myself.'

The trouble deepened in her face. 'I've never heard you talk like this before.'

'You didn't hear it now. Forget it. I'm tired, and the weight of the world is heavy on my shoulders.'

'Take it off. Atlas did.'

'Only for a minute. He wasn't very bright: he let Hercules trick him into taking it back again. Maybe I'm not so smart after all . . .'

There was a long silence, the effortless kind that can only exist between close family or lifelong friends. His arm was round her; he tightened his grip, pulling her against him as if for reassurance.

'You're in trouble,' she said. Not a question: a statement of fact.

He did not bother denying it. 'Don't worry,' he said lightly. 'I'm not risking my skin, only my immortal soul.'

'In the army,' she said, 'you risked your skin a good deal, but it never made you look the way you look now.'

'That's old age,' he retorted drily.

'I hope so,' she said.

After a while, she returned to more mundane subjects. 'How

119

long are you staying?'

'I was planning to leave after lunch on Boxing Day.'

'Off to Scotland?'

'Mm.'

'Your chum Henderson, I suppose. Doesn't he occupy some frightfully superior position in the government.'

'Chief Whip.' He sat nursing his Ovaltine mug, swilling the dregs of coffee around in the bottom. Watching him, she recalled him as a boy, employing the same tactics to make his drink last as long as possible and delay the advent of bedtime. When Henry glanced up he saw the thought in her eyes, shared her smile.

'Merry Christmas,' she said. 'Whatever comes after.'

'Merry Christmas.'

He listened to her climbing the staircase to her room, waiting for the familiar squeak of the seventh tread. An ache that was more than nostalgia stabbed at his heart. He tried turning his thoughts to Charlie but she was too remote and unreal, unattainably young, untouchably clean, someone who could never absorb his chequered experience or compass the murky spectrum of his feelings.

Charlie woke on Christmas morning in the bedroom where she had grown up. The curtains were not quite closed and the early sun slanted in across the quilt, dazzling her opening eyes. She rolled over, pulling the duvet up to her ears, dozing for another half-hour while her waking mind ran through a résumé of events of the last few days. The scene at Sticky Fingers seemed, even at that short distance, less humiliating, less crucial, invoking only a flicker of the murderous fury which, at the time, had almost destroyed her. What remained was not a scar but a blot, a stain on the golden path of her new career, as if the challenge that confronted her, the acceptance she fought for, would be irrevocably marred by that one grotesque incident. They had made of her a victim, a target, a clown, and whether it was an ugly joke or rites of passage hardly mattered; the aftertaste would be in her mouth every time she entered the offices of Fitzgerald Denton. 'Well done,' Hugo had said, her solitary crumb of comfort. No other individual had offered understanding, no other words had expressed appreciation. Andrew, supposedly her friend, had been too hopelessly drunk to care. She thought about quitting and knew it would be running away. In any case, she did not want to quit: the goals on which she had set her heart still shimmered ahead of her, the adrenalin thrill and the glittering rewards. The game was worth the candle, provided she did not scorch herself too badly.

She got up and wrapped herself in her old red dressing gown with ladybird buttons, a leftover from childhood, now far too short. Involuntarily her thoughts switched to Henry, mature and sophisticated, certainly too sensitive to have abandoned her to the schoolboy torment of her colleagues, had he known anything about it. He would expect, she was sure, a clinging négligé, a transparent wisp of chiffon and lace with a hand-embroidered tendril tracing her nipple. Would he still want her, she wondered, dressed in the red fluff and ladybirds of little-girlhood? She smiled to herself for all her doubts, a smile which broadened as she caught sight of her stocking at the foot of her bed. It was one of her father's old army socks, stuffed with tangerines, walnuts, a bar of chocolate and a couple of small presents, a pot of jojoba night cream and a black case containing the Mont Blanc pen which was in traditional use at Lloyd's. She had said she was too old for a stocking but her mother never took it seriously. 'I believe,' she whispered, remembering Henry and a moment of pure exultation, and for a few seconds the scenario at Sticky Fingers vanished without trace.

Charlie's Christmas Day officially began with uplift as the Christies sang their way, enthusiastic and occasionally in tune, through family service at eleven o'clock, then degenerated comfortably into a bonanza of eating and drinking. There was an opulent turkey, covered in scrunchy golden skin and oozing calorific juices, Brussels sprouts and chestnuts, roast potatoes spitting in fat, thick bread sauce made with cloves and garlic and cream. Wine succeeded sherry, port succeeded wine. Presents were exchanged and crackers pulled, and they all laughed at puns that normally wouldn't have raised a smile and perched paper hats on their heads.

Christmas for Charlie was always a family affair; even when

living in Paris she had ignored Michel's pleas to stay with him and caught a plane home. She found the predictability of the seasonal agenda infinitely relaxing: 'Hark the Herald Angels' on the old-fashioned record player, complete with crackles and scratches, her father applying his military expertise to tinkering with the fairy lights, adjusting decorations, topping up glasses, her mother whisking mince pies in and out of the oven. Granny sat and watched, interjecting the odd piece of practical advice but taking no active part in the proceedings. Charlie was not quite happy about her: she seemed quieter than usual, curiously withdrawn, apologising for cheaper gifts than in previous years, apparently counting the pennies. The sale of Ballards should have left her more in funds than ever and Charlie wondered if she was growing a little peculiar about money, as she had heard old people sometimes did. The stock anecdotes about Grandpa's escapades in India were also absent; instead, she had moments of distraction, an increasing vagueness, an evasive response to direct enquiry. Charlie had a feeling she should find out what, if anything, was going on, but festive euphoria reduced the worry to a niggle and she felt it could be put off to the New Year. Full of turkey and mince pies, and with the bouquet of the port in her head, she could not believe there was anything seriously amiss.

Once she was back in London, Caroline came round to the flat a couple of days after Christmas prior to flying off to Aspen for the skiing. They cracked a bottle of champagne and Charlie told her about her experience at Sticky Fingers.

'Men!' Caroline said bitterly. 'There are times when I wonder if the male sex developed from chimpanzees or simply retrogressed. Of all the insensitive, immature, imbecilic – I can't believe the way you kept your cool. I'd have screamed until the walls cracked and inundated them all with enough litigation to cram the courts for a decade. Do you think your dress will be OK?'

'The dry cleaners are fairly optimistic. It should be out of intensive care shortly.'

'Are you going to leave?'

Charlie said flatly: 'No.'

'*Darling*! Look, I could get you into PR overnight; you'd be ideal. How to sell some frightful new drink with an albino elephant and three cocktail parties. Or a sports car with a brace of cheetahs, a mountain landscape and a charitable marathon. It's a crazy game: you'd love it. Shake the dirt of the City – and I do mean dirt – from your feet and join the party. Come on, darling; you can't go on cosying up to a bunch of louts who think business is a rugger scrum and women should be underneath. Get out before you get hurt.'

It was advice Charlie would remember later. For the moment, she could only reiterate: 'No.' Her small chin jutted and her mouth was set in a stubborn line. 'I'm not giving up now. I've come this far and I won't – I *won't* – throw it all away. I know, I know, they're a load of upper-class yobs and I'm a sucker to work, let alone play, with them. But you don't understand. This job means a lot to me. It's something I've always dreamed of, and I'm not going to chuck it because of a few hiccups *en route*.'

'Hiccups!'

'That's all it is. They were stupid and cruel but I don't think that's what they intended: it's just the good old classroom sense of humour. I'm the first female they've ever had to work with above the level of a secretary or a tart and I think – I *think* – it was their way of showing me I'm accepted, making me a member of the club.'

'Give me strength!'

Charlie paced up and down, tugging her hair, groping for motives which she feared were only excuses. 'Please listen, Caroline. I'm not saying I condone what they did – I was so angry I could have killed them all – but it has to be put in its context. I've demonstrated that I can be what they call a sport, I can *muck in*, I'm one of them. From now on, things should be a lot simpler.'

'Is it such a good idea,' Caroline said, 'to be one of them?'

'This is very important to me –'

'Yes, darling, I know. I only wish it wasn't.'

'Hugo says I'm doing really well. He sent me out broking much earlier than is usual and I know that's aroused a certain amount of petty jealousy. I don't want to ruffle the water any more than I have to. If I just forget the incident, if I just shrug and laugh – well, I've come to the conclusion that's the best way to handle it.'

She stuck out her chin – and some of her lower lip – still further and Caroline emitted a sigh of resignation. 'Come home, Emmeline Pankhurst, your gender needs you. Oh well, darling, it's your funeral. Give me some champers and fill me in on Henry Marriott.'

Charlie smiled at her with real affection, and complied.

CHAPTER ELEVEN

The lodge owned by Douglas Henderson was situated just beyond a hamlet called Dunbean, its solid stone walls braced against the winter gales. On a clear day it overlooked the Solway Firth. When Henry Marriott arrived, however, the day was not clear: flurries of snow swept across the landscape, a stinging, gritty snow that felt more like powdered hail; a grey fog smothered the Irish Sea; the wind was Force 6. The blowing mists almost obscured the crenellated façade, with the stolid tower to the right and the sprouting turret on the left-hand corner of the building.

The front door opened at the sound of the car and Henry hurried inside, shaking hands heartily with his host, probably in an attempt to maintain his circulation. The native caretakers, traditionally frugal, had been compelled to turn up the oil-fired central heating on Henderson's arrival, but high ceilings and prevailing draughts did much to abort the warming-up process and Henry relinquished his coat with reluctance. A dour Scotsman with an accent as thick as porridge disappeared upstairs with both coat and baggage and Henderson led his guest into a former banqueting hall which now functioned as a drawing room. Oak beams spanned the ceiling, mullioned windows excluded the darkening day, and a large section of pine tree burned merrily on the wide hearth, its wayward smoke evading the chimney and blackening the plaster above. A long-haired retriever, sprawled on the goatskin rug within singeing distance of the fire, lifted its head an inch or two and thumped a plumed tail in welcome but did not move from its prime situation. The manservant reappeared presently with two chunky crystal tumblers and a bottle of Aberlour; Henderson poured generous measures of the dark gold liquor and Henry sipped gratefully.

'The others won't be here for a couple of days,' Henderson was saying, 'but I've got some good sport lined up for tomorrow.

Stuart, the head keeper – remember him? – he's going to be here first thing in the morning. Apparently there's an older stag he's had earmarked for culling for some time. I spoke to him just before Christmas and he's pretty sure he can locate it for us. Quite a monarch of the glen: it should make an exciting target.'

Henderson was a dour Scot, man whom few things appeared to excite, least of all shooting stags. The cultivated blandness which had stood him in good stead in his younger days had acquired, with the march of time, faint imprints of character, suggesting the core of toughness vital for political survival, the pomposity of vaunted convictions, and a potentially ruthless will. Tension'lines stiffened his mouth and his eyes were permanently narrowed as though focusing on his future prey. For the rest, his waistline was disciplined, his ginger hair was receding. He had a handsome and forceful wife much given to supporting his career and a long-term mistress of such extraordinary discretion hardly anyone knew she existed. His background was not quite as upper class as his foreground: he had gone to Gordonstoun on a scholarship and, after his stint in the army, had made money juggling company assets before standing for Parliament. His hobby was collecting directorships. Thinking of his sister, Henry knew she would have treated Douglas with the wry tolerance she reserved for those she did not like. His own association with the Chief Whip was based not so much on a trade in favours as the memory of their army past, a bond outside ordinary friendship, admitting no moral disapprobation.

'Tomorrow ought to be good.' Henderson was saying 'it makes a pleasant change to hunt a quarry you can see. You and I spend too much time in pursuit of chameleons.'

'You could call it that,' Henry conceded. 'Camouflage is certainly what it's all about.'

'Ah, no more business,' said Henderson, draining his glass. 'Not tonight. Should I ask after Helen or would you prefer I left it?'

'Leave it,' Henry said.

He woke the next morning out of a dream so vivid it left him trembling. He had been sitting on a long grey beach under a

126

louring sky. The tide was coming in, hungry wavelets lapping at his feet, but he could not move his chair: he had given his word. A large stag came up out of the water, shaking the droplets from its antlers; twenty yards away, Douglas Henderson was crouched behind a rock, taking aim with his rifle. Henry cried out in warning but either it was too late or his voice made no sound: the gun exploded, the stag fell. Before his eyes its flesh seemed to melt away, crabs nibbled its entrails, the white bones were washed clean by the tide which now covered his ankles. Somehow, he was alone again. He wanted to go but he knew he must not; it was his duty to remain and reason with the sea. The dream faded into broken images which Henry could not recall on waking and then the picture re-formed with startling clarity. The beach had become a garden, the sea a lake. A motorbike reared up: the rider was visored and helmeted but Henry knew the face underneath would be that of his son, though he could no longer visualise James. Henderson was there, lurking behind a rhododendron bush. Something terrible was going to happen, something he must avert, but he could not move, and the lake was rising over his knees, rising, rising . . . In the moment of waking the worst thing, he realised, was that one aspect at least was true. He could not picture his son's face.

He got up and went to the window. Outside, the snow was settling; a pallid gleam dimmed the landscape. He tried to summon the recollection of Charlie, warming his thoughts on an agreeable memory, but instead he found he was seeing her in his car, chattering in a desultory fashion about the parting of the traffic and the behaviour of King Canute. *Canute*. Had it been so desultory after all, that casual mention? A coincidence – a flash of intuition – a veiled warning? If the latter, that must mean that Charlie was not what she seemed. She could be a plant, an unauthorised investigator working for the Opposition, or maybe Spooner had tipped her off. She had made such an issue of her repulsion for him: perhaps she had protested too much. He might have the evil fascination of a De Flores, with Charlie in the role of Beatrice'Joanna. Involuntarily, Henry smiled. His imagination was going too far. He did not really believe that Charlie, his radiant and innocent Charlie, had any ulterior motives.

127

Beneath his window he watched the arrival of a Land Rover; it disgorged the vaguely familiar figure of John Stuart, the head keeper, followed by a liver-and-white English pointer. He looked up, and Henry gave him a wave to which he responded with a cryptic Scottish nod. Then he disappeared inside the house and Henry went in search of a wash and a shave.

An hour or so later, having consumed a substantial breakfast prepared by Mrs McGurtey, she of the dour husband and frugal habits, they emerged from the lodge to find that the snow had stopped and a bleary sun was struggling to disperse the fog. Henry found himself relegated to the back of the Land Rover with the pointer, which promptly deposited its chin on his knee and fixed him with a soulful pansy-brown gaze. In the front, Stuart and Henderson talked shooting, Henderson with the loquacity of a politician who feels silence is a sign of weakness, Stuart with contrasting brevity. Henry, relieved of the need for conversation, ruffled the dog's ears and lapsed into private reflection. As they left the tarmac road and the vehicle bounced and bucked its way on to the moor the pointer uttered whimpers of anticipation and Henry, chilled despite his Barbour and his breakfast, wondered why the hell he had come.

When they finally stopped and clambered out the mist had evaporated and an ice-blue sky had opened above them. Snow sugared the heather and lay thickly in every fold of the ground. The wind had slackened but the cold was intense, pinching nose and ears in an iron grasp. Stuart had parked under the needle-fringed boughs of a pair of conifers on the rim of a small fir plantation. He clipped a leash to the pointer's collar in case it decided to attempt a solo expedition and they set off through the trees, breaking cover after a short while and crossing the flank of a ridge, keeping to the high ground, following the contours of the valley. Every so often Stuart would stop and scan the opposite hillside through a three-section telescope, closely observed by the dog. The fourth time both man and dog stiffened: the stag was grazing some four hundred yards away, a dark silhouette against the unmarked snow.

It was a large ten-pointer, a Highland Royal, with majestic antlers and the musculature of an eland. The dog lowered itself into a stalking position but did not attempt to advance; the man also crouched down. Some way below them was a knoll overlooking the clearing where the stag, as yet oblivious to its audience, was pawing at the snow with its foreleg to uncover a patch of grass. They descended cautiously, knowing that if their quarry scented them, or heard a human footfall, all their effort would be wasted. Behind cover on the knoll Stuart set up the telescope again while the rifle was loaded. The stag had ceased tearing at the short grass; its head was lifted, its eyes wide and dark. A plane passed overhead, a minute glint of silver with the white ribbon of its contrail fading in its wake; the distant rumour of jet engines washed over them like an invisible wave. As the sound diminished the animal, calmed by the renewed stillness, returned to its grazing. Satisfied that their ambush was undiscovered, Stuart indicated to his companions that they should find a vantage point on the incline and prepare for the kill. Henry offered Henderson the first shot, aware that if his host's aim was true he would have to be content with being merely a spectator. 'Make it quick and clean,' Stuart had said in the Land Rover. 'Like an execution.' Douglas raised his rifle, took aim. Henry saw that the target had shifted, presenting his haunches, making a heart shot impossible. Henderson waited a moment, and then some slight noise or sixth sense triggered a warning and the stag half turned, its coronet upraised, muscles tensed for imminent flight. Henderson fired too soon; the bullet thudded in below the left shoulder; the stag stumbled but did not fall, forcing itself upright, reeling away despite its crippled limb. Blood spots dappled the snow, crimson on white.

Henderson swore. But Henry had already taken the gun and had the animal in his sights: he squeezed the trigger, felt the kick of the rifle against his shoulder, saw the stag momentarily frozen in flight, then sinking to the ground. As always in the act of killing he knew a terrible sense of power and wonder, a race-memory from the days when men were hunters and death meant life, and yet with it an ache of unbearable loss, because through his agency something beautiful and splendid had perished from the world; and the power and the magic and the pain were twisted up inside him, so that for a few seconds he thought he might weep. But grown men do not cry. Not for the downfall of a king or the decay of faith or a twinge of the heart. 'I think that's it,' Stuart said, and that was it. The pointer, unleashed, scouted the stag with prudence and then sat down awaiting its master, shivering at the blood-smell which excites all creatures, tame or wild. The men approached slowly, as if out of respect for a noble death.

But the illusion was fleeting. Stuart went to work with chill efficiency, bleeding, disembowelling, and trussing the carcass before thrusting the sharpened end of his stick through its nostrils and between the bound forelegs. In that manner his two companions could drag it down to the point where the track petered out, perhaps half a mile away, while he went to fetch the Land Rover and drive up to meet them. Stuart took the rifle and strode off, the pointer at his heel; Marriott and Henderson began the back-breaking process of bringing the dead animal down the hill, sliding it on the snow, hefting it over out-thrust boulders, disentangling the antlers from obstructions. Behind them, a solitary bird hovered high in the air, its far-off gaze focused on the bloody mound of discarded entrails. The two men presented a bizarre spectacle, accoutred for the modern day yet engaged in primitive activity, heaving and tugging at their cumbersome burden in an ungainly fashion, not merely out of breath but ill at ease with such a crude proceeding. When they finally reached the track they were sweating, speechless with exhaustion. Henry sat down on a rock beside the carcass, avoiding the stag's glacid stare, extracting a hip flask from an inner pocket and offering it first to his friend. They appeared isolated and incongruous in the midst of this huge wilderness, lost in a Siberian tundra a thousand miles from the civilised technopolis which was their normal habitat. At their feet their prey was already cold; the wheeling bird had dropped; only the sky listened to their talk.

Douglas did not mention bungling his shot but Henry sensed the extra reserve in his manner. The Chief Whip did not like to bungle anything. It took a couple of drams of neat whisky before he spoke in an altered voice, no longer the bland host or the piqued sportsman but the politician underneath, hard-edged and professional, a jarring note in this kingdom of untouched nature. 'So,' he said, 'what are we going to do about Spooner?'

130

It was the question Henry had been waiting for ever since he arrived; he sensed now that the morning's shoot, the struggle with the carcass, everything had been simply a deliberate build-up to this question, this instant. He made no answer, refusing to be hurried.

'Hugo Wingate phoned me just before Christmas,' Henderson added. 'I presume he contacted you?'

'Yes.'

'Well?'

'Well . . .' Henry refilled the cap of the flask, took another mouthful. 'We have very few options. A further warning might prove effective, but only in the short term. Once he gets his teeth into something he isn't likely to let go, and a cornered rat must be dealt with promptly.' Like any other wounded animal, or so said the tiny pause that ensued. 'Buying him off, in my view, could also prove a short-term measure. Spooner, like so many of us, has an almost unlimited capacity for greed, and unlike most he makes no bones about it. He'd keep coming back for more. If *we* didn't pay, the press most certainly would. Suppressing that kind of leakage would be very difficult. Failing to suppress it would be disastrous. None of us wants to go down that road.'

Douglas shuddered at the spectre of the intrusive media, glancing over his shoulder despite their desolate surroundings. 'No indeed,' he said. 'That's a nightmare we must avoid at any cost. My God, Henry, there used to be honour among thieves. Blackmail becomes meaningless if the blackmailer can't keep his word.'

Unreal conversation, Henry thought. 'Spooner,' he said very drily, 'never wore an old school tie.'

Unlike other blackmailers, presumably.

But Henderson's mind had moved on: he was targeting useful details like a magpie searching for baubles. 'Let's look at it from another angle,' he said. 'What have we got on Spooner? What can we use to pressure him? He's hungry, dishonest and unreliable. With those star qualities, there's bound to be some dirt in his past. The Intelligence boys can dig it up –'

'It won't be enough,' Henry said. 'Canute is far bigger than any small-time cheating or deals in the grey area between

131

legality and fraud. We could never get a hold on him to match the hold he has on us.'

'In that case,' Henderson snapped, riled by the use of *us*, 'we'll just have to implicate him. That should limit the pay-off and guarantee his discretion at the same time. Unless he's a complete fool. If he is –'

'He's no fool,' Henry said. 'But I don't like the idea of involving him. There's plenty of shit under the carpet without adding Spooner.'

'Henry, this is not the moment to turn fastidious. That's a luxury you can save for your private life. I gather there's still some crucial paperwork to be done?'

'I believe so.'

'Recruit him. Use him. Get him in it up to his neck. When it's his balls on the chopping block he won't be in such a hurry to lift the axe. Come on, Henry, you can handle it. Didn't someone tell me he's a Freemason? That means he has the club mentality, Boy Scout rituals, all that crap. Make use of that weakness. Offer to admit him to the inner circle, give him the confidentiality spiel, secrets of government, Queen-and-country, you know the line. The way I hear it, he's an outsider trying to worm his way in. All you have to do is open the door.'

'It'll be expensive,' Henry said, smiling faintly at the aspersion cast on Freemasonry. He and Henderson were members of the same lodge.

'We have very little choice.' Henderson stood up; Henry, too, had heard the approaching engine. 'I only hope he hasn't talked to anyone else. Is there a girlfriend in the picture?'

'No.' But an image of Charlie flashed into Henry's mind, with her glancing reference to Canute and the waves. She claimed she disliked Spooner intensely. Would he have hinted anything to her, of all people? What could she have overheard? As he screwed the cap on the flask he saw there was blood on his hands; he had inadvertently smeared his sleeve.

'Back to the weight-lifting,' Henderson was saying as the Land Rover pulled up. 'Anything wrong?'

'Nothing,' Henry said.

CHAPTER TWELVE

On New Year's Eve, Charlie had a social aberration. Caught out by her own good nature, she had accepted an invitation from an old college friend to a party where she would know virtually no one, only to discover, on arrival, that Berenice, a former pupil of Cheltenham Ladies' College and pillar of the *haute bourgeoisie*, had acquired a boyfriend who was an unemployed revolutionary and had joined the trendy Left. Gone were her designer clothes, the Vidal Sassoon haircut, the diamond rings remaindered from former engagements, the suntan left over from a recent skiing trip. Her face was pale and made up only round the eyes, her hair was half grown and half tinted, her partywear was Oxfam chic. A desperate and faintly artificial gravity, more suited to discussing the issues of the day, infused her once languid manner. She had spent Christmas in Romania, studying conditions.

Charlie had met few of her old friends but she could see immediately that Berenice – now pronounced Berry-nee-chay – had traded them in for a more politically correct social circle. There were Rastafarian hair extensions, intellectual beards, female couples holding hands, Caribbean accents reciting ethnic poetry and Oxbridge ones extolling the primitive lifestyle in locations with names like Cappodocia, Oahu and the Puerile Islands. The clothing was predominantly earnest and Charlie, in split skirt and plunge neckline by Jasper Conran, felt as if both she and her outfit were committing an actionable piece of bad taste. The champagne and caviar of earlier days had vanished; instead there was red wine, presumably brought back from Romania, vegetarian canapés, sushi, and something that looked alarmingly like quiche. The unmistakable aroma of marijuana assailed her nostrils. She was introduced to the new boyfriend, who wore a hangdog expression and talked at length about the difficulties of finding a decent job. She sympathised: after all, there could not be many career opportunities for a revolutionary in Belgravia, which was where Berenice's flat was still situated (she had clearly been unable to move to a more appropriate address, like Brixton or Clapham). After that, she was sucked into a rather one-sided discussion with her hostess on the democratic potential of Eastern Europe; Berenice, like most converts, had gone too far, and was obviously unable to chat on frivolous subjects without feeling guilty. Escaping from an uncomfortable jeremiad, Charlie collided with a bottle of Stoli and an Asian babe, in that order. The Stoli was peppered and the Asian babe was masculine, with an amber velvet complexion, high cheekbones, and eyes the colour of black honey.

'You don't remember me,' he said in an accent which, if not Oxbridge, was definitely Eton.

'No,' Charlie admitted.

'Good. I don't remember you either. Let's do something about it.'

Charlie followed him to an unoccupied sofa well clear of all meaningful conversation, emptied her red wine into a pot plant, which promptly wilted, and started on the vodka. Her companion asked her who she was and what she did, paid her charming and improbable compliments, and doled out casual items of personal information. His name was Amrit, his family were all stockbrokers, he was writing a novel and working as an unemployed actor in the meantime.

'This seems to be a party for the unemployed,' Charlie remarked. And, to herself: 'Perhaps I should join them.'

'If you mean Berenice's boyfriend,' Amrit said, 'he's not exactly unemployed, it's just that it's bad for his image to confess to a job at a shoe repairer's. As for me, I feel regular work – or indeed any work – is detrimental to my lifestyle. Besides, my father and brothers work quite hard enough; it's my duty to rectify the balance. Any philosopher would understand the need to maintain a universal equilibrium. Why do you work? You are much too pretty to fritter away your youth in a fusty office. It's time you took things more seriously and had fun.'

Charlie giggled. She had not eaten and the vodka was going straight to her head. 'I like what I do,' she insisted. 'At least . . .'

'At least?'

'Nothing.'

Amrit hijacked a passing joint and some time later Charlie

found herself confiding in him: her experience at the Christmas party, her ambitions, her doubts.

'The problem with the British,' he sighed, 'is that they never grow up. During the time of the Raj we did our best to teach them the wisdom and maturity of an ancient civilisation, but all they ever learned was a taste for cheap curry and high-rise mountaineering. We tried, we really tried, but they have remained unhappy barbarians, stubbornly ignorant and entrenched in a state of permanent adolescence. Even now, they visit our gurus only to drink urine; they idolise Rushdie, but have never heard of Tagore. My poor sweet, your fellow countrymen are a lost cause. They go to school in search of education and their minds are closed, their growth stunted, their inhibitions fixed. I should know; I went to one of those schools.' He took a long drag on his spliff; the glow inched towards his lips. 'Where was I?'

'Tell me about your novel,' Charlie said. 'Is it very traditional – back to your roots – that kind of thing?'

'Good God, no. It's a thriller: sex, violence, international terrorism, the usual formula. I want to make money.'

'I thought you were a philosopher?' Charlie quibbled.

'I want to philosophise in comfort.'

'How much have you written so far?'

'Three pages.'

'*Three pages?*'

'When my ex-girlfriend moved out she took the word processor,' Amrit explained. 'She said it was hers but that was hardly the point. She may have owned it originally, she may even have paid for it – I won't argue about that – but *usage* made it mine. In the dictionary, usage justifies the existence of new words, alternative spelling, the acceptability of slang; therefore it should certainly justify possession of a word processor. Alas, she was very petty about the whole business. Her father was in the Foreign Office; it just shows you. Anyway, until I get a computer or at the very least a typewriter my blockbuster is stymied. The creative process is one long struggle.'

He met Charlie's sceptical eye with a gaze like molten toffee and a smile to liquefy the hardest heart. She could not help responding. 'I tell you what,' she said. 'We've got some old typewriters at work – I've seen them in the store-room – I'm

135

sure I heard they were going to be chucked away. I expect I could get one for you, if that would be any good.'

'I'd prefer a computer.'

'No luck.'

'Never mind. Anything will help. What an angel you are.' He kissed the tip of her nose. 'Let's have some more vodka.'

By midnight she was regarding the party with increasing approval. A belated attempt to insulate her system against the Stoli had led her to try the quiche, which proved to be a superior specimen of onion tart. After a couple of generous slices and some salad she felt – mistakenly – that it was safe to go on drinking. She discovered too late that successive joints contained pure cannabis resin. Her subsequent impressions were blurred, but she would retain a hazy recollection of telling her hostess, with distressing sincerity, how delighted she was to see her again, kissing the boyfriend and saying they must all meet for a revolution some time, and extracting herself with difficulty, and a certain reluctance, from a parting embrace with Amrit. She got home somehow, presumably by taxi, set off the alarm on her way in, and subsided muzzily into bed.

It was not until the following morning that she found the hand-delivered letter in her mailbox.

She did not recognise the writing on the envelope and yet, at the same time, a curious lurch of the stomach told her instinctively whose it might be. *Charlotte Christie*, it said, in slanting black script on cream-coloured manila. After so much vodka her insides felt slightly fragile and the lurch of anticipation did them no good at all. She sank on to a chair, tore open the flap. Inside was a short note inscribed in the same sloping, elegant hand, dated and timed for nine the previous evening.

Dear Charlie,

Called round on the off-chance that you were at a loose end to-night. Unlikely, I know. I'll give you a ring shortly. I trust the Fitz-gerald Denton party went well after our little shopping spree. Will return your other clothes on our next meeting. Happy New Year.

Yours,

Henry Marriott

136

The elusive memory of her clinch with Amrit receded into the realm of light entertainment: this was reality, intriguing and improbable though it might seem, a tentative romance that had yet to reach a kiss, infinitely more tantalising than any chance encounter. She spent some time indulging in speculative fantasy, visualising the sophisticated, self-assured Henry Marriott, socially in demand according to David Chater, spending the early part of his New Year's Eve roving Notting Hill in request of her company. An exercise in ego massage and she knew it, telling herself not to be idiotic: ten to one he had simply been *en route* to a party on this side of town. But there was a warm glow inside her that persisted against all the logic of her sterner self.

The next day she would be back at Fitzgerald Denton, face to face with those colleagues who had jeered and cheered her in Sticky Fingers before the holiday. She knew it would require courage to laugh off the inevitable jibes, shrug off the sneers, to pretend that it had all been good clean fun and she could take it like one of the boys; but if she was to continue in her chosen career that courage must be found. Charlie had never considered herself deficient in nerve but she felt a tightening of the gut at the approaching ordeal. She tried and failed to put it out of her mind, distracting herself with thoughts of Henry. 'I trust the Fitzgerald Denton party went well . . .' The words carried a barb that she was sure he had not intended; Henry, she was convinced, would not have stood by while she was victimised and humiliated, would not have howled with drunken mirth or swayed to the tune of 'She's a jolly good fellow.' Not like Andrew. She and Andrew had been friends, or so she used to believe: after their Italian lunch together there had been shared sandwiches, amicable drinks, career advice from him, girlfriend advice from her. It had been a platonic relationship spiced with a latent mutual attraction which would probably never develop into anything. A cosy situation without the heights and chasms, perils and pleasures of her association with Henry. Risk-free. She was not really interested in pursuing an affair without the excitement of risk, but she had valued their friendship and would be sorry to lose it. Yet she did not know if it could survive the sense of betrayal that still nagged at her.

Over Christmas, in passing, her mother had brought up the old familiar subject of marriage and children. Ever since the break-up with Michel she had put out a feeler, once in a while, wanting to know whom Charlie was seeing, what did he do, how much did he earn, was he tall, short, dark, fair, single, divorced? Charlie's parents had married young and stayed together and her mother had a lingering distrust of divorcees. 'If he's walked out once he'll do it again' was her attitude. Half the time, Charlie pointed out, it was the wife who walked out, dumping middle-aged domesticity for a career and a toyboy; but she knew Susan Christie could not really accept that. Women, she believed, had a greater capacity for caring and suffering – as Anne Elliot had said, they could love on when all hope was gone – whereas men might be rogues, rakes, or the salt of the earth, but their emotions ran less deep, their passions had less stamina. She would not say that if she met Henry, Charlie thought. She had mentioned Andrew now and then, more in a teasing spirit than because there was anything to talk about, but she had never made any reference to Henry. She wondered how her mother would react to him, daydreamed hypothetical conversations, sensed in advance an aura of disapproval. The age gap. 'He's too old for you, darling. He'll be sixty when you're thirty. Just imagine it . . .' But Charlie did not want to imagine it, not yet. She was too busy trying to picture, a little guiltily, what he was like in bed.

Charlie's first day back at work coincided with the start of her period. It was a particularly bad session: she felt bloated and heavy, with a looming headache, chronic dizziness and a desperate craving for chocolate. Not for the first time, she was baffled by references to the radiance of women in early pregnancy; if she found regular menstruation this tiresome she was doubtful if she could ever cope with nine months of an expanding belly and constant oedema. Her mother had always told her having children was a miraculous experience, but Charlie suspected the existence of subversive propaganda, probably masculine in origin. Imagine a parasite growing deep inside you, feeding off your body, finally refusing to budge and having to be shifted by the contraction of unpractised muscles through several hours of unbelievable agony. Inevitably, her thoughts switched to Bianca, apparently anticipating this state of affairs with rueful satisfaction despite a lover who was married elsewhere and her own need for a continuing salary. Charlie had been touched by her confidence, touched and disturbed, emotions lost in the later events of the evening. Now, she wondered not only how her relationship with her colleagues would have altered, but whether there would be any difference, an additional warmth or an embarrassed cooling, between herself and Bianca.

'Glad to be back?' grinned the security man, as she entered the building.

'Thrilled,' Charlie grimaced. 'I should have come in yesterday.'

'Your boss did,' he responded surprisingly. 'Mr Spooner too, and Miss Leach. I had to show up special to let 'em in. That's taking overtime too far if you ask me. But you spent the day with your boyfriend, didn't you, Miss Christie?'

Charlie laughed automatically, privately disturbed by the puzzle of her associates' behaviour. She knew Spooner lived insurance, but surely not on New Year's Day. And Hugo? and *Bianca*?

In the loo later that morning, Bianca joined her at the mirror. Charlie glanced at her abdomen and noted it looked flatter than her own. There was a momentary hesitation between them, a pause while each waited for a *rapprochement* that did not come; then Charlie enquired conventionally: 'Did you have a good Christmas?'

'Family stuff.' Bianca shrugged. 'It was OK. My sister was there with her little boy. Sick on chocolate and torn-up paper everywhere: he loved it. Christmas is really great for kids.'

Oh Lord, thought Charlie. 'Any progress,' she asked with a delicacy which she knew to be absurd, 'on your . . .?'

'I've given up the fags.' Bianca nibbled a fingernail, a childhood habit reasserting itself. 'Look – you haven't told anyone, have you?'

'Of course not.'

'Well, don't. I haven't decided anything yet. I –'

Charlie laid a hand on her arm. 'You ought to speak to Hugo.

Didn't you get a chance when you were in yesterday?' Still bewildered by the security man's information, Charlie admitted privately that she was taking the opportunity for unobtrusive query.

'*Yesterday?*' Was Bianca shocked, or merely surprised?

'I heard you were here – you, Hugo and Spooner.' For no reason that she could explain Charlie studied her own reflection, affecting uninterest.

'Someone made a mistake.' Bianca was curt. 'I was at home yesterday. New Year hangover. I expect Hugo was in the same condition. Can't answer for Spooner.' She went into one of the cubicles and Charlie heard the click of the lock. Returning to her desk Rupert, who was in the vicinity, caught her eye. 'I took a call for you,' he said. 'Some chap called – Amrit, was it?'

Charlie nodded. Under the influence of all that drink and dope, she must have shelled out her business card. A reflex action. The inventor of business cards had a great deal to answer for.

'He left a number,' Rupert said. 'Who is he, anyway?'

'An Asian babe.' Charlie smiled faintly. 'I suppose I'd better call back.'

The atmosphere at work had changed, she concluded, after her baptism of foam. There was none of the expected ragging, no below-the-belt humour, no aftermath of derision. 'Well done,' Hugo had said, and that seemed to be the consensus. She had been promoted, at least in spirit; she was one of the lads now. On the floor at Lloyd's, she was greeted as a regular; Rupert himself seemed to acknowledge her as his partner, not simply an apprentice; their exchanges were shorn of the usual suggestions and innuendoes. After the suspense beforehand her first week back at Fitzgerald Denton went by on a roll, as if she were a dancer who, having laboured to learn a complex sequence of steps, could now perform them without effort, without thought. On the Friday she went home by taxi, having appropriated, with an inexplicable sense of guilt, the nearest of the store-room's reject typewriters. The cab driver carried it into the flat for her and she uncorked a bottle of wine in preparation for the arrival of Amrit.

140

He showed up three-quarters of an hour late, looking far too beautiful for a man she did not fancy. She had planned to eject him gracefully as soon as possible but, just as at the party, something in his lustrous gaze and negligent charm of manner undermined her resolve, and she found herself explaining her distraction at unnecessary length, and even telling him about her note from Henry Marriott.

'Rich, successful, on the mature side of middle age, and definitely upper class,' Amrit summed up. 'He sounds like my father. Are you sure he *isn't* my father? These things happen.'

'Too pale,' Charlie said.

'Pity. It would have been wonderful material for a novel. Or possibly a TV play, BBC2, serious stuff with lots of guilt. I rather fancy that. The mad wife, a magnificent touch, so neo-Gothic . . . It'll all end in tears, of course. These things invariably do.'

'Why?' Charlie asked, mildly annoyed.

'A man like that isn't going to change the habits of a lifetime. He's used to tragedy: living happily ever after with a sweet young thing would throw his whole existence off balance. I dare say he's always presented a stoic figure, polite yet reserved, brooding on secret sorrows in the eremitic solitude of his luxury flat –'

'I happen to know,' Charlie interjected frigidly, 'he's very sought after by society hostesses.'

'Of course he is. A guest like that adds interest to any dinner party. I must cultivate a secret sorrow to brood on. Perhaps if I gave up smoking . . . Where was I?'

'Brooding,' Charlie snapped.

'Your Henry.' Amrit steepled his fingers and assumed a judicious expression which dissolved almost immediately into mischief. 'He'll find a reason to renounce you: see if he doesn't. You'd be far too disruptive, hanging your newly washed knickers in his pristine bathroom and using the *famille rose* fingerbowl as an ashtray. He won't ever admit it to himself, let alone to you, but he prefers tragic isolation; it's so much more restful. One day, he'll come up with an incontrovertible argument for sticking to it. He'll be desperately sorry, of course, probably heartbroken, but at peace: that's the main thing. Drop the whole idea, darling, before you get hurt. Come fly with me. I can offer you nothing but my dreams.'

'Thanks,' said Charlie. 'I prefer my own.'

It was well past nine before Amrit, the typewriter and the wine were gone. Charlie was standing naked under the shower, her hair in a desultory knot, when the shrilling of the entry-phone system intruded on her thoughts. Swearing profusely, she switched off the taps, reached for her bathrobe, and dripped into the kitchen to pick up the handset. 'Hello?'

'Hello,' echoed a familiar voice. Charlie reeled. 'It's Henry.'

'Hold on.' She covered the mouthpiece in an instinctive gesture, looked down at her unfastened bathrobe and up at her reflection in the window, face scrubbed bare of makeup, wet strands of hair evading confinement to channel droplets of water round her ears and down her neck. 'Just a minute.' She shot into her bedroom, gazed helplessly in the mirror, smeared on a little lip gloss and then returned to the dangling handset, pressing the button to release the front-door catch. 'Henry? Are you still –'

Of course he wasn't there. He must have come inside. She went to the front door, tying the sash on her bathrobe, pulling the towelling tight across her chest. But as soon as she moved the gap widened again, exposing the lower slopes of her bosom; the after-shower damp had chilled the peaks into a rigidity hopefully concealed by the thick material. She felt desperately conscious of her naked face, her dishevelment, above all of her breasts, presenting, under their insecure wrappings, an image of instant arousal, an invitation as reckless as a demand. When she eventually opened the door and saw Henry standing there she knew his eyes strayed involuntarily to that gap, and she pulled the lapels of her robe together, clutching at them with a nervous hand.

'So sorry –' they began simultaneously.

'You were in the bath –'

'Shower.'

'This is very clumsy of me.' He didn't appear clumsy. 'I had a late meeting, I was passing . . . I should have called first.'

'It doesn't matter. Please come in.' There was no wine. She had gin but no tonic. What on earth could she offer him to drink?

142

'I brought some champagne.' He produced a bottle from under one arm and handed her a vaguely familiar Harrods carrier bag. 'Your clothes.'

He was just passing, he had happened to pick up a bottle of Dom Pérignon: she didn't believe it. 'Wonderful,' she said, hoping it didn't sound like gush, hesitating between bottle and bag. 'The glasses are in the kitchen. I have to get dressed –'

'If you feel you must.'

As she fled from the room she was blushing like a teenager, a sudden heat irradiating her skin, making her cheeks glow and her breasts tingle. She prayed Henry hadn't noticed. In her room she scrambled into a pair of leggings, realised she had forgotten her knickers, tugged the leggings off and started again. She decided to put a sweater on over them, the casual, slouching-round-the-house effect, but she could not make up her mind which, trying and rejecting two at top speed before settling on a bundle of pale pink mohair which had been a Christmas present from her mother. She was in such a hurry she did not see that the label was still attached and dangled down her back, mingling with her loosened hair. She rubbed the shine off her nose with a concealing stick, daubed on mascara, almost poking the wand in her eye, applied a lavish squirt of scent. It was only when she was back in the drawing room that she registered the omission of a bra: the wide neckline of the jumper exposed too much shoulder for Henry to be in doubt and her breasts bounced as she moved in a manner unacceptable in these days of silicon and uplift. She was determined not to succumb to another blush but she was intensely aware of Henry's proximity, of the space between them which seemed to vibrate like water with their every motion. The touch of the wool prickled softly against her skin; the leggings clung to thighs still slightly damp from the shower.

Henry thought that with so little makeup on, ruffled, off guard, flushed from haste, she looked younger than ever, more girl than woman, and he distrusted his own corresponding arousal, barely able to restrain himself from a tentative caress. But it was too soon, much too soon. He was experienced, worldly-wise, a long way from impetuous youth. Now was not the moment to forget himself and behave like an oversexed Romeo. She must meet too many of those.

143

He handed her a glass of champagne, commented politely on the spaciousness and comfort of the flat.

'I bought it for the view,' Charlie said. 'That big double window looks out on a garden, just grass and trees but it's lovely to have it there, sort of calming after the furore at work. It's a pity it's dark and you can't see it.'

Henry agreed that it was a pity.

'I'll put on some music,' Charlie said, wishing he would talk, relax, do something to ease the subliminal tension in the atmosphere. She was very conscious of his superior height, his sheer presence dominating the room. It was the first time she had ever been interested in an older man and she tried not to fantasise about the physique concealed beneath his formal manners and inscrutable suit, the body visibly flat stomached and lean hipped, softened with age or hardened with exercise, she did not know and was almost afraid to guess. She skimmed along a shelf of CDs, dismissing contemporary pop, hovering over the classics. Vivaldi? Too predictable. Tchaikovsky? Too noisy. Ravel? Too sexy. In the end, she settled for a cassette of Natalie Cole, undemanding listening, a soothing background. She was slotting it into the music centre when she sensed him close behind her, leaning over her, touching her neck, his sudden nearness a tangible warmth, a subtle threat.

There was a minute when her heart beat faster; then came his voice, cool and unexcited: 'The label's still attached to your sweater. I'm no Sherlock but I assume it's a Christmas present. Here, I'll take it off for you.'

He produced a penknife from an inner pocket, flicked out a tiny blade, snipped the thread. The cold touch of steel against her nape made her shiver.

'Thanks.' She took the label, stared at it mindlessly for a few seconds, then deposited it in an ashtray. 'Yes. Yes, it was a present.'

'It suits you. Someone has good taste.' Was there a muted enquiry in his tone, an undercurrent of potential jealousy?

'My mother,' Charlie said. 'She's the only person I trust to buy me clothes. When I'm not there, I mean.'

'I should never dare,' he smiled, 'when you're not there.'

'Did you have a good Christmas?' Back to conversational

144

mainstays, she thought. Then she remembered his wife. 'I mean . . .'

'Seeing my sister was very pleasant: we're very close. The lunch with my wife was rather more difficult.' He told her about Helen's misconception of the new handyman, saying nothing of his own useless resurgence of guilt; but Charlie understood and found herself forgetting her nervousness, taking his hand in a swift, impulsive gesture. Later, she speculated that he might have engineered the moment, making a deliberate play for her sympathies. She shrank from the idea, not wanting to believe him so calculating; as for Henry, he admitted to himself that there was an element of calculation, if only subconscious: his intelligence was too quick for him.

As the tension eased and the level fell in the champagne bottle he glanced at his watch: it was almost half-ten. 'Have you eaten?'

'No.' Charlie confessed, aware that the champagne had gone to her head and it was probably too late to do anything about it.

'I had lunch –' he almost said with Hugo, but checked himself '- at the Saville. It feels like a long time ago. Where's your nearest restaurant for latecomers?'

'Julie's Bar.'

Secretly relieved to move to neutral territory, Charlie snatched a coat and scarf and they walked round the corner to the wine bar, which was warm and crowded, muzzy with smoke and dim with understated lighting. Ensconced at a table for two in the cosy gloom upstairs, they chose hastily before last orders, skipping a starter for steak and salad with red wine to accompany it. The last of Charlie's reservations had evaporated: she felt a glow inside that was not entirely due to food and drink. Her sexual hyper-awareness had not dissipated but mellowed, the menace engendered by his initial invasion fading in more impersonal surroundings. A softness of shadow gentled his face, stealing his age; she noticed with a pang of impossible sweetness that his tie had shifted slightly off centre. It was like a chink in the impenetrable perfection of his image, visible if sparse evidence of some inner vulnerability. She told him about her ordeal at Sticky Fingers, and was warmed by his thin-lipped outrage. 'Hugo Wingate should have stopped it,' he concluded. 'There

145

are times . . .'

'Go on.'

'There are times . . . when I look down into the central well at Lloyd's and imagine I'm gazing into a modernised version of Dante's Inferno. Each circle is for a different variety of malefactor. When it's all over, they'll ring the Lutine Bell for Judgment Day. It may not be very far off at that. Under their human exterior, my fellow dealers seem to have the instincts of animals: they band together like wolves, they cackle like screech-owls, they follow the herd like sheep. You should get out of there, Charlie. You can find better places to work.'

'I've wanted this job all my adult life,' Charlie said. Not a justification, more an apology. 'I'm not going to back out when they've just begun to accept me.'

'It's an unclean environment,' he persisted. 'You shouldn't be – contaminated.'

'It's your workplace too,' she pointed out.

'That's another matter. Nowadays it seems to be my duty to get my hands dirty. Or so they tell me.' A distant expression dimmed his gaze; Charlie looked bewildered. After a pause he recalled himself to the present. 'It's getting late. I'll walk you home.'

Back at the flat , Charlie offered some coffee and some cooking brandy which was all she had by way of a digestif. 'It's frightful,' she said. 'How embarrassing. I'm awfully sorry . . .'

'I've had worse,' he assured her, 'at the dinner parties of the rich and mean, masquerading as Rémy Martin.'

'Of course,' Charlie said. 'I expect you serve it yourself. Being one of them.'

'How you keep harping on that.' His faint smile mocked himself more than her. 'Infuriating of you to remember it. A revealing slip of the tongue early in our relationship. I've been trying my best to deceive you ever since.'

'To what further lengths will you go?' Charlie wondered. 'You made me believe in Santa Claus. What do I have to believe in next?'

'Us,' he suggested, stretching an arm along the back of the sofa behind her shoulders, surrounding but not yet touching her. His very restraint was curiously exciting. She looked into his eyes, pale as the smoke from an autumn fire, and some quality in his regard seemed to pierce right through her, stirring her nerve-endings like a caress.

'Us,' she said, low-voiced, uncertain.

The kiss ended her doubts, at first no more than a meeting of lips, then pressure, insistence, opening, the exploration of his tongue, his arms closing around her, drawing her towards him, the firmness of his torso under suit and shirt. He tasted dry from a recent cigarette, sharp from the brandy, warm with his own heat, flavours of masculinity, almost harsh after the farewell clinch with Amrit – an embrace she had been unable to evade – aqua vitae after mild wine. She felt herself yielding, not merely physically but mentally, an insidious surrender draining her automatic resistance, making her compliant, drowning emotion in sensation. Her muscles seemed to dissolve while a reawakened tension stiffened her nipples almost beyond bearing and throbbed between her legs. His right hand cupped her breast through the softness of her sweater, then bundled the mohair under her arm as he felt for bare warm skin, malleable flesh. Then somehow, they were on their feet, he was pulling her against him, his hardened penis, confined by his clothing, jutting at an angle, thrusting, awkward and insistent, into her lower abdomen. In a moment she would submit completely, and reach between his thighs . . .

'No.' She had broken away before she knew it, sticky with desire, plucked from the maelstrom of sensuality by something deeper and more compelling.

'Charlie . . .'

'I don't know you.' It emerged with the brutality of truth. The wrench with which she had torn herself free of passion – not only his but hers – had left her no energy for tact or pretence. 'You're all contradictions. Sometimes I feel I understand you, and then – it's as if you draw a curtain, and I can't see anything any more. I'm not sure what you want. I'm not sure what I want. I . . . I'm sorry.'

'Are you saying it's too soon,' he asked quietly, accepting his dismissal, 'or never?'

'Never say never.' Charlie's smile went awry. 'It's just too soon. That's all.'

'I'll call a taxi.'

147

'No – no, please. Don't go like this. As if – as if we'd quarrelled, or – Look, I'll make some more coffee.'

'All right.'

She made the coffee too strong but he did not comment. While they drank, she tried to elucidate some of her confusion.

'You keep telling me Lloyd's is full of shady deals and even shadier dealers,' she said, 'yet that's where you operate. I *know* you would never do anything you believed to be wrong, but –'

'Right and wrong are not always clear issues,' he said. 'Something which is wrong according to a certain set of rules, could be right according to a different ethos. The laws of the land are not moral absolutes: they exist purely for the convenience of society. A law can be overridden in great need. The wrong deed, for the right reason.'

'Eliot,' Charlie said instantly. '*Murder in the Cathedral*. It was the school play one year. But surely it should be the right deed, for the wrong reason?'

'It's more or less the same thing.'

Is it? Charlie wondered.

On an impulse, she said: 'There isn't anything wrong at Fitzgerald Denton, is there? I know Spooner sails a bit near the wind occasionally, but – I mean, anything really wrong?'

'Such as?' His eyebrows lifted, his tone was neutral.

Charlie turned pink, feeling suddenly melodramatic and rather silly. 'It was Bianca Leach,' she said hastily, shifting the blame and promptly ashamed of herself for so doing. 'At the Christmas party. We were just talking in the loo – girls do; we aren't even very friendly, most of the time. She was sort of hinting things.'

'Who's Bianca Leach?'

'Hugo's secretary. Sorry. I should've explained . . .'

'Even if there was anything unorthodox,' Henry said drily, 'I can't imagine a secretary would know about it, can you?'

'No.' Charlie relaxed at once. 'No, of course not.'

Secretaries know everything, Henry thought. His own PA was omniscient, telepathic, inscrutably confidential and remorselessly plain. She would guess much of what had happened tonight when he requested her to send Charlie two dozen roses on Monday. No man is an enigma to his secretary.

148

'It's very late,' he said abruptly, getting to his feet. 'You must be tired. I ought to go.' And, on the way out: 'I'll call you soon.'

He kissed her goodbye, but briefly. She was alone before she knew it, with the dregs of the coffee and an empty bottle of cooking brandy, feeling there was something she had missed, something on the tip of her tongue, a page turned over too fast, a few words whose significance she had overlooked. The next day, when she was sober, she would think about it again.

But the next day, all she thought about was Henry.

CHAPTER THIRTEEN

The roses arrived on Tuesday, a courtesy that would have touched her if she had not suspected it was automatic. They were the most expensive kind, long-stemmed, burgundy-red blooms, so identical that they might have come out of a photocopier. They even had an elusive scent, a distant whiff of the heady perfume of real roses, growing on twisted stems along a garden wall in summer. She arranged them in a tall vase and waited for the call that never came. Inevitably, she found herself indulging in soul-searching, agonising, picking through the fallout of every action in quest of a cause, a motive, a note out of tune, anything that might have been misinterpreted. Had her rejection discouraged him? Had she been too brusque, too apparently cold, too much for his ego? Surely a man of his age could take a first refusal in his stride? She knew she was not heartbroken but something more than her pride smarted, a secret corner of herself to which he had been tentatively allowed access, a place he had either ignored or chosen not to see, turning away from her in blind vanity or ruthless denial.

Work, as always, absorbed almost all her waking hours but at night she would lie sleepless from time to time, rerunning their every moment together, looking for her fault or his, fishing among her recollections for the *faux pas* that had thrown him off his stride. But she arrived at no conclusions, made no deductions. January lagged, February dragged. A harsh snow fell, blackening the pavements; icy surfaces slithered underfoot. The glass walls of Lloyd's admitted the grey daylight of an interminable winter. She and Andrew lunched at Mario's: he talked about the latest in a succession of girlfriends; she did not talk about the Christmas party, Henry Marriott, or her concerns over Bianca. Towards the end of February, Charlie and Rupert concluded the major deal they had been working on, earning Charlie her first commission and confirming to Hugo he had been justified in taking her on.

150

'Well done,' he said, and she wondered if it was his stock phrase, dished out for encouragement or praise, in crisis or in triumph, a compliment without overstatement, low-key, genuine, quintessentially British. A cricket captain might have used it on the playing fields of Eton, or a general to some gallant messenger who had braved the local *banditti* to bring crucial orders in the days of the Raj. But Hugo, she knew, had not been to Eton, and had certainly never fought on the North-West Frontier.

In March she took a week off, flying to Jamaica with Caroline to stay with her brother, Mark Elliott-Browne, an architect currently designing dream-houses in the tropical paradise of the Caribbean. They spent a couple of days visiting Negril, staying in a bungalow belonging to one of Mark's clients. A garden of lemon and mango trees ran down to a postcard beach: sugar-white sand, sea-moulded rock, sun-spangled water, shallows of emerald, deeps of sapphire. In such an Eden England seemed a distant memory etched in shades of winter, and Lloyd's was unreal, a nightmare of greed and chaos in a science fiction setting. Towers of crystal and steel, fragments of antiquity imprisoned in metal frame and concrete substructure, vast sums of money whirled from syndicate to syndicate like clothes in a washing machine, and at the epicentre the silent bell, waiting on the trembling air to ring in the apocalypse. Ludicrous fantasy.

At night they had a beach barbecue, and Charlie lay on her back in the tepid water, gazing up at a huge yellow moon, listening to the rhythmic pulse of the reggae band and drifting into a state of half fancy, half dream. She pictured brave ships riding the oceans, tempests tearing at their sails, typhoons cracking their masts, a solitary albatross beating the gale ahead of them, the tentacles of giant octopuses clutching at stern and side, mermaids ringing them to their doom. Some struggled on, some sank; the storms blew themselves away; still waters closed over shattered hull and broken spar. Coral polyps rooted there, fish finned through empty portholes, green weeds waved in the current like dead men's hair, the blue lobster and the conga eel laired in the hold. A single shark circled the wreck, idling death in a tranquil sea. Floating farther from the shore Charlie dreamed on: somewhere below her, lidless eyes goggled from stalk or socket, seeing her shadow against the moon-glimmer, slenderer and less perilous than the cruising shark, many-limbed, her fanning tresses reminding them of the mermaids who had gone long ago, or the handsomest of the sailors who slept beneath the coral, sea-slugs kissing his hollow cheek. Had he heard it, she wondered, in his last moments, the great bell tolling in the deeps, the booming echo that sounded through wave and wind, all the way to England and the heart of the City, the Lutine Bell ringing for disaster, for Doomsday, for the world's ending? And on that thought the reggae music faded, and the sea-throb was in her ears, and she saw she had been carried too far from the beach. She rolled over and began to swim, and the gentle rollers bore her inshore and deposited her on the silver sand.

'Where have you been?' asked Caroline.

'Dreaming,' Charlie said.

'What was he like?'

'He was dead,' Charlie murmured, unusually fey. 'Drowned in the deep sea. 'Those are pearls that were his eyes . . .'

'Have some more rum punch,' Caroline said kindly.

The next day they returned to Kingston, to be greeted by an agitated housekeeper whose Caribbean English left Charlie baffled at the best of times. She was presented with a piece of paper on which was scrawled a garbled interpretation of a telephone message, evidently from her father. Trouble at work, Charlie deduced, grimacing. Even before she read the note, England drew nearer, only a flight away; the science fiction environment became fact. She unfolded the paper, scanned the printed capitals. Caroline saw her blanch under a four-day tan.

'Charlie – ?'

Wordlessly, she handed Caroline the note, sank into the nearest chair. 'SUDDEN DEATH GREAT MOTHER,' Caroline read. 'FUNERAL FRIDAY. Oh, darling . . .'

Charlie wanted to cry but couldn't; she felt numb inside, she supposed it was shock. It seemed so impossible that Granny should die like that, without prior notice, without preparation, without a chance for her to say goodbye. Granny who had always been there. Suddenly, the sunlit paradise all around her had become anathema, entangling her in visible hypocrisy.

Mark poured her a large tumbler of rum but although the fire in her throat scorched it did not warm her. Caroline hugged her; Charlie shivered as if at a glimpse of an abyss deeper than death.

'How old was she?'

'Seventy . . . eight, I think.'

'It's a good age,' Caroline suggested.

'For what?' A good age to have lived, a good time to die?

'She's had a long life.'

The measure of life, Charlie had read somewhere, is not in its length but in its depth. Her inchoate disquiet about her grandmother, which had been accumulating over so many months, crystallised abruptly into a conviction that for all her years Granny's measure had not been full, she had been deprived of something indefinable, essential, something to which every human being has a right. Self-expression, maybe. Tears came at last, but they were tears of anger and frustration, tears for an existence cut short before it was complete. Charlie was too young to know that death is always like that, sneaking up with his sickle and snipping the thread half spun; no one ever has time to tie a knot in the tenuous strand of their fate. Eternity is a tapestry of loose ends whose continuing pattern – if a pattern is there – is too vast in scale, too minute in detail, too intricate and too simple for any solitary mortal to see or comprehend it. And so Charlie cried her anger, and Caroline stroked her arm, as people do, and the practical Mark got on the plane to expedite flights home.

They were on the plane the following morning, Caroline having insisted on accompanying her friend. In England, it was raining. Charlie collected her car from the long-stay car park and drove the two of them to Chichester. 'You need me,' Caroline informed her. 'If you had sisters it would be different: God knows I can't stand Patsy but at least she's always there in a crisis. Even if I don't want her. Anyway, good friends are better than family. As someone or other once said, you're stuck with your family but you get to choose your friends.'

'I like my family,' Charlie said, producing an unsteady smile. 'I wanted to be stuck with Granny a bit longer.'

'I know, darling. I didn't mean –'

'I know you didn't.'

'My trouble is,' Caroline sighed, 'I talk too much. You get into the habit in PR: it sort of goes with the job. You spend plenty of time avoiding damage to over-inflated egos, but you tend to forget that in the real world people have feelings to hurt, not just vanity to dent. I'm sorry if I was offensive; I seem to be about as sensitive as a Chieftain tank today. Call it jet lag.'

'It's all right.' Charlie switched her gaze momentarily from the road ahead to Caroline's face. 'Keep talking. It's never too much for me.'

The funeral was held in St Peter's near Ballards, the church Granny had attended virtually every Sunday since she and Grandpa returned from India. Charlie's father read the lesson rather like an officer issuing orders; his was a martial God, a moral disciplinarian for whom compassion was something of an afterthought. In contrast the vicar, having known Granny for many years, gave a eulogy that was sincere in its warmth and regret, concluding with a humour which robbed his sentiments of banality that he was sure she would be happy up there with the harps and angels, well away from the ravers down below in brimstone and sulphur. The congregation launched valiantly into 'Onward Christian Soldiers', clearly determined to drown out the choir. Finally, David Chater read a special prayer, beginning: 'The journey is not long, from Here to There,' and ending: 'Give us strength to walk without fear into the dark. Give us faith to hold out our hands, though we cannot see to Whom. Give us Love to sustain us, Love to walk beside us, Love awaiting us beyond the shadowy gate, for neither life nor death endure, but Love is for ever.' David read very well and Charlie cried throughout, grateful for her friend's encircling arm, undeterred by the fact that, carried away by the atmosphere, or so she said later, Caroline wept steadily too.

Outside, the mourners processed into the churchyard and stood around the grave, collars upturned and hands in pocket or sleeve, the wind plucking at hemlines and invading every fold. Rain battered at the coffin lid. Granny had always disliked the wet, Charlie remembered; she would recall with a shudder the monsoons in India, 'the whole sky turning black, and ragged lightning, and the rain so heavy it seemed that the trees and

154

houses would be beaten into the ground'. The obligatory handful of dust turned to mud, spattering the wooden coffin; Charlie hoped it could not get in. She imagined the earth beneath her feet liquefying into a swamp-like ooze, closing over the grave, smothering her granny in sludge, and it was all she could do not to cry out, begging them to haul her out again.

Saturday was the worst. Caroline went back to London and in the afternoon Charlie's father sat staring at Granny's favourite coffee-cup – she wouldn't use a mug – and suddenly broke down, sobbing the hoarse ungainly sobs of a man who has been taught he must never cry. Charlie joined her mother in trying to comfort him, knowing there was no comfort to be had, feeling painfully adult in the face of unmanageable parental weakness. Ritual protects, she decided, thinking of the funeral, it preoccupies you, distracts you, providing a pattern of behaviour to which you can conform, but when it is over there is still the grief, and the strongest of men cannot run away from that. She had never seen her father weep before, not even when Grandpa died.

On Sunday she drove back to Ladbroke Gardens. Her face in the bathroom mirror looked all wrong, not pale with tragedy but tanned from the tropics, golden with forgotten sun, an incongruity in the urban winter and the wretchedness of her heart. She scrubbed at it furiously with exfoliant, in an attempt to erase the colour of happier days.

As soon as Charlie arrived at the offices of Fitzgerald Denton the next morning, she knew there was something wrong. She helped herself to a cup of vending machine coffee and took it to her desk, aware of a watchfulness all around her, whispers instead of chatter, undercurrents of vague tension. Andrew Kendall caught her eye from across the room; he smiled conspiratorially and came over, parking himself on the corner of the desk.

'Good holiday?'

'Not really. Jamaica was fun but I had to cut it short and rush home.' And she concluded, a little unwillingly, knowing how death embarrasses people: 'My granny died.'

'Oh Charlie, I'm so sorry.' He looked sorry too, more sorry than embarrassed. In that moment she forgave him for doing nothing at the Christmas party. He reached out to squeeze her shoulder; she changed the subject.

'What's happening? You could slice the atmosphere in here with a chain-saw.'

'Not sure, really. Spooner's been closeted with Hugo ever since start of play. Every so often he sidles out, makes a covert phone call, then sidles back in again. Bianca's been in there most of the time, too.'

'Ah.' Had she told Hugo about her pregnancy? If so, why the need for Spooner? Perhaps he was arranging the abortion? Preposterous.

'Sounds like you know something I don't.'

Charlie shook her head. At that juncture, Bianca came out of Hugo's office and crossed the room, plainly aiming for the Ladies. 'Excuse me,' Charlie said hastily, 'I need a pee.' She sauntered nonchalantly after Bianca, leaving Andrew staring.

When she entered the Ladies, one cubicle was occupied, pre-sumably by her quarry. Charlie waited several minutes before she heard the cistern flushing and Bianca emerged, an uneven colour staining her cheeks, showing distinctly under careless makeup. 'It's you,' she said, not pleased, Charlie thought, but not bothered either. 'Bloody baby. One coffee in, one coffee out. It's like that sometimes.' She was dressed to hide her stomach, loose sweater sagging over any telltale bulge.

Charlie said: 'You've told Hugo?'

'No. I'm saving it.'

'Till it's too late to abort?' Charlie said with a flash of percep-tion.

'Suppose so.'

'Are you sure – do you think that's wise?'

Charlie had gone too far and she knew it. Bianca turned towards her, switching eye contact from the mirror to her face. Under the heavy auburn hair she looked angry, vulnerable, painfully human. Unconsciously, Charlie had always seen her as 'the secretary', wiggling her bottom, screwing her boss, an office cliché; now she found herself seeing an individual, a girl on the make, insinuating herself into Hugo's confidence and his daily routine, taking root there, shrewd, uncertain, patient, resenting, maybe, somewhere deep inside, that she had to scheme and screw for a lifestyle to which another girl – a girl like Charlie – was automatically entitled by birth and education and class. And then she had been caught out by a stray sperm, and an unobtrusive fusing of DNA had woken in her a love and hunger like nothing she had ever felt for Hugo. When she spoke her voice was raw, the discarded accent of childhood leaking through.

'*Wise*? Of course it's not *wise*. It's fucking stupid: you don't have to tell me. *I'm* fucking stupid. God, you make me spew. You're such a smartarse – such a slick, chic, stuck-up, fucked-up –'

'I'm sorry.' Charlie rushed into speech, dismayed not by the insults but by Bianca's pain. 'I shouldn't have said anything. It's none of my business. I really am sorry.'

Bianca had broken off, clutching her temples. 'It's all right,' she said. 'My hormones are up the creek. Anyway . . .'

'If you haven't told Hugo,' Charlie said, anxious to move on to another issue, 'what's the flap about?'

'Oh, nothing.' Bianca's shrug was careless, but a shade of wariness slid across her face. 'Petty theft in the office. It happens.'

'You mean, we've got a kleptomaniac? Is there a lot of money missing?'

'Not money, equipment. Someone's nicked a typewriter, that's all. It's no big deal, but you know how paranoid they are in here –'

'*What*?' Charlie checked herself, stammering. 'All this fuss over a *typewriter*? But – but I thought they were going to chuck those old machines out. They can't be worth anything: they're obsolete. Everything's done on computer now . . .'

'Paranoia,' Bianca said. 'I told you.' She went out, leaving Charlie alone with her reflection, horrified and completely at a loss.

She had little leisure for thought during the remainder of the day, but by the time she left work she had come to a decision. No one knew she had taken the typewriter, of that she was certain; she had left the building late that evening and the reception area had been temporarily unoccupied. The taxi-driver whom she had persuaded to help her carry it would hardly have confided the matter to the company management. She had been half tempted to go to Hugo and confess her action, baffled by the importance it had suddenly assumed; yet instinct told her this would be no easy admission of a minor peccadillo but something disproportionately serious, and she preferred to keep silent. However, it would be best if she could return the typewriter on the quiet, with no questions asked or answered.

When she reached her flat she found Amrit's number, scrawled on her notepad when he had come to collect the stolen goods. She tried it, but the machine at the other end informed her, in Amrit's lazy voice, that it was dysfunctional and callers should not bother to leave a message. Try next year. There was an address with the number – 'In case you want to send me a birthday card' – so Charlie, determined to solve the problem as soon as possible, got into her car and drove round there.

It proved to be a first-floor flat in Kensington; either there was someone home or the owner had left the lights on in his absence. She rang three times before Amrit responded, opening the door naked to the waist with the top button of his jeans undone. 'It is always a pleasure to see you, moon of my desire,' he said, kissing her rather abstractedly. 'Your timing, however . . .'

'Sorry,' Charlie said curtly. 'Can I come in for a minute?'

'Well . . .'

She stepped over the threshold; he retreated perforce.

Upstairs, she entered a living room littered with clothes, unwashed cups and glasses, a plate with the remains of a sandwich, newspapers and magazines, videos and cassettes, and enough unopened mail to date back a decade. A television set peeped out from beneath a crumpled jacket, an empty wine bottle, and a half-melted candle. The typewriter might have been buried almost anywhere. As Charlie began explaining the position to Amrit a girl appeared from what was presumably the bedroom, face veiled in hair, loose T-shirt concealing her essentials, stick-insect legs. 'This is Bijou,' Amrit said. 'She's changed my life – I'm sure she has – if I could only remember in what way.'

'About the typewriter – ?'

'You can't know how sorry I am you had to ask me that. I would do anything in the world for you, Charlie – show me a lion's den and I will walk into it – but your typewriter, alas, is gone for good.'

'How?' Charlie said.

'My ex,' Amrit sighed. 'Unfortunately, she still has a key. She came round while I was out, probably to forgive me every-thing and suggest a fresh start, and read the opening chapter of my novel. Apparently she decided the superbitch on page 4 was meant to be her; I can't imagine why. Anyway, she took my bud-ding masterpiece and your precious machine and I believe she dumped them in some sort of pulveriser which would reduce them to a minute lump of useless matter, rather like the universe after the end of time. All I can give you is the ribbon – it's here somewhere –' he fumbled among a heap of cassettes, proffered his trophy with a disarming grin – 'It ran out and I'd removed it to change it. Did you ever *try* buying something as antiquated as a typewriter ribbon? Honestly, darling, I was reduced to the flea-markets –'

'Thanks,' Charlie said vaguely, thrusting the ribbon into her bag although she had no use for it, realising there was nothing more she could do. It was typical of Amrit, she felt, that both his novel and his typewriter should come to such a violent end. He possessed an elusive brand of fatal attraction which must frag-ment his love life and disrupt his environment: he was too beautiful for profound emotion, too indolent to suffer hurt. Both his womenfolk and his belongings could hold only a tran-sient place in his existence. Charlie was deeply grateful he was not her type. She bid him farewell with relief on both sides and left without having exchanged a word with the morose Bijou. On the way home she reviewed her position and came to the conclusion that as there was nothing she could do, there was little point in saying anything either. Why damage herself with vain recriminations over a valueless piece of office junk? Surely a disappearing typewriter could not *really* be of any significance in the mysterious workings of Fitzgerald Denton? Bianca was probably right: her superiors were afflicted with paranoia. Millionaire businessmen, she had heard, were often obsessive about purloined paperclips, wasted photocopies, overlong tele-phone calls. No doubt this was the same syndrome.

*

Having rationalised matters to the satisfaction of her conscience if not her nerves, Charlie was mildly alarmed two days later when Hugo emerged from his office and propped himself against her desk. She wound up a telephone conversation and replaced the receiver, producing her best smile against a quickening of her pulse. 'This new flip-chart presentation you've developed,' he said, 'it seems to have made a favourable impression on the client.' Her nerves unclenched; Hugo, observing the subtle relaxation of her smile, notched up a mental query as to the cause of her previous tension. 'I've got a presentation to Van Lewen in Amsterdam in a couple of weeks and I wondered if you'd like to put it into practice again, maybe give me a hand with my pitch? We'll arrange a split commission, of course. I've prepared all the figures: it's merely a case of transposing them on to your system and having a brief rerun to make sure we've got it right. How about it?'

'Fine,' she said with sincerity, brightening at the prospective challenge.

'Be in my office first thing tomorrow.' He removed himself from her desk, turned to smile down at her. 'When we've gone through all the bumf perhaps I could take you to lunch?'

'Thank you.'

'By the way, Emily tells me Reggie McAvee asked to be remembered to you. I promised her I'd mention it.'

'Who?' Charlie looked blank.

'Emily's Irish vet. That appalling dinner party I inveigled you into attending? I'm so glad you've forgotten.'

'Oh. Oh yes.' He wanted to be remembered, did he? How dare he!

'Emily seems to think he has a fancy for you.'

'It isn't reciprocated,' Charlie said tartly.

'Good,' Hugo said, his smile lingering. 'I didn't think a rustic animal doctor with straw in his hair and horse-dung in his pockets would be quite your style. I've always thought vets were at their best restricted to television drama – where you can switch them off.'

CHAPTER FOURTEEN

They had been booked into the Amstel Inter-Continental Hotel, with separate rooms on the fifth floor a safe distance apart. Charlie wondered if it was chance or Bianca being careful. Hugo was welcomed with a familiarity that indicated previous visits; maybe he had been there with her on an earlier trip, sharing a penthouse suite, lounging in a jacuzzi between bouts of selling insurance, strolling beside the canals in the Venice of the North. If so, she must feel wretched indeed, left alone in England with a secret that could not be hidden much longer and all its attendant problems, while the ignorant father went off with another woman, if only on business. 'Just business,' Charlie said to herself, secure in her room. 'I can promise you that.' A promise to Bianca, whom she didn't much like and who didn't like her, Bianca to whom she owed nothing, yet even if she had been in love with Hugo the promise no one had heard would have held her, fantasising Bianca's pain.

Charlie's horizons had widened in the last year: new job, new associates, trauma and tribulation had stretched her spirit, enlarging the parameters of her potential, providing her with fresh perceptions and insights, not yet increasing her strength and understanding but giving these qualities room to grow. She was conscious of a momentary panic at her broader vision, the glimpse of places she had never imagined, her strange empathy for the girl with whom she had little in common save their mutual humanity. Yet humanity, she realised, was the ultimate bond: if you rejected it, if you disregarded or overrode the feelings and needs of others, you had scenes like that at Sticky Fingers, people like Spooner, manipulative and unscrupulous. And Henry Marriott, whose behaviour was still incomprehensible to her, the vintage knight who had ridden away, leaving her to confront her dragons alone. The wound had been to her pride more than her heart; she resolved daily not to think of him; yet the puzzle of his unexplained defection still tantalised her.

Turning from her thoughts with an effort, she unpacked and laid out her flip-charts. Spring was in the air; her room was full of tulips; outside, the River Amstel was wind-creased, blue-rippled, catching slivers of sky on its trembling surface. White gulls wheeled and dipped above it, the gangsters of the air, fighting for the tastiest scraps, screaming with their childlike voices, high-pitched, harsh and sad. It was a lonely sound, she thought, lonely and free, and it pierced her heart, though she did not know whether with sorrow or longing, or something like desolation, here in this opulent hotel in a beautiful city, something she could not quite define. She tried to think of one person in the world whose image might warm her – father, mother, Caroline, Andrew – but the only face that came to mind was that of her granny.

An hour later she met Hugo to work on their presentation. They finished late, supping in the Riverside Terrace Bar off steak followed by coffee and brandy, chatting companionably. With a heavy agenda the next day Charlie pleaded fatigue and went to bed early.

After early morning meetings she had a couple of hours clear to explore Amsterdam. She walked for some time with no particular destination in view, leaving the Amstel river and entering the network of canals criss-crossing the city, street alternating with water, cyclist with bargee. The atmosphere was bustling but unhurried, apparently stress-free; the people she passed showed no sign of the niggling frowns and thrusting pace so often in evidence in London. There was an opening of leaf-buds in the trees, the sparkling of sunlight on water. Charlie stopped for coffee and a croissant in a pavement café, absorbed in the scene around her, feeling comfortably anonymous. No one bothered her; the waitress smiled and let her be; she flipped through a magazine but did not read. It was an essential lull in her work schedule, a moment to feel restful and inexplicably empty. She watched a young couple crossing a bridge nearby, cycling side by side, then switching to single file, the man in front glancing over his shoulder to check on his wife, who had a small child on a seat behind her. She had long fair hair, a scrubbed, unmade-up face, trousers that did not fit. She was

162

laughing, not at any mere joke, Charlie was sure, but because she was happy. For a second, Charlie experienced a ridiculous pang of envy for that unknown woman, with her husband, her child, her blatant happiness. Even she, Charlie Christie, who had an exciting job, a glamorous social life, chances and opportunities few other women would ever know. When the family had gone she paid her bill, returning the waitress's smile on autopilot, and walked slowly back to the hotel.

She was about three hundred yards from the entrance when she saw them, heads together at a table in an open-air café. Hugo was sitting facing her, if he looked up he must see her; but somehow she knew he would not look up. His companion had his back to her, yet she recognised him at once: the set of his shoulders, the nape of his neck, the quiet certainty he always exuded. Henry Marriott. He was doing the talking; Hugo appeared uncharacteristically silent, staring down at his hands with peculiar intensity. She was too far away to see his precise expression and too shaken by the sight of Henry to be sure of her own judgment, yet it seemed to her that there was something in the attitude of the two men which looked horribly out of kilter with their surroundings, a jarring note in an otherwise gracious panorama. Like one of those Dutch still lives of a vase of flowers or a cornucopia, with somewhere in the picture the hooked claw of a half-hidden beetle, the sly head of a newt, the beady eye and grasping paw of a rat. They leaned together like conspirators, obviously keeping their voices down though no one near was listening. They looked not simply guarded but almost furtive, though neither was a furtive man, as if whatever they were discussing must be kept close, buried deep, lest it return to appal and accuse them.

Retreating into a shop doorway she faced the fact that both were capable of ruthlessness, Hugo for his career, Henry, more dangerous still, for his convictions. She knew they must not see her, though she could not have explained why. When a flock of tourists approached she joined them, using them to screen her passage. As she drew level with the café a quick glance through the crowd showed her the two men still absorbed in their sinister conference. Henry's face in profile appeared concerned, the cold, irritable concern of a man forced against his will to take account of human failings. Hugo had lost some of his colour. Charlie's heart beat faster, perhaps because of Henry's proximity, but she was not sure.

In the bar later, Hugo did not mention his visitor.

'Where have you been?' he enquired, superficially casual. 'Seeing the city?'

'Some of it.' She hitched herself on to a bar stool beside him. 'Actually,' she continued with an air of candour, 'I just sat in a café for a while watching the world go by. How about you?'

'I'm afraid I slept in.'

Charlie flicked him a quick glance but offered no demur. 'You should get some fresh air,' she said, 'to blow the cobwebs away.'

'You sound just like my mother,' he joshed her.

After lunch, they went to meet the directors of Van Lewen at their offices near the airport. Charlie was introduced, hands were shaken, conventional phrases exchanged, Charlie and Hugo speaking English, the directors impeccable American. Then they repaired to the conference room for Fitzgerald Denton to present their proposals. Hugo seemed content to remain in the background, as if he were there in a purely supervisory capacity, allowing Charlie to make their pitch. She flipped through her flip-charts, spelled out her spiel, talking about their marine expertise, their customer base and industry contacts, their relationship with the principal specialist underwriters at Lloyd's. She sounded confident and concise, very much in command of the situation. The men seated opposite were attentive, making notes throughout and interpolating an occasional question. Once or twice she referred them to Hugo, requiring his supplementary knowledge, and he responded quickly and fluently, recalling his thoughts from she knew not where; but in the main he was silent. The meeting lasted almost two hours, and when the final glitches had been sorted out there was an offer of drinks and a general relapse into informality. The president of Van Lewen stepped aside with Hugo, and Charlie was left to turn on the charm with the others.

'Intelligent *and* decorative,' the president commented. 'Has she been with you long?'

'Not very.' Hugo was amused but guarded, never a man to dole out information on tap.

'She's quite a girl.' He relinquished the subject with evident regret and moved on to other matters. 'This looks like a pretty good deal for us all, Hugo. We'll retain our Dutch brokers for some of our other business, naturally, but I'm more than happy to let your people handle all our shipping insurance. I think we can leave the final details to others now. Maybe something can be arranged, say, for next week?'

'Fine.' Hugo raised his glass. 'Here's to it.' They clinked and drank. 'Perhaps you and your colleagues would join us for dinner tonight – a little celebration?'

'I'm real sorry but I have to decline. There's a company function later: duty calls. I was hoping, when we're next in London, we could have a – er – night out with the boys? And Miss Christie, of course.'

'I'll fix it,' Hugo promised.

They took their leave amid suitable compliments and cordial wishes for a further meeting soon. 'How did it go?' Charlie demanded on the way out. 'Do you think we'll hook them?'

'They're hooked.' He put his arm around her and gave her an impromptu hug. His tone was light, almost teasing, but his eyes rested warmly on her, betraying pride, satisfaction, or something of both. She had vindicated his judgment; he could not fail to be gratified. 'You did a bloody fine job. I'll bet you could convince Amazon Indians to insure their canoes against woodworm. Congratulations.'

'Th-thank you,' Charlie stammered, slightly stunned by her own success. 'I didn't know – I didn't think they'd make their minds up so quickly.'

'Nor did I,' said Hugo frankly. 'But you were impressive, and they were impressed. Good girl.'

In the heat of the moment, Charlie forgot the mystery of his clandestine encounter with Marriott. 'I owe a lot to you,' she said on impulse. 'You believed in me – you employed me against the advice of other people at Fitzgerald Denton, I know you did. You gave me my chance. Whatever I've done, I couldn't have done it without your backing.'

Hugo smiled, clearly enjoying the ambience of mutual ego

massage. 'In that case,' he said, 'since Van Lewen are busy elsewhere, I suggest we go and celebrate together. I'll see you in the
bar about 7.30.'

Back in her room, Charlie undressed and slid into a bath. The
steaming water soaked away the physical tension, but her mental
inquietude remained. If Henry had been in Amsterdam on legitimate business, and had bumped into Hugo casually, why
should Hugo deny it? Unless he knew about their aborted affair,
and omission stood for tact. I'm here with Charlie Christie,
Hugo might have said. Don't mention me, Henry could have
responded. She and I – well, it was one of those things. Just
didn't work out. I don't want to throw her off her stride. It was
a feasible scenario, Charlie supposed, except it didn't take into
account their conspiratorial air in the café, the blank look on
Hugo's face, his subsequent abstraction. Maybe she had imagined all of that, over-reacting to an encounter that was really
quite innocuous. But she could not disentangle herself from a
maze of conjecture: her thoughts ran away from her, roaming
down improbable avenues where Bianca's pregnancy, Henry's
desertion, the disappearing typewriter and the Amsterdam ren-
dezvous were all jumbled together, and somewhere along the
line the exhaustion of a stressful day supervened, and she
slipped into a dreaming doze, supported by the water, drifting
deeper and deeper into unconsciousness. Hypothesis was transformed into mirage: Henry was telling Hugo he would have to
marry Bianca because a wife could not give evidence against him
in court, and Charlie was sitting at the next table, Henry kept
pretending not to see her, and the cassette of typewriter ribbon
was protruding from her bag, she could not hide it, and then his
eyes met hers, more in sorrow than in anger, distant as mist, cool
with regret. 'Why did you have to take it?' he said. 'Don't you
know we would have been married, if you hadn't stolen the
typewriter?' *I told you so*, said Amrit, smiling at her, satyr's
horns jutting from his black curls. Bianca arrived in a barge,
wearing her wedding dress, and the Lutine Bell was ringing, and
the ferryman was Spooner, peering sidelong from under his
cowl, pale and haggard as a skull with his nostrils rotting. And
then his nose fell away and his face was bone and the dream

turned to nightmare. Charlie woke abruptly to find herself lying in a chilling bath, shaking all over.

When she was out and smothered in a towel she rang room service for hot coffee, blow-dried her hair, and fished her Valentino dress out of the wardrobe. The coffee did much to revive her and she took pains with her makeup, abandoning her anxieties for the soothing routine of preparation. It was always possible that Henry was actually staying in the Inter-Continental – it was reputedly the foremost hotel in Amsterdam – he might even put in an appearance during the course of the evening, and although her feelings about him were hopelessly confused she knew she would confront him with more confidence if she were looking her best. She discarded her bra on the discovery that the straps showed and went downstairs feeling suddenly reckless. She had just pulled off her first big deal in record time and whatever the undercurrents, she should be on a high.

Hugo was waiting at the bar, a cigarette smouldering in the ashtray at his elbow and a newspaper open in front of him. Yet Charlie, observing him from across the room, thought he was not actually reading: his gaze seemed to be fixed, unfocused, seeing something far beyond the columns of the *Herald Tribune*. She threaded her way between the tables towards him; when he noticed her approach his face changed, clothing itself in a suitable expression as if assuming a latex mask, his usual charm lighting up like an autoreactive lamp. 'You look sensational,' he said obligingly. She might have thought the compliment genuine if she had not seen him seconds before, sitting there almost like a zombie, as if the person inside him had moved out and only a shell remained, immobile, insensible, holding the paper in its petrified grasp. Surely he could not return to himself so quickly as to register her appearance and respond with actual admiration all in an instant. Suddenly there seemed something inhuman about him, a body occupied rather than owned by a glib, volatile spirit. She was reminded of her feelings about Spooner, whose soul appeared shrunken and inadequate in its fleshly casing. Too many of her associates at Fitzgerald Denton were lacking in humanity; it was bizarre that the one person of whose human quality she was convinced should be Bianca Leach.

Hugo had already laid on champagne: he filled two glasses and they toasted her success with Van Lewen. The conversation meandered naturally enough from Holland to London, from work to play. Charlie asked after Emily, unable to quash the fleeting thought that Bianca's pregnancy might soon wreck that carefully preserved marriage for good. Emily, no doubt, would have the dogs, but what would Hugo have? The company? Suddenly, she wondered if he would. Emily was a Denton; perhaps it was she who owned the shares . . . Emily, said Hugo, was fine. 'We lead fairly separate lives. She's a country person; I'm a city person. I'm supposed to switch roles at weekends but to tell you the truth I get so tired I just want to unwind. I don't have the energy for touting my daughter to gymkhanas or going to cocktail parties with horsy women and doggy men. You know how it is in this job; it tends to take over your life. Emily's a sensible woman: she understands. I doubt if she'd like it if I was around all the time.'

Just how much *does* she understand? Charlie speculated. How sensible is her sensibility? A grey vista seemed to open in her imagination, a glimpse into a marriage run on common sense, passionless and empty. No differences to compromise, no arguments to make up, no gaps to bridge – no squalls, no sulks, no fury, no fire. Only a weary acceptance, a daily divergence, two parallel lines that could not coincide, hands within touching distance that never reached out to touch. Are you happy? she wanted to ask him, filled with an overwhelming compunction.

They went in to dinner.

Hugo ordered extravagantly, escargots, Châteaubriand, and '66 Hermitages. Charlie let him take charge, noting with secret amusement how masterful men always feel when they have control of the menu. First Henry, now Hugo. She mopped up as much garlic butter as possible on each snail; it was, after all, the principal justification for eating the soft but flavourless spiral of flesh. He studied the flexing of her lips as she sucked each of the escargots from the miniature fork, mouth pursing as if in a kiss. For a fatal instant he visualised lips and tongue preoccupied elsewhere, exploring harder flesh, devouring his very essence.

168

Try as he might he couldn't banish the vision quickly enough; his penis nudged at his loins, stirred to a violent hunger. He had to discipline himself not to stare at her skimpy neckline, where below the delicate defining of her collarbone her breasts swelled unsupported. The colder images which had invaded his mind all that day, appearing to drain his very manhood, were thrust away, relegated to a filing cabinet at the back of his thoughts. He felt warm with food and drink, flooded with returning appetites, his blood surging once more strongly in his veins. For all his distrait manner, her effective performance that afternoon had both pleased and aroused him; he felt a purely creative pleasure in her, Pygmalion with Galatea, Svengali hearing Trilby sing for the first time. Creation is the ultimate power, Man become God, and although he knew her to be a separate being with a separate identity proprietorial lust tensed his erection almost beyond bearing.

'Are you happy?' Rash with wine, warmed to an impetuous intimacy, Charlie plunged into the forbidden subject, her low-toned question diverting him from his erotic absorption but doing little to mitigate it.

Hugo was touched by her sincerity, by an enquiry which he saw as endearingly naive.

'What is happiness?' he asked rhetorically. 'If this is a philosophical question, I pass.'

'No, no.' Charlie waved philosophy aside. 'I meant, in your life, your work, your home. You must have set yourself certain goals, as I do now, but are you happy now you've achieved them? *Have* you got what you want, and do you still want it now you've got it?'

'No one ever gets everything they want,' Hugo said casually. 'It's probably just as well. They'd have nothing left to strive for.'

'In other words,' Charlie said, 'you won't tell me. I had an awful cheek to ask: I know that. It must be the Hermitages.'

'It wasn't a cheek,' Hugo said, at his most tolerant. 'It's just a difficult issue. I enjoy what I do, in that sense I'm happy, but –' he paused, giving his answer real consideration '– how can I put it? There are momentary highs, thrills, clinching a deal, skiing down a mountain, seeing a controversial judgment vindicated –' and he grinned pointedly at her – 'yet overall, I don't know. No more or less than other men. I love my children when I have time; that may sound terrible but my spare time is short, I work hard to provide them with things other children don't have: better food, a better education, ponies, bikes, holidays. When they're older it'll be cars and mortgages. If I stayed home and played they would have none of those things. As for my marriage, it's comfortable rather than exciting. Emily and I get along. Well, you've seen us.' He half shrugged, half smiled. 'There, that's frank indeed.'

And Bianca? Charlie wanted to ask. Are you happy with her? But that would be a cheek too far.

'What about you?' Hugo retaliated. 'Are *you* happy, Charlie? What is it you want?'

'I'm not sure. Maybe a husband and children, one day. Sometimes I think it would be magical, and sometimes I think it would be hell; it depends on what mood I'm in. But right now, what I want most is to succeed. Today –' she sparkled with her own triumph – 'today was the best feeling I've ever had. I want that high again. I want to gamble, and win. So – yes, I'm happy.' Her brightness dazzled him. 'Now, this minute, I'm happy. I could – I could light up like a Christmas tree – I could shout like a peel of bells – I could dance like a Spanish gypsy –'

'This calls for brandy,' Hugo said.

They took their drinks on to the terrace but a cool air came off the water and Charlie shivered.

'We could look in on the disco,' Hugo suggested. 'It's a lot warmer down there.'

They found themselves a table in the basement lit by a squat candle in a glass goblet. The tiny flame flickered and grew as Charlie drew on it to light her cigarette; Hugo experienced a deep shudder of sensuality at the sight. He moved close to her so they could talk privately, without raising their voices against the music, though neither had much to say. It was still before midnight and the disco was fairly empty, only two or three couples cavorting on the dance floor. Charlie had long ceased to look for Henry and decided to go with the flow, relishing sumptuous food, potent wine, the appreciation and confidence of her boss. She was vaguely conscious that the rapport between them had gone beyond the strictly professional but suddenly she didn't care. Charlie was aware she was no *femme fatale*, just a pretty girl working in an alien environment, surrounded by wolves. Hugo had always held himself a little apart from the pack, smiling where they bayed; she felt at ease with him.

'How about a dance?' he said.

He didn't cavort, merely shuffling from foot to foot before admitting, on a note of self-deprecation: 'I'm no John Travolta.'

'Never mind,' said Charlie. 'Straight men hardly ever dance well. At least you don't have delusions about it.' Nearby, another dancer was writhing his haunches and tossing his embonpoint from side to side. 'He thinks he's Baryshnikov.'

They both laughed; Hugo pulled Charlie towards him, easing her into a smooch. But his hands remained at waist level and any meeting of nether limbs seemed to be accidental. When the music switched to a record she didn't like they returned to their table.

'Drink?' Hugo said, flourishing a cocktail list.

They ordered Manhattans. When the drinks arrived, Hugo offered Charlie his cherry, filling her in on the American joke. She found herself giggling and concluded she was mildly drunk. Back on the dance floor, Baryshnikov's flies had come undone.

More people had migrated from upstairs, crowding them in; Hugo and Charlie were forced closer and closer together. Her rhythmic swaying was becoming unsteady and she clung to him for support, the pulse of the music vibrating on the air, shuddering in their blood, binding them thigh to thigh, throb to throb. His crotch was pressed against her and a slow molten heat seeped into her groin despite all her self-admonitions. He was attractive, he was powerful, the situation smouldered with possibilities, and it had been so long, much too long, since her body had known total fulfilment. She ached, not for Hugo but for his erection, for a desperate thrusting union, for urgent foreplay and lingering afterplay, for mingled sweat and hungry kisses and tumbled sheets. She was young and lovely and too much unloved, and the adrenalin boost of earlier in the day had left her with its inevitable aftermath. She pressed herself against him. His grip slid down to her buttocks, and then he was pushing against her, out of rhythm with the music, his breathing quick and rough, his penis stimulated almost beyond restraint. He had

171

come in his pants once, dancing with Bianca in a similar disco a year ago: the crowd, the dark, the public location and private arousal had all been too much for him. He wanted to come now, right now. His hand rucked up her skirt, a questing finger explored her moistened briefs. She started to push him away but her gesture was fragile and half hearted; he pulled her on to him so that but for a flimsy barrier of clothing intercourse might have already begun, they had welded together in a shuddering impaction. Her libido was taking over; her thoughts spun away into the night.

She did not know where it came from, the recollection of Bianca – Bianca retching in the ladies loo, flushed under ill-applied makeup, not liking Charlie but trusting her. Trusting her. A sisterhood stronger than any Masonic handshake. I promise, Charlie had vowed on arrival in Amsterdam. Some promise. She wrenched herself from Hugo's arms and fled without apology, out of the disco, up the stairs, all the way to her room, leaving him baffled, frustrated, faintly ridiculous, alone on the dance floor.

A man who had been watching for several minutes drew back as she passed, unrecognisable in the shadows with which the basement was amply provided. She did not notice him, did not see the frown in his eyes, the shade of annoyance, the glimmering of pain. When Hugo followed shortly after, he was stopped by a hand on his arm.

'That wasn't very pretty,' Henry said.

Hugo did not attempt an answer. 'I thought you'd gone.'

'First flight in the morning. You need a drink.'

I need a fuck, Hugo thought. He knew he should appreciate Henry's breaking the news to him personally, giving him time to prepare his public face for the shock and provide whatever cover-up was necessary, but equally, he was aware there might be other interpretations of his friend's behaviour. Henry could have come to watch his reactions, to check on him, to ensure he kept his nerve. At that moment, however, it didn't seem important. He took the drink he didn't want and drank it down in one. What he wanted was sex – with Charlie, with a prostitute, with anyone – frenzied immediate sex, blotting out the image of

Bianca, Bianca on the dance floor, Bianca in a jacuzzi. Bianca who had been dragged out of the Thames just east of Wapping the previous day, pale as a fish with mud in her Coppertone hair. She had been dead for thirty-six hours.

CHAPTER FIFTEEN

Charlie and Hugo spoke little on their flight home the next day, keeping communication to a polite minimum. Back at her flat, Charlie ran through her telephone messages and was startled to find one from Andrew Kendall, sounding disquietingly urgent. 'Charlie, Andrew here. Tried to reach you at your hotel but you'd left. Must speak to you before you get into work tomorrow. Call me at home. Doesn't matter how late.' He'd left his number, although Charlie already had it in her Filofax, and she dialled immediately. A female voice answered, presumably Andrew's mother. Charlie identified herself and waited while Andrew was summoned to the phone.

'Your message sounded a bit desperate,' she said. 'Is anything wrong?'

'Have you just got in?'

'Yes.'

'So you haven't been in contact with anyone at the office?'

'No. But –'

'You haven't heard, then?' Andrew had lowered his voice and Charlie felt a sinking sensation in her stomach. Whatever had happened, it was serious.

'Heard what?'

'About Bianca.'

Bianca? So the cat was out of the bag, or rather the status of the embryonic kitten, still in the bag, had been made public. It might be a juicy piece of gossip, but it hardly merited so much urgency. Charlie began to relax.

'She's dead.'

'Sorry?'

'Charlie, she's dead. Fished out of the river near Wapping yesterday morning. They seem to think it's suicide; apparently she left a note. I don't know what it said but we had the police in the office looking for Hugo. It's all been pretty grim. Can't picture it myself, I mean, Bianca drowning herself out of

174

unrequited love. Shouldn't have thought she was that type at all. Charlie? You still there?'

'Yes. Yes, I'm here. Oh dear God. Has anyone told Hugo?' Henry. Hugo and Henry, nose to nose in the café, Hugo's subsequent abstraction, the way he looked in the bar, behind the newspaper, as if his soul had moved out. And then he had tried to make love to her. He had tried to make love to her within hours of learning of his mistress's death, caressing Charlie's warm body while Bianca's was chilling on a mortuary slab. And she wanted him, she had pressed herself against him. Suddenly, she knew she had to get in the shower. Immediately. She had to wash away even the memory of his touch . . .

'That's just it,' Andrew was saying. 'Old Spooner's bound to be on the line to him sooner or later, but as you've just been away with him, well, I thought it might come better from you. A bit of womanly sympathy; that sort of thing.'

'Oh. I don't know. I don't think I –'

'Come on, Charlie. Poor old Hugo: I'm sure it's not his fault. We all knew about him and Bianca, but he wasn't the kind to – well, drive her to it. He's a pretty decent sort really. He's been decent enough to you, hasn't he? Don't you feel you owe him one?'

'You could say so,' Charlie said. 'I'll think about it.'

In the shower, she lathered every inch of her body, working a mixture of fury and self-disgust out of her system in a savage skin massage. Her mind was spinning out of control: she kept picturing Bianca, floating in the river, face up – or should it be face down? – with her mouth full of silt and the mascara leaking from her empty eyes. Would she have worn mascara to kill herself? Would she have done it that way? Surely she would have preferred an overdose, the slumber that deepens to coma and death, the chance of a stomach pump, a messy awakening, Hugo, guilt-stricken and adoring, beside her hospital bed. That was a scenario, Charlie felt, much more suited to Bianca's temperament. Except that she would never have taken the risk with the baby. And in a sudden flash of clarity Charlie knew that whatever Bianca might have wanted to do to herself, she would not have harmed her child, that cluster of growing cells that had seized on her love even before its soul uncurled, a bud that would never open, a life that died unborn. And a vague anger surged through her not just for Bianca but for the baby, and the dead girl's love which had been disregarded, denied, thrown away. Charlie came out of the shower, reached for her towel, padded into the living room. Somewhere on the way her thoughts took the next step, and then froze. If Bianca had not committed suicide, could it have been an accident? There was a note, Andrew had said. No accident. The note revealed planning, deliberation, intent. Anyone could write a note. If not Bianca, then who? If not suicide, then . . . murder?

Henry. Henry and Hugo, poring over secrets in an Amsterdam café. Bianca in the Ladies at Sticky Fingers, saying something about the Serious Fraud Office, and how she 'knew too much'. In novels, people who knew too much invariably got killed. And she, Charlie, had mentioned it to Henry, the night they didn't make love. She had talked about Bianca's hints, and was there something wrong at Fitzgerald Denton. She had named Bianca as her source. And Henry had lifted his eyebrows and discounted her suspicions, and never called her again. Henry who had compared the Lloyd's insurance market to Dante's Inferno, who wore the disillusioned look of someone who has gone too far in the cause of duty. Henry with his understated arrogance, his unscrupulous convictions, his belief in his own rectitude. A knight without a quest, a saint without religion. Henry . . .

Charlie poured herself a large vodka and drank it down much too fast. Paranoia. The pressure of work had affected her; strain had thrust her imagination into overkill. Henry was Hugo's friend: it was natural he should want to break bad news to him personally, not preparing him for some obscure deception but merely easing him through a period of trauma. As for Bianca, she had said herself that her hormones were up the creek. Pregnancy, Charlie had heard, often unbalanced otherwise reasonable people. A bad dose of hormones, depression about her love life, such things could make anyone act out of character. Charlie was experiencing no such biological disruption but she knew she was behaving oddly, she could feel her mind reaching into unknown territory, the stretching of her spirit that might yet become a warp. She must get back to the safety of a smaller view, a narrow normality, away from this dangerous world of strange empathies and fantastic imaginings.

She did not phone Hugo. She could not face the charade of breaking the bad news he had already heard, listening to his affectation of shock, playing out hers of sympathy. She went to bed and slept fitfully, jerked awake by creakings and rustlings that would usually have left her undisturbed.

She arrived at Fitzgerald Denton early the following morning. The atmosphere was subdued: everyone appeared to be working industriously yet she had the feeling nothing was being done, it was all in pantomime, a cover for the whispering and watching that was the real business of the day. Spooner stepped in her way as she headed for her desk, looming in her path, forcing her to speak to him. To her surprise, he made no allusion to Bianca. 'I hear you pulled off quite a coup with Van Lewen,' he said. His attention was always on the job in hand, she thought; an office suicide was an irrelevance. 'Nice work.' He looked her over as if the compliment meant something quite different, she wasn't sure what, and she half expected him to continue, but a wave from Rupert distracted him and he moved away. She felt a sense of release.

At her desk, she was joined by Andrew.

'Did you call Hugo?'

'No.'

'Charlie . . .'

'Is he in?' she interrupted, anxious to avoid castigation on her lack of womanly sympathy.

Andrew nodded. 'Been here for hours, according to Rupe. Shut up in his office brooding.'

'So he knows?'

'Well, yes, I suppose so . . .'

Charlie tapped on Hugo's door and went in without waiting for permission. He was sitting behind the desk with a company report in front of him and a cup of vending machine coffee, testimony to Bianca's absence, to one side. Both appeared untouched. The ashtray was already replete with cigarette ends. His mouth was set in an unpleasant line but the eyes that lifted to her face were bleak.

'You know,' she said.

177

'Spooner rang me at home. A ghastly business. She was so young – she had so much to live for. Why do people do these things?'

The clichés grated on Charlie's ears but his bewilderment and distress sounded sincere enough. *So much to live for.* Ironic words. He couldn't know about the pregnancy, or he would have picked his banalities with more care.

She said: 'I gather the police were here looking for you.'

'They'll be in later this morning. They've already rung. A chief inspector from the Limehouse lot. Seemed a fairly civilised human being. God knows what I'm to say to him. Did Bianca appear at all depressed to you?'

'No,' Charlie said ruthlessly. 'Hugo – did she tell you she was pregnant?'

'*What?*'

'She was pregnant. If the police don't know they will soon. Pathologists check that kind of thing. It'll come out at the inquest. Hugo –' She was not sure if she was trying to warn him or making an implicit accusation.

'Dear God. I didn't know.' Caught off guard with no façade prepared, he tripped over his own honesty. 'I suppose that explains it . . .'

'It doesn't explain anything,' Charlie said, but Hugo wasn't listening.

'Poor Bianca. Why the hell didn't she tell me? Why –' he turned the question on Charlie – 'why should she tell *you*? I didn't know the two of you were particular friends.'

'We weren't,' Charlie sighed. 'There's a shortage of female confidantes in here; I dare say that was why. She was hardly going to tell someone like Cynthia Greenslade. She must have known I wouldn't pass it on. Anyway, it was at the Christmas party, she was a bit drunk, I expect she needed to talk.'

'*Christmas?*' Hugo was appalled. 'But that was ages ago! You mean, she was four or five months gone? She couldn't be. I never noticed – it didn't show –'

'Not much,' Charlie said. 'They say a first child doesn't sometimes, particularly if you're fit and tight-muscled. I saw she had a bit of a tum, that was all.' He slept with her, she thought. He slept with her and he didn't see. Perhaps they had always

178

done it in the dark.

Hugo rubbed his forehead with the heel of his hand. After a few minutes he said: 'I assume you didn't . . . pass it on?'

'Of course not.'

'So no one else knows?' At no stage, she reflected, had he either admitted or denied paternity; the unspoken secret lay between them, an invisible hazard that both avoided.

'She may have told a member of her family,' Charlie said. 'In any case, the police will find out. I warned you . . .'

He ignored the verb, his frown shifting, confusion resolving itself into an uncertain determination. 'Look, I'd prefer it – I think it's best if you don't spread this round the office right now. For Bianca's sake. Everyone's talking about her: there's no need to fuel the fire. I'm sure the police will be discreet if – well, if they think a lot of unpleasant exposure isn't really necessary. Better for her family – better for her – if we play the whole thing down.'

'Nothing's going to be better for her,' Charlie said brutally. 'She's dead, Hugo. She's bloody dead. Her lungs are full of Thames filth and a pathologist is sifting through her guts –' She stopped abruptly, horrified at her own outburst, sick at the phantom it engendered, ducking her head between her knees.

Hugo said: 'Shut the fuck up.'

'I'm sorry.' She straightened up slowly, gazing at him with unhappy eyes, and for a minute they were no longer boss and employee, superior male and subordinate female, but two people on the same level, caught in the same trouble, confronting each other in naked doubt, apprehension, suspicion, groping for some fellow-feeling and finding none.

She thought: He really believes it's suicide. That's why he's being such a rat: he feels guilty and he doesn't like it. Hence the urge to hush it up. I'm the only one who thinks of murder. (*Henry and murder.*) I must stop this crazy fabrication . . .

'It's all right,' Hugo said. 'I dare say we're all a bit on edge. It's a dreadful business. Such a waste of a young life.' He appeared to find clichés reassuring. Charlie stood up, feeling the discussion had run its course. 'Incidentally,' Hugo said, changing key, 'I'm afraid your success in Amsterdam has been rather overshadowed by all this. You did a fine job and I appreciate it.

I just wanted you to know that.' The versatile mask was back in place, the smile switched on, the regrettable incident in the hotel discotheque evidently forgotten.

Charlie walked out.

About half an hour later the police came and went in a relatively unobtrusive fashion, leaving Hugo looking relieved. The inquest would subsequently opt for suicide, citing the pregnancy but failing to enquire into the identity of the father. At the funeral, a depressing affair which Charlie would have preferred not to attend, there was a certain amount of muttering about Bianca's prodigality in the sexual department, something to which Charlie could not give credence. For Bianca, she was convinced, it had been Hugo, the whole Hugo, and nothing but the Hugo. She wondered where the rumour had started but decided to acquit her boss on hearing the word spread by a secretary from another company, one of Bianca's regular cronies, to whom he would not have had access. It must be easy to start a rumour, Charlie thought; a lie, a nuance, that was all it would take. And Bianca was no longer around to defend herself. The erstwhile crony, Charlie knew, worked for a colleague of Henry's, but surely that meant nothing. The contents of the suicide note were never published and the media, usually hot on the trail of tragic girls seduced by their employers and killing themselves in consequence, accorded the matter no more than a perfunctory paragraph in the broadsheets. Charlie knew stories could be suppressed by the powers-that-be 'in the interests of security' but that gave Bianca's death a significance which she did not want to contemplate. Nothing is good or bad, someone had once said, but thinking makes it so. Charlie determined to give up on too much thinking for a while, clear the debris out of her mind, let go of imaginary problems. Bianca's body was cremated, Coppertone hair, flexitongue, baby and all. Within a fortnight everyone at Fitzgerald Denton appeared to have forgotten her. Everyone but Charlie. Charlie couldn't forget.

'There was a bad-taste nursery rhyme circulating the office,' Hugo told Henry over lunch. 'Fuck-a-bye baby, Hugo's on top; I can't repeat the rest. I'm supposed to think Rupert penned it but I suspect Spooner: he's more malicious, also more devious. Besides, Rupert couldn't possibly write verse that would scan.'

'I thought we'd dealt with Spooner,' Henry said.

'His loyalties, like his treacheries, are two-edged. Anyway, it's history now. Poor silly Bianca. She didn't have to get into a stew over a baby; there's no problem about abortions these days. God knows I'd have done all I could to help. You know, until I heard about the pregnancy I was thinking . . . She'd done all that confidential work for us, and she was getting a bit demanding lately. If I'd only realised it was her condition . . .'

'No point in agonising over it now,' Henry said. 'As you say, it's history. She can't have kept back any paperwork and we've confirmed she didn't take the typewriter. She couldn't have had any documentary evidence.'

'Odd about the typewriter,' Hugo remarked.

'Mm. I don't like loopholes. Some time, it's got to be traced . . .'

After Hugo had gone Henry sat for a while over coffee, smoking and thinking. Principally, he was thinking about Charlie. 'Well?' Elizabeth had said at their last meeting, in the course of a brief visit to London. 'Any progress?'

'On what?'

His sister gave him a minatory glance, dismissing hedging and pretence. 'Don't beat about the bush. You know perfectly well what I'm talking about. This girlfriend of yours – David Chater's god-daughter – Charlotte.'

'Oh, that. I'm afraid it came to nothing, Lizzy. Sorry to disappoint you.'

She was silent for a moment, surveying him with that remorseless perception which is only possible between siblings. 'There's something wrong,' she deduced eventually. 'You were really keen on her: I know you. Don't tell me she didn't respond, any woman would, I've seen them. Unless she found a nice young man her own age . . . but no; what girl wants that?'

'Leave it, Lizzy,' he said. 'It just didn't work, that's all. I made a mistake. Perhaps I'll have better luck next time.'

But Elizabeth had not been convinced, and Henry, shrinking from further discussion on the subject, had not even telephoned her for several weeks. Thinking of Charlie still caused a flinching in his emotions, a mental withdrawal from an area of unwanted sensitivity. He concluded for the thousandth time that he must distance himself from her at any cost, to himself or to her; whatever she knew, no matter how little, was too chancy for him, too dangerous for her, too much. Her presence at pivotal moments in the chain of events he was determined to manipulate might be pure coincidence, but he could not be sure: she might be a plant by some investigating agency, or she could have an agenda of her own. He strove not to remember her sweetness, her openness, the sparkle of challenge with which she dared or questioned him, her quickness in retort, her facility for sympathy. It occurred to him with a gleam of bitterness that maybe he was not intended for that kind of happiness: girls like Charlie, lovely and loving, would always remain unattainable, whether they were youthful *allumeuses* or deadly innocents, meshed unknowing in a web of deception. Perhaps it was cruelly appropriate that he should be bound for all time to Helen, Helen who lived in a dimension apart, whose eyes saw beyond reality, whose ears heard only the voices of the dead. And in that instant he knew there would never be anyone but Helen: she was his millstone, his punishment, his soulmate, blind, deaf, dumb to his failings and his needs, charging him with an old guilt to take away the savour of the new. As the princess spellbound in ugliness was kissed only by the blind prince so Helen alone could fulfil him, his other half, life's partner, life sentence. Charlie had always been an irresistible impossibility. For her own sake, he judged, it would be better if she was removed from his vicinity, from the domain of Lime Street, ideally from Fitzgerald Denton. She was bright and well qualified, other avenues would open up for her. He made a note to obtain a copy of Fitzgerald Denton's staff handbook at the earliest convenience. Surely something could be engineered. A compromising situation, a calumny with no evidence to refute. Spooner would help. Hugo might not be pleased but by the time the deed was done it would be too late for him to object. It was a pity Charlie had set her heart on Lloyd's, but she was still under thirty, the direction of her heart could easily change. In any case, he had different priorities. That, too, was his burden.

He recalled Henderson, that day in his Westminster office,

talking about duty, stability, the Party – 'Labour would wreck the economy in weeks: we both know that' – the unforeseen threat to the government's majority in the Lower House. The asbestosis scandal had hit the fan, Names were going bust, MPs menaced with bankruptcy. A bankrupt cannot sit in Parliament; too many insolvents could leave the government bereft. And there were wider implications, for Lloyd's, for the City. Financial services formed a vital part of the economy – huge tax revenues – Britain's reputation abroad – market confidence - potential cataclysm. Huff and puff, sweat and spiel, cold facts and hot air. Something must be done, and Henry was the man to do it. No mention was made of the 1982 Act giving Lloyd's immunity from prosecution, of favours owed, of an under-the-counter trade-off; Henderson was more subtle than that. He talked of army days, loyalty under fire, standing by one's friends. It would be for the health and wealth of the nation; the end justified the means; *dulce et decorum est, pro patria Tory*. Reluctantly, Henry had agreed. The alternatives alarmed him almost as much as Douglas. In a necessary rather than a good cause, for a secure future, he would dabble in the mire. The worrying part, he reflected as he jabbed his cigarette into the ashtray, was how easy it had become.

The offices of Granny's solicitors were just off the High Street in Dorking. Charlie and George Christie attended for the reading of the will on a suitably grey afternoon; they were shown into a stuffy room insulated with unopenable windows, antique filing cabinets, stacked folders thick with legal verbiage, the moth-eaten correspondence of decades. Charlie did not dare to smoke for fear of smothering what little air there was. She knew that there would be a sizeable inheritance both for her father and herself but Granny's death was too recent and too painful for the occasion to be anything but depressing. Mr Pilchard, Granny's lawyer, sat behind a welter of yellowing paperwork resembling a figure out of Dickens, with his rotund belly and the white tufts of hair sprouting like wings on either side of an otherwise hairless cranium. He reached out with difficulty to shake hands, said 'Dear me' several times and even 'Good gracious'. He burrowed in a mass of documentation while his visitors moved stray files to sit on the available furniture.

'Well, well,' he was saying. 'This is a terrible business. Terrible. Of course, I've done what I can to keep the jackals at bay, but –'

'You mean the Inland Revenue?' Charlie's father queried. 'They're after inheritance tax?'

'Inland – inheritance – dear me no. I'm talking about the Official Receiver.'

'Official Receiver?' Charlie looked blank. 'But that means –'

'My mother was an extremely wealthy woman,' Mr Christie insisted, rather too loud. 'What is this all about?'

'You don't know, then.' Mr Pilchard ceased his burrowing and tugged at one hair-tuft, evidently unhappy with the situation. 'She didn't tell you. Oh dear. She was a proud woman, you know, in her way. An old and valued client. There aren't many left of that vintage. A great pity. If she had asked my advice – however, there's no point in discussing that now. She had a taste of independence and, well, it meant a lot to her. You might say it went to her head. She –'

'What exactly are you talking about?' Mr Christie interrupted.

'I'm afraid your mother died insolvent.'

'*Insolvent*? But – but – she had at least a quarter of a million even before she sold Ballards. This is preposterous. How on earth –'

'You see,' Mr Pilchard steepled his fingers together, unsteepled them, pulled the other hair-tuft, 'not long after your father died, Mrs Christie became a Name. I don't know that it was wise; she was pushing her boat out into unfamiliar seas, and at her time of life – but there you are. I dare say she thought of it as an adventure. And of course, the profits should have been enormous. I expect she looked forward to surprising you.'

'I'm sorry,' Mr Christie said carefully, 'but I don't follow any of this. What do you mean, a Name?'

'He means a Name at Lloyd's,' Charlie said, conscious of a hollowness inside. As if, because of her job, she was somehow responsible for all this.

'That's it,' said Mr Pilchard, gratified by her understanding. 'Of course, it's not my field, but I gather everything was going

184

fine until last year. Then her syndicate was – er – "run off". I don't know the jargon but I infer that means it went bust.'

'It ceased trading because of lack of funds,' Charlie said. 'I work at Lloyd's; I speak the language. But – look, normally, unless there's a huge claim against it, the business of that syndicate would either be merged with another, or the outstanding risks would be gradually reinsured over a three-year cycle.'

'I don't know about that.' Mr Pilchard briefly stopped tugging and scratched. 'As far as I can tell, it's got something to do with an old insurance that sort of came home to roost. That dreadful asbestos business in America, all those poor men terminally ill and deciding to sue: well, you can't blame them, can you? Anyway, Mrs Christie's syndicate was deeply involved and most of the Names seem to have been wiped out. She was devastated, of course. I didn't know she hadn't told you. She must have felt too ashamed. Oh dear. Poor, poor woman . . .'

'She *should* have told me.' A flicker of real anger, born of frustration, crossed George Christie's face. 'I'm her son, for God's sake. Didn't I deserve to know? It's a damn thing about the money, but –' He'd have been furious, Charlie thought. He'd have supported her but there would have been resentment underneath. And subconsciously he knows it, he feels guilty, that's why he's so upset. He feels guilty over a fault he never actually committed. The level of her own perception frightened her: she was seeing things she did not want to see, understanding too much.

She said: 'At least it's over. Granny's dead now. She can't be worried any more.'

'I'm so sorry,' murmured Mr Pilchard deprecatingly, 'but it's not – quite – that simple. You see, the insolvency people have traced the gift she gave to you and your wife, Mr Christie, to pay off the outstanding mortgage on your property. I believe it came out of the proceeds from the sale of Ballards.'

'Yes, that's right.'

'Unfortunately, as a member of Lloyd's, she wasn't really entitled to dispose of such a large sum – I gather it was in the region of £100,000 – in case the syndicate was ever called upon to pay up on a risk. Not without covering it in some way, for example with a second mortgage. And I'm afraid as all this hap-

185

pened so recently, within a year of her bankruptcy . . . She probably saw it coming and wanted to do her best for you. I expect she just didn't understand. I'm sure she never intended –'

'You mean,' Charlie intervened, 'they can reclaim the money. The money she gave Daddy.'

'Exactly so.' Forgetting himself for an instant, Mr Pilchard beamed at her quickness. Then the beam was expunged as he extracted a letter with a familiar heading from the chaos on his desk. 'This arrived yesterday. From Lloyd's.'

Charlie almost snatched it from him, skimming the formal paragraphs, her gaze coming to an abrupt halt about halfway down. 'They want £400,000,' she whispered.

'I fear so.' At this juncture, Mr Pilchard tugged both hairtufts simultaneously, as though trying to pull some consolation out of his head. 'Of course, Mr Christie, you are only liable for the sum given to you, but I regret that your inheritance . . .'

'But I only have my army pension.' For the first time in her life, Charlie saw stark panic in her father's face. 'I'd always been led to expect . . . My mother always told me . . . I'd *counted* on it, dammit. Charlie too. It's her future security.'

Charlie said: 'It doesn't matter.' She took his hand and felt him squeeze her fingers till they hurt, yet she realised he was oblivious to what he was doing. He looked suddenly much older, ineffectual, not the strong soldier-figure she had always respected but helpless and desperate. She turned her face away.

'I'm so sorry,' Mr Pilchard was saying, 'but I don't think there's anything I can do.'

CHAPTER SIXTEEN

Charlie's parents were ill-equipped to deal with catastrophe. They had lived all their lives with financial security, irritations rather than worries, bills paid on the nail, debts few and regularly discharged, minor luxuries taken for granted. George Christie had anticipated an agreeable retirement free from the daily niggles that afflicted those less comfortably situated. It took him a while to accept the idea that his expenses could be reduced, his lifestyle altered; his wife, with the innate realism of her sex, adjusted far more quickly, curtailing her weekly shopping list, cutting back on hairdressing appointments and unnecessary purchases of clothing. Friends offered optimistic platitudes: 'Always darkest before dawn', 'It'll turn out all right in the end', 'It all comes out in the wash'. In fact, what came out appeared increasingly unpleasant. 'Under section 357,' according to the law, 'a person who subsequently becomes bankrupt is guilty of an offence in making a gift within the five years preceding the commencement of the bankruptcy, unless he can prove that at the time of making the gift he had no intent to defraud or conceal the state of his affairs. But if the person making the gift does so in the full knowledge of an impending insolvency for the purpose of putting the assets beyond the reach of creditors, or potential creditors . . .' and so on. Granny's death changed nothing; her son, in receipt of a possibly fraudulent gift, could be liable to repay it completely.

David Chater took over from Mr Pilchard, much to Charlie's relief, but his attitude was far from hopeful. 'They could be forced to sell the house,' he told Charlie. 'With prices falling there may not be much equity left once the debt's paid. If I've done my sums correctly they should be able to count on an income of about £18,000 a year, but of course that's a lot less than the kind of money your father has been used to. What with having to scrape together the funds for a new home, it could all be a bit of a struggle.' David had never before been compelled to envisage existence on such a meagre pittance, and the picture distressed him.

'Is there nothing we can do?' Charlie said, knowing there wasn't.

'To tell you the truth,' David continued, pursuing his own train of thought, 'I don't really understand the panic over this particular claim. I gather there's a whole bunch of Names on this and a couple of other syndicates who are being pushed really hard. Funny thing, most of them are relative newcomers, like your grandmother, not the old established members. Lloyd's seems to be hell-bent on getting their assets.'

'Are they?' Charlie said on a reflex. She had a feeling there was something she was missing, something which ought to be obvious, but she couldn't think what it was.

The following afternoon she walked round to Lime Street with Andrew Kendall. She had poured out most of her family troubles to him in quiet moments over a pub sandwich or coffee at Corney and Barrow's and he had responded with stiff-upper-lipped sympathy, moral support, and comments like 'Jolly bad luck' and 'Anything I can do', all of which soothed but did not help Charlie. That day, on an impulse, she passed on David Chater's remarks about the syndicates which had been run off. 'I know this sounds a bit far-fetched,' she said, 'but . . . would it be possible to shove a load of bad risks on to the less important Names, like poor Granny, in order to keep the influential ones in the clear?'

'You know it wouldn't,' Andrew said. 'How can you identify a bad risk in advance? You only find out it's a dud when it's too late. We don't check the bottom of a ship for holes: we just wait till it sinks.'

'This is the asbestosis shenanigans,' Charlie said. 'Couldn't someone have smelt the shit before it hit the fan?'

'May have done,' Andrew replied, 'but so what? The insurance was already arranged: they couldn't cancel it. Just bad luck a few people seem to have carried the bulk of it.'

'*Was* it just bad luck?' Charlie clung to her *idée fixe*, working out possible ramifications. 'Supposing . . . supposing it *had* been spread around the market, and some real heavyweight members

188

were going to lose a lot of money. Somebody could have rigged reinsurance and backdated it.'

'Difficult,' said Andrew. 'For one thing, you'd have to make the documentation look right. We're computerised now but in the old days it would have been typewriters and Tippex.'

'Anyone can get hold of a typewriter,' Charlie said idly, remembering how easily she herself had absconded with one of these sought-after antiques. 'That wouldn't be a problem.'

Halfway up the steps to the Lloyd's entrance she stopped short.

A typewriter. A *typewriter* . . .

Inside, she returned to the business of placing the insurance for Van Lewen. Over the last few days she had presented the slip to thirteen of the underwriters and most of the cover was completed; she hoped to finish the deal that afternoon. She headed for the underwriting box of a marine syndicate, currently manned by a florid individual named Simmonds. His style of insurance involved writing a good deal of small business, and this was what Charlie needed. Two or three lines would complete the slip; Simmonds, she decided, was just the sort of underwriter to take a quick punt with a line of maybe 5 per cent. She approached him with a smile, launched into the preliminary courtesies. He did not smile back. 'I wonder whether you'd like to have a glance at this for me,' she persisted. 'It's the hull risk for Van Lewen of Holland. I'm sure you know their reputation . . .' She had begun her spiel, intending to remind him, when he cut her short.

'I'm very sorry, Miss Christie, but with effect from this morning I'm afraid you have been banned from our box.'

Charlie just stared at him, uncomprehending, confused. 'I beg your pardon?'

His eyes flicked from side to side as though checking for eavesdroppers. Inevitably, people were beginning to turn and look at them, work slowing, sensing the sudden tension. 'I regret,' Simmonds went on, 'I have been instructed by the members of my syndicate not to discuss the matter further with you. You will have to take it up with your employers who, so I'm told, are aware of the situation.'

189

'What situation?'

Simmonds's flabby cheeks flushed with embarrassment. 'I repeat, I can't discuss the matter further.'

'Why not?' Inwardly, Charlie was starting to shake, but face and voice held steady. It was a misunderstanding, a cock-up, a nightmare. And, as in a nightmare, her feet were weighted, and she could not find the right words to break the spell.

'I'm sorry,' Simmonds echoed.

'But –'

'Miss Christie, I would urge you to make further enquiries at your office. I can't say any more. I really am *very* sorry.' He flinched away from her, diving into a folder like an ostrich seeking for sand. The conversation was evidently closed. Charlie tried not to look about her, unwilling to see the eager curiosity and vicarious Angst on the faces of her work fellows. There was a strange silence in her head; her thoughts were numb. As if in slow motion she felt herself turn and walk towards the escalator, her gaze fixed on some nonexistent point in midair, oblivious to the muttering and speculation that pursued her. *You have been banned from our box*. The escalator bore her downwards, her feet aimed for the exit as if of their own volition. Daylight flooded her senses. *You have been banned from our box*. She heard the open-tread steps pattering beneath her, ignored a wave from someone she knew. And then her walk had become a run and the familiar cityscape skidded by and she was back at Fitzgerald Denton, forgetting to exchange the usual pleasantries with the security man, ascending in the lift with the silence growing louder in her head. Hugo was out. The temporary secretary who had replaced Bianca did not know where he was, no one knew where he was, he was just out. There was a letter on her desk marked PRIVATE AND CONFIDENTIAL. ADDRESSEE ONLY. She tore it open.

The first paragraph danced before her eyes. 'I am writing to confirm that your employment with the company has been terminated with immediate effect for reasons of gross misconduct, as described in the staff handbook. You will receive payment of your salary up until the end of this calendar month. Your P45 and final payslip will be forwarded to your home address by our accounts department.' She skimmed the other details – holiday entitlement, expenses – saw Hugo's signature at the bottom. Belatedly, she sat down, the shakiness inside her becoming uncontrollable. The desk nearest to her was vacant; if covert eyes studied her she did not notice them. She was reading and rereading the relevant passage, numb with shock and increasingly bewildered. Gross misconduct as described in the staff handbook? What was he talking about? Had she been blamed for someone else's dirty dealing – probably Spooner's? Or had she been set up, deliberately, cynically, and if so, why? She couldn't think clearly: the questions spiralled round and round in her brain, bumping into each other; she seemed unable to disentangle them. She reached for the telephone as for a lifeline, called Lloyd's, left a message for Andrew. Of all the people at Fitzgerald Denton he was the one she thought she could trust. Then she rang Caroline.

'Darling, you sound very peculiar. What's the matter?'

'I can't talk now. You know that little wine bar round the corner from your office? Could you meet me there in about an hour?'

'It's urgent, isn't it?' Caroline had assimilated the undercurrents immediately.

'Yes.'

'I'll be there.'

Charlie hung up, stuffed the letter of dismissal into her bag, picked up her briefcase and marched out of the offices of Fitzgerald Denton. She had every intention of coming back.

In the wine bar, with the invigorating warmth of cheap claret pervading her system, Charlie told her friend about the day's events. She had already covered her success in Amsterdam and the scene with Hugo on the dance floor, but it was Caroline who began constructing theories in an attempt to produce a logical explanation. 'You've had enough trouble with the male ego in that job already,' she pointed out. 'What if *that's* what this is all about? You reject the boss and his vanity is so paper-thin he can't bear seeing you round the office all the time. Therefore, out you go. How's that for a scenario?'

'I don't know.' Although she did not really believe the hypothesis, Caroline's suggestion was forcing her to think, prodding her intelligence back into action. 'Hugo's pretty

191

tough, ambitious, short on moral scruples, and I dare say he's fairly conceited, but not to the point of idiocy. I mean, afterwards he just behaved as if nothing had happened. He didn't try to pressure me or anything.'

'Well, darling, you've been sacked,' Caroline said. 'Take it lying down by all means, if that's how you feel, but personally I think you might have a case.' She had a litigious streak a mile wide, as Charlie well knew, and a familiar gleam was invading her eye. 'You've had plenty of hassle since you went to work in that circus; now, they've fired you for no reason. And it's pretty clear Hugo's a schmuck after that business with his secretary, what's-her-name who drowned herself.'

'Bianca,' Charlie said. Bianca who knew too much.

'If I were you,' Caroline said, 'I'd go to the Industrial Tribunal. Take the buggers to the cleaners. Hugo went for your pussy, darling; you go for his balls. Kick him right in the profit-and-loss department: he's asking for it.'

'Mm.' Charlie, pursuing another train of thought, was paying only limited attention.

'Believe me,' Caroline went on, 'I know what I'm talking about. I'll lend you my lawyer. Better still, call that godfather of yours, keep it in the family, he'll make them an offer they can't refuse. Darling, are you listening to me?'

'Yes, I am,' said Charlie. 'It's just . . . I've an idea that for once this has nothing to do with sex.'

'OK,' Caroline said, refilling their glasses, 'Drop the sex. What haven't you told me?'

'You'll think I'm going barmy,' Charlie said doubtfully. 'Sometimes, *I* think I'm going barmy. It's about Bianca. And Henry. I forgot to mention, Henry was in Amsterdam. At least, I didn't exactly forget . . .'

'Out with it,' Caroline said.

Charlie unburdened herself of her paranoia, uncomfortably aware how tenuous were the grounds for suspicion, a matter of nuances and evasions, tiny details that jarred, broken jigsaw pieces that would not quite interlock. When she had voiced her fears there seemed to be only a nebula of doubt with little or no substance hidden in the mist. But Caroline did not look either scornful or sceptical. She pounced.

'Let's recapitulate,' she said, ticking items off on her fingers. 'Bianca tells you she knows something discreditable about Fitzgerald Denton. We assume she's making herself awkward with Hugo. In due course, you pass this on to Henry. Then Bianca turns up dead. All right, it's a couple of months later, but Henry could have been checking up on her, or examining alternatives: dead secretaries tell no tales but they do tend to stand out. In addition, Henry goes to Amsterdam to inform Hugo and prime him for the visit of Inspector Knacker, who isn't in on the secret. (And who else *is* in on it, by the way?) I've heard a thing or two about your Henry: they say he's so cold you could chill ice on his heart. And I don't know if it's relevant, but he has political connections, very high up. Do you think this scam – whatever it is – could have something to do with the government? The way Bianca's death stayed out of the tabloids smells a bit. Discreet pressure from above, maybe. I rather fancy the idea of backroom plotting in Westminster.'

'I don't know about the government,' Charlie said, 'but I thought I had a brainwave today. About Granny's syndicate, and the small Names going bust while the big ones were kept in the black. All to do with backdated reinsurance. It fitted in with that silly business of the typewriter, too, or so I thought; but a typewriter isn't like a computer, it doesn't have a memory, so I don't see how it could provide incriminating evidence no matter what you typed on it.'

'Fingerprints?' Caroline suggested. 'The typewriter ought to fit in somewhere. If this were a thriller it would be the key to the whole mystery.'

'This is real life,' said Charlie. 'It's probably not important. Just the object of corporate meanness. Reality is never as tidy as art. And I've lost my job . . .'

There was a short pause while both of them returned to the bald fact, undecorated by cobwebs of conspiracy.

Then: 'Darling,' Caroline said, her tone altered, suddenly devoid of inflection, 'I've just thought of something. Bianca knew something; Bianca's dead. You've been sacked. Supposing . . . they think you know something too? Maybe they're not absolutely sure yet. Maybe . . .'

'Stop it,' Charlie said. 'This is ridiculous.'

'Is it?' Caroline was thinking visibly, her normal affectations discarded. 'Listen: call your godfather. Have him write to Fitzgerald Denton saying you'll sue for unfair dismissal. Act all aggrieved innocence.'

'I *am* innocent.'

'That's not the point. And that guy you're so pally with, Andrew Kendall, you'd better steer clear of him for a bit.'

'He's my friend,' Charlie said indignantly.

'Not when his job's on the line. He works for Fitzgerald Denton; he won't sup with the enemy.'

'He's not like that,' Charlie insisted.

'Most people are like that,' Caroline said, 'given half the chance.'

Charlie rang David Chater the next morning. 'Don't worry,' he said to her. 'I'll fight your corner. I think the whole affair is disgraceful. First we need to get them to clarify the issue of gross misconduct. Are you certain there's nothing you've done that could have been in any way misinterpreted? There's a very fine line in business between what is and is not acceptable. Or maybe someone else instigated your actions and has compromised you without your knowing it?'

'I've been racking my brains half the night,' Charlie said. 'I can't think of anything. Anything reasonable.'

'Anything unreasonable?'

'No.' She didn't like to lie to him but she couldn't possibly tell him her real suspicions; he would think she was on hallucinogens.

'Right. Have you cleared your desk?'

'Not yet.' She couldn't bear to contemplate such a final move, erasing the last traces of her presence from the office she had entered with high hopes and blossoming ambition less than eight months before.

'Do so. Or better still, get a friend to do it for you. You want to avoid unpleasant confrontations: leave all that to me. I'll write to Hugo Wingate and ask for all the relevant correspondence to be sent to my office, also a precise statement of the grounds for your dismissal. That should give him something to think about. Stay clear of Fitzgerald Denton; don't get in touch with any of your former colleagues. If Hugo tries to communicate with you, refer him to me. I'll handle it from now on. And don't lose your nerve. The Christies seem to be really in for it at the moment, but we'll win through.'

'David, you're a dear,' Charlie said. 'I can't thank you enough.'

'Frankly, you may be well out of it. I've always thought Lloyd's a small pond with too many sharks. I don't want my god-daughter torn apart in a feeding frenzy. Which reminds me, concerning the case, you could start jotting down a few details now. Any incidents that spring to mind, with a date if you can remember it. At some stage we're going to have to prepare an affidavit, and the more accurate it is the better. You may as well make a start immediately. Give yourself something positive to work on. I'll be in touch. We'll have lunch soon, darling, just the two of us. Take care.' When he rang off Charlie had to fight back an idiotic urge to cry, he had sounded so kind.

David drafted the letter to Fitzgerald Denton that afternoon, sending a copy by fax as well as by registered post. Referring to Charlie as his client, he said they were to treat this letter as notice of her intention to appeal against her dismissal. He requested a copy of the staff handbook whose contents Hugo had cited to justify his action, and pointed out that in accordance with section 53 of the Employment Protection Consolidation Act, as she had been dismissed without notice, his client was entitled to a full statement of their reasons for so doing: the term 'gross misconduct' must be properly elucidated. Piling on the pressure, he indicated that the above-mentioned statement should be treated as a matter of the utmost urgency and should be produced within the fourteen-day period prescribed under law. That letter dispatched, he wrote another to Charlie's parents telling them that the date for the insolvency hearing had been set for early the following month. They come not single spies, he reflected, correcting a slip of the keyboard on the part of his secretary, but in battalions. He only hoped he had enough big guns to stage something more than a last stand.

Hugo, in receipt of the fax later that day, studied it with a marked lack of enthusiasm. He had not been expecting formal retaliation quite so soon after Charlie's departure, if at all. He reached for the telephone and dialled Henry Marriott's number.

Although both David and Caroline had warned her to remain incommunicado as far as Fitzgerald Denton was concerned, Charlie was relieved to hear from Andrew. The previous evening she had accompanied Caroline to a party, but once she was in bed she still found herself worrying fruitlessly at her problem, replaying a dozen different incidents, trying a hundred computations to make sense of the incomprehensible. And whenever thinking stopped there was the unpalatable truth, glaring in her face: she had lost her job. The job she had dreamed of and longed for, the opportunity she had reached out to grasp with eager hands, her entrée to the steel towers of fairyland – in less than a day, it had all been wiped out. During the slow hours of that night she felt as if her life was over. She was young: this was the first time she had built something up only to have it fall to pieces between her fingers. She remembered how bravely her parents, much later in life, were facing financial ruin, and hoped she would be able to emulate their courage in her own lesser disaster, but it was too early for such comparisons to bolster her nerve and she could not kick herself out of despair. Failure was still new to her, sickeningly real, a terminal condition. Sleep came at last, to be succeeded by a grim awakening. Her red-wine headache vanished with her father's wonder-cure but even David's brisk confidence could not disperse her depression. When she heard Andrew's voice on the phone it was a contact with the world she missed; not everyone at Fitzgerald Denton had rejected her; she felt insensibly reassured.

'What happened?' he wanted to know. 'Why aren't you here? Are you ill?'

'Not exactly. They've given me the push. We can't talk now. Could you get round here this evening, and . . . would you mind clearing out my desk?'

Andrew arrived around 7.30. Charlie found herself ridiculously pleased to see him. His handsome, essentially English face, clean-shaven and clean-cut, appeared to her an open book in which every trait of his character, every feeling he experienced, could be easily read. A little shyness, a little strength, none of Henry's power and mystery or Hugo's relentless opportunism but other, gentler qualities, qualities she was learning to value more, or so she believed, kindness, loyalty, honesty. 'I'm so glad to see you,' she said with genuine warmth, and, noticing he had come empty-handed: 'Did you manage to get my stuff?' Presumably he had left everything in the car. 'Can I help you bring it in?'

'I'm sorry,' he said. 'The fifth column got there before me. There was nothing left.'

'I don't understand.'

'I waited till the staff had thinned out a bit and then went over to your desk. It was empty. Clean as a whistle. I'll swear they'd done your drawers with a hoover to get the fag ash out. It was as though you'd never been there.'

Involuntarily, Charlie shivered. 'Did you ask anyone what had happened to my stuff?'

'I pumped that chap Lyle, the office manager. He said Hugo had ordered him to clear your desk space, sort out the personal stuff and forward it to you here. You should get it soon. Anything pertaining to the company was to be sat on. He'd been told to do it pronto, top priority. Charlie, what the hell's going on?'

'I wish I knew.' Automatically, she poured two glasses of wine, offering one to Andrew. 'First Granny dying, and then my parents being stung by Lloyd's for the money she gave them, and now this. I feel as if everything's coming apart at the seams. The people I trusted – the things I was sure of –' To her horror, she realised there were tears running down her face, spilling into her wine, the first she had wept since opening Hugo's letter. Andrew tried to put his arms around her and there was a moment of confusion as she attempted simultaneously to deposit her wine glass on the table; then she buried her face in his shoulder and for a few minutes she allowed herself the luxury of heaving, bellowing sobs. When she pulled herself free her eyelids were swollen, her nose pink, and there was a damp patch on Andrew's jacket. She mumbled an apology and dived into the kitchen in search of paper towels to mop up the mess. To her surprise, Andrew followed her.

'For God's sake, don't apologise. I mean, you've had such a

lousy time, if you want to cry, you cry. Think of me as a sponge. I just stand here and soak up the tears.'

Charlie laughed rather shakily and although she showed no further signs of weeping Andrew took her in his arms again for good measure. A kiss found its way on to her cheek, then another located her mouth, and she responded with an ardour that startled her, vaguely remembering that she had read somewhere there is nothing like a good cry to spark off the libido. 'We mustn't do this,' she murmured between kisses. 'We've been such good friends. I don't want to spoil it.'

'We're not spoiling it,' Andrew said. 'We're improving it.'

'No –' Charlie detached herself resolutely from his embrace – 'this isn't the right moment, I'm too upset, off balance. I need to calm down, think things out . . .'

'All right,' Andrew said equably. 'Let's just talk for a bit.'

They sat down in the living room and resumed their wine. Charlie's tasted slightly salty from the addition of her tears and Andrew gallantly offered to swap, claiming he liked salt in his wine. 'In a bar, I always eat the crisps,' he declared. 'You've just cut out the potato.'

Inevitably, the conversation returned to the subject of her dismissal. Although she failed to touch on her more extravagant imaginings they did discuss Bianca's suicide, its inherent implausibility – 'There's a rumour she was pregnant,' Andrew interjected – and, by a natural progression, the phantom typewriter.

'Maybe she stole it to type her farewell note,' Andrew suggested.

'Actually,' Charlie admitted, a little shamefaced, 'she didn't steal it at all. I did. The whole thing was so silly. They had no use for the bloody machines; I'd heard they would probably be dumped. And I met this guy at a party, a writer . . .'

Andrew enjoyed the saga of Amrit and his ex-girlfriend and they agreed that the typewriter should be consigned, metaphorically speaking, to perdition. Charlie made some toasted cheese which they washed down with the rest of the wine. Then Andrew gave her a goodnight kiss, withdrawing his tongue chivalrously when it began to get out of hand; Charlie, indeed, wondered privately if she really wanted him to be quite so chivalrous, despite her misgivings. 'I'll find out anything I can,' he promised her on his way out. She heard his car engine start and the purr of a vehicle retreating down the silent street.

She was left feeling suddenly very alone.

CHAPTER SEVENTEEN

A couple of days later Spooner cornered Andrew over a large gin in Corney and Barrow's and suggested a quiet chat. Andrew had no desire for a chat with his least amiable colleague but Spooner was insistent and, perseverance being one of the qualities which had ensured his professional success, eventually he got his way. Charlie's dismissal was now common gossip both at Lloyd's and at Fitzgerald Denton but although an intriguing variety of theories had been put forward no hard evidence was forthcoming. Spooner always claimed to be one jump ahead of the rest of the City; maybe he would be able to tell Andrew something.

They found an isolated table, and Spooner told him something.

'Hugo wanted me to have a word with you,' he said. 'On the side, so to speak. It probably isn't necessary. You're a bright boy, you're doing well, you've got nowhere to go but up.' The faint ambiguity missed Andrew, who was frowning at the gentle menace underlying Spooner's tone. 'As long as you don't stumble on the lower rungs and fall flat on your kisser. If you take my meaning.'

'No,' Andrew said bluntly. 'I don't.'

Imbecile, Spooner thought, the glimmer of contempt showing in his expression. 'Listen, boy,' the scorn was all but naked, 'I gather you were friendly with Charlie Christie. Possibly you still are; I don't know. But it is not a good idea to remain too chummy with an ex-employee who has left under a cloud. It could bring your own reliability into question. Clear?'

'As mud,' Andrew responded. 'Charlie and I are friends and we intend to stay that way. Why not?'

'And you won't discuss company business with her ever again? Even though you've been accustomed to doing so? Get real. She's probably using you to keep herself informed of our activities.'

'She doesn't even know *why* she was fired –'

'Are you aware she's entered into litigation with Fitzgerald Denton?'

'N-no . . .' Andrew's confidence faltered and Spooner, sensing weakness, tensed himself as if to spring. 'She didn't tell me that.'

'When did you see her last?'

'Wednesday,' Andrew admitted.

'We heard from her lawyers on Wednesday. She's suing us – and she didn't bother to mention it. Use your head, Kendall. She's playing you for a sucker.'

'Charlie isn't like that,' Andrew insisted. 'Anyway, she was very upset.'

'I'll bet she was.' Having located the crack in Andrew's certainty, Spooner continued to hammer away at it. 'What *did* you talk about? Fifty quid says she turned on the tears and begged you not to desert her. You're the only friend she has left in the world and by the way, could you give her the inside dope on whatever her old employers are up to. Right? Don't bother: I can see it in your face. Of course I'm right. These days, every bimbo thinks she can play Mata Hari. Lyle told me you tried to clear out her desk. What else did you promise to do for her?'

'Nothing,' Andrew said. 'Bill, for Christ's sake – ! Yes, we talked about the company but there wasn't anything confidential involved. As it happens, we were discussing Bianca's death and that stupid affair of the disappearing typewriter. She told me –'

'Told you what?'

'Look, it's not important. She's left now, and –'

'*Told you what?*'

'The bloody machines were practically decrepit, no one had any more use for them. She took one for some writer she met at a party, he needed it for that great novel they're always working on, and when the fuss started and she tried to get it back she found his ex-girlfriend had swiped it and had it mashed up. Apparently she objected to something in the great novel. Anyway, poor Charlie was too embarrassed to say anything. She didn't mean any harm. It was just a generous impulse on her part.'

So that's that, Spooner thought. The phantom typewriter

traced. And the evidence tidily destroyed. He ought to pass the information on to Hugo and Henry Marriott but his conspiratorial instincts told him to sit on it for a while and see if there was anything more to be extracted from the situation. He would have to think it over.

'In other words,' he said to Andrew, 'she stole office equipment and you covered up for her. You've landed yourself right in it, my boy. If I were you, I wouldn't be in too much of a hurry to see Charlie Christie again. Better to concentrate on keeping your job – if you can.'

George Christie received the letter from David Chater informing him of the court date that same week. He didn't tell his wife, not out of cowardice, or so he assured himself, but to keep her from anxiety for just a little longer, as if, by hiding her eyes from approaching cataclysm, he could somehow delay it. It was futile and he knew it, but he clung to his futility because it was all he had.

In the same way Charlie could not bring herself to tell her parents what had happened at Fitzgerald Denton. She spent her days mooching around the flat, feeling too humiliated to talk to most of her friends, with nothing to do and too much time to think, to agonise, to turn events inside-out and upside-down in a desperate attempt to fit them into a logical pattern. Bianca's suicide, Granny's death, the financial ruin hanging over her family – all these were thrust to the back of her mind: the wretched end to her glittering career monopolised her thoughts. When Andrew did not call again she was at first mildly surprised; later, remembering Caroline's admonition, perturbed, furious, hurt. She tried to believe he had a work overload, or was waiting until he had learned something definite about her dismissal, but by the following Monday she had given up. A dispatch rider biked round the dregs of her desk contents: there was little of significance but rifling through the pile of oddments she had a dreadful sensation of finality, as if her last toehold in Fitzgerald Denton had gone. She plunged into a wallow of despondency from which Caroline, telephoning that afternoon, resolved to rescue her, inviting herself to lunch on Tuesday and planning a course of parties and a diet of dinner-dates to cheer her up. Secretly, she was deeply concerned for her friend: she had rarely seen Charlie down in the mouth, let alone close to breaking point, and although it was understandable that did not make it any less disturbing.

Within fifteen minutes of her arrival she had coaxed the truth about Andrew out of Charlie, a confession accompanied by a few angry tears.

'I'm sorry to be such a wimp,' Charlie said, gazing savagely at a damp tissue. 'I wasn't in love with him or anything like that, but I *trusted* him. This is all so horrible. You think you know someone, you confide in them, and they let you down. And don't say *I told you so*.'

'Would I do that?' Caroline protested, injured. 'Am I the sort of person who scores cheap points at the expense of afflicted friends?'

Charlie managed a valiant smile and nodded enthusiastically.

Caroline achieved an expression of haughty superiority and resumed: 'All right, so what did you confide in Andrew?'

'Not much, really. We touched on Bianca – apparently the whole office knows about her pregnancy now; I suppose someone talked after the inquest – then we got on to the flap about the typewriter. I – I'm afraid I told him the truth. But I don't see that it matters much; after all, the typewriter's been destroyed.'

'Bloody nuisance about that,' said Caroline. 'By sheer fluke, you land a vital piece of evidence, and your Amrit's ex has to have it pounded up and turned into horsemeat.'

'I still don't see what evidence you can get from a typewriter,' Charlie reiterated. 'I've got the ribbon somewhere, Amrit said it ran out and he had to change it. He gave it to me, God knows why, and I think I hung on to it, but –'

'Where?' Caroline interrupted in sharpened accents. 'What have you done with it?'

'I don't know; it could be anywhere; but I don't understand –'

'Look for it. I'm thinking.' Caroline clutched her temples, her face squeezed into an expression of anguished concentration.

Charlie surveyed her with interest. 'Don't do that. You'll hurt yourself.'

'Listen. You said something vital might have been typed on

that machine, forged contracts, backdated documents, that kind of stuff. Only a typewriter has no memory so we couldn't use the machine to read whatever it was. But Charlie, it *does* have a memory; don't you see? *It's all on the ribbon.* From what Amrit said it must have been the sort you can only use once; it looks like an ordinary cassette, right? So every letter typed must be imprinted there, clear as paint. Darling, find that ribbon and we've cracked it! God, I'm a genius. Move over, Poirot; I'm wasted in PR.'

'It's a wonderful theory,' Charlie said more cautiously. 'I'm simply not sure – anyway, how come you know so much about typewriters?'

'I used to type up my class notes when I was in the sixth because I couldn't read my own handwriting,' Caroline explained. 'It just goes to show: all experience is valid. Where the hell did you put that ribbon?'

After half an hour of fruitless investigation they took a break for wine. Caroline had brought some smoked salmon and Charlie made a side salad, and they sat down on the sofa to revive themselves. Caroline, too far from the low table for convenience, placed her glass on top of a stack of videos. 'What's this?' she said. 'It doesn't look like a proper tape: it's too small. Charlie –'

'That's it!' Charlie yelped. 'Of course: I knew I'd put it somewhere logical. It's a cassette, so I stowed it with other cassettes.'

'Very logical, darling.' Caroline thrust her plate away, fiddled with the reel, and unravelled a short section of ribbon, holding it up to the light. 'See: as each letter came in contact with the ribbon it removed the ink, leaving a transparent impression of itself. Some of them are a bit blurred but they should all be legible. I'm right, I tell you; I know I'm right. Once we've got Amrit's blockbuster out of the way whatever comes before that must be the incriminating material. No wonder they went apeshit when it disappeared. Bianca probably did the typing: she'd have understood the significance of the missing ribbon. Maybe she drew their attention to it. Maybe they thought she'd nicked it herself, for blackmail purposes. That could be why –'

'Why she died,' Charlie supplied. 'It all comes back to Bianca, doesn't it? And me. I took the typewriter; I told Henry what she said in the loo at the party. I did for her both ways. If all this is true, and not some crazy nightmare we've both imagined – then it's my fault. It's my fault she's dead.' To her horror, she found the facile tears, too frequent of late, were welling in her eyes.

'Stop fantasising,' Caroline said bracingly. 'You don't know that, darling. If she typed the fake contracts and was making herself difficult about it – and she did give you that impression – they would have got rid of her anyway. Whoever *they* are.'

'I wish I was sure of that.'

'And who *are* they, anyhow? Hugo, the slimy Spooner, Henry as the *éminence grise*, but I detect other figures in the background, pullers of strings, wielders of power . . . Charlie, Bianca's dead, there's nothing you can do for her, but you've got to start looking out for yourself. Don't make that face; I mean it. If Andrew's spilled the beans they must know you had the typewriter. Sooner or later someone may decide to verify its state of disintegration. Darling, you could be in real trouble . . .'

'My granny died, my parents are going broke, and I've been fired,' Charlie said, 'and *now* you tell me I'm in trouble.' The words were flippant, but there was no laughter in her voice. 'Well, I can't run away and hide, can I, so I hope to God this is all a bad dream. What are we going to do with that ribbon? I don't fancy unwinding it myself, inch by inch, and trying to make out the lettering. It could take years.'

'No problem,' said Caroline. 'All we need is a big light box and a tame photographer with a rostrum camera. Give me the ribbon: I can lay my hands on both. I have a friend –'

'You always do,' Charlie smiled, rather wanly. 'How long do you think it will take?'

'No idea. Depends when he has some free time. Eat that smoked salmon; it's from Harrods.'

'I thought it was Scottish?'

'Only by birth.' Caroline, setting an example, resumed her plate and fork. 'Meanwhile, darling, you've got to watch out for yourself. What you need is a bodyguard.'

'That would be lovely.' Charlie's sigh melted into sudden warmth. 'Do you know a saphead who wants the job?'

*

Caroline's deductions might be melodramatic and potentially alarming but at least they provided a stimulus. Three days later she was sent to New York on business and Charlie was left to her own devices, declining social invitations, skimming the Sits Vac columns in the *Times*, the *Telegraph*, and the *FT*, waiting in vain to hear from David Chater, and fretting over her parents' misfortune. She did not ring them for some time, delaying till she felt brave enough to make light of personal calamity, unwilling to tell polite lies about her progress at work. One evening, she came in from a late expedition to the supermarket to find a message from her father on her answering machine. She debated calling back but she had rented a soothing video and felt that she would be better able to tackle painful communications in the morning. She settled down to her film, feeling guilty, flinching from the proximity of the telephone. After a bad night's sleep – one of many – she woke early, worried pointlessly, and finally got up to make her call.

Her mother answered, her control breaking as soon as she heard her daughter's voice. She told Charlie how she'd found David's letter when looking through Daddy's desk for the gas bill, which she was sure was incorrect, and the letter said the hearing was only a week away, and Daddy hadn't told her, and they'd had a terrible row, really terrible, and George had walked out. Something he'd never done before. Apparently he'd simply roamed the streets for hours and then, discovering he'd gone out without his house-key, he'd gone to sleep in the garage in the front seat of the car. She'd found him in the morning, slumped over the wheel; for a dreadful minute she'd thought he was dead. Anyway, they'd decided they needed to talk things through, to envisage the worst and make what her father called contingency plans. Could Charlie take a couple of days off work and come down? Her heart sinking, Charlie said yes, she would come immediately.

On arrival in Chichester she broke the bad news as soon as possible, to get it out of the way, but she said nothing of the darker suspicions she had discussed only with Caroline, or the off-chance that Granny's insolvency might somehow be part of it. Her mother hugged her and her father's face grew rigid, stiffening with pent-up anger and frustration. 'Why did it have to happen *now*?' her mother protested. 'Everything's so awful, and now this; I really feel fate has got it in for the Christies. But we'll manage somehow, won't we? At least we have each other.' She produced this sentiment as though unaware of its triteness, and on her lips it sounded both original and heartfelt.

'If the house has to be sold,' Charlie said, reverting to practicalities, 'where will you go? You're welcome to my spare room, that goes without saying, but I couldn't take the furniture, and I think it's quite expensive keeping things in store.'

'No point in incurring unnecessary costs,' said her father. 'We don't want you to be saddled with us, either. No, don't argue about it: we've made up our minds. We'll find a little place to rent, a cottage or something, maybe out in the country. We may have to make a few economies but we'll do very nicely, you'll see. The important thing in life is to be flexible. I learned that in the Marines. You ride out the bad weather and wait for the wind to change.'

'It certainly isn't blowing our way at the moment,' Charlie said.

'It will,' said her father. 'It will.'

Back in London, she took a call from David Chater. 'I'm so glad you've rung,' Charlie said. 'I've been going crazy wondering what was happening.'

'Not much,' David said, sounding inexplicably ill at ease. 'I still haven't received anything official from Fitzgerald Denton. Look Charlie, I'm terribly sorry – I can't tell you how sorry – but I'm going to have to shelve this case. I've got a hell of a lot on my plate at the minute and, well, it needs more attention than I have time to give. When you first got in touch with me I sort of rushed in without thinking – I'm very fond of you, I wanted to help – and I'm afraid I got rather carried away. Trouble is, business is business, and I've just got too many commitments already. I'll send you copies of the letters I've written on your behalf and anything I get from Fitzgerald Denton and then you can pass them on to someone else. I think that would be better all round. Charlie? Are you still there?'

'Yes.'

'I do hope you understand my position. This is a very delicate problem and I simply don't – don't have the time.'

'I see.' She didn't see. He knew she didn't, and it was probably just as well. 'Will you have the time for my parents' affairs, do you think? Because if not, perhaps you would be good enough to inform them of it – immediately.'

She pressed the button to cut him off, disgusted to find herself trembling and on the verge of tears, though whether from hurt or rage she did not know. Then without giving herself an interval to calm down or reflect she dialled her father's number.

David Chater hung up more slowly, a spasm of unaccustomed hurt creasing his comfortable face. He had failed his god-daughter, whom he loved very dearly, and in so doing he knew he had failed himself, betraying the unspecified creed of affection and principle to which most men try to adhere, one way or another, through the temptations and pitfalls of an uncertain world. There are moments in everyone's life too shameful to recall, moments of humiliation and cowardice, of self-inflicted defeat, which the mind must obliterate for the soul's respite; but David knew he would have difficulty forgetting that day. His existence was habitually easygoing, unruffled, the stresses of his profession restricted to office hours; unhappiness sat awkwardly on him. The lines on his brow were new and poignant; his eyes winced. 'It's done,' he said. Of course Charlie didn't understand. She never would.

Henry Marriott nodded brusquely. 'It's unpleasant,' he said. 'It's unpleasant for both of us, but it's necessary. She's young: she sees everything in black and white. We live in a greyer world. She'll learn.'

'I don't want her to learn lessons like this,' David said. 'I love her the way she is: candid, open, impulsive, thinking she's sophisticated when really she's so bloody innocent. I thought you liked her that way too.'

'I didn't come here to discuss that.' Henry's voice was chilly; he had memories of his own to erase. 'Candour is merely a euphemism for indiscretion, innocence for ignorance, and personally, I never acted on impulse without regretting it. There's no point in plaguing ourselves: what's done is done. The quicker this is straightened out the better for all concerned.'

'"If it were done when 'tis done, 'twere well it were done quickly,"' David quoted absently.

'Macbeth,' Henry said, lifting his eyebrows. 'Vaulting ambition . . . Is that to my address?'

'Not really. You remind me more of that chap in *Measure for Measure*, the one "whose very blood is snow-broth". As I recall,' he continued blandly, 'the girl in the case turned him down: that was the root of the trouble. But he was planning to double-cross her anyway.'

'*Measure for Measure* is a comedy,' Henry pointed out drily, 'and therefore improbable. If I were you, I would have a quiet word with Charlie in the near future. For her own sake. Persuade her that the benefits which might accrue from dropping her claim could far outweigh any compensation she imagines she might obtain.'

'What benefits?'

'Just do it.' Henry had walked over to the window and stood looking out. In the street below a couple of beggars, pale from bad diet, ragged from sleeping out, cupped their hands for small change, calling friendly greetings both to those who gave and those who did not. He did not attempt to put himself in their place: it was not in his nature. He merely felt that it was deplorable they should be there. Society had disinherited them, and he was an instrument of that society, but he saw no way to improve the situation. In a less well-regulated world the beggars might have been impolite. 'We've been friends a long time. I don't want to have to twist your arm –'

'You already did,' David retorted bleakly. He knew – they both knew – Henry was too influential a man to offend or refuse.

A shade of annoyance crossed Marriott's face. 'Don't think of it that way. I owe you a favour, and you – well, you're nudging your god-daughter out of a situation which could turn very nasty. Discourage her from poking her head over the battlements. Better for both of you. Charlie, I'm sure, will be much happier if she keeps clear of the City in future – and of Lloyd's.'

'I'll do my best,' David said with a sigh, 'though opinions may differ as to what that entails.'

When his visitor had gone he sat for a while as though mummified, ignoring the clamour of the telephone. He felt cheap,

209

compromised, but professional survival was too high a price to pay for his integrity. Every man has his price, as he had told Charlie once before. He could not imagine a life outside the walls of this office, deprived of his customary luxuries, perhaps even of necessities, reduced to the level of a dole queue or the homeless boy to whom he had given a fiver that morning. Yet he envied that boy his conscience, imagining, in the seclusion of his ivory tower, that only the rich have cause to feel guilt.

Presently, his secretary came in to see if he had thrown himself out of the window or collapsed with a heart attack. He apologised for troubling her, and consented to pick up the phone.

'It's Mr Christie,' the receptionist told him. 'He sounds rather upset.'

He would. 'Put him through.'

'I could say you were in court, sir.'

'No. Just put him through.'

There was a pause, and then he heard the voice of his friend of forty years, the father of his godchild. Anger had deprived George Christie of civilian fluency and his words emerged in short bursts, like the shouted orders of a drill sergeant. 'David – what's going on, man? – Charlie phoned – floods of tears – says you're too busy – too busy to help her – your own god-daughter – what the hell are you playing at? How dare you – letting us down – what the fuck – what's the game?'

Cringing inwardly, David achieved what he hoped was a placatory tone, doling out the same excuses he had offered to Charlie, embroidering the theme that litigation would be time-consuming, time-wasting, potentially fruitless. 'The problem is that when the case comes up before the tribunal, it'll be Charlie's word against that of Hugo Wingate and his cronies, and the burden of proof will be on her. That could be tricky.'

'What are you saying, David? You think she's making it up? Is that it?'

'No, of course not. I just think – look, they're bound to make all kinds of allegations, anything to discredit her. You've got enough to deal with right now. She'd be better off well out of it.'

'Bullshit!' The oath exploded out of the telephone; David thought the receiver shuddered in his grasp. 'You've got no gumption: that's it, isn't it? No balls. You're too chicken to

210

challenge the bigwigs at Fitzgerald Denton. One of my oldest friends and you won't even defend your god-daughter. She's been treated damned badly and you know it. Pull yourself together – *make* a case for her – get the bastards. If you don't I will – with or without the law.'

David did what he could to calm George Christie down, gave a mendacious promise to reconsider his position, and brought the conversation to an unsatisfactory end. In Chichester, his caller was racked with emotion he could not suppress, whipping up anger as a purgative. In London, David nursed the bitterness that corroded him as if it were a precious thing, knowing it would fade soon enough.

The long-awaited statement from Fitzgerald Denton relating to Charlie's 'gross misconduct' arrived the next day. It accused her of having misrepresented information to the managing agent of a marine syndicate who, David learned later, just happened to be a contemporary of Henry Marriott from his schooldays. The testimony of the principal witness was attached and the covering letter quoted the relevant section of the staff handbook at some length. It was plain that the fine Italian hand behind the indictment had covered all the angles and paid attention to every detail. To refute the charges Charlie would require support from the enemy camp, support that was hardly likely to be forthcoming. David was sure the statement was a string of lies; equally, he knew that with the best will in the world he would be batting on a very sticky wicket. Even if he were to take a moral stand, reverse his decision, defy Marriott and place his career and lifestyle in jeopardy it would almost certainly be in vain. The true crusader does not reckon up the odds, but David Chater had no taste for rash adventure; his was a temperate spirit, flourishing in moderate climes. He promised himself to do what he could to avert financial calamity from the Christie family, but into wilder waters he would not stray. Neither he nor any other advocate could help Charlie: of that he was convinced. Yet his conscience still plucked at his sleeve, no matter how he tried to ignore it.

CHAPTER EIGHTEEN

The bankruptcy proceedings were held in Chambers, presided over by a district judge. Charlie had expected both judge and lawyers to be bewigged and gowned and was vaguely relieved when only suits were in evidence. The opposing sides sat facing one another across a wide space of table; the judge was installed at the top. He had a high domed forehead, a low-slung jaw, and a portentous expression in between. From time to time he accorded a certain amount of sympathy to Mr and Mrs Christie, but the law, he maintained, is the law. In the hope of making staggering profits the deceased, Alice Hilda Christie, had taken on certain commitments, commitments which she had perhaps not fully understood but which were, nonetheless, legally binding, and the court had no alternative but to recognise the fact. Staggering profits, Charlie thought; he makes Granny sound like a yuppie on the make, or some crazed market speculator. She was torn between horror and a desire, born partly of nerves, to giggle.

David Chater pleaded George Christie's ignorance of his mother's position and reiterated that she had not intended to place her assets beyond the reach of creditors, simply because she did not appreciate the extent of her liability. No mention was made of Mr Christie's service for Queen and country in the Marines, or his commendation for gallantry at the battle for Goose Green during the Falklands War. Such information, David had explained beforehand, would be considered irrelevant. 'The law,' he had concluded, 'isn't always fair or just, it's merely legal. No law is any better than the society which effected it; burning witches used to be on the statute books.' Presumably Charlie's father was meant to be grateful that he wasn't going to the stake, but the reflection did little to hearten him. His role in the case seemed to be totally passive; he felt he was losing the battle without even being allowed to fight. The Christies sat in silence, a dumb audience at an adjudication

212

which would uproot the foundations of their world. The whole proceedings took only thirty minutes. The judge, discarding portentousness for a mien of lofty regret, decreed that the transaction between George Christie and his late mother must be reversed and the monies repaid to the representatives of Lloyd's. Mr Christie's sole asset was the unencumbered freehold of his house; it was duly ordered that the property in question must be sold at the earliest opportunity. If necessary at auction.

Charlie went cold inside. Although they had been prepared for the worst, both she and her father had nurtured a secret conviction that it would never happen, something would turn up, disaster would be averted, a system that was supposed to dispense justice must perceive that George Christie was a victim of chance and his erring parent had been distraught rather than dishonest. But this comfortable solution had not materialised; the system, like all systems, was uninterested in the rights and wrongs of the business, rolling on indifferently as it had been programmed to do. And on the far side of the table was the solicitor for Lloyd's, making his life-changing demands in clinical accents, as implacable as the machine in which he was a minor cog. Charlie felt a terrible guilt that she had once worked for that institution, she too had been a cog in the machine, and although none of this was her fault she knew she had acquiesced in the process that was now destroying her parents. The glamour of her old job faded in the light of a harsh reality. There was a price to be paid for everything – for the foreign trips, the high life, the caviare, the champagne – and her father and mother were paying it. A slow rage burgeoned under the coldness, but it did her no good. George Christie's face was rigid in defeat, muscles working along his jaw, looking for someone to harangue, someone to blame, someone to hate. They left the room slowly, Charlie supporting her mother, who clung to her like a refugee. For lack of another target, her father rounded on David Chater.

'So that's it, is it? That's the whole show? How you can have the nerve to charge such exorbitant fees for a bit part in a farce I can't imagine.'

'I'm sorry. I did all I could . . .'

'Did you? Perhaps if you'd stated the facts with a little more conviction you might have persuaded the judge to come to a fairer and more compassionate verdict.' David forebore to point out that compassion was not part of any judge's mental equipment. 'It's perfectly obvious you haven't the balls for a tussle in court any more than you had the heart to back your god-daughter when she needed you. All I can say is I'm glad, after all these years, to know how much value you set on our friendship. Send me your account. And don't worry: whatever happens, it will be paid.' He stalked off, evidently finding some satisfaction in such an exit. David tried to speak to Susan Christie, to offer commiseration, but Charlie murmured 'Not now' and the two of them walked away, following her father. David Chater was left alone with his inadequacies.

Charlie took her parents to lunch, and after stiff drinks their appetite began to return. They discussed the advantages of rental as opposed to buying a small place on a low mortgage, attendant costs like buildings insurance or ground rent, issues they had hoped never to have to consider again. Charlie's father's attitude was superficially bracing but underneath she sensed a fatal loss of confidence; her mother, outwardly more shattered, pulled herself somewhat shakily together and faced their prospective move with wan practicality. 'We could go to the West Country,' she said. 'Devon maybe, or Dorset. A cottage on the coast. I've always fancied living in sight of the sea.'

'We've got to sell our place first,' her husband said briskly. 'Better have the estate agents round as soon as possible. Don't like the idea of an auction but I suppose we have no choice. We don't seem to have much choice about anything now.'

'Daddy, don't rush at it,' Charlie said. 'We needn't go to auction yet; they must give us a little time.' An auction, she knew, would mean selling the house for much less than it was worth.

'No point in hanging about,' her father maintained, a dogged look about his mouth.

'Daddy . . .'

In the end, she coaxed him into a more reasonable frame of mind. Impatient to get over the worst, he was apt to precipitate matters, charging at hurdles that might never have to be negotiated. He finally agreed to put the house on the market at a fairly low price and pray for a quick sale. He would get in touch with several agencies in the immediate future and, at Charlie's suggestion, would also advertise the place himself in the local paper and possibly one of the nationals. It was a desirable residence, in the jargon of the trade; Charlie devoutly hoped the right buyer would come along as rapidly as one had done when her granny sold Ballards. Prices were slipping all the time and there was no indication as yet of an upturn. She left her parents at length, having done her best to be positive, and returned to London in a depressed frame of mind. No glittering job offers waited on her doormat and Caroline was still in the States. She did not feel like the company of those friends with their careers still on track and nothing to worry them but whether to take their summer holiday in St Tropez or Portofino. What she needed, she decided, was a congenial loser with whom to get drunk. She rang Amrit, but he was out, and his machine, as usual, informed her that it was out of order.

Over the next couple of weeks she spent a lot of time in Chichester, helping her mother to pack crockery and glassware in wooden tea-chests – 'We may as well get started now: it's going to take ages' – and offering as much emotional support as she could. In turn, she felt strengthened by their uncritical affection, the concern for her which seemed to override other considerations. In trouble, in doubt, in tribulation it is your family alone, Charlie learned, on whom you can rely, who will love and believe in you without question and without reserve. She was suffering a good deal from doubt: after further communication with David she had faced the fact that her chances at the industrial tribunal were slim; he had also intimated that Lloyd's would not hesitate to initiate a smear campaign against her to forestall her aims. The thought of the tabloids doorstepping her parents, either vilifying her or portraying her as a victim and wringing vulgar pathos from their plight, made her blanch. They had problems enough, she concluded, without the addition of all that. Her instinct was to fight, but when she saw her mother's weary resignation and her father's would-be flexibility, when she watched him attempting to sweep aside the past and, military-fashion, evolve a stratagem for survival, she knew

215

she could not drag them into what might prove to be a last stand. The very fact that they would have backed her whatever course she chose made it imperative that she should do nothing to further damage their lives. Caroline would find her another lawyer, if that was what she wanted, but her confidence was ebbing fast. She had never felt suicidal before, not even on the day she was fired, but now, dividing the family possessions into 'things to keep' and 'things to sell', she thought she understood the despair that made oblivion appear sweet relief.

Hugo and Emily Wingate were about to go on their annual holiday. Normally, their summer migration was accompanied by offspring, slotted into the school holidays, and involved villas in Greece, Italy or the south of France, chaotic plane journeys or endless hours diverting the infantry from car sickness and tedium. This year, however, Emily's mother had been deputised to mind the children and the dogs, assisted by a trained nanny, the au pair, and her own cook/housekeeper whom she was bringing with her.

Possibly from a sudden access of guilt, possibly because he had had enough of extramarital adventures, successful or otherwise, Hugo was striving for the ambience of a second honeymoon, with a three-week luxury package in Antigua including everything from guaranteed sunshine to gourmet cuisine. Emily, who had not particularly enjoyed her first honeymoon, kept any misgivings to herself. Hugo had chosen the tropics because in his view they represented the ultimate in romantic hedonism, but Emily would have preferred mountainous scenery, bracing walks, horse-riding, simple food in family restaurants; sunbathing and sea-bathing were not her style. She grew bored lying on the beach, and although she was a competent swimmer she had been nervous of the sea since she was stung by a jellyfish off the coast of Cornwall when she was a child. Nonetheless, she appreciated the effort her husband was making and responded accordingly, stocking up on the latest from Dick Francis, Joanna Trollope and Jilly Cooper to pass the time. If she guessed his motives she was not profoundly hurt; it was a flesh wound, a mere scratch, no more, she was far beyond letting him hurt her. She did not realise that the pain was too

216

deep to be truly known or consciously felt, an ongoing ache that was so much a part of her life she had forgotten what it was like to be without it. Preoccupied with preserving her frayed marriage, she knew only surface anxieties.

Hugo had told her about Bianca's suicide and Charlie's rapid exit from the company, but she had other sources of information, specifically a friend of her late father who, like herself, was a major shareholder in Fitzgerald Denton and who had contacts there and within Lloyd's. For her father's sake he kept in touch with her, and, unknown to Hugo, gave her whatever snippets he had amassed which he thought would be of interest to her. Thus he had reluctantly divulged the story of Bianca's pregnancy, also the off-the-record suggestion that Charlie might be intending to sue. Thank God, Emily reflected without humour, that men were far more addicted to gossip than women. At least she knew the position. The problem of Bianca she dismissed; poor Hugo was obviously feeling remorseful but he would get over it, he might even be more careful next time, which would be all to the good. Charlie Christie, however, could still pose a problem. Out of the company, there would be no reason in the future for her to maintain discretion over anything that might, or might not, have happened between her and Hugo. She had always known Charlie was trouble: presentable enough, if a bit dolled up for Emily's taste, but too bright, too aggressively modern, one of those people who like to have everything open and above board regardless of the damage they cause. Emily had seen Reggie McAvee was very taken with her, that was obvious from his patent hostility whenever Charlie's name came up – she had even tried to nudge him in the right direction, hoping to distract Charlie from Hugo, but without result. She was still mulling things over when he arrived to check a minor infection on Nutters' rear.

'He'll do fine,' Reggie said when the examination was over, ruffling floppy golden ears. 'Lovely creature, aren't you? I hear you're off on holiday, Mrs Wingate.'

She nodded. Although she knew him well, she remained slightly shy of asking him to call her Emily. She offered coffee, then changed it to Scotch. 'We're going to Antigua,' she said, splashing an excess of Chivas Regal into a tumbler. She had no

217

idea of suitable measures, not drinking whisky as a rule, and it was on an impulse which she could not explain that she poured an equivalent amount for herself. 'Mummy's coming to look after the children. Hugo wanted me to have a real break.'

'Thoughtful of him.' Reggie tried, and failed, to keep the sarcasm from his voice. He was diverted by the proffered whisky, which he surveyed with appreciation. 'Cheers.'

'Cheers.' Emily took a large gulp and decided it tasted as unpleasant as ever but felt agreeably warming on its way down.

'Antigua sounds wonderful,' Reggie continued conversationally. 'Palm trees, sun – bliss.'

'It's supposed to be very glamorous,' Emily said. 'Apparently, the hotel where we're staying is frightfully popular with people like Joan Collins and Liz Taylor, film stars, you know, and celebrities. I'm not sure I'm going to fit in with that sort of person. I'm not really a glamorous type.'

'Nothing to worry about,' said Reggie. 'Women like that don't suit the tropics: their makeup runs in the heat and their fancy hairdos go all limp. On the beach, what matters is your body. I'll bet you look fine with your clothes off.'

Startled, Emily swallowed too fast and began to choke. Reggie patted her obligingly between the shoulderblades.

'No need to be embarrassed. A vet, it's like a doctor. You see the anatomy from a purely clinical angle. I look at every woman as if she were a horse.'

'Th-thank you.' Emily got her breath back. 'Of course,' she resumed, dropping the subject of anatomy, 'it's Hugo who really needs the break. He's had a few problems at the office lately.' And, on her second impulse of the day: 'You remember that girl you met here at dinner?'

'Which girl?' Reggie remembered very well.

'Charlotte Christie. I thought she gave you a lift home?'

'So she did. What about her?'

'They had to fire her. I don't know exactly why. One of the underwriters complained, he said she wasn't quite frank about something, I didn't really follow all the details. Anyway, it's caused a bit of a flap. She was handling some big deal with a Dutch company; Hugo's had to take over in midstream. He's in town with the directors now, probably wining and dining them.

218

Of course, he's good at that sort of thing. Mixing business and pleasure.' I'm sure he is, Reggie thought. 'Still, losing Miss Christie has made a lot of extra work for him. I gather she may sue, too. Unfair dismissal. It must –' Emily hesitated '- it must have been rather upsetting for her.'

'Mm.'

There was a whisky-laden pause. 'I thought you quite liked her?' Emily said, with an air of artless enquiry achievable only by the naturally vague.

'Not much.' Reggie shrugged. 'A bimbo with attitude. Fancy packaging, but just another woman underneath. Have you ever seen a poodle without a perm?'

'Hugo says she could stir up a lot of trouble for herself,' Emily persisted tentatively.

'Or for him,' said Reggie. Absentmindedly, he said it out loud.

The unaccustomed liquor had removed a layer of inhibition from Emily's behaviour. She said abruptly: 'You don't like Hugo, do you?'

'No,' Reggie responded with equal bluntness. 'Do you?'

'He's my husband.' She forgot to sound indignant. 'I – no, I don't really think I do.'

'Why do you stay with him?'

'He's my husband,' Emily repeated, benumbed by the unexpected turn of the conversation.

'The kids and all that?'

'All that,' she affirmed, resorting to the whisky again.

'Did he and Charlie Christie – ?'

'I don't *think* so,' Emily said, having already given the question serious consideration. 'I imagine he was attracted, but I doubt if it went any further. I should have thought she was the all-or-nothing kind who wouldn't have settled for just being a mistress. Unless . . .'

'Unless that's why he gave her the boot,' Reggie supplied. 'Because she asked too much.'

'It's not very likely,' Emily said. 'You see, he had this secretary . . .'

'I see.'

Emily omitted to mention Bianca's suicide: it didn't seem

219

very important to her. 'It's rather novel to be actually discussing these things,' she went on. 'I dare say it's dreadful of me, but I'm so tired of pretending. Sit down, Ginge.' She stroked the nearest dog, evidently deriving comfort from the physical contact. 'I think it must be the whisky. I really shouldn't drink it. I'm going to be awfully embarrassed when I sober up.'

'Never mind,' said Reggie. 'Have some more.'

He left half an hour later, with Charlie's address and telephone number on a piece of paper in his wallet.

Charlie got back from Sussex late one evening to find a note from Caroline thrust through the letterbox: *Darling – dropped round to say hello on return from Injun territory. Called Trevor –* Trevor was her tame photographer – *but he's gone to Tunisia on a shoot. Will ring you tomorrow. Keep your chin up. Caroline.* Charlie knew she was meant to be heartened but her normal resilience had deserted her; the clue of the typewriter ribbon seemed to belong to the realms of fantasy, bearing no relation to the dull, real-life tragedy unfolding in Chichester. Inside the flat, even the misbehaviour of her alarm system failed to arouse her beyond irritation. She went listlessly to her answering machine, pressed the 'play' button.

There was only one message.

'It's Amrit: remember me? Of course you do; how could you forget? Thought I ought to let you know someone came round about that typewriter. An unattractive individual named Spooner; said he was a colleague of yours. I gather he'd rung on half the doorbells in the street looking for me. He didn't seem to know the flat number or my surname. Anyway, I told him the bloody thing had been pulverised but I'd given you the old ribbon back. The tongue of the dead dragon, you might say, by way of a token. He got very interested at that point and left in a hurry. Sorry if I've landed you in it; let me know what's going on some time. Incidentally, has the middle-aged father-figure ditched you yet? Bye.'

'Oh shit,' Charlie said out loud.

CHAPTER NINETEEN

Charlie called Caroline later that night but she was out. 'Something's happened,' she told Caroline's machine. 'Call me. Urgently.' She was not panicking, or so she told herself, and she kept the tone of her plea as light as possible, but Amrit's message had transformed fantasy into unwelcome fact and she felt suddenly vulnerable, alone in the flat with no one near to help her. Before going to bed she checked windows and doors, peered out into the shadows of the garden. The friendly plane trees looked suddenly ominous, their leaves huddled together in whispering masses, hiding secrets. A cat emerged from beneath them and slipped over the wall: the swift flicker of white startled her, almost making her cry out. Ridiculous.

She drew the curtains against the night and sat watching a late movie, hoping for diversion. Unfortunately, it was a Hammer House of Horror. Usually, she found such films pure entertainment but this time, watching Christopher Lee prowling the woods in search of maiden victims, she felt vaguely uneasy. She tried to restore her equanimity by picturing Spooner in the role, flicking a fag-end aside as he showed his canine teeth over a vodka and tonic. Henry would be more appropriately cast as Dracula: Henry at his most aristocratic, brows lofted, cheekbones highlit, pale eyes gazing down at his victim with a faint, cool regret as he bared her white throat. 'I'm sorry, my dear,' he would say, 'but it's for the greater good.' And then someone screamed, jerking her from the doze into which she had relapsed without knowing it, and it was a few seconds before she realised that the sound had come from the television. She switched off and headed for bed, thinking sleep would come at once; but instead she just lay there, listening to the remote throb of traffic and the little creaks and groans of a house at night. Shortly before dawn slumber finally took over for a few short hours.

She was up and half dressed – jeans and a bathrobe – when

221

the doorbell rang. It might be Caroline, she hoped it was Caroline; but she could not avoid a shiver of apprehension as she picked up the entryphone. The voice that answered her was masculine and unfamiliar, with a slight brogue. 'Charlie Christie?'

It seemed sensible not to commit herself. 'Who is that?'

'Reggie McAvee. You know: that boorish vet who behaved so badly to you after Emily Wingate's dinner party. Can I come in?'

Relief flooded through her. Tiresome he might be, but at least he wasn't sinister. She slipped into routine annoyance. 'What the hell are you doing here? It's 10.30 in the morning and I thought you lived in a remote hamlet in the wilds of Surrey . . . and who gave you my address?'

'I will answer all questions, madam,' said Reggie, 'when you let me in.'

'I never buy things at the door!'

Nonetheless, any company was reassuring, even his. Charlie pressed the button to release the lock and went to the door of her flat. She wasn't looking her best, her hair still damp from the shower and her face scrubbed and shiny, but for Reggie McAvee it hardly mattered. Anyway, she had other things to worry about. It was only as she admitted him that she realised her bathrobe, as usual, was coming open. She yanked the lapels together irritably and ignored his appreciative grin.

He did not appear to have made any effort for the visit; fragments of what looked like straw clung to his army surplus jacket, his denims were both grubby and faded, and he had either been too busy to shave that day or he considered designer stubble a prerequisite for his careless image. With the tousle of hair in his eyes and his faintly wolfish smile he resembled a Corsican bandit and, Charlie thought, he probably knew it. The awareness did nothing to soften her mood. 'I don't know what you're doing here,' she reiterated, 'but you may as well have some coffee. It's on.'

'Christ,' he said. 'I've walked into a Gold Blend advert.'

Charlie giggled. 'Actually,' she said, 'it's the real McCoy. Wait here while I put on a sweater.'

On this occasion she did not waste time on selection, merely snatching the nearest to hand, an undersized lambswool V-neck that had shrunk disastrously in the wash. In her haste, inevitably, she forgot her bra, but she could not be bothered to worry about it.

Back in the kitchen, she poured coffee. 'You promised me some answers.'

'So I did. What am I doing here? We rustics like to venture up to the Smoke once in a while, gaze wide-eyed at the city folk enjoying their sophisticated pleasures, that sort of thing. Emily Wingate gave me your address, and I decided to look you up. And down,' he added, suiting the action to the words. 'I hear the charmless Hugo has dispensed with your services.'

Charlie bristled at what she thought was a deliberate ambiguity; but Reggie gave her no time to interrupt. 'I got the impression you weren't having much fun. I thought I'd bring some fun into your life, that's all. We Irish bumpkins know how to have a good time. And now it's your turn to answer a question.'

'Perhaps,' Charlie said cautiously.

'When you spoke to me through the entryphone, until you knew who I was, why did you sound so scared?'

Charlie hesitated fatally before replying: 'You're imagining things. It's early for visitors, I wasn't expecting anyone – I was cross, that's all it was. You must have travelled up on the heels of the commuters. You were obviously pretty eager for your jaunt to the city.'

'I'd been up all night ministering to the sick – a mare with colic, poor darling, her idiot of an owner left it till the last minute to call me. Anyway, there didn't seem to be much point in going to bed. I just got straight on the train. Now, why don't you stop sidetracking? That wasn't a satisfactory answer.'

'It's the only one you're going to get,' Charlie said, but both her vexation and her hostility were evaporating rapidly. Reggie looked physically tough, obviously fit, a solid shoulder between her and any threat. She remembered Caroline's words: 'What you need is a bodyguard.' Suddenly, she was very glad he was there.

'All right,' he was saying. 'How about a drink? I know a grand place in the Fulham Road. I usually head that way when I'm in town.'

'To gawp,' Charlie suggested, 'at the city slickers?'

'That's it.'

The grand place proved to be a pub called the Elm, evidently patronised almost exclusively by building labourers and Irish navvies. The long dark bar ran the length of the long dark room, supporting long dark pints of Guinness and several members of the clientele. Charlie removed her jacket in the stuffy atmosphere and then wished she hadn't: with her shrunken sleeves pushed up to the elbow and the skimpy knit clinging much too tightly to bare breasts she felt like a grown woman bulging awkwardly from the clothing of a ten-year-old. Heads turned, stares followed her, there was a subdued guffaw which might or might not have been aimed at her. Reggie, unabashed, greeted the barman by name, swapped a joke with one of the regulars, and took her arm in a gesture she did not repulse. 'Gin and tonic,' she said, when he asked her what she wanted.

He shook his head. 'They do serve it here,' he explained, 'but only to aliens. Wherever you are it's good manners to drink the local poison, and this is a piece of Ireland. Anyway, you need something to build up your red blood corpuscles; I can tell. Try a half. It'll do you good.'

Charlie submitted and they retired to a corner table with two tankards of stout. She drank valiantly, rimming her upper lip with froth; the Guinness tasted as thick as stew and felt somehow comforting inside her. 'Hey, it's not bad,' she exclaimed, agreeably surprised.

'*Not bad*? It's the best you can get this side of the water. For the real stuff you have to be at home, of course. It always tastes different there. It's the rain, you see, the clean Irish rain, with the clouds drifting up from Tir na nOg and the water as pure as when God first decided He was thirsty. He tapped on the rock and out the spring came bubbling, clear as diamond and cool as the dew, and when He saw there was room for improvement He turned it into Guinness. And that's the honest truth.'

'The honest truth?' Charlie echoed. 'I'll bet God made that too – and when He saw there was room for improvement He turned it into blarney.'

'Too right.' Reggie's face split into the bandit's smile, all wicked mischief and glinting laughter, tilting the corners of his eyes, dazzling her with the sudden shock of overpowering attraction. 'I could dish it out all day, but I won't. Now you've got some good liquor inside you, you're going to tell me what's up. Start with your job – and why you lost it. You'd never have done the dirty on anyone so presumably they did the dirty on you. Tell me about it.'

'I hardly know you,' Charlie protested.

'We're working on that,' he pointed out, 'all the time.'

So she told him, slowly at first, with reservations and omissions, about Fitzgerald Denton, and Lloyd's, the job she had wanted so badly, the high of pulling off a coup, the events in Amsterdam, the horrifying moment when the ground beneath her feet seemed to vanish without warning. Then somehow she strayed on to her granny's death, the discovery of her bankruptcy, the terrible consequences for her parents – and the whole hideous mess came spilling out. David Chater, Andrew Kendall, her sense of betrayal, of loss, of utter futility. Everything except Henry Marriott, the query over Bianca's suicide, she and Caroline playing detectives over a typewriter ribbon. He had enough to be going on with.

'Were you keen on this Kendall git?' he wanted to know.

'Not in the way you mean. He was my friend; that's all. Or so I believed.'

Reggie evidently deigned to accept this. 'Right,' he said. 'You've explained why you're upset, unhappy, and your life is hell. You still haven't explained why you're frightened.'

'Reggie –'

'Let's have lunch. You need proper food – none of this *nouvelle cuisine*, morsel-of-salmon-with-puddle-of-green-sauce crap. We'll eat here.'

They had steak-and-kidney pie and mashed potatoes because that was the only dish on the menu. Charlie nibbled to begin with and then decided she was starving and polished off the whole plateful. It occurred to her she had not eaten much for several days. 'Better?' he asked.

'Much better.'

'Another half?'

'Well . . .' she faltered, 'it's a bit heavy. Really, I'd like some wine.'

'Not here you wouldn't,' said Reggie. 'It'll take the lining from your stomach.'

Again Charlie paused, knowing her next words would sound like an invitation. 'We could pick up a bottle on the way home.'

'And so we could,' said Reggie.

Timing is everything, Charlie thought. For no reason that she could elucidate she felt that Reggie's timing, and hers, was perfect. She was in trouble, perhaps even in danger, defenceless and desperate, her veteran knight was wearing the colours of the enemy, and now the woodcutter's son had turned up, right on cue, to come to her aid. She had no idea if Reggie was any hand at slaying dragons – in view of his profession he was more likely to physic their injuries – but he was there, and that was all that signified. He was there and after her initial recoil she accepted him, needed him, wanted him without question or doubt. She drove home quickly, careless of speed limits, pausing in transit for Reggie to collect a bottle of Sancerre from a passing off-licence. At the house, she fiddled with the keys, entered the hall, went to disarm her front door while Reggie followed with the wine. Then she stopped short.

It was open.

As far as she could tell the locks had not been forced and there was no visible damage. Her temperamental alarm system was mute. But the door stood a couple of centimetres ajar and beyond it, inside the flat, *her* flat, she could hear someone moving about. The last trappings of fantasy evanesced; the thriller was not only real, it was here, crossing her threshold, invading her private sanctum, rifling through her possessions. She turned a blanched face to Reggie and saw his savage frown.

'You should have told me the lot,' he said, 'shouldn't you? I suppose I'd better charge in and get hurt. Wait here.'

He deposited the Sancerre on the stairs, opened the door a little further, and slid quietly through the gap. Charlie groped for her mobile phone and then remembered she had left it behind. She looked round for a potential weapon, helped herself to an umbrella from the hall stand; she thought it belonged to a tenant upstairs. It did not look particularly useful, but there was nothing else to hand. Then she followed Reggie into the flat.

As she entered the living room there was a crash: a table went over, taking Reggie with it. She glimpsed a tall man with a bunched fist calling to an accomplice, then another man came out of her bedroom and they both pushed past her. She tried to jab with the umbrella, heard one of them swear, and was thrust violently from their path. It all happened too quickly for her to register many details but she was conscious of surprise that they appeared so respectable, clean-shaven, grey-suited, professional types rather than thugs. Then the house door slammed and she realised she had been pushed to the ground. She picked herself up and hurried over to Reggie, who was trying to disentangle himself from the table. There was blood trickling from his nose, welling from a split lip, blood on his hands, on the carpet. As he sat up the trickle became a flood. 'Fucking hell.' His voice, to her overwhelming relief, sounded as strong as ever, irate and unshaken. 'What the fuck are you mixed up in? Don't just stand there; do something. Get me a towel, tissues – whatever. I'm bleeding like a fucking abattoir.'

'You're all right,' she gasped thankfully. 'I'm so glad you're all right.'

'Of course I'm not all fucking right. Get moving, wench; I've only got eight pints and a couple have gone already.'

Dragons one, woodcutter's son nil, Charlie thought with a flippancy that was probably a nervous reaction. She brought her bag of cotton wool from the bathroom and attempted to block both Reggie's nostrils and his mouth in order to dam the fountain. 'Jesus,' he complained. 'Now she wants to smother me.'

'Maybe I should take you to Casualty –'

'What you should do,' he intervened, mopping his hands on a gory sweatshirt, 'is to shut and lock the door to this flat –'

'Seems a waste of time.'

'- putting the chain on so any burglars, even with skeleton keys, will rattle on their way in. Then open the Sancerre, wash my sweatshirt, tell me what the fuck's going on, and suck my cock, not necessarily in that order.'

'I *beg* your pardon?'

'Sorry. The last one's optional. Fighting always makes me a bit brusque, especially when I lose.'

'*Brusque?*' Charlie yelled, finding an outlet for weeks of

227

tension in a sudden upsurge of glorious fury. 'You call that brusque? I call it bloody rude, I call it obscene, unforgivable – insensitive – disgusting. Who the fuck do you think you are? Do you know what you can do? You can get out of here, you can get out now, this minute, this fucking minute, and you can take your bloodstains with you – and your sweatshirt – and your Sancerre –'

'Charlie, stop it. Stop it . . .' He was cupping her face between reddened fingers, planting kisses in the vicinity of her lips even as she tried to thrust him away. 'I'm sorry. I'm really sorry. The trouble is, fighting always makes me want to fuck, too – and I wanted that bad enough *before* anyone hit me. The wanting is getting a bit out of control, I'm afraid. If you don't want it, one word is all it takes. All you have to do is say no. Just one word. Charlie . . . Charlie . . .' His tongue was in her mouth, she tasted blood; the taste, the fear, the fight excited her, anger melting into lust, and then she was kissing him back, licking his wounds, and they were rolling on the carpet, clinging to each other, clawing each other, the urgency of their need overriding all else. 'Forget the Sancerre,' he said, pulling back for a moment to remove his sweatshirt, fumble with his zip. 'Just shut the door.'

She went to close it and found him behind her, his arms around her waist. 'The bedroom –' she indicated.

'Here. No point in getting blood on the sheets. Here. Now. On the floor. *Now* . . .'

This is unreal, Charlie thought. No. No, this is real. Everything's real. This is the most real time of my life.

Between them, they dragged her jeans to her ankles; she kicked her legs free. Her briefs had gone with them. He felt for her clitoris, beginning a rhythmic insistent massage. She was already wet with desire, her senses dissolving into pleasure, her pussy open as a flower oozing pale nectar. He put his tongue between the petals, teasing, probing, and she thought how long it was since she had allowed anyone to do this, and how pleased she was that it was so long, because this one time, this moment, was exquisite beyond comparison, and this man, this one man was someone she had been looking for, waiting for, without knowing it, maybe all her life. She did not say the word 'love'; nor did he. But she felt *love*, she sensed *love*, and his feeling and sensing met

228

hers; and then his tongue took from her all power of thought, locating the very heart of the corolla, the nucleus of sensation. She writhed and gasped and cried out: 'Stop! Don't stop! No!' and 'Yes!', torn between the longing to succumb and the wish to prolong every last second short of ecstasy. Afterwards, he found a condom in an inner pocket of his jacket, waited for her to catch her breath, pushed the tight sweater up over her breasts, and then he was easing himself into her. Gradually, he became less gentle and his body seemed to be invading her, thrusting deeper and harder, kisses falling on cheek and throat while he pounded into her, speared her, stiffened beyond enduring, imploded, shuddered, relaxed. Then they lay on the floor, sweat-streaked, laced in each other's arms. Reggie murmured: 'Wow!' and 'That was lovely . . . lovely . . .' It was *real*, Charlie thought, in a blissful state of shock. None of the games with Michel, no lovemaking with anyone else had ever been as real as this.

'Now,' Reggie said at length, 'we open the Sancerre.'

When they had recovered, showered off the blood, left Reggie's sweatshirt to soak and salted the stains on the carpet, Charlie remembered to check her machine. 'Darling,' said Caroline's voice, 'what's happening? You sound *frightened*. Hope you're OK. Call me at the office.'

'Aha,' said Reggie. 'Someone else knows you're in the shit. Who is she?'

'My pal Caroline. I'd better phone her. She's the one with the little grey cells.'

'Sorry?' Reggie was confused.

'Know your Poirot,' Charlie said. 'It eez zee leetle grey cells, *mon ami*. Caroline has been detecting with a typewriter ribbon, and it looks as though she's been spot on. It's all so incredible I couldn't bring myself to believe it, not till those men came. You probably won't believe it either.'

'Try me,' said Reggie, probing gingerly at swollen lip and nose. 'I seem to have the medical evidence already.'

By the time Caroline came round, in the early evening, Reggie had had the leisure to digest the whole story.

'Who is he?' Caroline demanded *sotto voce*, as he went into the kitchen to uncork the champagne without which she never

229

travelled. 'You didn't tell me about this!'

'He's my bodyguard,' Charlie said innocently.

'You said he's a vet,' Caroline hissed darkly. 'How on earth did you meet a vet? You don't even own a goldfish. One doesn't bump into vets at press launches or in Stock's or Tramp. I've never met a vet in my life.'

'Your loss,' Charlie sighed.

'I admit, he's gorgeous – but that's just it. How come this gorgeous man, about whom we know nothing, turns up out of the blue, in the nick of time, claiming to be a vet and offering to act as your bodyguard? It's far too convenient. He's obviously a suspicious character. And don't tell me which parts of your body he's been guarding; I can guess.'

'All of it,' Charlie said. 'He's guarded absolutely every inch of me. It was divine.'

'What's more,' Caroline pursued, 'he's Irish. How can you trust a nation where half the place names begin with *Bally*?'

'As it happens,' Reggie said, returning opportunely with the champagne, 'I come from Donegal.'

'The only Donny I ever heard of,' Caroline said, undeterred, 'was Donny Osmond – and that isn't a recommendation. Look at this man, Charlie: he's too good to be true, therefore, he isn't true. He has to be working for *them*.'

'I don't really care,' Charlie said blithely. 'If that's the case, we'll give him the ribbon and to hell with it.'

'Anyway,' said Reggie, 'I'm not one of *them* – whoever *they* are – and I've had the nosebleed to prove it.' ('Diabolical subtlety,' Caroline muttered.) 'I want to know what's going on as much as you do. The heavies who came here seem to have done a pretty slick job, at least until they were interrupted. Nothing's missing, as far as we can tell. They only wanted the typewriter cassette, and as they didn't pinch anything else we can assume they weren't from the light-fingered classes. Amateurs would have done some damage on entry, possibly sparked off the alarm, so it's clear they were trained in this kind of thing. Where do you get formal training for breaking and entering? It has to be Intelligence. Those thugs must have worked for the government at some stage.'

'It might fit,' Caroline conceded, abandoning resistance to

Reggie's collaboration. 'I always fancied the idea of conspiracy at Whitehall. I told you, Henry Marriott has the contacts, but – It's no good: we need more information before we can get the whole picture. I'll go round to Trevor's studio first thing tomorrow.'

'You said he was in Tunisia,' Charlie reminded her.

'His assistant may be there, or his partner, or *somebody*. If push comes to shove, I'll just have to fly out to Africa.'

Reggie grinned at her. 'I really believe you would.'

He returned to the country the following morning, promising to be back as soon as he had arranged a locum to mind the surgery. Charlie was left invigorated by wild sex and an extraordinary sneaking happiness, a hint of something more enduring than lust, flourishing improbably on the brink of disaster like a rose-tree on the lip of a volcano. She only hoped that when the volcano blew, the rose-tree might somehow survive. It seemed unlikely according to the laws of science, but Charlie remembered her grandfather's stories: she knew there were forces stronger than biology, legends truer than fact. It was as if she had suddenly rediscovered the faith and wonder of childhood – a remembrance of things forgotten – pearls in oysters, apples in Eden, spring after winter, a monster in Loch Ness, a sea-song in the whorls of an empty shell. Henry Marriott had spent nearly £2,000 to make her believe in Santa Claus, but in the end she had found nothing to believe in but the dry-cleaning bill. Reggie had bought her a half of Guinness and a steak-and-kidney pie and made love to her with a bleeding nose and ruptured lip, and now her broken world felt whole and full of possibilities.

She rang her parents, wanting to pass on her newfound confidence, offering encouragement by inference if not by word.

'The estate agents are starting a big advertising campaign,' Charlie's father reported. 'It's all going to take time. We may have to go to auction after all.'

Charlie's buoyance subsided; her own tentative happiness would be no consolation when they were losing their home. She said what she could, knowing it was not enough, and rang off feeling once more wretched with frustration. Reggie called shortly after to say he would be back in two days, and she was smitten with guilt because the mere lilt of his brogue chased every cloud from her horizon.

'Got it!' The triumph in Caroline's voice vibrated down the wires. 'Nick -Trevor's partner – had the negs; I wheedled him into printing the lot. Can you come round to my office now?' It was three o'clock the following afternoon and Charlie, alone in the flat, was trying to focus on the Sits Vac columns.

'I'll be there.'

When she arrived at Caroline's office, she found most of the floor space tiled with black-and-white ten-by-eight photographs. Caroline herself was laying out more with methodical enthusiasm. 'Good God!' Charlie said faintly. 'How many are there?'

'Ten rolls, twenty-four exposures to a roll. What we'll have to do is start in the bottom right-hand corner –'

'Of each picture?'

'No: the floor – and transcribe every letter on to paper before we can try to make sense out of it. They're in reverse order, don't forget, and there won't be any gaps between words, though punctuation and capitals should help a bit. It's all here, the entire ribbon. The guys did a great job.'

'It'll take forever,' Charlie murmured in horror.

'The sooner we start, the sooner we'll finish, as my dear grandmother used to say. Though come to think of it, she was referring to the gin. Come on, Charlie, grab a pen and pad. I'll sing out the letters and you write them down. Then we can sort them out afterwards.'

They wasted some time on Amrit's blockbuster before a string of consecutive capitals revealed the title – FATAL KARMA, initially mistyped as FATAL KORMA – and they could get on with something which they hoped would be more significant. Copying out the letters was less arduous than arranging them in acceptable words, allowing for the errors and misprints that invariably accompanied old-fashioned typing. When they had finished with the photos Caroline enveloped them carefully in order – 'We may need to verify something and if we mix them up we've had it' – and they took Charlie's notepad to Caroline's house in Hollywood Road to decipher at leisure. 'This is awful,' Caroline said. 'Like one of those game shows for crossword nutters, or breaking a code in the war. Given a mistake or three, a string of letters becomes complete gibberish. How about some champers?'

'No,' said Charlie. 'I need a clear head.'

It was midnight before she thought she was getting somewhere. Familiar words had begun to emerge – 'risk', 'liability' – and then a promising company name, The Union Asbestos and Rubber Company of Chicago. The date was 1982.

'Progress,' Charlie reported.

'Jolly good show,' said Caroline, acceding to the prevailing atmosphere of wartime drama. 'If we can work out how much their chaps know about our chaps, then maybe we can pull our chaps out before their chaps pull them in. Lives depend on chaps like you. Ready for refreshment? What about pizza?'

'Everything except pepperoni.'

'Good chap.'

'Shut the fuck up,' Charlie said good-humouredly.

By the time the pizza arrived she reckoned she had incomplete versions of the brokers' cover notes relating to three syndicates underwriting a health and safety at work policy for an American consortium. They took a break from fiddling with letters to eat and study their handiwork. The reinsurance appeared fairly straightforward bar the date. 'I'll bet that typewriter hasn't been sitting in the store-room unused since 1982,' Charlie said, 'but how the fuck do I prove it?'

'Your language is deteriorating rapidly,' Caroline said. 'It's not like you.'

'I'm tired and cross.'

'Let me have a go. I think . . . I've got the germ of an idea.'

She pored over the notepad, scribbling, swearing, crossing out and writing in. Charlie ate two slices of pizza down to the crust, picking off a morsel of pepperoni that had been introduced on the sly. 'Look,' Caroline said at last. 'This is the section before all that stuff. It's just a letter, probably quite standard, nothing incriminating . . .'

'So why the gleam in your eye?'

'The date, Charlie, the date.'

'Of course –'

'Of *course*!'

'16th January 1986,' Charlie read. 'But it must have been typed *before* these covernotes, because it's earlier on the ribbon. We've done it! This is *proof*!' They hugged each other, laughed, caught their breath.

'Now,' Caroline declared, 'the champers.'

'I wonder,' Charlie mused, several bubbles later, 'if I could get hold of the originals. What we've got here is such a muddle: I'd like to see the finished copies.' Boosted by the success of their initial labours, a task she would never have contemplated beforehand suddenly seemed feasible.

'Where are they?'

'In the storage vaults at Fitzgerald Denton, under some old railway arches. You've never seen such a place: endless filing cabinets stacked with endless files, going way back to the beginnings of time, when a nervous apeman insured his coracle against a revival of the Ice Age. It looks like a nightmare of obsessive paperwork but it's all in order, finding things isn't difficult. I wouldn't need long . . .'

'How would you get in?'

'Key,' Charlie said simply. 'The security guy on the front desk has it. He *might* give it to me. He always seemed to like me – and although he must know I'm not there any more ten to one they haven't told him I left under a cloud. Why should they? He's only the guy on the door. Nobody gossips with a security man, not even Cynthia Greenslade. I could say I need to check the documents on some deal I was involved in – it could overlap with something I'm doing now – that sort of line. It sounds natural enough. I ought really to have some sort of verification – a letter from Hugo, something like that – but I might just get away with it. If I smile nicely. After all, I look honest, don't I?'

Caroline did not comment. 'A letter,' she mused, chin on hand. 'I don't suppose you were the sort of employee who pinched the company notepaper to impress your friends?'

'Of course not.'

'Pity. Still, you must have a letter from them somewhere. What about that charming little note of dismissal? That was from Hugo, wasn't it?'

'Yes, but –'

'Find it. The master detective is about to become the master forger. There's nothing like some champers to give genius a second wind.'

Charlie duly produced the letter and Caroline pored over it, bright-eyed with inspiration, her energy clearly undiminished despite the evening's exertions. 'Two pages . . . never mind. This is what we do. First thing tomorrow, we go into my office, take a photocopy, blank out everything between *Dear Miss Christie* and Hugo's signature, then take another copy with both sections on one sheet. A bit of Tippex to cover any joins and marks, then yet another copy, this time on to posh paper, and there you are. In the blank space, we print out a nice police note saying *Please admit one to Fitzgerald Denton storage vaults* and you flourish it at your security man to obtain the magic key. Boy, am I a loss to the world of crime!'

'The address is supposed to be embossed,' Charlie said a little doubtfully. 'What if he notices?'

'He won't,' Caroline asserted confidently. 'Hand him the letter holding the corner, then he'll take the sheet lower down. If he doesn't actually feel it he won't know the difference. In any case, as you said, he *knows* you, you're not a suspicious character, so why should he suspect? It'll work, darling, believe me.'

'It's worth a try,' Charlie said.

In the morning, feeling rather less confident now the champagne had ebbed from her system, Charlie drove into the City. She was dressed in jeans and a T-shirt, with her hair in a cap of a pair of Caroline's largest sunglasses hiding most of her face, not so much a disguise as civilian clothing in marked contrast to her former uniform of suit and blouse, or the cocktail dresses she had sometimes worn to socialise. She had expected to feel like a discharged soldier returning to barracks, awkward and out of place without his regimentals, but in fact she experienced not embarrassment but invisibility. Walking round to Fitzgerald Denton from the meter where she had parked her car she saw two or three acquaintances, none of whom even acknowledged her: they saw the clothes, not the woman, and dismissed her accordingly. No one in the Square Mile came to work in jeans. Charlie did not attempt to greet them; she could only trust that the staff at Fitzgerald Denton would prove similarly blind, should she run into any of them. She knew Hugo was abroad but there was always Spooner, Rupert, Andrew. Strange how she was no longer angry with Andrew; however, since the advent of Reggie McAvee the Andrew Kendalls in her life had ceased to matter. She approached the swing door, waited till the reception area was clear, and then walked boldly in.

The security man, she thought, looked as reassuring and as friendly as ever. She was assailed with a sudden impression that time had slipped, she was back on that first day, late for the interview, and everything in between had merely been a delusion, the chimera of an idle moment. In a few seconds he would enquire her name and her business, escort her to the lift, tell her to 'let 'em wait'. She banished the fancy with an effort, produced her usual smile. 'Hello.'

'Hello, miss – why, it's Miss Christie! I shouldn't hardly have known you, dressed like that. You look like my granddaughter, and she's only fourteen. They told me you'd left, a real shame, I thought, you always brightened up my day. Anyhow, she's probably getting married, I said to myself, a pretty girl like that. Is that it, miss?'

'We-ell . . .' Charlie temporised, snatching at a convenient straw.

'It's all right, I won't tell nobody. Now, what was you wanting today? Left something behind, have you?'

'Not exactly,' Charlie said. 'The thing is, I'm doing some work for another company, just for a bit, and there's a client making overtures whose name I've seen here, I think he may be pulling a fast one, and I wanted to check up on him. I rang Hugo a week ago and asked him to get me copies of the relevant documents and he said he would, but he didn't have time before he went on holiday so he's authorised me to get the keys to the storage vault and fish out the bumf myself. Here, I've got his letter.'

The security man duly glanced at it, holding the single sheet well clear of the telltale address. 'That looks fine, miss. I'd better just check . . .'

'With Mr Spooner?' With no leisure for panic, Charlie achieved a comical grimace. 'Must you? He doesn't like me – he doesn't like anyone – and he's bound to make himself difficult.

236

It could take ages – and I'm a bit short of time.'

'All right then, miss. Since it's you . . .'

'*Thank* you.' Charlie smiled dazzlingly, gave him an impulsive kiss on the cheek, and departed with her trophy jingling in her pocket.

She had been shown the vault in her early days at Fitzgerald Denton but had never had occasion to visit it since. The room was long and very high, strip-lighting kept to the barest minimum, shadows hugging the narrow alleyways between rows of cabinets. There were signs denoting each section – general insurance was to the right of the door – date labels on every cabinet, portable wooden steps for reaching the topmost racks. A dim, dusty, musty smell pervaded the atmosphere, the smell of staleness and age, of mouldering files, yellowing paper, browning ink. History was buried here, a history of a thousand futures, of numberless gambles on hypothetical disasters, planes that had not crashed, ships that had not sunk, a whole range of things that had never happened preserved for posterity in this mausoleum of paperwork. Here and there, of course, a cataclysm had come to fruition, the folders were ruffled, the dust stirred, the cobwebs blown away. But Charlie, searching along cliffs of filing for 1982, felt as if she was the first person to come there in a decade.

The echo of her footfalls was smothered, stifled out of existence under the weight of paper. But once or twice she heard other sounds, furtive rustlings which could not be human in origin, possibly rats. She shuddered at the thought. When she had located the right cabinet she began to check the racks; the material she wanted was at the top, she had to fetch the steps in order to reach it. She skimmed along the files until she came to the one relating to Union Asbestos and Rubber, pulled it out, leafed through the contents where she stood. The three documents she wanted were in there, with the underwriters' signatures and the official stamps of the syndicates that took the cover. But the paper looked newer than anything else in the file and the scratch marks lacked the underwriters' customary flourish. She did not recognise their names and wondered suddenly if they had been chosen because they were senile, or dead, and forgery would be difficult to prove. She saw the name of her

237

Granny's syndicate; she would have to verify that the others, too, had been run off, suffocated under the liability overload from asbestosis. The deal, as she had suspected beforehand, was a reinsurance from another syndicate, a standard enough procedure in normal circumstances, disseminating the risk. But the other syndicate, the one passing the parcel, losing the liability, was the one headed by Henry Marriott.

Charlie took the cover-note slips and thrust them in her bag, returning the folder to the cabinet. Then she left the vault, glancing round as she locked the door, hurrying back to Fitzgerald Denton so she could return the key before the lunchtime exodus.

'That was quick,' said the security man. 'Get what you want?'

'Yes,' said Charlie. 'Yes, I think so.'

She got back to the flat to find Reggie on her doorstep.

'Where've you been? It's twenty minutes I've been waiting here.'

'Sorry – I went to the City, to raid the storage vaults at Fitzgerald Denton. I'll explain properly in a minute.' As always, she got her keys mixed up. 'My nerves are in pieces. I don't know how regular private eyes stand it: one little adventure and I'm a wreck. Come on in. I'm so pleased to see you – so pleased –'

In the end, her pleasure outweighed the necessity for an explanation, and they tumbled into bed and made love with the passionate intensity of Romeo and Juliet, trying to fit a lifetime of loving into a single encounter. Afterwards, exhausted, they swapped endearments, nuzzled, cuddled, and slipped inadvertently into sleep.

On the floor at Lloyd's, Spooner ran into an acquaintance who enquired: 'What really happened about that girl at your place, Bill? Charlotte Christie – I always fancied her. Funny thing: saw a student in the street today looked just like her.' The remark pricked at Spooner's thoughts like a splinter, nagging and worrying. Back at the office, he cornered the security man.

'Haven't seen anything of the late Miss Christie today, by any chance?'

'She popped in,' admitted the security man reluctantly.

'Didn't half look different. Jeans and a hat.'

'What did she want?'

'Something to do with a client she wanted to check on, old documents, I didn't get the details. She'd brought a letter from Mr Wingate saying it was okay, so I didn't see the need to bother you.'

'Saying *what* was okay?' Spooner was scowling with impatience.

'To give her the keys to the vault,' he explained with vague apprehension. 'Mr Wingate had authorised it; I saw the letter. It was plain enough. Anyway, she wasn't gone more than a few minutes . . .'

'Christ,' Spooner blasphemed. 'Christ. *Christ.* You senile old fool, you're fired. The letter must have been a fake. I suppose if she'd batted her eyelashes a few more times, you'd have handed her the books. Give me that key.'

'You can't fire me. Ten years I've been here –'

'*Give me the key!*'

In the vault, Spooner found the cabinet for 1982, zoomed in on the correct file. His excitement was so violent he had to take a break for a line, cutting it with his credit card on the cover of the folder, snorting a liberal helping of dust with the priceless white powder. When he had inhaled the required uplift he checked the documents in the file. It took him no time at all to realise what was missing.

CHAPTER TWENTY

It was the rattle of the door chain which woke her. Since the discovery of her uninvited guests she had taken Reggie's advice and formed the habit of double-locking and chaining the door whenever she was in the flat, even during the day. The clatter of metal links jerked her alert instantly; she shook her companion and hissed: 'They're back. Reggie, they're back. I can hear the door.'

'What the fuck –'

'I took some documents from the vault this morning. I was going to tell you about it but you distracted me. We've got to get out of here.'

'Back way?' He was already zipping into jeans, having dispensed with underwear. She followed his example, hastily retrieving her handbag with its precious contents from the living room. Fortunately the chain, instead of merely sliding into place, was also locked in position with a miniature key so it could be fastened from inside or out. In the past Charlie had rarely bothered with the extra precaution, relying more on the two main locks and the alarm. Ordinary burglars, she had been given to understand, did not usually come equipped with skeleton keys. This particular brand of illicit visitor obviously did; happily, they were having some trouble finding a skeleton for the miniature. Charlie invoked a silent blessing on the head of the conman who had sold her on the siege mentality. The hindrance, though temporary, gave them vital seconds: she and Reggie had cut through the garden and back to the street before the invaders had found any evidence that they had ever been there.

'I think I've got my car-keys,' Charlie said, fumbling in her bag.

'Good. I'll drive.'

She smiled a little shakily. 'I love it when you're masterful.'

'What did you say you pinched?' he asked as they drove off.

She told him, interspersing the recital of recent events with directions to Hollywood Road.

'Where?'

'Caroline's pad.'

'Tell me something,' he said, as they parked outside the house, 'is it always this exciting, working in the City? If I'd known when I first met you, I'd have been rather more respectful.'

'How boring,' Charlie grinned.

Back in Charlie's flat, the visitors surveyed the bed, still warm from recent occupation, the stains on the sheets, the used condom which still reposed in a bedside ashtray. They unearthed two pairs of pants, 'His and hers', as one man said, and a bra. They checked cupboards and drawers, under the mattress, behind the radiator. In the living room, they stripped covers from cushions, pictures from walls, books from shelves, tapped into Charlie's PC, played every message on the answering machine. They were equally thorough in the kitchen, emptying sugar from the packet, coffee from the jar, listing the damage for future replacement. When they had examined the apartment down to the bone they knew all they needed to. One of them extracted a portable phone from his pocket, dialled a number.

'Nothing,' he reported. 'They must have made a quick exit. We were a little slow getting in; they could have heard us coming.'

'They?'

'Christie and the boyfriend. At a guess, the one we met before. Scruffy type, early thirties, no ID as yet. Or another. Depends how prolific she is.'

'It's not important.' The voice on the phone was taut rather than tense, dispassionate, cold. Charlie would have recognised it. 'She must have the documents with her. Do we know where she's gone?'

'No. We ran the tape on the answering machine: there's a load of messages from someone called Caroline, sounds posh, could be her best girlfriend. Not much help, I'm afraid. Can't find an address book anywhere. How many posh-sounding Carolines are there in central London?'

'Is there a PC?'

'Yes, but we can't find anything relevant on it.'

241

'Destroy it,' said the mobile phone. 'Hard disc, floppy disc, everything. There mustn't be any loopholes. We'll get her another. Something more up to date. Put Sheila on to it. And tidy up afterwards. I want the place left so immaculate it looks as if it's been ironed.'

The voice terminated the call and the two men went back to work.

Henry Marriott cradled the receiver in his hand for several minutes after cancelling the call. He was thinking of Christmas at Kirkby Pelham, his sister's teasing, warm red wine, shared confidences. And now Charlie had a boyfriend: scruffy, early thirties, no ID. He felt a vague sense of pain which he knew to be meaningless, self-indulgent, the sentimentality of a middle-aged man recovering too slowly from a vain infatuation. What, after all, had Charlie Christie meant to him? A pretty girl, a younger Helen, an echo of youth and happiness made all the sweeter by distance and unavailability. She had not been his soulmate or his bedmate, only an elusive fantasy, something he thought he must have been chasing, without knowing it, for a long while. *Though I am old with wandering Through hollow lands and hilly lands, I will find out where she has gone, And kiss her lips and take her hands* . . . But Henry Marriott was no obsessive wanderer in a mythical landscape: he was a man in the real world, with responsibilities and a job to do, and the phantom he pursued had become an obstacle of flesh and blood, a tangible stranger. He pressed out the number of Douglas Henderson's mobile.

'We have a problem,' he said.

In Caroline's house, Charlie was trying to explain the insurance market to her co-conspirators. 'You have a ship,' she said, 'and you insure it, in case it sinks. Then you insure the insurance. Then you reinsure that insurance. And so on, and on, more or less indefinitely if you want.'

'Why?' asked Reggie.

'If the ship doesn't sink, the client pays the premiums and everyone makes money. If it *does* sink, ideally you've spread the load. That's the theory of it.'

'So what happened here?' Reggie persisted.

'The syndicate headed by Henry Marriott got stuck with a staggering liability for the asbestosis claims. They had no re-insurance, so they decided to fake it. Henry got on to his chum Hugo at Fitzgerald Denton – Spooner must've got in on the act too – and they forged contracts, backdated to 1982, passing on the mess to three other syndicates, probably selected because the underwriters are now dead and can't complain. I haven't checked that but I don't know any of them. Anyhow, what happened was that people like Granny, Names who obviously weren't considered very important, got landed with someone else's bill. Clear?'

'I suppose so,' Reggie conceded grudgingly. 'I prefer horses.'

'They insure those too,' Charlie said brightly. 'Racehorses, stallions put out to stud, pedigree dogs who win at Crufts, prize bulls laden with top-quality sperm. Everything in life can be insured. Pick a risk. You could toss a coin and cover yourself if it doesn't turn up heads 50 per cent of the time.'

'Life is unpredictable,' said Reggie. 'What if it never turns up heads?'

'That's when you get the present balls-up,' Charlie sighed.

'And where did the girl come in,' Reggie resumed, 'the sec-retary who drowned?'

'She typed the forged documents,' Charlie indicated the papers in question, '*on* the typewriter. They had to be done that way because Fitzgerald Denton wasn't computerised in '82.'

'In other words,' Reggie summed up, 'she knew what was going on, she made things difficult with Hugo the supergit who was her lover, and so she died. Seems to me we could do with some insurance of our own.'

'Absolutely,' said Caroline, who had been thinking furiously throughout their exchange. 'The ribbon, the photos and negs, and these –' she tapped the documents – 'go in the bank. Copies of the documents will be lodged with my lawyer – *not* your use-less godfather, darling – and we'll keep some ourselves. That's the first priority. While I fix that . . . Charlie, do we know exactly who's on Henry's syndicate? Can we find out? I think it's vital we learn which Names are being baled out, otherwise we're only going to have half a story when we go to the press.'

'The *press*?' Charlie flinched at the thought.

'Don't look so horrified: I deal with them all the time. I can get you the right contacts; all you need is a long spoon. This is major fraud, people are suffering, it's got to be exposed. And with Henry's connections the government, even if they aren't actually involved, will probably try to smother it. Besides, editors will pay the earth for something as hot as this – maybe enough to help your parents. And finally –'

'Yes?'

'Publicity is your best safeguard. There's no point in silencing someone who's already talked.'

'The Mafia wouldn't agree,' Reggie said.

'We aren't dealing with the bloody Mafia,' Caroline retorted. 'Thank God. Charlie, about Henry's syndicate –'

'The Names are in the Blue Book,' Charlie said, 'in the library at Lloyd's. I could look it up. But there's a problem.'

'What?' queried two voices.

'I can't get into Lloyd's without a pass. That might be ticklish. Nobody at Fitzgerald Denton would lift a finger for me but I could ask someone from another company; a few people have called since I was fired saying they didn't believe that misconduct business. Only . . . I don't want to get anyone else into trouble. I'm awfully worried about the security man, he was so nice to me, and I didn't even know his name.'

'Stop being so squeamish,' Caroline said. 'This is war, and we don't take prisoners. Get on the phone.'

The following morning, wearing yet another hat, a trilby of Caroline's which was rather too big and kept sliding down over her eyes, Charlie sat in the library at Lloyd's leafing through the Blue Book and glancing warily around from time to time. She was dressed in the same jeans with new underwear purchased from Harrods – 'I'm buggered if I'm going to lend you my knickers, darling, even if they'd fit' – since a return to her flat for a change of clothes was inadvisable. Unlike on the previous day, she felt not only visible but conspicuous, a Martian astray in a flock of terrestrials. When she had found what she wanted she got into a fresh panic because she had forgotten to provide herself with a piece of paper on which to write it all down. Eventually, she scribbled down the Names on the receipt for her lingerie which was still in her wallet, overspilling on to her chequebook, and then hurried out. In the lobby, she collided with Rupert Lambeth.

'Charlie! What on earth –'

'Hi! Too wonderful to see you –' And she planted a hasty kiss on his astonished cheek and fled down the open-tread stair to the street below.

'Wonderful,' Rupert murmured blankly.

In Hollywood Road, Caroline had taken the afternoon off, pleading a hospital appointment with such tragic conviction that several of her colleagues were now persuaded she was either pregnant or terminally ill. 'I never go to the hospital,' she told Reggie. 'It just shows you. They've probably started a collection – for a wreath.' She was so immersed in the plot they were unravelling she had omitted to restock her liquor cupboard and they were driven on to the ropes with vermouth and chocolate cream liqueur. On Charlie's return, shaken but triumphant, they sat down to go through the list of Names she had obtained. Coffee grew cold in the mug and ashtrays overflowed with cigarette ends. 'I've met *him*,' said Caroline, pointing to a duke who had recently featured in *Hello!* magazine. 'Nasty old man. And *that's* a familiar name.'

'High Court judge,' Charlie said promptly. 'I saw him on the news the other day, sentencing somebody to a hundred hours' community service for rape or something like that.'

'There are at least a dozen MPs,' Reggie concluded. 'Probably all Conservative, although it's getting increasingly difficult to tell them apart. Here's a cabinet reject . . . *that* bloke's an incumbent minister, though God knows what for . . . this one was in the shit lately over that porn star with no tits. It's quite a collection. Charlie, you say without that reinsurance fiddle all these people would have been ruined?'

'Absolutely. The asbestosis affair went through the ceiling. With unlimited liability they could have lost everything. Like poor Granny . . .'

'Well, well. No wonder everyone's been jumping through hoops over this. We aren't just talking money, we're talking power.'

Caroline frowned. 'I thought the two were synonymous.'

'Not always. Nowadays, information is power. We have

245

power, right here, that you cannot buy. It's on this list.'

'Explain,' Charlie said.

Reggie's eyes gleamed satisfaction. 'If these Names had had to fork out for the asbestosis claims, some or all of them would have gone bankrupt. Correct?'

'I told you that.'

'A Member of Parliament isn't allowed to be insolvent. All this lot would lose their seats. It could bring down the government. Throw in a public exposé of the fraud scandal and no one would ever trust the Party again. It might fuck up the entire political system in this country. The Opposition might even be tainted with it too: there's a socialist millionaire on this list. People would vote in Screaming Lord Sutch 'cause at least they know he's honest.' He paused to let his words sink in, took a mouthful of cold coffee. '*This* is power, Charlie. Real power. What are you going to do with it?'

In the Directors' loo at Fitzgerald Denton, Spooner had just snorted his third or fourth line of the day – he had lost count, and anyway it didn't seem to be doing much good – and was waiting in vain for a resurgence of his normal sanguine outlook. His busy brain was revolving possibilities, probabilities, improbabilities, testing what few options he possessed, latching on to slim chances, clutching at straws in the wind. Was it too late to change sides, grass to the Fraud Office, sell to the press? Could he, natural traitor though he was, bring himself to betray the world where he had striven and thrived for so long? If the racket was made public it could destroy not only Fitzgerald Denton, but Lloyd's, the insurance market, the City itself. Confidence, that mysterious intangible, would vanish overnight, and with it the nerve centre it sustained. There could be no future for a City that lost its nerve. And where would he go, what would he do, deprived not only of his job but his entire universe? Without the swamp, the crocodile must perish; without the jungle, the ape has nowhere to swing. Thinking with vicious but futile satisfaction of the day he warned Hugo and Sewell not to employ a woman did little to improve his mood. He was facing the abyss, and under the frantic spiral of his thoughts his terror grew.

*

In Antigua, Hugo had risen to take his tan for an early morning swim. Emily was still sleeping, curled firmly in her half of the bed, looking younger and almost childlike in a light gentled by translucent curtaining, the sun-flesh imparting a deceptive glow to her thin face. He told himself that he was fond of her, they were used to each other, she was easy to have around, not knowing, since such perception was beyond his range, that the woman behind the face was a stranger and always would be. Comfortably oblivious to imminent disaster, he headed for the beach, the palm trees, the crystal sea. Emily rolled over as soon as he had gone, stretching to fill the whole bed, the illusory innocence vanishing with the opening of her eyes. She itched with boredom without her children and dogs, walks and rides, shopping and cooking, all the things with which she sought to fill up the emptiness of marriage to Hugo. Here in this tropical paradise she was confronted with the tedium of their conversations, the charade of their sex life. As she lay there in the filtered morning, gratefully alone, she wondered for the first time what it would really be like to leave him.

On the terrace at Westminster, Henderson took a mouthful of Scotch. Behind him, the sunsparkle on the water turned the brown river into a glinting mirror; the background of bridge and farther bank might have been a picture postcard. But the Chief Whip was indifferent to both the cityscape and the whisky. 'They must find her,' he was saying. 'If they don't – if she talks to the wrong people –'

'She won't,' said Henry Marriott, trusting he was right. 'She's not completely irresponsible.'

'This business about her grandmother,' Henderson wasn't listening, 'why the hell wasn't I informed? Christie worked in the market, for Christ's sake, she was bound to get nosy. The old lady goes bust and then drops dead and her parents are let in for a debt-load they never incurred: it's hardly surprising she starting poking around. This young man she confided in –'

'Kendall.'

'– does he know anything?'

'I don't think so. He's confused. Spooner has seen to that.'

'Thank God.' Henderson sounded positively devout. 'Let's keep it that way. We've got enough to worry about. If I have to tell the PM we've fouled up –'

'Not yet.' For a man facing catastrophe, Henry was curiously relaxed. He knew when there was nothing more to be done. 'As I see it, we were unlucky. No amount of planning can take account of chance. We all learned that in the army. When the luck goes against you, all you can do is keep your head down, and pray. Miss Christie heard something – we don't know what – from Hugo's secretary, she acquired the typewriter by pure fluke, her grandmother's death handed her another piece of the puzzle. As you say, it wasn't surprising she began to fit the jig-saw together. Now, we have only one course of action left.'

'What's that?'

'We wait,' said Henry.

'You have the power, Charlie,' Reggie repeated. 'Use it.'

'You could wipe out those bastards you worked for,' Caroline said with vengeful ferocity. 'Remember Sticky Fingers. Send them a fax: *Crazy foam is for kids. You're playing with the big girls now. Hang on to your jobs if you can.* They'll be finished.'

'Lloyd's would be finished,' Charlie said quietly. Thinking.

'Wow,' said Caroline. 'The government and the establishment in one fell swoop. Fucking wow. That's so fabulous it's scary.' Her face was alight with glee. Could we? dare we? said her tone, as if they had been schoolgirls plotting a midnight flit from the dorm, or teenagers contemplating their first gin, their first joint, their first sex.

'I'm scared,' Charlie said. Her voice was low and level.

'Don't be!' Reggie seized her by the shoulders; his rough beauty was illumined by maverick passion, his eyes were grey as storms. 'Think of what they did to your grandmother, to your father. Think of how they betrayed and slandered you. Is that blood in your veins or milk, faintheart? Are you going to prove them right after all? Will you let them think, because you're a woman, that you're too soft, too weak, too cowardly to fight back? You've got them by the balls, colleen. All you have to do is squeeze.'

'Shut up,' Charlie said. It came to her in that moment that

she was genuinely in love with him, no passing fancy but the real McCoy, and if she let him browbeat her, if she was seized with his convictions and swept along in his ardour, she would lose herself just as surely as she might have done with Henry Marriott. She had to slow him down, make him listen, make him think. 'It's *my* fightback: remember? *I* decide.'

'You have the power –'

'I know.' There was no glee in her voice, no daring, no satisfaction. 'I could bring the world down about their ears.'

'We ought to do something soon,' Caroline said. 'They'll be looking for us. Can they trace me?'

'With difficulty. My Filofax lives in my bag. I wonder . . .' She took it out, leafing through the telephone numbers. Then she picked up Caroline's phone.

'The next move?' Reggie queried.

'What's a good place for a meeting?' Charlie said. 'Somewhere public. Safe. Out in the open.'

'We're near enough to the Fulham Road,' Reggie said. 'I defy the British establishment to infiltrate the Elm.'

On the terrace at Westminster, Henry Marriott's phone began to ring.

'Convince me,' Charlie said.

Henry Marriott glanced round the dim interior of the pub. He was too poised to betray any obvious *gêne*, but he had not expected to make his pitch in such unlikely surroundings, and Charlie sensed he was disconcerted, off balance, on guard. Whether in the army or in the City he was used to an established terrain, a war where he could make the rules, call the shots, pick the battleground. The problem with always being in command, she reflected with an inward smile, is that if the command shifts it is difficult to learn how to fight from a subordinate position, where someone else is making the rules, the territory is unfamiliar, and the choices are out of your hands. She recalled thinking once that Henry Marriott had probably never travelled on the Underground; now, she knew that all she had ever needed to do to unnerve him was to put him on a tube. He was a rarefied animal, a successful predator in a specialised environment. Move him only an inch outside those invisible boundaries and he was immediately disorientated, potentially lost. She saw him eyeing the navvies at the bar, the men in donkey jackets and shapeless jeans, with bad teeth in broad grins and dirt under their nails, who eyed him back, grins fading, suspicious of his suit, his hair-cut, his small Irish whisky and the uppercrust English accent in which he had ordered it. Amongst them was a young man in a combat jacket who looked up from time to time, staring at the corner table where Henry and Charlie were seated. A long cool stare from sea-coloured eyes, naturally insolent, or so it seemed to Henry. The young man was dark, unshaven, with a misshapen nose and a discoloration on his lip. The boyfriend.

Henry's gaze reverted to Charlie; he thought: She's changed. What a pity. The perfect bud unfurls, the fledgeling sheds its down, the tiger-kitten unsheathes killer claws. What a pity . . .

'Convince you?' he said, and a little extra frost was injected into his hard voice. 'Why should that be necessary? You will have to take my word for it; the stakes are too high for you to understand. You have evidence which, after all, you stole: namely the documents and the typewriter ribbon. That makes your position very suspect. Hand them over and I will see to it that your family receives a complete reimbursement for your grandmother's losses, plus some sort of compensation for you personally – I'm sure we can agree a figure – from Fitzgerald Denton. After that you must – you *must* – keep silent about this whole business. If you talked, I would be unable to protect you any further.'

'You haven't convinced me,' Charlie said with cold gentle-ness. 'I know the stakes. The government's majority in Parliament. The future of Lloyd's. Tell me why I should care.'

'I realise you must feel very disillusioned. I'm sorry about your grandmother, truly sorry. If I had known, I would have averted it somehow.'

'How?' Charlie's voice was still gentle. 'By passing the bill on to another syndicate, another unsuspecting Name? Someone else's grandmother?'

'Don't give way to bitterness.' There was sincerity in his plea, but it did not touch her. 'Your godfather once described you as – open, candid, innocent. Don't lose that, not yet. You're so young . . .'

'That was all you ever loved in me, wasn't it?' she said, understanding. 'Youth. Not even the real thing, painful and unsure, but an idealised picture. Like a rose that withers in your hand, something you can never hold on to. I'm not disillusioned and I'm not bitter: I leave those to you. I've grown up. Innocence is only ignorance in a white dress.' Almost his own words. And: 'When did David say that? Henry . . . *when*?'

He accepted the implied accusation, without attempting denial.

'Poor David,' Charlie said. 'No wonder he sounded so wretched.'

'He loves his comforts,' Henry said with a sudden spurt of cruelty, 'better than you.'

'No,' Charlie said, warm with comprehension. 'He *needs* his comforts. He *loves* me.'

He looked into her face and saw awareness, insight, tolerance, the antithesis of the ambition and eagerness which had once adorned her. The infantile physiognomy had matured, even in so short a time: her mouth appeared less obstinate than resolute, the flesh seemed to be moulded more closely against her bones, her eyes had learned concealment, no longer transmitting her every thought. The girl had become a woman; it was the girl he had wanted. Rose-white youth, spotless, self-centred, blind . . .

She was drinking Guinness. It was the final degeneration.

'What would happen,' she speculated, 'if – for instance – I gave my story to the press? What would happen, not to the state of the nation – to hell with that – but to you, Hugo, Spooner? Even if you didn't go to gaol, you'd all be ruined. The way you tried to ruin me. Right?'

He nodded curtly.

'And if I say nothing, what happens to you then?' she pursued. 'Will you survive and thrive?'

Henry shrugged. 'Probably. Is our collective ruin so important to you? Hugo's career will continue on the up: that's predictable. Spooner will come a cropper once in a while but so what? He always has. And I . . .'

'And you?' There was no emotion in her tone, only mild enquiry.

'I was Canute,' he said. 'They told me to turn the tide and I

251

dug them a river. If the truth comes out, I will probably get my feet wet. If not, no doubt there are those in the City who will continue to believe in my omnipotence. It hardly matters.'

Canute? What did that remind her of? Of course: driving through traffic with Henry that evening when she had confused Canute with Moses parting the Red Sea. She said with a flash of inspiration: 'Was that what they called it? Operation Canute? Like a military exercise.'

'That was it.'

'Not a very good choice,' Charlie said. 'The king was no fool: he knew he couldn't stop the sea. Any more than you can stop the future. The tide is rising and it cannot be turned. Yet you made people – innocent people – suffer. Convince me that was right.'

'It was *necessary*.' His lips thinned with vexation. 'Stop saying *convince me, convince me* like a child asking for a story. You are no longer a child, I can see that. Convince yourself. If even a small part of this is made public, it could destroy not only the government and Lloyd's but maybe the City itself. When confidence starts to seep away that is the beginning of the end. Do you want revenge so much that you are prepared to inflict permanent damage on your country? You see us as guilty: does everyone else have to share in our punishment?'

'You *are* guilty,' Charlie said. 'If you hadn't cheated there would be nothing for me to expose. You're just trying to transfer liability again. Stop – stop playing games.' Her voice shook slightly, possibly with anger. 'If confidence is eroded it will be your doing. Not mine.'

'I never play games.' Henry sounded stiff with the effort of self-restraint. He might indulge in private doubts but no one else had ever doubted or challenged him. Indignation filled him at being required to justify himself. Unconsciously, he had always considered Charlie his inferior, in intellect, in standing, in *savoir-faire*, a creature to be protected and insulated like a rare bird in a gilded aviary. He had expected to be confronted with tears and ideals, emotional pleas, emotive harangues, a scenario where he could overawe and control. Instead, he faced remorseless accusation, calm, deadly understanding. He said: 'I acted from the best of motives,' and for all his convictions, it sounded like an excuse.

252

'The wrong deed,' Charlie said, remembering a conversation months ago, 'for the right reason?'

'If you like.'

He saw her eyes move to the bar, seeking support; saw the young man there raise his glass in response. His lips moved on a phrase which only Charlie assimilated. *Your decision.*

The stab of irrational jealousy which Henry experienced almost destabilised him, making him feel suddenly crude, farouche, hideously vulnerable, correspondingly bitter.

Her next question was one he had not looked for.

'What about Bianca?' Charlie said, her carefully preserved cool chilling to ice. 'Was her death acceptable, because your motives were pure?'

'It was suicide,' Henry said sharply. 'She was just a silly little secretary who got herself pregnant –'

'Hugo got her pregnant. It's a two-person job.'

'It had nothing to do with this.'

'Bullshit!' The intensity of Charlie's reaction surprised her. 'She wasn't just a *silly little secretary*. She was a woman – she wanted the baby – she loved it – she might have killed herself but she would never have killed the baby. If you lie to me – if you lie about this – I'll go straight to the press. I'll go *today*. Let Lloyd's go to blazes, let the City crack up; I don't care. Don't you dare dismiss a human being like that, as if she were nothing, as if she were dirt. She was killed, wasn't she? *Wasn't she?* She was killed and you ordered it.'

'No.' Involuntarily he shuddered. 'I wanted her frightened, pressurised. I ordered minimal force. No one knew she was pregnant. She over-reacted – it was an accident . . . The river seemed the best solution.'

I'm listening to a confession of murder, Charlie thought. And I once believed I could love this man. Dear God . . .

She said: 'Someone fixed the path report.'

He didn't bother to confirm it. 'It was an accident,' he reiterated. 'I swear . . . Do you think I wanted any dead bodies drawing attention to us?'

'You made it happen,' she said. 'You and your heavies. You made it happen, because she was just a silly little secretary, who didn't matter. Do you deny it?'

253

'I am not afraid to take responsibility –'

'You and God,' she said.

'I haven't lied.' He saw her anger and could not comprehend it. It was impossible that Charlie should care about someone like Bianca. 'I do not wish to shirk one ounce of blame, nor have I tried to do so. The burden is mine –'

'I see,' Charlie said. 'Amrit was right: the burden is yours because you want it so, you enjoy your martyrdom, you take the weight of the world on your shoulders to make you feel important, loftier than us lesser mortals. But it is not your world; you have no right –'

'You're a child – a stupid, crass, ignorant child –'

Eye to eye they faced each other, stripped of courtesy and respect, ruthless in their mutual disillusionment. A juddering sigh came from her as she let go of her rage; he remained tense, unspeaking.

'I'll make a deal,' she said. 'Not for your sake or Lloyd's or the bloody national interest but for the people who would suffer, the lives that would be damaged if I burst the balloon for good. Too many people have been hurt already; I don't want to add to it. You'll pay my father – not me, my father – all the money he should have inherited from Granny; I think it's about £400,000. Check it with David Chater; he can handle it. And don't put any more pressure on him. You never know, you might have another accident. I don't want any compensation for myself but I want my name cleared; Fitzgerald Denton can circulate a statement or something, saying the accusation of gross misconduct was a complete fabrication and they offered me my job back, only I refused. You'll know how to phrase it.'

'That might be difficult . . .'

'Do it. That's the deal, and it's not negotiable. In return, I'll give you the documents I abstracted, the typewriter ribbon, and my guarantee of silence. The photos and the negs will stay in the bank, just in case.'

'Don't you trust me?' he snapped back, without humour.

'Yes, I do,' she conceded, knowing it for the truth. 'I trust your given word, as I expect you trust mine. This will be an old-fashioned arrangement.' Lloyd's as it used to be, when a man's

254

word was his bond and a handshake meant more than any legal verbiage.

'Very well.' A faint, painful smile lined Henry's face: he held out his hand.

Reggie, seeing the gesture, knew the die was cast, the deal made. Charlie was right and he accepted her decision, but there was a grimace of regret for the débâcle he had missed. An imp in his nature would have relished the havoc that daunted Charlie.

She waited a moment before responding; Henry's handclasp, as before, felt light and strong. They had shaken hands when they met, the day of her interview at Fitzgerald Denton; they shook hands now, to bargain and to part.

Then she stood up to leave. At the bar, Reggie finished his pint.

'Since you trust me,' Henry said, 'why keep the photos and the negatives?'

She looked down at him: the smile that lit her face was radiant and knowing, far beyond the innocence of youth.

'Insurance,' she said.